RELENTLESS

A Kate Preacher Thriller

MICHAEL MALOOF

Scan the code to join the
Michael Maloof VIP Readers Club

"The Art of War teaches us to rely, not on the calculated likelihood of an enemy's coming or not, but on our continual readiness to receive him, no matter what he does."

Sun Tzu

CHAPTER I

FRIDAY, APRIL 17, THE PRESENT
6:15 AM EDT

UNDISCLOSED LOCATION

NOMAD FLEXED HIS RIGHT wrist, and with the palm of his hand, eased the joystick forward. The motor on his wheelchair hummed, and he maneuvered toward the center of the workstation. This environment was his creation. The height set to accommodate his chair with room beneath to manipulate the joystick. With subtle right or left pressure on the stick, he could navigate the full semicircle desk and jump between clients and projects.

There were traditional keyboards and mice, but the layer of fine dust revealed little use. Nomad's world was one of proprietary speech recognition technology and the pressure-sensitive controls he designed and added to his chair. His forearms, wrists, fingers, head and voice all served as system navigation and command-and-control interfaces.

A matrix of monitors, stacked three high and eight across, spanned the arc of the desk and formed his window on the outside world. As a C6 quadriplegic, what he lost in physical mobility he regained in the virtual world. He chose the name Nomad for the irony, and believed his world offered freedom, control, and safety.

Nomad scanned the monitors. His building's security cameras, global news feeds, random engineering musings of a few MIT grads on Slack. Another monitor was hammering away on a client's file with one of his decryption algorithms. No challengers yet on any of his virtual chess boards, and that brought him to the Frenchman, his favorite opponent.

The central monitor was a live, split-screen camera feed from the Frenchman's Paris apartment. One feed came from the Frenchman's laptop, and the other from the camera embedded in the smart TV. It was Nomad's practice to plant malware on the systems of anyone in his inner circle. What began as a safety protocol became something more, and he watched and lived vicariously through his contact's living rooms and their digital and social media lives.

Nomad glanced at the camera feed's system clock. Twelve-fifteen. It was almost time. He hoped the apartment would be empty, but saw Francois scurrying about, preparing for the meeting. Nomad knew it was pointless, but he had to try one more time.

Francois's laptop rang with Nomad's encrypted call request. He watched the Frenchman approach the laptop and press cancel. Nomad tried again, and this time he watched Francois accept the call.

"I admire your determination," Francois began, "but there's nothing left to discuss."

"Look, I know how it sounds, but I'm begging you to trust me," Nomad said. "You need to leave."

"You ask for trust, but hide in the shadows."

"Who I am is not important. All you need to know is that your life is in danger."

"Nonsense," he said. "For one thing, I know who you are, but rest assured, your secret is safe with me. Why you've chosen this life, I will never understand, but that is your business and now you must leave me to mine."

"Is that a threat?"

"No, no, my friend. You misunderstand," Francois said. "This is just a promise that I will keep you out of the discussion, but Moore Industries needs to know what you found. They believe the device is impenetrable, exceeding even the capabilities of quantum computing, and with millions relying on this technology, I have no choice. There is no room for debate."

"You're missing the point," Nomad said. "Tens of millions of customers is exactly why Moore will do anything to protect the NanoVault's reputation."

"Again with the conspiracy theories," Francois said. "You watch too much American TV. I am a respected academic meeting with a representative of a major corporation, not the KGB."

"I pray I'm wrong," Nomad said.

"Au revoir, my friend."

"Wait," Nomad said. "Before you hang up, what makes you think you know who I am?"

"I understand some hackers have a signature, patterns of behavior, code or techniques they use, that help identify the author."

"Yes, that's true."

"So do chess players."

Nomad heard the knock at the Frenchman's door. Francois called out to his visitor, and the call ended.

Chapter 2

PARIS, FRANCE

FRANCOIS LEGRANDE IMAGINED HIS meeting with the Moore Industries representative. *They'll want to see my research and review my findings. A lucrative offer for my work would be nice, but it would be an honor to receive one of Moore's Distinguished Fellowships.*

Francois rushed to answer the door. He never saw what the masked man pressed into his side, but the effect was immediate. His body convulsed, knees buckled, and his head struck the floor. Next came the duct tape over his mouth and around his wrists and ankles. He lay on the floor of his apartment, dazed and in pain, only half-aware of the large black boot that passed over his face.

Adrenaline surged. His heart raced. He fought to focus his thoughts. Blinked and squinted to clear his vision. He squirmed and wrestled against the restraints. Tried to call out, to scream. Nothing worked. In the futile struggle to free himself, his breathing was rapid and shallow. His vision blurred, and the room spun. *Don't pass out*, he thought. *Just breathe. Slow down. Listen.*

From the hallway, it was difficult to know what the stranger was doing. *Was Nomad right? No. Can't be. If he was here to kill me, I'd be dead already. Then what? What does he want?* His head throbbed as he thought back to the fleeting image of opening the door and looking up at the face. *There was no face. Just a blur of gray and white rectangles.* The man's ball cap and hoodie obscured any chance of street cameras catching his approach to the building, and the camouflage mask stretched tight from his forehead to his neck prevented facial recognition.

Francois tried to follow the sound of the stranger's steps. The attic apartment, converted from an 18th-century mansion, was elegant but small. While it suited the Frenchman, it took only moments to explore. He heard the wheels of the office chair as they rolled across the hardwood floor. *He's in the bedroom.*

The bedroom served as his home office. Stacks of books and papers shared his bed, and most of the floor. He pictured the stranger seated at his laptop and cursed his decision to close the connection with Nomad. *If he knew, if he saw, he would call the police.*

There was an odd sound. An electronic chirp beeping slowly at first, then faster and louder, then slow again. Finally, a solid tone for a moment, then silence.

Francois heard the tones of a cell phone. *Too many digits,* he thought. *Not a local number.*

"I have it," the man said. "No, it has to be tonight. And count yourself lucky I could make this work on short notice." There was another brief pause and then the call wrapped up. "Yes. Yes. I'll keep it safe. Now, send me the drop site."

American, Francois thought, and at that moment, all hope vanished. The businessman he thought might still arrive, might somehow intervene. The man he was expecting was already here. Despair wrapped him in an ice-cold blanket and he trembled. He stopped fighting back the tears and sobbed.

The American dragged Francois down the hallway and into the living room, and the tears gave way to terror when he surveyed the room. A chair from the small kitchen table was in the center. A rope stretched over the ancient oak beam that framed the ridge-line of the apartment's ceiling, and a noose hung above the chair.

The duct tape muffled his attempts to cry out, and the masked man had little trouble setting the slight Frenchman on the chair. He slipped the noose over Francois's head and pulled on the rope. Francois stiffened his back, lifted his chin, and gasped for air. The man kept one hand on the rope and the other drew a knife. With a flick and click, the blade locked into place, and in one sudden move he cut the tape binding Francois's feet. He pulled the slack from the rope and Francois's only escape from suffocation was to climb up on the chair.

The American tied the rope to the radiator, then stood directly in front of Francois and stared. The mask was disorienting, and Francois found it difficult to focus. He saw a black leather jacket and a gray hoodie. He saw dark blue jeans, and the boots. Large black boots. *He could be anyone on the streets of Paris, even one of my students. What is he waiting for? What does he want?*

"Let's talk."

The words startled him and Francois wobbled atop the wooden kitchen chair. The noose made it difficult to breathe, much less answer questions. When he raised up on the balls of his feet, he could almost take a full breath, but the old chair flexed and creaked when he moved. He knew at any moment it might collapse and he would hang.

"I'm going to remove the duct tape," the masked man said. "I suggest you remain still. And quiet," and he gave the rope a slight tug. "Understand?"

Francois nodded, and the stranger ripped the duct tape off the old man's face. The Frenchman scrunched his eyes, gritted his teeth, and wrinkled his nose. Tears and snot seeped into his mustache. The American balled up the tape and noticed the collection of gray hair.

"Trust me," he said. "Faster is better." And then he reached into his jacket, fished out the shiny black device, and held it out for the Frenchman to see.

"Did you crack it?"

Laying in the palm of his glove was a Moore Industries NanoVault. The polished black onyx device, about the size of a woman's lipstick, was ringed with seven combination dials that controlled access to the device's unique properties. For the first time since the masked man crashed through his door, Francois thought he understood what was happening. *He thinks I'm after the bounty. He thinks I've cracked the encryption.*

The offer of a bounty, paid in anonymous, untraceable, and tax-free Bitcoins, intrigued cryptographic researchers and enticed the hacker denizens in every corner of the Darknet. Crack the encryption on a Quantum NanoVault, known affectionately as a portable Swiss Bank account, and you'd learn the location of 1,000 Bitcoins. What started as a clever promotional stunt became a worldwide phenomenon when Bitcoin values rose exponentially, and the bounty, still unclaimed, grew to tens of millions of dollars.

"No. No, Monsieur. I assure you, this device is worthless."

"My client insisted I retrieve this specific device," he said. "And paid handsomely to recover it immediately. I'd like to know why. What makes this device so valuable?"

"Please. Just take it and go."

Francois imagined his ordeal might soon be over. *He has what he came for. He can just leave.*

The American slipped the device back into his pocket and glanced at his watch.

"What's the combination?"

"It's not locked."

"What's on it?"

"Nothing. I assure you, it's completely blank," and Francois nodded toward the laptop. "Go. See for yourself. You will see. It's empty."

The American took the device back to the desk, and the NanoVault connected automatically. He returned moments later.

"You're right, it's blank," he said. "But if you're not using it, why have one?"

"Research," and Francois nodded toward the back wall. The American turned to see a lifetime of achievement and accolades. Among the faded degrees hanging on the wall were journal clippings, edges curled and fraying, a small shelf of dusty mathematics awards, and a handful of student group photos. Missing was any semblance of a life outside of academia. No wife. No family.

"Then, tell me *Professeur*," he said, exaggerating the Frenchman's academic position. "What makes this device so special?"

"Oh, but it's not. It's like any other. Available at any— [22]

The slap caught him before he could finish.

"You're lying."

"I swear. I'm telling you the truth."

The American pulled out a phone, launched an app and hit a few keystrokes, and there was the noise again. The same as before. When he extended his arm and pointed away, the tone was low and slow. When the phone was closer, the chirp grew higher and faster until he came within an inch or two of his jacket pocket.

"They sent me to retrieve this specific device," and he tapped his pocket. "It's different alright, and if you want to live, you'll tell me why."

Francois lifted his heels, and balancing on his toes, took a deep breath. His lower lip quivered.

"I want to live. If I knew anything useful, anything at all. I would tell you."

"OK. Have it your way," he said, placed a boot on the chair and pressed.

"Stop. Please. I beg of you."

"I'm listening," and he let the chair settle back on all four legs.

Francois closed his eyes and cleared his throat.

"He warned me," he sobbed. "I didn't listen."

The American remained silent.

"He found it. He said it was dangerous," Francois said. "I didn't believe him."

"What did he find?"

But Francois wasn't listening anymore. He coughed and lifted his heels again. He thought about the decision that brought him to this moment. *Did he really believe contacting Moore was the right thing to do, or was it just the pride of an old man at the end of his career?*

"He said I was a fool, and he was right," Francois muttered. "An old fool."

"Who? Who were you working with? What did he find?" The urgency of the questions crept into the American's voice. "Tell me and I'll set you free."

"Le Nomad," he spat out with such force the chair shook and rocked onto two legs, but the American caught him and steadied the chair.

"Who is Le Nomad?"

Francois just closed his eyes.

***

NOMAD OPENED AN AUDIO-ONLY channel to the Frenchman's laptop.

"He can't help you," echoed a synthesized male voice. From the TV camera feed, Nomad saw the masked man draw his knife from behind his back and scan the room.

"Over here," Nomad said, calling the man to the Frenchman's computer. The masked man grabbed the office chair and sat down.

"Nice of you to join us," the man said. "I assume I'm speaking with Le Nomad."

"Just Nomad, and you are?"

"Well, 'just Nomad', they call me Ronin."

"Ah, the wandering samurai, no lord or master," Nomad said.

"Shall we focus on the matter at hand?" Ronin asked. "You say Frenchy can't help me, but I'm guessing you can."

"I could, but we both know you'll kill him, anyway."

"Then why speak up?" Ronin asked. "Why not just grab some popcorn and watch the show?"

"Because I believe in second chances," Nomad said and paused. "I was given a second chance. Now I'm offering one to you. Just take the device and go."

"That's not much of an offer. I have the device. I can leave any time."

"I've been watching you," Nomad said. "The laptop's camera and the apartment's TV."

"That's clever, but it doesn't change anything."

"You've checked your watch three times since you arrived," Nomad said. "You're in a hurry. Perhaps the client is waiting, or you're expected elsewhere.

And now you're wondering when the police will arrive, which should be any minute now. So, I think we can agree you're running out of time."

"Smart, and correct," Ronin said. "I do have another engagement, but I also have my reputation to consider. The contract was quite explicit, and failure has consequences."

"There's nothing to be gained by killing an old man. You have what you need to satisfy your employer."

"You don't know my client, but this is interesting," Ronin said. "It makes no difference to me if the Frenchman lives or dies, but it means something to you."

"Then let's make this meaningful for you as well," Nomad said. "I see your client is someone calling him or herself, Grandmaster. That's amusing. And I see you received $100,000. That's a tidy sum, and I assume you'll collect more on delivery. No wonder you're curious."

"What the hell!" Ronin said. "How could you know — you hacked my NanoVault."

"Just take the device," Nomad said. "Cut the Frenchman loose and walk away. You can keep the money. But if you kill him, everything on your device will vanish. You'll lose it all. Do we have a deal?"

"No can do," Ronin said, and stepped away from the laptop. "Mission first," and with a swift kick, the chair flew out from under Francois.

The Frenchman's body bucked, his legs flailed, and eyes bulged. Within seconds, Francois was unconscious, and his limp body swayed on the rope. Ronin cut and removed the duct tape from Francois's hands and monitored his pulse. Two minutes later, the Frenchman was dead.

Stuck in his chair, continents away, Nomad watched and cried. He never felt more helpless and powerless. *Where were the police,* he wondered, and sobbed? *Why hadn't they come? There was time. They could have saved him.*

Nomad struggled to clear his throat and find his voice. "I'm so sorry, my friend," Nomad whispered, but the synthesized voice from the laptop echoed cold and distant. *This is all my fault,* he thought. *I never should have asked for your help.*

Ronin pocketed the duct tape and scanned the room. He returned to the computer.

"Nomad?" Ronin asked. "You still with me?"

"Yes."

"You know it doesn't end here."

"I know."

"This client is rich, resourceful," Ronin said. "He will find you."

"I'm counting on it."

CHAPTER 3

FRIDAY, APRIL 17
6:46 AM EDT

UNDISCLOSED LOCATION

Nomad spun away from the workstation when he heard Keisha's footsteps. The wheelchair's motors hummed, and the tires whined at the sudden, sharp, turn. She blocked his retreat and his effort to shield her.

Keisha Mobatu kept Nomad fed, clean and, most important, out of the hospital. His live-in companion had the nursing skills he required, and a past that pushed legitimate employment out of reach.

"What's wrong" she asked and looked over his shoulder at the monitor.

"My God. Is that," she began. "Is that Francois?"

"Yes," Nomad said, and the tears returned.

Keisha grabbed some tissue and blotted Nomad's eyes and cheeks and wiped his nose. While Nomad had partial use of his arms, his range of motion was limited. She placed a hand on his shoulder. Nomad flinched, and she withdrew.

Nomad looked down, embarrassed. The touch was unexpected. The twitch uncontrolled. Even after two years, her friendship and warmth remained startling.

"I heard you two arguing again last night."

"I tried to warn him," Nomad said. "But he is, was, so damn stubborn. Brilliant, but stubborn."

"I know the type," Keisha said. "Have you eaten?"

"No," he answered. "I can't."

"Then we better check your blood sugar."

"My Dex thinks I'm fine."

"So, your Dexcom 'thinks' now? Oh, great," she said. "I've seen those things be off thirty, forty points, and if you crash, you won't be helping anyone."

Keisha hunted around in her bag for a test kit. "And if you die, what happens to me? Back on the streets? No thank you, that is not an option, so give me your damn finger."

Nomad released his grip on the chair's joystick and extended a finger. For all his body's failings, he knew it well enough to sense that his blood sugar was fine, but this was a ritual Keisha performed to mask awkward moments. She pressed the softclix device against his finger. Nomad waited for the lance to prick his finger, but it never did, and he looked up at Keisha.

"What is it?" he asked, wondering what caught her attention. There was movement in the Frenchman's apartment.

"Who's that?" Keisha whispered.

"I was expecting the police," he said. "But you don't have to whisper. Whoever it is, can't see or hear us."

Nomad tucked back into the workstation. He studied the man's movements and waited for a glimpse of his face. The Frenchman's body obscured the view from the apartment's TV, and they saw little more than a partial profile. The man's actions were swift, methodical. *Definitely not the police*, Nomad thought. *Then who?*

The man brushed past Francois's swaying body. Ignoring the Frenchman's tortured expression and urine pooling on the floor. The man entered the bedroom and approached the laptop.

"Oh no," Nomad said, and he captured a screenshot of the man's face.

"You know this guy?"

"Not personally, but we've crossed paths," Nomad said. "That's Mikhail Zhukov. Former Russian Spetsnaz."

"Spets-what?"

"Russian special forces. Think Navy SEAL, only savage, ruthless."

"You worked with the Russian military?" Keisha asked.

"No. Zhukov's military service is ancient history, and so is his prison time," Nomad said. "He's a mercenary now."

They watched Zhukov search the desk and the room.

"What's he looking for?" Keisha wondered.

"Doesn't matter. He's too late," Nomad said. "There's nothing left for him here. What I want to know is who's holding Zhukov's leash? Someone new has joined the hunt for the device and probably me."

Zhukov appeared ready to leave, but stopped and studied the professor's gallery of plaques, articles, and photos. Something on the wall, some moment in Francois's past, caught Zhukov's attention, and he leaned in for a closer look. He lifted an old photograph off the wall.

Nomad strained to see what Zhukov was handling and recognized the chess team photo.

With a flick of the wrist, Zhukov smashed the frame. Glass shattered and crashed to the floor. He removed the photo, examined the back, then folded and slipped it into his jacket's vest pocket.

Zhukov returned to the bedroom. The video feed from the Frenchman's laptop caught a flash of shadow and flesh, then disappeared.

"What just happened?" Keisha asked.

"He took the laptop."

Nomad weighed the implications like an opening chess move.

"The laptop will have trace evidence of my link to Francois," he said. "And Zhukov has the technical resources to piece together my location, but that was always a risk. There's still time."

"You sound worried."

"It's probably nothing."

"I know that voice," Keisha said. "It's something. Something bad."

"Years ago, I did some contract work for Zhukov. He was in Syria at the time, and when it looked like he was orchestrating a chemical weapons attack, I passed his location to an analyst I knew at the CIA."

"Jesus. What happened?"

"I don't know. Not really," he said. "A few rumors surfaced. My contact was captured and interrogated, later hospitalized. The rescue team incurred casualties. And Zhukov disappeared. The details would be in the CIA's after-action report, but it was buttoned up tight and buried so deep even I couldn't find it."

"Does Zhukov know you set him up?"

"No. I was invisible then, like now," Nomad said. "But there's a chance he recognized her. Why else would he take the team photo?"

"Her? Who are we talking about?"

With a couple of flicks on his chair's control system, Nomad opened a folder and displayed a photo.

"This is the photo Zhukov just took," Nomad said. "It's the MIT chess team the year we won the PanAm Team Championship."

"You think somehow he recognized her?" Keisha asked, pointing at the young woman in the photo.

"That is Katherine Preacher, my contact at the CIA."

Keisha studied the photo and said, "I recognize Francois. Younger, of course, but the same broad smile and that mustache."

She leaned in and scanned the group standing alongside the professor.

"Christ, is that you?" she asked, noting the shortest boy in the photo. "How old were you? Twelve?"

"Fourteen," Nomad said, and he peered into the eyes of his friend and mentor. *Francois would still be alive if I hadn't asked for his help,* he thought, and swallowed hard.

"You went to MIT at Fourteen?"

"Yes," he said, grateful for the distraction. "MIT has an early admissions program, and I was one of the youngest accepted."

"She's young, too. Not as young as you, but younger than the others."

"We were the youngest on the team," he said, "and the best."

"You were just kids at the time," Keisha said. "I doubt she looks anything like the skinny girl with the ponytail."

"No, you're right," he said. "She's gorgeous."

When Keisha raised an eyebrow, he realized he'd slipped and tried to ignore it.

"You had a crush on her, and apparently still do," Keisha said. "But there's no way Zhukov recognized her from a teenage photo."

"I hope you're right."

"I know I'm right," Keisha said. "The photo means something, but she's not it. Who's the tall kid in the middle?"

"That's Devin Moore."

"No way," she said, and pushed in for a closer look. "That's THE Devin Moore? The Sexiest Man Alive Devin Moore?"

"The very one."

"I had no idea you knew him."

"That's another—" he began.

"I know, I know. Another life," she said. "Let's get back to this life. Could he be in danger?"

"No. Moore's untouchable," Nomad said. "And besides, Moore has his own agenda."

"Then it has to be you," Keisha said. "Zhukov sees an old photo of Francois standing with a bunch of pimple-faced MIT nerds, and he thinks Nomad might be one of them."

"Maybe, but the boy in that photo is dead. Anyone looking for him is ghost hunting."

"That boy may be dead, but the man sitting here is still breathing," she said. "And that reminds me."

Keisha took his hand, pricked his finger, squeezed a drop of blood onto a glucose test strip, and waited for the result.

"Eighty-two. You'll live, but let's get you something to eat before you go any lower," she said. She took a step toward the kitchen, but turned back.

"He's coming, isn't he?" Keisha asked. "The Russian. He's coming for you."

"Yes," Nomad said. "And he's not the only one looking."

"How long do we have?"

Nomad hesitated. It was a race now. Zhukov had a network of contacts with global reach, yet somehow Francois's killer beat Zhukov to the device. Nomad knew both adversaries were resourceful and determined, and neither would stop until they found him.

"A few days, a week at most," Nomad said. "You should pack a bag."

"Do you have time to finish what you started?" Keisha asked. "I mean without Francois?"

"I'll try," Nomad said. "But I honestly don't know. If I can't do it. If I need help. There is one person I'd trust with the truth."

"You're thinking about contacting her, aren't you?" Keisha asked. "The girl in the picture."

"Yes," Nomad said. "If there's no other choice."

"Then you better think twice," Keisha said. "This crusade or vendetta or whatever the hell you're doing just cost a man's life. If you bring her in, then Katherine Preacher could be next."

CHAPTER 4

FRIDAY, APRIL 17
6:50 AM EDT

RICHMOND, VA

KATHERINE PREACHER ACCEPTED THAT she'd become predictable. No alternating routes from home to work. She didn't need to glance at the reflections in shop windows or in the side mirrors of parked cars. No one was following. Of course not. But some habits are hard to break, and some lessons too painful to forget.

She walked to the Starbucks on the corner of Seventh and Byrd as she did most mornings, and waited for her usual mobile order. They were busy today. Kate glanced at her watch. *There's time.* She was early, but today was special. Jake was calling from Paris and she wanted to take the call in her office.

A Tesla screeched to a stop and drew Kate's focus to the windows. Her threat assessment was instinctive. *Excessive speed. Blocked fire hydrant.* The front door flew open, and the driver brushed past a couple trying to exit the coffee shop. They stepped out of his way, juggling the coffee cups in their hands.

Both hands visible. Empty. Fitted designer suit. Thin fashion belt. He's not armed.

He approached the mobile order desk and scanned Kate from head to toe. She followed his eyes, noting where they paused. His half-smile, half-smirk conveyed Kate crossed his "doable" threshold. She glared and turned away.

"What the hell is this?" he yelled at the barista, and Kate turned back in time to see him shove the coffee back across the counter. The cup tipped and the lid popped off. Hot coffee and steamed milk flew at the barista and she lurched back.

"I ordered a grande almond-milk flat white no whip no foam," he said. "I don't know what the hell this is, but it's half foam. Now do it again and do it right, or find someone who can."

Kate approached the counter, grabbed some napkins and helped the young woman wipe up the mess. Kate could see she was flushed and fighting tears.

"Amy, are you alright?"

"Thanks, Kate," she whispered. "I'm OK," and turned to prepare the man's drink.

Kate reached into the canvas messenger bag slung over her shoulder, withdrew a small android tablet, and started typing. The junior digital evidence investigators at the firm called it her bag of tricks. Kate preferred to think of it like a country doctor's bag of instruments. Password cracking, Wi-Fi sniffing, disk imaging, vehicle data recovery, Faraday bags and more, each selected and prepared to help exonerate or convict. But given the law firm's mix of high-profile clients, the goal was often shades of gray.

The more attractive Kate's outfit, the more obvious the unsightly appendage, but she went nowhere without the bag. Kate's red DVF pencil skirt and silk wrap top were stunning and hugged her tall, svelte figure. But the messenger bag, a mix of faded khaki ballistic nylon and cracked leather, looked like it belonged to Gunny, the homeless vet that lived in the alley around the corner.

Tesla-man, as Kate now thought of him, took a call, and she used the distraction to edge closer.

"Yeah, I know I'm late," he said. "A blond bimbo screwed up my espresso, but I'll be there soon, and if they want the deal, they'll wait."

Everything about the conversation confirmed Kate's initial assessment. *Self-important man.* Within seconds, she cloned his Tesla keys and hacked into the car's control system. His default PIN made the effort rather trivial. Kate added *moron* to her assessment and her fingers flew across the tablet, composing a series of vehicle system commands.

Tesla-man ended the call and turned back to the barista, but before he could say another word, his car sprang to life. The Model X's Falcon Wing doors opened and flapped and *Flight of the Bumblebee* blared from the audio system. He dug into his pocket, rummaging for the key, and raced toward the door. Pointing and pressing the remote triggered more trouble. The hood popped open, windshield wipers flicked, lights flashed all while the car alarm wailed, and when the car moved, he panicked and screamed.

The whoop-whoop siren of the Richmond police was Kate's cue to wrap up. She stopped the car's erratic back-and-forth movement and shut down the hack while Tesla-man struggled to turn off the car's alarm. The police car's flashing lights flickered through the coffee shop's windows. Two more quick yelps on the siren alerted the gawking crowd to move on, and Kate slipped the tablet back into her bag. Tesla-man was on his own now, and she suspected the police would be less than sympathetic about his choice of parking spots or the urgency of his big deal.

Kate turned back to the mobile order counter. Everyone frozen, transfixed by the show outside, but Kate's order was ready and Amy said, "I added a little something extra for Gunny. I hope he likes it."

"Whatever it is," Kate said, "he'll complain about it, but he'll love it."

Amy smiled, but hesitated when she handed Kate the paper bag. "Did you have something to do with that?" she asked, nodding to the scene outside.

"Me? No." Kate looked out the window and smiled. "Just karma."

CHAPTER 5

FRIDAY, APRIL 17
7:00 AM EDT

RICHMOND, VA

GUNNERY SERGEANT TYRONE WALKER, known to the locals as simply Gunny, or Grumpy, made his home in the alley between Starbucks and the office building where Kate worked.

"You're late," he said when he saw Kate approaching.

"Car trouble," she said, and handed him his morning coffee.

"That racket yur doin?" he asked, looking up the street when a tow truck arrived.

"Why does everyone keep asking me that?"

"Figured as much."

"Just take your coffee."

"Black?"

"Of course."

"Three sugars? The real stuff, not that pink crap?"

"Yes, your highness," she said with a half-curtsy, "and Amy added something for you in the bag."

"Somethin fruity I 'spect," he said. "That girl's always pushin' fruit."

"She's concerned about you. We all are." Kate glanced up the alley to the makeshift structure of cardboard, plastic and shopping carts that Gunny called home.

Kate pulled back the bag before Gunny could reach it. "And when you see her, be sure to thank her."

"Alright. Alright. I will."

Kate extended the bag, and Gunny snatched it before Kate could change her mind.

"Are you sure there isn't something more we can do, something you need?"

"You ask me every day. Nuthin's changed. Now leave me be."

Kate's phone rang. "Oh no. Jake's call. How could I forget that?"

Kate answered the FaceTime video call, "Hi, honey."

"Where are you?"

"Well, hello to you too."

"Oh, sorry," he said. "I just thought you'd be at work. What's going on in the background?"

Gunny interrupted, "Tell that squid of yours what you been up to," he said. "Go on."

Jake laughed. "Now I know where you are. Turn the phone around."

Kate turned the phone so Jake could see Gunny. Tesla-man's car alarm died, and the street grew quiet.

"Hey Gunny. Whatever's going on, it's best you and I don't know," he said and laughed. "We need plausible deniability."

"OK. Very funny, you two," Kate said, and she turned the phone back around. "Give me ten minutes to get to my desk and call me back."

"That works," Jake said. "I'm on my way to meet Marcus at some cafe. I'll call you when I get there."

"Love me?"

"Always."

Chapter 6

RICHMOND PINNACLE BUILDING, RICHMOND, VA

KATE STEPPED INTO THE ground floor lobby of the Richmond Pinnacle building, eighteen stories of glass and steel overlooking the James River. Frank, Burman and Dodd, the law firm where Kate worked, had the entire top floor and the best views in the city. Kate readied her access card for the lobby turnstiles and waved to the guard at the front desk.

"Hey Pete, working days now?"

"Just filling in today," he said, "but if you'll be pulling all-nighters again this weekend, I'll be here. Feel free to bring more of those chocolate chip cookies."

"Your wife says you're on a diet."

"What she don't know won't hurt her."

Kate winked, waved her access card over the turnstile scanner, and headed for the elevator.

"Katherine Preacher!"

Kate turned back to see Leslie Dodd, her boss and one of the firm's partners. As always, Leslie was a vision of style with a sleek, confident look. Knee-length, black knit skirt, ivory silk blouse, delicate gold necklace. At five feet eight inches, she was taller than Kate, and black patent leather stiletto heels added to an already impressive air of authority. But Leslie was a bit technology challenged. She struggled with the access control kiosk, and Kate stepped up to her through the building's electronic gate-keeper.

"I hate those damn things," she said. "And I know the enhanced physical security was your recommendation."

Leslie led the way into the elevator, but she took Kate's elbow and directed her into the back corner. When the doors closed and the elevator began rising, Leslie lowered her voice and leaned in.

"What I want to know is how you managed it," Leslie asked. "Never mind. I don't want to know. I mean, I do, but I don't. I can't. The less I know, the better."

"Leslie," Kate said. "What are you talking about?"

"This," she said, tilting her phone so that Kate could see the *Wall Street Journal* article. "This is what I'm talking about."

Kate glanced at the headline. *Dominion Investments CFO Roger Smiley Resigns.*

"Good. The guy's a crook," Kate whispered. "He should be in jail, but I suspect Dominion wouldn't want the publicity."

"That's it? That's all you're going to say?"

"What do you want me to say?"

"It's not just Smiley's resignation," Leslie said. "It's the money. All thirty million."

Leslie's voice dropped even lower, and she added, "Last night, the Bank of Belize transferred thirty million dollars into Dominion's escrow account, and—"

Leslie paused and looked around the elevator. "And this morning Smiley resigns."

"I'm sorry," Kate said. "I'm not following."

"Let's just say it's a remarkable coincidence. Smiley's assistant is accused of embezzling the money. It appears obvious, and she's taken into custody. But your digital forensic investigation can't find any trace of the money. It's gone. Completely untraceable."

"Yep, vanished into thin air," Kate said. "Probably moved offshore."

"Exactly. Offshore. And untouchable. Legally," Leslie said. "Next thing we know. The money's back and Smiley resigns."

"Dominion must be thrilled to have their money and their thief."

"Indeed, they are," Leslie said. "In fact, they're so thrilled they're not asking questions about how it was done, or who was responsible."

"Well, clearly," Kate said. "Smiley had a change of heart. His conscience couldn't allow an innocent woman to take the blame.

"Oh. Yes, clearly," Leslie said. "He's a changed man."

"What happens now to his assistant?" Kate asked. "I imagine Dominion could be facing an expensive and pretty embarrassing wrongful termination suit."

"I've advised Dominion to wrap things up quickly and quietly with an NDA."

"In exchange for a generous severance package," Kate asked.

"Yes. Yes. Of course."

"You know her son was taken into foster care?"

"That was out of our control, but we've already reached out to child protective services."

The two women were moments away from reaching the eighteenth floor when Leslie turned back toward Kate.

"That's it, isn't it?" Leslie asked. "In our world, it's rarely black and white. We deal with it, but Smiley crossed the line. Your line. When he accused his assistant."

"In digital forensics, we look past the legal briefs and study the people," Kate said. "Maya Washington is a single mother, struggling to work and pay for her son's special needs. I think Smiley figured that made her the perfect scapegoat."

The elevator doors opened and Leslie stepped out. This is where the two women usually parted. Leslie heading left down the mahogany-paneled hallway toward the executive wing. Kate turning right toward the cubicle bullpen, break room, and her interior office. Kate had only gone a few steps when she felt Leslie's tap on her shoulder and turned.

Leslie gave Kate an awkward and unexpected hug.

"I'm glad you're on our side," she said and strolled toward the executive wing.

The sentiment caught Kate off guard. The normally aloof Leslie Dodd was a partner in one of the most powerful law firms in the country, with an impressive client list of politicians, lobbyists and Fortune 100 executives. Kate saw her as brilliant, tenacious, and feared by most. *Bitch was the term the boys in the cubicles would utter,* Kate thought, but she admired Leslie's style.

Leslie was tough but fair, and she paired high expectations with zero tolerance for incompetence. She was quick to reward excellence and mercilessly cut the deadwood. These were attributes Kate could respect. Leslie was also the only one at the firm fully briefed on the unclassified portions of Kate's CIA background and injuries. When Langley orchestrated Kate's placement, Leslie's no questions asked acceptance earned Kate's trust and respect.

CHAPTER 7

FRIDAY, APRIL 17
7:15 AM EDT

FINANCIAL NEWS NETWORK STUDIOS, MANHATTAN, NY

DEVIN MOORE WAITED OFF stage. A sound tech clipped a lapel mic to Moore's suit jacket and handed him the battery pack and transmitter. *Last one*, Moore thought and reached around behind his back to attach the transmitter to his belt. This was the last interview of a grueling week-long press tour, but the publicity was an essential part of his plan.

A handful of newsroom staff gathered nearby to catch a glimpse and Devin didn't disappoint. In a trim dark blue suit, and signature black t-shirt, Moore looked like he just stepped off the cover of a men's fashion magazine.

Moore glanced at his private security detail and shrugged off the attention. This same scene occurred at every news station in town, so this morning's group was no surprise. Moore was comfortable attracting attention, and most of it was harmless, but he understood that a billionaire's high-profile lifestyle came with a unique set of risks. A quick nod from his close protection operator was all it took to ensure the room was secure.

With Moore's sound check complete, he approached the edge of the studio and listened. The show's host, Stephanie Larkin, was wrapping up a panel discussion on China's manipulation of SEC reporting requirements.

Stephanie Larkin at FNN owned the morning business news market with the highest rated financial news show in the country. Moore was looking forward to the interview, but was no fan of the talking-head panels that were a staple of the 24/7 news cycle. In the PR firm's negotiations with Larkin, Moore agreed to come on the show, but only face to face with the host.

During the commercial break, Moore was escorted to the seat immediately to the left of the host. He wondered if the seating favored Stephanie's "good side," and makeup artists scurried around her eliminating any hint of unwanted shine. They gave Moore a quick dash of powder and a final mic check. He straightened his jacket and waited for the producer's countdown to his introduction.

"Welcome back," Larkin said, addressing the audience, and the camera held in tight on the engaging blonde who prepared to introduce her next guest.

"From international magazine covers to the top of New York's most eligible bachelors, this CEO has one of the world's most recognizable faces," Larkin began, and the cameras pulled back to bring Devin into the shot. "In the corridors of MIT he's remembered as the wunderkind who shattered barriers in quantum computing and artificial intelligence, but in financial circles he's the man that set the FinTech world on fire and rocketed into the top ten of the world's richest men."

Larkin pivoted in her chair to address Moore directly.

"I'm joined today by the founder and CEO of Moore Technologies, Devin Moore. Devin, it's always great to see you. Thanks for coming in this morning."

"It's a pleasure to be back."

"Before we dive in, congratulations on cracking the top ten. At an estimated net worth of over one hundred billion, you're among an elite group of global entrepreneurs, and easily the youngest self-made billionaire on the list."

Right on cue, Moore thought, and launched into his prepared response.

"Thanks, Stephanie. I'm humbled to be among so many remarkable people, literally household names, but don't forget, I also hold the distinction of being the youngest person to both make and lose a billion dollars before I was old enough to drink."

"It's true. Your story is a blend of tremendous success, spectacular failure, and unconventional thinking."

"I'll take that as a compliment."

"We're here today to discuss a remarkable milestone, but let's start at the beginning," she said. "Two years ago, in a move that stunned Wall Street, you took Moore Technologies private, betting your entire fortune on a product that no one outside a select group of private investors had even seen or fully understood. Few thought you would survive, much less succeed."

"As I recall, you were one of many who predicted my demise."

"It's true," Stephanie said. "I believed that exiting the capital markets was a fatal mistake, but you were right. The company has literally risen from the ashes, and that brings me to the reason for your visit today."

Larkin reached into a compartment beneath the studio desk and pulled one of Moore's products out of her purse. She held the small black cylinder between her thumb and index finger. The camera pulled in to show a smiling Larkin holding a device that resembled a designer tube of lipstick, and she addressed the audience.

"In the interest of full disclosure," Leslie said, and placed the device on the desk. "I'm a Moore Tech customer and this one is mine. And judging from the sales figures, many of you watching already own one, but for anyone that's been living under a rock, Devin would you take a moment to explain the product's unique appeal and phenomenal success?"

"In simple terms, the Quantum NanoVault is your personal cloaking device," he began. "We're all digitally connected to a remarkable network of information, communication and commerce. But the price of admission was our privacy. I would say even our dignity. It seemed a fair trade, at first."

"So would you say that digital privacy is the NanoVault's primary benefit," Leslie asked.

"It's where most customers start. We all have secrets, and the NanoVault's Quantum Key encrypted storage is the one place you know you can trust,"

Devin said. "Whatever you store, documents, photos, videos, digital currency, it's safe, secure and impenetrable."

"I understand the NanoVault's encrypted storage is state-of-the-art, but many of us have used password management tools before. The concept isn't new, but no other product or service has even approached the NanoVault's level of distribution and widespread acceptance," Leslie said. "How do you explain that success? What motivates your customers?"

"Freedom," Devin said. "Our customers are cutting the cord to the corporations, financial institutions, and governments that have been spying on us. Those entities have had a monopoly on our personal data. Every search, text, post, message. Absolutely everything in the digital world. And what have they done with all this data? We're categorized, divided, manipulated and controlled. Our customers said, 'Enough. You don't own me.' And this week we're announcing that global shipments have crossed the one hundred million mark."

Larkin turned away from the camera and twisted back toward Moore.

"Devin, congratulations! That's a remarkable achievement for any product, and to hit that threshold in nine months is simply stunning."

"Thank you," Moore replied. "Naturally, we're..."

"But the product, the company, and you personally have more than your share of critics."

Moore shifted a bit in his seat. *She's going off script*, he thought. *Interesting opening. Let's redirect.*

"Yes, in fact, both the product and I have been banned in China. A move that screws up my vacation plans."

"Isn't it true that China banned the product because you refused to disclose to the CCP the full breadth of the device's capabilities?"

"As you know, being banned in China is a badge of honor I now share with several actors, activists, and politicians."

"Yes, but this isn't about a stance on human rights or on Taiwan's independence. My sources tell me that China sees your product as a threat."

"China fears anything it doesn't control," Devin said. "In my view, their tenuous grasp on the people is already slipping. Attempts to block independent news sources, their Digital Great Wall, if you will, is crumbling. So it's not unreasonable for China to fear that the Quantum NanoVault could accelerate that collapse."

"So while corporations in every major sector build factories and open offices seeking access to China's vast markets, you're content to ignore that enormous opportunity?"

"China has one business model. They 'rob, replicate and replace' - a phrase that is finally gaining momentum," Devin said. "The CCP would demand I hand over source code, setup R&D centers in China, and create backdoors into the hardware and software. Only the foolish, or the greedy, would take that deal."

"And you're neither?"

"I try not to be."

"How do you respond to speculation that you took the company private solely to avoid the scrutiny and oversight of a board of directors, and that adhering to SEC regulations would have crippled your ability to operate in total secrecy?"

There it is, Moore thought. *The real reason she booked the interview and insisted her show was the last stop.* Moore's momentary pause was all the time Larkin needed to change the tenor of the discussion and begin her assault.

Larkin continued, "Mr. Moore, isn't it true that China is only the first country to ban your product, and that other countries are considering similar actions, because the device's encryption and communication capabilities stifle law enforcement investigations and empower criminals and terrorists?"

"Stephanie," he replied. "You have one of my devices. Is there anything on it you need to keep private? Anything that would be embarrassing if it leaked to the press?"

"My personal life is not the issue."

"But it is. How much money you make or who you sleep with may be juicy fodder for the tabloids, but there are countries where reliance on the

NanoVault's encryption integrity and secure communications is a matter of life and death," Devin said, and he pushed on before she could interrupt. "There are entire communities throughout Africa and the Middle East entirely dependent on the NanoVault's ability to get work, sell goods and services, shop in open markets, all without government intervention or relying on corrupt or non-existent financial institutions."

"Doesn't it bother you that terrorists allegedly used your device to communicate, coordinate and fund several devastating attacks and political assassinations, and still, you refuse access requests from both the FBI and Interpol?"

"I'm horrified by the acts of the insane and the irrational who justify violence to achieve their goals," he said. "And I'm terrified by the despots, tyrants and dictators who use information to control their populations, enslave the weak, and murder political opponents."

"That doesn't answer my question."

"Listen," Moore said. "For decades, personal privacy fell victim to the illusion of safety and security. What have we learned? That the very agencies tasked with ensuring our safety have their own agendas and often collude with global corporations to further personal ambitions."

"Despite the growing body of damning evidence, you refuse to cooperate with any lawful investigation?"

"I will never provide the CCP, FBI, CIA, NSA or any other so-called intelligence agency unfettered access to the device because someone must draw a line in the sand. Someone has to say no."

"But you're comfortable working with Ukrainian Oligarch, Vitali Moshenski, an alleged arms dealer, and suspected war criminal? Is he the billionaire 'white knight' that rescued Moore Technologies? Are Moshenski's illicit activities and his investment among the secrets you're so determined to protect?"

"Mr. Moshenski is a respected business executive and member of Ukraine's diplomatic mission, and through that mission we have discussed economic development efforts, but no, he's not an investor in my firm," Moore said. "As you noted at the start of the show, I leveraged every asset at my disposal to take the company private. Had I failed, I'd be holding a cardboard sign outside your studio, not sitting in it."

That's a decent sound bite, he thought. *Let's wrap this up.* He pushed away from the desk, but Larkin pressed on.

"Mr. Moore," she began. "Devin, my sources in Washington..."

This is her endgame. Let's see how she plays this.

Moore pulled back into the desk and gave her his attention.

"My sources tell me that Senator Cahill, the Ranking Member of the Senate Subcommittee on Homeland Security, is calling for an investigation into Moore Technologies and the Quantum NanoVault's potential threat to National Security. Care to comment?"

"I'm not surprised, though I admit I'm disappointed."

"You're not surprised a subpoena might compel you to answer, under oath, the very questions you're determined to evade?"

"No, I'm not surprised that your Washington sources would leak an obvious attempt to grab a headline," he said. "I know Senator Cahill is facing a tough reelection, and with the mid-terms looming, there's a good chance he'll soon be out of a job, but I'm disappointed you took the bait."

The show cut to a commercial, Moore smiled and stood. He extended a hand to Larkin, which she hesitated to take, but then relented. *Firm, sweaty,* he thought. Moore held the handshake, and with his left hand on her elbow, stepped closer, and whispered in her ear.

"Shall we call it a draw?"

"Is this just a game to you?"

"Off the record?"

"Alright," she said. "Off the record."

"Acknowledging that it's a game, doesn't mean I don't take it seriously," he said. "The country, the world, is at crossroads. A handful of powerful elites have a near monopoly on all of our personal data, and with it they intend to shape the very future of our planet."

"So in this grand conspiracy, Devin Moore is both saint and savior?"

"No one who knows me would suggest I'm a saint, and I can't save anyone. But I can offer the means for people to save themselves," Devin said. "Think of it like that Matrix movie. I can't make anyone take the Red Pill. If they don't want to wake up, that's their choice."

"And this game you're playing. You think you can win?"

"As a student of history, war and chess, I know nations rise and fall on the moves of a few key players," he said. "We're all playing, but to win, we must decide what risks we'll take. What sacrifices we're willing to make. So, the only question now is, are you a pawn or a queen?"

Moore let go of her hand and stepped back.

"Don't worry, that's rhetorical," Devin said. "But when your divorce is final, call me."

CHAPTER 8

FRIDAY, APRIL 17
1:17 PM CEST

LE CAFE PIERRE, PARIS, FRANCE

MIKHAIL ZHUKOV TUCKED THE Frenchman's laptop under his left arm, keeping his right arm free to draw his weapon. He exited via the rear of Francois's building to avoid the Paris street cameras. On his way to the cafe, he placed a brief call and in Russian instructed one of his men to pull the car into the alley behind the cafe. He ended the call with a warning, *"Bud' nastorozhe"* — *stay alert.*

Mikhail threaded through the lunchtime throng with remarkable ease. The pedestrians appeared to sense the Russian's determined strides and stepped aside. He arrived at the cafe a few minutes later and approached one of the sidewalk tables.

Of the three occupants at the table, only one glanced up when Mikhail approached. The Ukrainian Oligarch, Vitali Moshenski, a distinguished gentleman in his seventies, wore a finely tailored dark blue suit. His neatly trimmed gray hair and beard completed the look of both European sophistication and wealth. Mikhail waited. When he observed Vitali lift his right index finger, he approached, leaned in and whispered.

"The Frenchman is dead. The device is gone."

"What do you have there?" Vitali asked, nodding at the laptop.

"A lead. Our people will examine, but this location is compromised. We should go," Mikhail said, as he straightened up and scanned the area. He expected Vitali would follow his suggestion, make his excuses and proceed to the car staged in the alley.

"Monsieur Zhukov, allow me to introduce my grandson, Stephan. And this lovely young woman I've just learned is his fiancée. Desiree."

Stephan stood, smiled and extended a hand. Mikhail was struck by the young man's firm handshake and engaging smile. The strong jaw and rugged face reminded him of Vitali, and he didn't dress like a university student. The navy blue blazer, striped shirt, gray slacks and leather loafers was a look of sophistication Mikhail didn't associate with Paris youth.

"Congratulations," Mikhail said, and he summoned a smile for the bubbling young couple and turned back to Vitali. "My friend. I'm sorry to interrupt the celebration, but I must insist. You are needed elsewhere."

"Dedushka, if you must go, please don't let us detain you," Stephan said in Russian. "We only wanted to take this opportunity to share the news."

"Nonsense," Vitali said. "We have time. Mikhail, please join us."

"Your Russian is excellent," Mikhail noted, and he took the chair next to Vitali.

"*Merci*," Stephan replied, and smiled.

"Stephan speaks several languages fluently," Desiree said. "That's how we met. But sometimes I have to insist he pick one and stop bouncing around."

"Mr. Zhukov. My grandfather mentioned you might join us, and I was hoping to meet you," Stephan said. "Is it true you two met in prison?"

"It is, but —" Mikhail began.

"And you saved his life?"

"Yes, a Russian prison is no place for soft men like Vitali," Mikhail said, and the men laughed. Vitali Moshenski was one of the most feared and respected of the Ukrainian Oligarchs. There was never a moment anyone would mistake him for soft, and the men at the table knew it.

"But let us not dwell on the past," Vitali said. "Today, we celebrate the future." He raised his glass and toasted the young couple.

"May your love guide you and bind you, and grow stronger with every breath."

Mikhail recognized the joy and love in the young couple's eyes. He pictured his wife, and the sparkle in her eyes. Nadia was a concert violinist. So beautiful and talented. She could have had any man she desired and she chose a soldier. Few understood why, and Mikhail was among them. He still carries her photo, and of one his baby girl. *How long has it been,* Mikhail wondered. *Eighteen years? No, Nineteen.* He still sees them in his dreams and hears their screams in his nightmares.

In prison, Zhukov learned of Vitali's wife and her death. It was one of many things that bound the men together. So he understood Vitali's desire to stay and bask in the radiance of the couple's love, but he knew it wasn't safe to stay. Not for his friend or his family.

"Mikhail, just before you arrived, Stephan was telling me of their plans," Vitali said. "Oh, to be young and in love in Paris. Stephan, when you have a date for the wedding, you must let me know. I wouldn't miss it for the world. And, if I can do anything to assist, you have only to ask."

"That's kind of you to offer, Grandpapa," Stephan said. "And we will, of course, coordinate with you and your schedule as things progress."

Mikhail stood as a signal they had delayed long enough.

In Russian once again, Stephan insisted Mr. Zhukov attend the wedding as well.

"It would be my honor," Mikhail replied.

Moshenski stood, and the young couple did as well.

"Please, stay. Finish your champagne. I insist," Vitali said, and he stepped forward to hug Stephan. He extended a hand to Desiree, took hers and kissed it, but she pressed forward, placed her hands on Vitali's shoulders and kissed both cheeks.

Mikhail was happy to see his friend smiling, and they turned away from the table. It was a rare, tender moment in a life filled with darkness and punctuated by loss. He hoped the couple would never know the pain that he and Vitali knew all too well.

When the two men were far enough away, Mikhail noted. "He has her gift for language."

"Yes," Vitali replied. "And his mother's eyes. Don't you think?"

"Will you ever tell him?"

"I think not. His life is his own, and that's best," Vitali said. "And a new life is about to begin."

CHAPTER 9

FRIDAY, APRIL 17
1:22 PM CEST

LE CAFE PIERRE, PARIS, FRANCE

JAKE CHURCH APPROACHED THE cafe at the corner of Rue de Tournon and Saint-Germain and scanned the popular French bistro's sidewalk tables. No sign of Marcus. That was perfect. Jake was early and now he could call Kate without Marcus trying to steal the show. He grabbed a table, caught the eye of the waitress, and ordered an espresso.

With his clients all safely tucked into the Global Economic Council's regional meeting, he and the rest of the close protection team wouldn't be needed again for a few hours. He could relax a little and wait until the drivers were ready to review the conference exit routes. The daily practice runs on the primary and alternate routes ensured the team was prepared for unscheduled road work, unusual congestion, or unexpected protests.

Jake checked the time and pictured Kate's morning routine. Knowing she would be settling in at her desk, he launched a FaceTime call.

"Good timing," she said, propping her iPad on the desk. "I just sat down."

"You doing OK?" he asked. "You look tired."

"That is just about the last thing any woman wants to hear. Especially one that's been sleeping on the couch while her husband's running around Paris."

"Right. Let me try that again," Jake said. "You look great. You know I love that blouse."

"Nice save," she said. "Hang on."

"Are you recording?" he asked. "Again?"

"Yes, smart ass," she said. "Maybe you don't miss me, but I love these little videos. They keep me company when I need to hear your voice and see that smug face."

"You're right. I'm sorry."

"Nice," Kate said. "I think that's going to be my new ring tone."

"Now, who's the smart ass?"

"Fair enough," she said. "Where are you?"

"A little sidewalk cafe," he said. "It's packed. I was lucky to grab a table."

"Oh, hold the phone up," she said. "I'd love to see it."

Jake panned the bustling street scene in front of him and turned the camera toward the cafe. The sidewalk in front of the cafe was lined with wrought-iron tables, each adorned with white tablecloths that fluttered in the breeze, and nearly all were occupied. Ceramic flower pots hung from lampposts, and overflowed with vibrant blooms, adding a touch of natural beauty to the dense urban scene.

The call captured the tapestry of sounds. The clinking of porcelain cups and saucers, the symphony of laughter and conversation in various languages. Tourists wandered past, eyes glued to their phone's walking maps, while couples shared a bottle of wine and students hunched over books, sipping coffee and nibbling pastry.

"It's beautiful," she said. "I can almost smell the croissants at the table behind you. And here comes your espresso."

He turned to see the waitress, tray balanced in one hand, skillfully weaving her way through the maze of tables, her gaze locked on to his table.

"Merci beaucoup," Jake said, and the petite espresso cup landed on his tablecloth.

"Nice try," Kate said. "Remind me to work on your pronunciation."

"Yeah, that's not going to happen," he said, and they both laughed.

Jake propped the phone up on the table and took a sip of the espresso.

"I do have some good news," he said.

"You're coming home?"

"Good guess. Looks like the conference will wrap up on Monday."

"Wow, celebrating our anniversary in the same room," she said. "Just like normal people."

"And this time, I have an actual present."

"Just come home," she said. "You know that's all I ever want."

"I know, but five years is a big deal, and I've got a little something right here," he said and tapped his suit jacket's breast pocket.

"What is it?"

"I'm not saying, and don't even think about using your tricks on me."

"It's jewelry," she said, closing her eyes, concentrating. "A bracelet."

"Hey! Don't spoil the surprise."

"OK, no more," she said. "I have a little something for you as well."

"I'm counting on it," Jake said, and smiled.

"I know that smile. That's not your present."

"Well, that's disappointing."

"Trust me, big boy, you won't be disappointed, but we better change the subject before neither of us can get back to work."

"Copy that," he said. "How did your investigation go?"

"Let's just say the score is good guys thirty million, bad guys zero."

"I'm proud of you."

"Thanks, my love," she said. "What about the conference? Any trouble?"

"So far, so good. The usual array of protesters, but the police are keeping them at bay. The French team handles all the close protection work inside the conference. We just get the clients from the hotel to the pavilion and back again in one piece. You know the drill. Lead and trail cars. Mix of live and decoy vehicles. Private entrances."

"Yes, I know the drill," she said. "You take all the vehicle interdiction risk while the French CPOs stand around eating croissants?"

"I love having a spook for a wife," he said. "You cut right through the BS."

"Former *Analyst*," she said. "And I know deflection when I hear it."

"You gotta admit, three weeks in Paris beats six months in the sandbox."

"I'll let that slide, for now, but the next trip to the City of Love we take together. Deal?"

"Let me make sure I understand the mission parameters," he said. "Romantic location, fine wine, fabulous food, and you expect to be swept off your feet by your bodyguard?"

"Smart boy," she said. "You catch on quick."

"Marcus. Over here," Jake called out, and waited for his teammate to turn around and zero in on Jake's table.

"What are you doing here?" Marcus asked.

"Waiting for you, dumbass."

"You're in the wrong place," Marcus said, and pointed. "Le Parisien is across the street. Come on, let's go."

"I've already got a table. Just grab a chair."

Kate interrupted. "Jake, you're not listening."

"What did I miss?"

"It's not what Marcus said, it's the way he said it."

"Hey Preacher," Marcus said, and stepped behind Jake to look directly into the phone. "Happy almost anniversary."

"Ah, that's sweet," Kate said. "Thanks for remembering."

"Are you kidding? Who do you think reminded Jake?"

"Hey buddy, what are you trying to do?"

"I'm just kidding, Preacher. Jake's been working on your present all week."

"It's OK Marcus. With or without your help, I'm just happy he'll be home," Kate said. "But tell me about the high value target across the street."

"Do you ever stop being an analyst?" Marcus asked.

"Nope," Kate said. "What's her name?"

"I don't know her name yet. And I won't if we miss her," Marcus said, squeezing Jake's shoulder to signal time to move.

"Then go," Jake said. "Lord knows you don't need my help."

"You're missing the point," Marcus said. "Next to you, I look like a real catch."

"Ouch," Jake said. "Now, you're definitely on your own."

"Jake, it's OK," Kate said. "I need to get to work and you can go play wingman. Call me tonight after you put the clients to bed. I don't care how late it is, just call me."

Marcus stepped away from the table and waited for an opportunity to cut across the traffic. The intersection was a collage of motorbikes, taxis and delivery vans, and on the sidewalk a sea of university students, local businesspeople and tourists juggling shopping bags.

"Don't hang up," Jake said. "Not yet. I love the sound of your voice."

"I miss you too," she said, but her instincts said there was something more. "Jake, is everything all right?"

Jake was distracted. He watched Marcus fuss with his phone and weave through the lunchtime scene. A dozen three-foot tall primary school kids, with backpacks half their size, cut across Marcus's path and beat him to the street. The kids, linked hand-in-hand, trailed behind their teacher, and Jake watched Marcus turn to admire the attractive woman leading the group.

"That boy has the attention span of a goldfish."

"What's that?" Kate asked.

"Never mind," Jake said. "I'll let you get back to work, and I'll call when we wrap up tonight."

"Love me?"

Jake's focus shifted to a speeding cargo van. The former SEAL, and now Close Protection Operator, knew you stayed ahead of trouble by keeping your head on a swivel, and details mattered. Three men were visible in the van's front row. Tinted windows obscured their faces, but not the unmistakable silhouette of an AK-47's curved magazine.

"Jake?" Kate asked. "Are you still there?" For a moment, there was only the road noise blending with the chatter of random conversations, and the phone's camera pointing straight up at the sky.

Jake sprang to his feet. The cast-iron cafe table flipped over, and his cell phone flew into the street. He looked at Marcus, who pivoted back toward Jake when he heard pedestrians screaming, and saw the van plowing through the crowd. Most jumped clear, but the van bounded over an elderly man and screeched to a stop halfway up the curb.

"The kids!" Jake yelled. "Get the kids." Marcus moved without hesitation. Years of teamwork, training and battlefield lessons had formed a nearly psychic link that kept their team alive. Jake watched Marcus scoop up two screaming kids, and herd some others away from the road.

Now it was up to Jake, and the decision to move was instinctive. The attack vector was obvious. Those who froze would die where they stood. The indiscriminate spray of high velocity AK-47 rounds would shred those who ran. The only chance of survival, the only chance that any of them had, was for Jake to charge.

The Israelis taught their citizens to swarm and overwhelm terrorists with sheer numbers. A wall of bodies surging forward would shield those behind, at the cost of those who led the way. Many would die, but not all, and those that survived would prevail. In this place, at this moment, Jake knew he would be alone, but the principle was the same. Violence of action wins the day.

Cries of "Allahu Akbar!" rang out and the van's panel door slid open. Two hooded figures jumped out and opened fire. Two more slid out of the front seat and charged down the alley. The continuous explosion of automatic gunfire muted the collision of screams and shattered glass. The cafe patrons seated closest to the van were the first hit. A wave of destruction washed over the tables and chairs, filling the sidewalk with bodies and blood.

Jake's phone laying at the edge of the road caught flashes of shoes and clothing on a canvas of blue sky and cloud while Kate's screams for Jake vanished in gunfire and chaos.

CHAPTER 10

FRIDAY, APRIL 17
1:30 PM CEST

LE CAFE PIERRE, PARIS, FRANCE

AT THE FIRST SCREAM, Mikhail drew his weapon and never looked back. Whatever was happening behind him in the cafe, he had one goal. A massive left hand gripped Vitali's shoulder like the talons of an eagle and he drove Moshenski toward the waiting SUV.

When gunfire erupted, Vitali tried to stop and turn. "Stephan!" he screamed, but Mikhail kept pushing. The car was near, and nothing and no one would stop him from reaching it.

Vitali's elbow struck Mikhail's face. Blood spurted from his nose. He didn't flinch. He wrapped both arms around his friend in a massive bear hug, lifted him, and dashed for the car.

The man stationed at the passenger door shouted a warning, opened fire and took out a terrorist charging down the alley. Mikhail shoved Vitali to the ground behind a dumpster. A second terrorist appeared and a burst of gunfire echoed down the alley. Bullets struck the car and ripped through his man.

Dropping to his belly, Mikhail rolled out from the dumpster onto his left side. The maneuver worked. Several rounds buzzed over his head and he returned fire. The man's AK clattered on the pavement and he sunk to the ground.

Mikhail grabbed Vitali's suit jacket, yanked him to his feet, pushed him toward the SUV's open door and shoved him into the back seat. The driver yelled. Another man appeared at the top of the alley. Mikhail jumped on top of Vitali and the SUV rocketed forward. The passenger door slammed shut and another volley of fire ricocheted off the bullet-hardened exterior.

"Are you hit?" Mikhail asked, and he scanned and scoured Vitali's body for any sign of impact or blood. He saw nothing, but he couldn't be certain. Not yet.

"The Embassy," Mikhail yelled at the driver. "Alert the medical team." He turned his attention back to his friend. "Vitali, answer me. Are you hit?"

"I'm fine," Vitali shouted. "Leave me be."

The tears flowed, and Vitali moaned, "Stephan. My Stephan. Dear, sweet boy. And his fiancée."

"Mikhail," Vitali begged. "Please. Stop. We must go back."

"*Niet.*"

He hoped the clarity and brevity of the response would be enough, but Vitali persisted. "But if there's a chance, any chance at all they survived. I have to see. I must know."

"I will go," Mikhail relented, knowing the couple's survival was unlikely. "But not until I know you are safe."

"What are you saying?"

"The two men in the alley were hunting you," Mikhail said. "You were the target. If we had stayed any longer, you would be dead."

The fortified gates of the Paris Ukrainian Embassy parted, and the ram barriers dropped as Vitali's vehicle approached. The SUV sped into the underground garage, where a heavily armed security detail flanked the medical team. Vitali waved them off and refused both the gurney and the wheelchair they had stationed.

"I'm not injured, but stay where you are. You're still needed," Vitali said. "Mikhail. Please. Go!"

CHAPTER II

LE CAFE PIERRE, PARIS, FRANCE

JAKE EXPECTED GUNMEN TO pour out of the van using every door. He charged the rear loading doors and arrived just when they were opening. Jake's two hundred pounds of battle-hardened muscle hit the doors and crushed the first head that appeared. Jake then ripped the doors back open. A dead man fell out and Jake jumped inside. The lone terrorist still in the van fell back and lifted his rifle. Jake's left hand deflected the barrel. The terrorist fired, bullets shredded the ceiling. Jake drove his right thumb deep into the man's eye. A scream ricocheted off the van's interior. Jake stripped the gun free, pointed at the bloody face and fired.

From the van, Jake saw one of the hooded figures run down an alley. He would have to wait. The immediate threat was about to enter the cafe's front door. The restaurant's confined space was a chokepoint offering little real cover, and Jake knew everyone inside was about to die. Jake leapt from the van, shouldered the AK and pressed the trigger. Click. He yanked on the magazine. It was secure. Pulled the charging handle, and pressed the trigger again. Still nothing. The gun's malfunction left him with only one choice.

"Hey Asshole!" Jake yelled. "I just killed your friends."

The gunman turned and opened fire. Jake dove back inside the van. A burst of gunfire swept across the back half of the van and ripped the sheet metal like paper. Fragments of glass, plastic, and lead showered down, but the bodies of the two men he'd killed provided cover. And the bodies concealed Jake's slithered escape out the back doors. He scooped up the dead man's rifle and rolled under the van.

Wait for it, Jake thought. *Here he comes.* From under the van, Jake stared at the bloody destruction on the sidewalk and the lone pair of desert combat boots weaving through the forest of tables, chairs, and bodies. When the gunman stopped to scan the van's interior, Jake fired. He watched the gunman's knee explode, and the leg buckle. For a moment, the two were lying face to face. The gunman's eyes locked on Jake's. The predator had become the prey. Jake fired and the gunman's face vanished

Jake rolled out onto the far side of the van and approached the front. The driver was gone. Jake tried to wipe the sweat from his eyes, but the sleeve of his jacket was dripping blood. *Not my blood*, Jake thought. He couldn't be sure, but it didn't matter. *Stay in the fight. Focus.* His ears were ringing, but the sirens were getting louder. *Were they gone? Was it over?* He knew that wasn't his call. The fight's not over until the bad guys know it's over.

With the AK pressed to his chest in a low ready position, Jake scanned the surrounding area. He spotted Marcus and the school kids tucked behind a cement parking barricade. Marcus rose, but Jake raised a clinched fist, for him to stand fast. Marcus crouched back down and signaled that he had no visual contact with any other combatants.

Jake edged past the front bumper of the van. He surveyed the battlefield scene. Blood and urine pooled around the dead and dying and hundreds of spent steel casings carpeted the sidewalk. A young man cried out, begging for help, cradling the girl in his arms, gingerly kissing her forehead as he rocked.

He remembered seeing the striking couple at a nearby table. The young man in the blue blazer and the girl in the crisp white blouse. They were laughing, sipping champagne, celebrating something. That moment, that joy was gone.

Her blouse soaked red. *He's wounded,* Jake thought. *And she's dead, but I'll do what I can for him.*

Jake didn't hear the first shot. He smelled the burning flesh and felt the blood soaking through his shirt. He heard the second shot, and the third. Now his back was on fire, and his face struck the sidewalk. It was cold and wet. There were footsteps. A kick in the ribs. A man stepped over him and approached the injured boy. *What is he saying?* Jake wondered, then he saw the pistol. The man that just shot him was about to execute the boy.

No! Jake thought and tried to yell, but failed. Then he felt it. The AK lying beneath him. If he could roll off the gun, he could fire, but he could barely breathe. Jake knew the symptoms. His lung was collapsing. In another minute or two, he'd be unconscious. In five, he'd be dead. Jake kicked his legs like a drowning man reaching for the surface. He rolled to his side. The gun was free. Jake's right hand was still on the grip, and he dragged the gun along the sidewalk until it pointed at the gunman. He didn't have the strength to lift the gun, and his left hand was useless. Jake pulled the rifle in tight and braced the butt stock against his hip.

The gunman turned toward Jake and raised his pistol. Jake tilted the AK off the deck and pressed the trigger. The gun cycled round after round and, with each explosion, lifted higher. The result was a devastating zipper of bullets striking the gunman from his groin to his throat. Jake's grip failed, and the AK crashed to the sidewalk.

Jake rolled on to his back, stared up at the sky, and listened. *Now it's over*, he thought, and struggled to breathe. He felt Kate holding his hand. He saw her face. She looked into his eyes. She had a way of peering into his soul, but it was warm, comforting.

"*Jake Church,*" he heard Kate say.

She's angry. She only uses my last name when I'm in big trouble.

"Don't you die on me," she commanded.

She knows, but how?

"You promised," she reminded him.

Yes, I promised, he thought. *I said we would grow old together, but always suspected that was a lie. I promised we would die in each other's arms and prayed that was true.*

The world grew silent, and the sky grayed. Kate's loving gaze remained a moment longer, then faded into darkness. The broken promise left Jake with one last thought before he lost consciousness. *I'm sorry.*

Chapter 12

LE CAFE PIERRE, PARIS, FRANCE

MARCUS KNEW THE SILENCE was his opportunity. He moved low and fast across the street while scanning for terrorists. Several civilians followed his lead. Most were unprepared for the horrific scene, but all were determined to search for family and friends. On seeing their approach, a few stunned and bloody survivors stumbled out of the restaurant, and the strangers helped them navigate through the labyrinth of the dead.

Marcus knelt beside Jake and launched into a field trauma assessment. *Rapid, weak pulse. Labored breathing. He's alive. Barely.* Marcus flicked out the blade of his knife and cut away Jake's dress shirt. He'd seen enough battlefield wounds to know he was looking at the ragged exit of a sucking chest wound. *Jugular distended. Trachea shifted.* And given his presentation, Jake was running out of time.

Even off duty, every member of the executive protection team carried an IFAK, a trauma kit, strapped around their ankle. Marcus grabbed Jake's kit and unwrapped the HALO chest seal. Once the exit wound was sealed, he grabbed his own kit, rolled Jake on to his side and searched for the entry wound. He found three. Another HALO seal was set near Jake's left shoulder covering two of the wounds. The last he packed with combat gauze and secured with a compression bandage, then eased Jake onto to his back.

Marcus looked up, hoping to see medics rushing in to help. There were none. Jake's mission briefing was short and to the point. *After the Bataclan massacre, it was thirty minutes before help arrived. If something goes down, assume we're on our own.* Marcus never felt more alone as he probed the ribs above Jake's wound, located the intercostal space between the second and third ribs, double-checked his alignment, and pressed a three-inch decompression needle into Jake's chest cavity. The protocol called for waiting ten seconds. It felt like minutes and Marcus counted out loud. On ten he removed the needle, checked the integrity of the catheter, and listened. *I'll never hear it,* he thought. *Not over all this noise.* Training called to listen for the whoosh of trapped air escaping Jake's chest. That wasn't going to happen.

Jake's chest rose. *That's it,* Marcus thought. *It's working.* The pressure in Jake's lung cavity was easing, and so was his breathing, color and pulse. Marcus took Jake's hand and prayed he would regain consciousness. "Hey man. I'm here. Just breathe," Marcus said, hoping a friendly voice would be reassuring. He needed to keep Jake calm. Jake's primal instinct would be to fight if he sensed danger.

Marcus felt Jake's fingers twitch. There was movement, pressure. "That's it. You got this. You're gonna be fine. Now, stay with me."

Jake's eyes fluttered, and Marcus held on tight. *Come on back,* he thought, and he imagined Jake fighting his way through the pain. Jake's hand shot up and grabbed Marcus's leather jacket. The move was so fast Marcus rocked back on his heels.

He cupped Jake's hand. "Hey buddy," Marcus said. "Just relax. Help's on the way."

Jake's grip tightened. He pulled Marcus in closer and struggled to speak. "Kate," he said, and then his grip loosened and slipped. Marcus caught Jake's hand, leaned in close, and stared into Jake's eyes.

Don't you dare die on me, Marcus thought, and then said, "Whatever you need to tell Kate, tell her yourself. Just stay in the fight, brother. Stay in the fight."

Jake took a deep breath, coughed, convulsed, and grabbed the back of Marcus's head. He pulled Marcus as close as he could. Marcus felt Jake's breath, hot and moist. He strained to hear what Jake was fighting to say, but heard only the death rattle of mucus and saliva building in Jake's throat.

"Kate's—," Jake said again, and took two more slow, deep breaths. Marcus sensed that from somewhere deep within Jake's core, he was summoning the strength to speak.

"She will—," Jake whispered.

Marcus listened to Jake's faltering attempts to speak. With his last breath, Jake spit out the message and let go.

Jake's hand hit the ground. Marcus pressed two fingers into Jake's neck, but that was a reflex. He already knew. The moment Jake let go, he knew. Marcus took one last look into his friend's eyes and brushed his hand across Jake's eyes and face. He kissed Jake's forehead with one last thought for his friend and warrior brother and said, "til Valhalla."

Chapter 13

FRIDAY, APRIL 17
7:42 AM EDT

RICHMOND PINNACLE BUILDING, RICHMOND, VA

Kate clutched the iPad in both hands and shouted over the explosive bursts of gunfire, children wailing and women screaming, "Jake! Jake? Can you hear me?"

She knew the effort was futile, but she had to try. She had to do something. As long as the video link held, there was hope, the possibility, that Jake would pick up the phone, that he was OK, that he was alive.

Kate stood and paced. Tears streamed down her face, her throat swelled, but she continued.

"Jake? Damn it! Pick Up The Phone!"

Every gunshot was an electric shock tearing through her body. Silence offered hope that shattered with the next explosion. She pressed her back against the office wall and slid down to the floor. The sounds echoing in her head were fading, her vision blurred. *Damn it! Don't you even think about passing out,* she thought and fought to stay conscious.

Focus on the video, she thought. Jake's phone was askew. There was a piece of the sky, some pavement, a streetlight. Rooftops in the distance. No one was in sight. No one in Paris could hear her screaming Jake's name or the sobs that followed each attempt. She ignored the whispers of the crowd gathering outside her office.

***

WHILE KATE'S COWORKERS STOOD back wondering what on earth was happening in Kate's office, the new receptionist ventured forward. She placed an ear on the door and listened. Then she kicked off her heels, ran down the hall, and burst into Leslie Dodd's office.

"What on earth…" Leslie began, but the receptionist cut her off.

"Kate's in trouble," she said. "She needs you."

"I'll call you back," Leslie said and hung up the phone. "This better be important, or this is both your first and last day."

***

WITH EVERY MOMENT OF silence, Kate held her breath as if she could freeze time and it would all be over. The next gunshot would snap that illusion, but not this time. This time, the silence held. Two seconds, five, ten. Then she saw them. People. Running. Crying. *It's over,* she thought. *It's finally over.*

"Can anyone hear me? Is someone there? Please, please, pick up the phone."

She shouted again, and again, praying that someone, anyone, would hear her and grab the phone.

The Parisian man who picked up Jake's phone was crying. Kate saw the blood splattered across his face and tie, the confusion in his eyes. He looked at the phone but didn't speak. *He's in shock,* Kate thought.

"Monsieur, s'l vous plait," she said, hoping her French would bring him back into the moment.

"Allo," he said.

Kate seized the moment, and in fluent French, she pleaded for help. "Monsieur, I'm looking for my husband."

"Dead. So many dead," he said, and Kate feared he was about to end the call.

"No, no, please. Don't hang up. I beg of you," she said. "I need to find my husband."

"American?" he asked.

"Yes. Yes. American. I'm looking for the big American."

"He saved them," he said. "He saved the children."

Kate's heart soared. He did it. Jake did what Jake does best. He charged in. Saved lives. Please, God, let him be alive.

The Frenchman turned the phone toward the cafe and Kate saw the carnage and the chaos. She'd seen war zones and civilian casualties, but nothing on this scale. Scattered among the toppled street side tables and chairs were dozens of bodies and rivers of blood. A handful of the walking injured were making their way past the dead, while civilians formed makeshift litters to carry others.

Then she saw him. Marcus kneeling on the sidewalk. The Frenchman approached and held out the phone.

"Monsieur," the Frenchman said, to get Marcus's attention.

Marcus turned and wiped the back of a bloody hand across his right eye. "Yes?"

"Your wife is on the phone," the Frenchman said, and handed Marcus the phone.

"My wife? I'm not... Oh my God. Kate."

Marcus took the phone and looked into Kate's eyes.

She could see he was searching for words that wouldn't come, but there was nothing he could say. The blood on his face, the tears he was fighting back, said enough, words wouldn't change anything.

She took a deep breath, the first slow, deep breath she'd taken since the first gunshot.

"Are you alright?"

"I... yeah. I'm OK," Marcus stammered.

"I need to see him."

"Kate, no," he said. "You shouldn't see him, not like this. Trust me, you don't want to remember him this way."

"Marcus, I need to see him," she said. "Please."

Marcus turned the phone so Kate could see Jake's face. There was a quiet peace that was unexpected. Amid the horror of the attack that had exploded in her ears and pulsated through her entire body, Jake was now still.

"I did everything I could," Marcus said, and turned the phone back to look at Kate.

"I believe you."

"He saved dozens, maybe more."

"And the terrorists?"

"Dead," he said. "All dead."

"That's my guy," she said. "I'll be there as soon as I can, and we'll bring him home."

The call ended, and so did the last pretense of control. Kate dropped the iPad and curled into a ball on the floor.

Chapter 14

RICHMOND PINNACLE BUILDING, RICHMOND, VA

THERE WAS A SOFT knock on Kate's door, and a moment later it opened. Kate didn't look and couldn't speak. She was on the floor, her body shaking with sobs. There was no containing the flood of tears that escaped. She clung to her arms, buried her face deeper, hoping to muffle the gut-wrenching sounds she couldn't control.

"Kate, what is it?" Leslie asked.

Leslie closed the door behind her, knelt down and placed a hand on Kate's shoulder. "What's happened?"

Leslie stroked the back of Kate's head and hair. "Honey, whatever it is, I'm here."

Minutes passed, and slowly Kate unwound from her cocoon.

Kate's arms relaxed. She turned to look up at Leslie, still unable to speak.

"It's OK," Leslie said, and handed Kate a few tissues. "Take your time. Breathe."

Kate attempted to dry her eyes, wipe her nose, and she dabbed at the mascara that streaked her cheeks.

"Jake's gone," Kate said, and between gasps for air she added. "Killed. In Paris."

"Oh Kate," Leslie said, and she scooped Kate into her arms. Both closed their eyes, hugged and rocked in silence.

Kate startled Leslie when she broke free of the embrace, sat up, and looked Leslie in the eyes.

"I need to get to Paris. I need to see him," Kate said, and stood. Kate headed for her desk and sat down at the keyboard. "I need to find the next flight to Paris."

"Kate, let me handle this. No one can get you there faster. I promise," she said. "How soon can you be ready?"

"Twenty minutes," Kate replied, and she yanked a small duffle bag from the closet's top shelf. Leslie pressed the cell phone to her ear.

"Hi John, it's Leslie Dodd... I'm fine, but I need a favor... I need the Jet... Now... Yes, seriously. It's an emergency... Paris."

Leslie turned away from Kate and lowered her voice.

"You know the young woman who recovered the missing funds... Her husband was just killed... How long until the jet's fueled and ready... Make it less. We'll be there in 30 minutes... Thanks."

Leslie turned back toward Kate. "Done. Dominion's jet will be waiting at the Richmond jet center."

"Dominion's jet?"

"We saved them thirty million dollars. They owe us," Leslie said. "They owe you. I'll have the car brought around, and we'll leave as soon as you're ready."

"We?"

"I'm coming with you," Leslie said. "I don't think you should be alone right now."

"I won't be alone. Jake's team is in Paris and Marcus will meet the flight."

"That's not the same, and you know it."

"Please, trust me," Kate said. "I've got this, and I need you to finish what I started. There's a confused and frightened little boy in protective services that needs his mother. They need you."

Kate pulled a shirt, pants, and shoes from her go bag, and slipped off her blouse. Kate's camisole did little to hide the pattern of scars carved into her chest. She watched Leslie look away.

"It's OK, Leslie," Kate said. "I know you've seen my jacket, so you know the story... at least the unclassified bits." Kate buttoned up a light khaki-colored shirt. "Jake always said whether the scars are on the inside or the outside, you need to face them to heal them."

Kate reached around to the back of her pencil skirt and unzipped. The skirt hit the floor and Leslie's eyebrows jumped.

"Is that loaded?"

"It's not a fashion statement," Kate said. She drew the Glock 43x from her Enigma holster and locked it into the gun safe in her desk drawer.

Leslie watched Kate unbuckle the odd-looking contraption that held Kate's gun pressed flat against her abdomen. "I had no idea you were armed."

"That's the idea."

"Are firearms even allowed in the building?" Leslie asked, but Kate didn't answer.

Within minutes, Kate transformed from office-chic to urban camouflage and slipped the messenger bag over her shoulder.

Leslie stepped forward, hugged Kate again, and pressed one last time.

"You're sure you don't want me to come?"

"I'm sure."

Leslie glanced at her cell. "OK, the car's waiting downstairs." They walked toward the elevator, and Kate stepped inside.

"Thank you," Kate said. "Thank you for the jet... for everything."

"Promise me you'll call if you need anything, anything at all." Leslie said. "Or if you just want to talk... any time... day or night."

"I will," Kate said. "I promise."

Chapter 15

UKRAINIAN EMBASSY, PARIS, FRANCE

VITALI MOSHENSKI'S SECOND-FLOOR OFFICE faced Avenue de Saxe. The normally quiet road echoed with sirens and emergency vehicles choked every route between the scene of the attack and regional hospitals. He knew the magnitude of the dead and injured would consume first responders for hours.

Ensconced within the Ukrainian Embassy, he was safe, angry. Vitali had never run from a fight, and would have stayed. He would have tried to reach Stephan. Now, all he could do was wait, cell phone in hand. Every few seconds he confirmed he had signal. *The towers will be overwhelmed,* he thought. *If they go down, I am going back to the cafe, and no one can stop me.*

Media accounts reported the attack was an isolated incident. For Parisians, he was grateful. The multiple, coordinated explosions of the 2015 Paris attack still haunted the city. This was different. The men who targeted him, the men Zhukov killed, were organized, trained, and equipped. Once again, he owed his life to Mikhail Zhukov, but he was an old man. It was Stephan and his fiancée that mattered now.

Zhukov's call shattered Vitali's internal rant, and he held his breath and answered.

"Stephan is alive," Zhukov said the moment the call connected.

"Thank you. Thank you. Oh merciful God," Vitali said. He dropped to his knees and wept. With those tears, the fear, the guilt, began to wane.

"Arriving in thirty," Zhukov said, and Vitali realized that message was directed to embassy personnel and Zhukov's security team.

"Alert medical," Zhukov added, and that brought Vitali back to his feet.

"Is Stephan injured?"

Zhukov returned to the call.

"Yes, but stable. He is shaken, and bloody, and —"

"And what?" Vitali demanded. "What are you hiding?"

"The girl," Zhukov began. "Stephan's fiancée —"

"Was she hit? How bad is it?"

"She is dead," Zhukov said. "Stephan would not leave her, so she is with us."

Vitali said nothing. The life he imagined for his grandson and future bride now shattered.

"Get away from the windows," Zhukov commanded.

It was Zhukov's tone that brought Vitali back into the moment, but his hesitation sparked another command.

"Now."

Vitali stepped away from the windows, and any possible line of fire. He often thought Zhukov too cautious, but knew he was right. Given the pursuit in the alley, he'd been foolish to parade so openly in his office. If someone would take countless innocent lives, just to mask killing him, they won't stop until they succeed.

"Alright. I am safe," Vitali assured his friend. "Tell me. What is happening?"

The call dropped, and repeated attempts to return Zhukov's call were met with busy signals and busy circuit messages.

Stephan is alive, stable and on his way, Vitali reassured himself, and the embassy's medical facility is well equipped. His mind was racing. He checked his watch. Mikhail said thirty minutes. It had only been two and already felt like hours.

Vitali sought distraction, anything to occupy his mind while the minutes crept by. He'd avoided the TV until now. On every channel, commentators warned of graphic images. Sensational video of the man the press had dubbed *Le American* consumed most of the broadcast news, but even knowing that Stephan was alive, Vitali feared what he might see.

His rapid, distracted, channel surfing landed Vitali on a rebroadcast of an American Cable News show. He recognized a smiling Devin Moore when the camera pulled in close. The attractive host appeared to be enjoying a lighthearted conversation. Vitali turned up the volume just when the interview grew more intense, and Moore was on the defense.

Vitali scowled when the host pressed Moore on rumors of a relationship with a Ukrainian war criminal and arms dealer. This was old news, but he was pleased with how deftly Moore deflated the accusation. Then the interview took an unexpected tact that drew Vitali's full attention.

"My sources tell me that Senator Cahill, the Ranking Member of the Senate Subcommittee on Homeland Security, is calling for an investigation into Moore Technologies and the Quantum NanoVault's potential threat to National Security. Care to comment?"

"I'm not surprised, though I admit I'm disappointed."

"You're not surprised a subpoena might compel you to answer, under oath, the very questions you're determined to evade?"

"No, I'm not surprised that your Washington sources would leak an obvious attempt to grab a headline at my expense," Moore said. "I know Senator Cahill is facing a tough reelection, and with the mid-terms looming, there's a good chance he'll soon be out of a job, but I'm disappointed you took the bait."

Vitali turned off the TV and retrieved a SAT phone. Devin Moore answered the call the moment it connected.

"Vitali," he said. "Thank God you're alright. The news is flooded with the most horrific images of the carnage, and I feared the worst."

"Yes. Tragic," Vitali said. "Fortunately, I was nowhere near the incident."

"Well, that's a relief. So, what's on your mind?"

"I saw your interview."

"Man, these press tours are grueling, but effective," Moore said. "Sales are literally off the charts."

"And Senator Cahill?"

"Oh, you saw the Larkin interview," Moore said. "Stephanie can be aggressive, even voracious, and that includes the bedroom," he said and laughed.

"Your liaisons do not interest me, but her sources do," Vitali said. "Has the committee initiated an investigation?"

"No, and they won't. Trust me, I have better intel on Capitol Hill than the NSA," Moore said. "The leak came from Cahill's campaign. By coming after the NanoVault, and me personally, they're hoping to generate some buzz and take the heat off Cahill's falling poll numbers, but it won't work. You'll see."

"You may be right, but I do not believe in coincidence. The attack today, and interest from Homeland Security, could be signs."

"So now you believe in signs? I never imagined you were superstitious."

"No. Just cautious. I have survived this long by learning to trust my instincts."

"You need to trust me," Moore said. "You'll see. The news on Cahill will turn in the next 24 hours, and no one will be talking about a Senate investigation."

"Trust isn't a toy you purchase. This is life and death. Mine and yours. That is why I will be sending Mikhail to New York. Tonight. I will follow soon."

"Zhukov? Are you kidding me?" Moore asked. "I have my own security. All former Special Forces. Younger. Faster. Stronger."

"Youth has its benefits to be sure," Vitali said. "But you know what they say, beware an old man in a profession..."

"Where men usually die young. Yes. Yes. I know the saying, but with all due respect to your instincts, and your proverbs, I don't need your Russian goon following me around."

"You misunderstand. This is not a request," Vitali said. "I will protect my investment, and a word of warning. If you wish to keep that boyish smile and all of your fingers, you will show some respect. Mikhail does not suffer fools."

A knock on Vitali's door brought the conversation to a quick close, and he rushed out to meet the ambulance transporting his grandson. While his focus returned to the boy's injuries, the events of the day and the conversation with

Moore were unsettling. *Moore's ambitious. Reckless,* Vitali thought. *He may be foolish enough to imagine that killing an old lion is a simple task.*

Chapter 16

FRIDAY, APRIL 17
8:30 AM EDT

RICHMOND JET CENTER, RICHMOND, VA

Kate's arrival at the Richmond Jet Center was choreographed precision. A representative of the jet center's executive support team accompanied her from the limo's arrival, through check-in, and past security. A member of the ground crew completed Kate's journey out to Dominion Investment's Gulfstream G650.

Kate climbed the stairs and could see the cockpit flight crew was completing the preflight checks. When she reached the top step, the lone member of the cabin crew welcomed her aboard.

"Good afternoon, Ms. Preacher," she said. "I'm Samantha Wells and I'll be on board today to assist you in any way that I can."

"Thank you," Kate said. "And, please, call me Kate."

"Of course, and everyone calls me Sam."

Kate stepped into the cabin and noted they configured the G6 for up to eight passengers.

"Please, take any seat," Sam said. "You're our only passenger today, and I'll be in the back."

That's a relief, Kate thought. She couldn't imagine trying to make small talk with anyone from Dominion, or worse, being grilled for details on their CFO's sudden departure.

Sam pointed to a pair of seats. "These two have a lie flat capability, so if you'd like to sleep, let me know and I will make up the bed, and draw the curtains."

"I don't think that will be necessary, but thanks."

"Can I get you something to drink before we take off?"

"Just water, thanks."

"Still or sparkling?"

"Still, please," Kate said, and anticipating more questions, she added, "No ice, or lemon or anything. Just plain. Thanks."

Kate took a seat, and the captain announced that they were cleared for takeoff, anticipated a smooth flight to Le Bourget Airport, with an expected flight time of eight hours, thirty minutes. *With customs and the drive, it will be almost midnight,* Kate thought. *I need to alert Marcus, and I should try to get some sleep on the flight. Tomorrow is going to be a long day.*

The call to Marcus went unanswered, so she left a voice message.

"Hey Marcus, it's Kate. My firm called in a favor and I'm flying in via private jet, but I won't hit the ground until after eleven, so don't even think about trying to meet the flight. I'll head straight to the hotel. We'll meet in the morning, and head over to the..." Kate froze. "I'll meet you in the lobby."

The aircraft had a wide selection of entertainment options, but Kate found it challenging to settle on anything. She longed for distraction, but her mind kept circling back through the morning hours like it was stuck on a loop. Breaking free of the loop wasn't much better. She imagined what it might feel like to arrive in Paris and step into Jake's room. The room where mere hours earlier he was alive.

Hours passed, and as lunchtime approached, Sam reappeared. "I didn't mean to eavesdrop on your call this morning, but I wanted you to know that your arrival in Paris will be as seamless as your departure. An agent will meet the flight and escort you through immigration. The car is booked and the hotel's aware that you're en route."

"That's very kind, thank you."

"My pleasure. Now, would you like something else to drink, perhaps something to eat? We have a full bar, a lovely selection of wines, and I can prepare anything from a charcuterie board to filet mignon."

Kate glanced at her watch. Day drinking wasn't her style, but a glass of wine with lunch might help her relax, and perhaps even take a nap. A bowl of popcorn and a glass of red wine was her go-to dinner when Jake was away. She thought about how often he would check on her. *Have you eaten*, he would ask, and she would just smile. Kate swallowed hard and cleared her throat. *Don't cry*, she thought. *Not now.*

"Do you have any Pinot Noir?"

"We have some beautiful Burgundies. Traditional, earthy. They go beautifully with everything."

"It doesn't need to be anything special, just a glass," Kate said. "I appreciate Mr. Farrow's generosity arranging the flight, and I don't want to be a burden."

"Nonsense," Sam replied. "Mr. Farrow was clear that you're to have anything we can offer, and we have a fantastic Clos De Vougeot Grand Cru 2012 that I know you'll love."

Sam returned a few minutes later, showed Kate the bottle and poured a taste in a Riedel Burgundy glass.

"I'm sure it's fine," Kate said. "You can just pour."

"Yes, of course," Sam said, and nearly filled Kate's glass. "Now, that's what I call a girl pour."

Sam disappeared with the bottle but came back with a charcuterie board.

"I know you said you weren't hungry, but we have some exquisite cheeses and cured meats. I'll just leave it here and you can nibble and sample with the wine," she said. "A little something to eat might help you get some rest."

Kate sensed a gentle mothering tone and smiled and nodded when Sam deposited the tray. *They must know*, she thought, but she was grateful no one asked or offered their condolences. *I'm not ready.*

The wine worked its magic, and Kate could feel her shoulders relax. She sampled some of the prosciutto and cheese, then tucked one leg under the other, leaned back into the plush leather seat and closed her eyes.

The echo of gunfire shattered Kate's nap. She bolted upright and sent the wine glass flying.

Sam appeared at her side and placed a hand on Kate's shoulder.

"It's OK. I've got this," and Sam picked up the broken glass and mopped up the remnants of the wine.

Just a dream, Kate thought, but something was out of place, and her mind raced.

"Sam, does the Jet have satellite Internet service?"

"Yes, of course. I'll get you the access card," she said.

Kate donned AirPods and fired up her iPad. With a deep breath, she braced herself to face the last recording. Jake's last moments. Kate opened the video file but waited. She closed her eyes and pictured the moment. She was in her office. Jake had just called. He teased her about recording his calls, Marcus interrupted. They agreed to talk later that night, and she asked, as she always did. Love me? But there was no answer, only gunfire.

Kate opened her eyes and slid the video time-line bar to the end and then back a few minutes. The French businessman had picked up Jake's phone. She was begging him to help locate her husband. *No, further back.* People running, crying, but no gunshots. *Back farther.* A blast of automatic fire, *AK47,* she thought. *It's just before that burst.* She skipped back another 60 seconds. Three shots, grouped close, a second later, one more. *That's it. That's what I heard in my dream, but why?*

She bracketed the two seconds of video and exported the audio track. Closing her eyes, she listened and looped through the audio again and again. The first three shots were familiar. *Small arms fire, a handgun, probably 9mm,* she thought. *But that last shot, that's something else... maybe from somewhere else.*

CHAPTER 17

FRIDAY, APRIL 17
8:47 AM EDT

DULLES AIRPORT, DULLES, VA

THE STARDUST MOTEL WAS more dust than star, but it suited the man who requested the corner, street-level, room. The hotel, directly in the flight path to Dulles International, was the domain of hourly occupants who paid cash and bought anonymity for themselves and their guests.

Former DEA agent Manuel Rojas was napping during one of the brief interludes between the whine of jet engines and squeaking bed springs. The hotel's paper-thin walls did little to mask the roar of aircraft engines or the mock ecstasy in the adjoining rooms, but Rojas hoped his proximity to DC would soon pay off.

When the New Bounty alert hit his phone, he smiled. *Joining the secretive online gaming group might work out after all*, he thought, and Rojas was quick to accept the contract. The prize was too lucrative to ignore, and on the face of it, ideally suited to his current location, skills, and bank account balance.

The entire encrypted transaction, from offer and acceptance to the Bitcoin deposit, was masked within the phone app's gaming interface and completed within seconds. Rojas confirmed the Bitcoin balance in his digital wallet, grabbed his tablet and logged on to the game. Then he clicked the link to the target package.

"Jesus," Rojas said when he saw the full package. "Rojas, what have you done?"

He recognized the man in the photo. He'd seen the guy on the news just this morning. The girl was nobody. Pretty, but just a child. *Fifteen, maybe sixteen*, Rojas thought as he scanned the extensive collection of digital images and target profile data.

Photos...dates...times...locations. It's all here, Rojas thought. The target package was remarkable. The level of detail surpassed the High-Value-Target (HVT) folders he'd seen in Iraq, and the DEA's Cartel member workups didn't come close. He wondered how something this precise and expansive even got assembled, but membership in BountyHunt came with a no-questions understanding. It also came with strings. Contract terms were non-negotiable, and there were only two possible outcomes.

Rojas studied the plan. He had little doubt he could complete the mission. The target, Cahill, John, had a DC behavior pattern that he repeated like clockwork. *Sloppy*, Rojas thought. *Seems the more prominent the target, the more untouchable they see themselves.*

The girl was another matter. Rojas had spent enough time embedded with the cartels to recognize the type. *Promised the world,* he thought. *Life in America, the land of opportunity.* He knew her journey was like hundreds, thousands, of others. Beaten. Raped. Addicted. Sold.

He couldn't watch the video of Senator Cahill and the girl. The photos were enough for Rojas to imagine he was on a mission of mercy. He would set her free. Not to the life she had imagined, but at least free of the nightmare she was living, and he would send at least one of her tormentors to the hell he deserved.

Or so he told himself.

Because he had to.

The app on his phone flashed again, only this time with an encrypted call. He jumped from the bed, grabbed his SIG from the nightstand, and approached the door. The app continued to ring, but he ignored the call and studied the parking lot. Nothing appeared out of the ordinary. He answered the call.

"I was beginning to worry," the caller said. "I thought perhaps you were having second thoughts."

"Who is this," Rojas asked.

"I'm the system moderator," he said. "You can call me Riley."

"What do you want?"

"Ah, direct and to the point. Lovely," Riley said. "Since this is your first high-profile contract, I just wanted to congratulate you personally and welcome you to Level One. I have a few preliminary details to confirm, and then you'll be on your way."

"What details?" Rojas asked.

"Well, let's have a look. I see that your contract calls for a drug overdose. Male adult. Female teen. Personally, I might have opted for murder-suicide, but the client was specific. Oh, dear…"

"What?"

"I see you have a daughter. Angela. That's sweet," Riley said. "And she's just a year older than the girl in your package."

"So?"

"In our experience, professionals such as yourself don't make tactical mistakes, but mindset and motivation can be important."

"What are you getting at?"

"It's just that contracts at this level are heavily scrutinized," Riley said. "Out of curiosity, how long has it been since you last saw your daughter?"

"Two years."

"It may interest you to know that she's a bright young woman. Doing very well in school. A future scientist, perhaps a doctor."

"How do you—"

"We take a keen interest in our players. I dare say that the fee for this contract alone may help mend broken fences. Imagine yourself moving out of the Stardust and finding somewhere more appropriate for your daughter to visit."

"What are you playing at?"

"I just want to be sure that you fully comprehend this opportunity and your engagement. Goals are important, and we find relationships are the key to motivation," Riley said.

"Are you threatening my family?"

"No, of course not. Your family is perfectly safe," Riley said. "But they are your collateral."

"What the hell does that mean?"

"We can't have players opting out of the game. Take that SIG in your hand. What is that a P320?"

Rojas looked around the room. *How does this guy know where I am, and the gun I carry?*

"Let's say you put that SIG in your mouth and pull the trigger. Game over, right?" Riley said. "Not quite. There's still the matter of your collateral. Men and women, professionals like yourself, often picture themselves alone in the world, and that can lead to rash decisions. Your collateral is there to help you see the big picture, the world beyond yourself."

"Touch one hair on my little girl, and you will beg me to kill you."

"Excellent. That's the attitude of a winner," Riley said. "Now, let's go over the plan."

When the call ended, Rojas was left to face the reality of his decision and the contract he'd just accepted. It seemed his whole life was one of choice and consequence and collateral damage. And here he was again, finally clean and sober but without prospects, and desperate. Somehow they knew. They knew everything about him. They knew what he was capable of doing, and what buttons to press.

There has to be something I can do, some way out, he thought. *I couldn't care less about the Senator. Given what I've seen, he deserves worse. But the girl. The girl deserves better.*

Rojas worked the problem for hours, considered every angle, but the risk was too great. If he failed to kill both the Senator and the girl, exactly as planned, they would kill his daughter. He was trapped. To save his daughter, to save Angela, another little girl must die.

Chapter 18

2ND ARRONDISSEMENT, PARIS, FRANCE

THE THICK RUBBER SOLES of tactical boots muffled Ronin's approach. The cobblestone streets near Rue Montorgueil were empty. All the shops and restaurants closed early. He imagined the locals that frequented the popular street were home, mourning the dead, or reassuring distant family and friends.

Ronin's black jeans and leather jacket merged with the shadows. The gray hoodie and ball cap pulled low hid his face from the street cameras. The day's events hadn't gone as planned, but the timing still worked to his advantage. There was little chance the package drop would be observed or interrupted.

He checked the time. *Ten-Ten. I'm late,* he thought, and turned down the alley.

A single light bulb flickered above a restaurant's service entrance. He watched a man step forward and into the light. *Short and fat. Dark blue suit. Looks like a banker.*

The banker flicked a cigarette into the alley, and smoke floated above his head. "You're late."

"All things considered, I'm lucky to be here."

"Do you have it?"

"I do, but —"

The banker raised a hand and said, "Be very careful. The next words you speak may be your last. Your contract was explicit and the consequences severe."

"Whoa. Relax. It's not that," Ronin said, and scanned the area for the man's backup. *Dumpster. Rooftop. Two, maybe three.*

"Do your friends speak English?"

"Enough."

"Good. That makes things easier."

With open palms Ronin kept both hands visible about shoulder height and addressed the figures hidden in the darkness.

"I'm going to reach into my jacket and retrieve the package. See, just two fingers," Ronin said, and reached into the jacket's interior.

With the device in his fingertips, Ronin presented it like a precious stone. The light reflected off the metallic cylinder and danced around the banker's face when Ronin rocked the device. The banker's eyes fixed on the device, and Ronin knew the others would do the same.

"Give it here."

"It's yours, as agreed," Ronin said and took a step forward, his right hand extended. With a magician's precision, all eyes were on the device in his right hand, and Ronin's left hand swept behind his back. None saw him draw the knife.

With the blade pressed against the banker's neck, he pulled the fat man back into the alcove from which he'd appeared. Shrouded in darkness, Ronin commanded the others to step forward. No one moved. He pressed the knife tight against the banker's throat and pulled back on the man's forehead. The razor-sharp edge drew blood and a few drops slid down the banker's throat.

"Tell them to step forward, and drop their weapons, or the next words you speak will be *your* last."

"Do as he says," the banker said. "Now."

Two men stepped out from behind the dumpster and dropped their handguns on the street.

"Kick them away."

Ronin watched the guns disappear into the darkness.

"Now the sniper," Ronin added, gambling on a decade of instinct and experience.

"There's no one else," the banker insisted.

Ronin tucked in close behind the banker's body, but it was little cover or comfort. *A headshot would canoe my head at this distance,* he thought and pictured the forehead shots he'd seen in Afghanistan. Heads split open in a V like the bow of a canoe. Officially, canoeing wasn't sanctioned. Just a head shot with unintended results, but the psychological impact was undeniable. Once you saw it, you never forgot it, and Ronin wrestled with the image of his head split open.

He focused on the man beneath the blade. There was tension in the banker's body. *Fear? Maybe. Anticipation? Possibly.* Ronin felt the jugular pulse beneath his blade. Listened to the shallow breathing, and made the call. *He's lying.*

"I won't ask again," Ronin said, and the curved blade edge rocked. Fresh blood trickled.

"Come down," the banker said, struggling to speak and keep his throat still.

A dark figure moved toward the roof top ladder and descended. The silhouette of a rifle barrel with attached suppressor was visible above the man's shoulder when he descended into the light of the alley.

The sniper joined the others, released the sling, and cradled the rifle as he set it on the street.

A craftsman cares for his tools, Ronin thought watching the precision with which the sniper handled the weapon.

"The pistol too," Ronin said, and a moment later, a handgun hit the street.

Ronin didn't need to see the pistol to know there would be one. The rifle might be the sniper's tool of choice, but transitioning between rifle and pistol is a skill you master if you want to stay alive.

"Good," Ronin said. "Now that we're all here, we can talk."

Ronin's left arm secured the banker in a choke hold, and he whispered, "Move and I will snap your neck like a twig."

With his right hand, Ronin swept the banker's waist. *Damn. He's unarmed.* Ronin couldn't risk carrying a gun but hoped the banker would help him level the field. *The knife will have to do,* he thought, and pressed the tip of the blade near the base of the banker's skull.

"Nobody else needs to die today," Ronin announced to the group. "But try anything heroic, and I will shove this steel into your boss's brain."

"What do you want?" the banker asked.

"I need to speak with the buyer."

"I am the buyer."

"You're lying," Ronin said, and tightened his grip on the banker's throat.

"No. I swear. It's my contract you accepted, and we can still do business. Just tell me what you want."

"Maybe you posted the contract, but there's no way in hell you're the 'Grandmaster' character that wants the device."

The banker's phone rang.

"I should answer that."

"On speaker," Ronin said.

"Mr Ronin," the caller said, using a voice modulation device that sounded male. "I see that your impeccable rank in the game is justified, and this evening has been both entertaining and illuminating, but you possess something that belongs to me."

He, or she, is watching the alley, Ronin thought. *Night vision cameras. Clever.* Ronin slipped the knife into his belt and took the phone.

"This conversation is best handled more discretely. I wouldn't want to spook the gentleman awaiting your instructions," Ronin said. "I do have something you want, but for the moment, it still belongs to me."

"Sir, let me remind you that access to BountyHunt contracts at your level required acceptance of the terms, and the consequences for failure."

"Oh, I understand."

"I'm uncertain you do," the Grandmaster said. "Your life is forfeit, and your collateral's life as well. Perhaps not tonight, but soon. There's nowhere you can hide from the other players, some of whom are surely your equal."

"Here's the problem," Ronin said. "The contract is only valid when payment's secured. Your deposit disappeared."

"Nonsense."

"Check the logs. Look at the balance. You'll see. The deposit vanished. Like it never existed."

"Impossible," the Grandmaster said. "The NanoVault's quantum key encryption is impenetrable, and the Blockchain transaction record immutable."

"Believe me. I thought these devices were perfect for gig workers like myself. That's all about to change."

"I wouldn't think a man of your reputation would frighten so easily. A single errant payment, which will soon be rectified, has you proclaiming the sky is falling?"

"Look, whoever you are, you're obviously connected. You've got money, reach, brains. My guess is that whatever the professor discovered, you wanted it for yourself, but you're late to the party."

"What are you talking about?" the Grandmaster asked, and the modulated voice couldn't mask the anger. *I struck a nerve*, Ronin thought. *Time to strike a deal.*

"The Frenchman wasn't working alone."

Silence. Good. I'll let that sink in, Ronin thought. The next move is his.

"I was assured the discovery was his. His alone."

"You were misinformed," Ronin said. "I knew the old man was hiding something. It took a little convincing, but I got a name."

"I'm listening."

"The Frenchman was working with someone he called Nomad."

"Nomad? Are you sure?"

"You know him?"

"Only rumors."

"Turns out this Nomad character was on-line. Watching. Listening," Ronin said. "And this is where it gets interesting. He tried to convince me to spare the professor. Just take the device and go."

"He wasn't interested in the device?"

"Nope, just the professor, but I declined. I have my reputation to consider."

"And your life."

"Yes, but that's when he took control."

"Control of what?"

"My NanoVault. The one linked to your contract. It's the only explanation," Ronin said. "I mean, he knew everything. Your Grandmaster avatar, which he found amusing. The contract fee. The deposit. Then it vanished. The money was gone. And that brings me back to the terms of our agreement."

"I'm listening."

"First," Ronin said. "full payment is due. Now. Second, I expect an excellent review for my services. Last, I would suggest a generous performance bonus. A little something to encourage a positive client rating. You wouldn't want others hesitating to accept your contracts."

"Is that all?"

"One more thing."

"Go on."

"When you find Nomad, and my gut tells me you will, I want first crack at the contract."

"When I find Nomad, his, or her, contract will be time sensitive," the Grandmaster said. "But I'll promise you this. If you're in position and can meet the timeline, the contract is yours. Do we have a deal?"

"Fair enough."

"Now, check your balance. You'll find I've doubled the fee and rated your performance."

Ronin released his hold on the courier's neck, slipped a phone out of his back pocket, used a thumb scan to open the app, and checked the account.

"Five-hundred-thousand. Five stars. Very nice."

"Assuming you're satisfied, please hand him the device and return the phone."

"I think it's in my best interest to put the phone back on speaker," Ronin said, but he handed it back to the courier along with the device.

"I have it," the courier said. "What do you want me to do?"

"Time for us to conclude our business. Get the bag."

The courier produced a small black bag about the size of his cell phone.

"Hold the device over the opening and let it drop inside."

Ronin watched the courier follow the Grandmaster's instructions and realized the cameras monitored the exchange and ensured the chain of custody. Once the device was inside, the courier folded the top inch, rolled another inch and secured the bag's Velcro seal.

That's a Faraday bag, Ronin thought. *He's shielding the device, but is he keeping something out or locking it in?*

"Now get to Le Bourget. There's a jet waiting for the package. When I have confirmation, the bag is on board, you will be compensated," Grandmaster said. "Tell the others to collect their weapons and leave. The sniper will drive you to the airport."

The call ended. The courier pocketed the phone and called out to the men in the alley.

"You two. Get your things and go. And you," the courier said, and pointed at the sniper. "You're with me."

Ronin watched the first two men scan the alley for their handguns, holster them and walk toward the street. The sniper remained behind, gathered and secured his weapons, and waited for the courier to step out.

"Hold on," Ronin said, and placed a hand on the courier's shoulder. "Let's give those two a few minutes to be on their way," and he nodded at the pair exiting the alley.

Ronin knew he'd made no friends tonight and considered what might wait for him when he left. *Why this alley? This entrance? The infrared cameras. One light. That took effort and planning or familiarity and easy access.*

Ronin released his grip on the courier. "OK, you and your escort can lead the way. I'll follow."

Ronin watched the courier approach the street. *Get off the X,* Ronin thought. *Never stay where the enemy last saw you.*

He stepped back into the alcove where the courier first appeared and tried the service door. *Nailed it.* Ronin slipped inside and took cover. The restaurant was dark, quiet. Under the glow of safety lighting, he dashed to the front door and peered outside. The aroma of butter and garlic still hung in the air. The same scent that lingered on the courier. *I was right. He'd been waiting inside.*

Ronin disappeared into the darkness of the deserted street. *The mission's complete... for now,* he thought, but there were arrangements to be made before morning. His pace quickened. Using parked cars for cover, he crossed the street, back and forth, several times. When he was certain no-one followed, he headed for the BMW1200 parked a few blocks away and strapped on a motorcycle helmet.

Rocketing along the Seine, Ronin could see the towering facade of the Orsay clock. *Nearly midnight. The device would be in the air by now,* he thought and wondered if the courier was dead. *Clients like the Grandmaster don't like complications or loose ends.*

CHAPTER 19

FRIDAY, APRIL 17
5:11 PM EDT

RITZ-CARLTON, WASHINGTON, D.C.

MANUEL ROJAS KILLED FOR a living. It suited him. First as an Army Ranger in Iraq, later as a DEA agent embedded in a Columbian cartel. He was proud of his work, once, and was always clear about the mission objectives. This was different. The man they hired him to kill was a United States Senator, not some third-world insurgent or cartel enforcer. And there was the girl. She was innocent, but the contract was explicit.

The contract's substantial deposit made it possible for Rojas to buy some new clothes, rent an innocuous dark blue KIA, and acquire the drugs he needed for the job. He left the Stardust motel behind and booked a room at The Ritz-Carlton, just a few blocks from the target. The digital package contained minute detail, but with his own daughter's life hanging in the balance, Rojas assumed nothing. He studied every element of Senator Cahill's weekend routine.

Saturday mornings were spent on the hill, and split between committee work, constituent meetings, and fundraising. The Senator's more personal encounters, in his suite at the Willard, began with the arrival of the Magic Touch janitorial company vehicle. The van had all the earmarks of a legitimate cleaning business, but it was the property of the Quimera Cartel. So was the girl that Cahill ordered.

The Magic Touch van would pull up to the hotel's service entrance. Two of the cartel's delivery men, dressed in cleaning crew uniforms, would enter the building, pushing a large yellow and black maintenance cart. The target package included a thermal image photograph of the cart's interior, and the body heat signature confirmed the girl was inside.

The cleaning crew used the service elevator to reach the hotel's top floor, where Senator Cahill maintained a suite as his DC residence and office. The suite's proximity to Capitol Hill facilitated the Senator's frequent escapes to freshen up or retrieve papers or whatever excuse he might offer his staffers. The Senator's car would arrive at the front entrance, where the doorman greeted and escorted him into the building. The driver appeared to be the Senator's only security, and he remained with the car until a text message summoned him back to the entrance.

The mission profile included the hotel's floor plan, photos of Cahill's suite, entry and exit routes, and contingency alternates. Even on this final mission review, the sheer volume and clarity of the material and the precision of the plan remained striking. *The room's obviously bugged,* he thought. *But this camera angle... these shots are so close, so direct. Damn. The TV. They hacked the TV's camera.*

It was the profile's inclusion of explicit videos of the Senator's proclivities and routine that Rojas found difficult to watch. With a daughter not much older than the child in the video, Rojas grimaced and focused his analysis on the mission-critical moments. The Senator's abuse was bad enough, but the two cartel delivery men took their time with the girl before shoving her back into the cage. *I'll bet Cahill thinks she's his private property,* Rojas thought. *And that she's dressed and served for his pleasure alone. What a fool. At least these two are careful not to damage the merchandise, or I imagine their cartel boss would literally have their balls.*

Rojas noted the girl's cloudy eyes and vacant stare. *An addict's eyes, but still pretty,* he thought. *Brown with flecks of gold.* He studied her face for a moment, trying to decide if there was still a hint of innocence or was it hopelessness? Rojas coughed and cleared his throat. Choking at the thought of his daughter trapped in the endless hell of addiction and abuse. *I can do this*, he thought. *I will do it... for this girl and my daughter.*

The Senator's predilection for bondage was cruel but convenient, and the series of recordings confirmed his pattern. The maintenance men would remove the girl from her utility cart cage. Bound hands and feet prevented running or injury, and the ball gag ensured silence before, during, and after. She would wear whatever costume the Senator ordered. The school girl's uniform, white blouse, red striped tie and short plaid skirt appeared to be Cahill's favorite. What intrigued Rojas was the Senator's exhilaration, almost euphoria. He watched the Senator shred the girl's clothes and strip her bare.

A recovering addict himself, Rojas recognized the signs. The target package identified exactly where the Senator hid his stash, and his drug use pattern was central to the plan. After witnessing Cahill's frenzy fuse with the debauchery, Rojas knew the plan was solid.

Chapter 20

FRIDAY, APRIL 17
11:47 PM CEST

HOTEL DE CRILLON, PARIS, FRANCE

KATE'S ARRIVAL IN PARIS was as choreographed as her departure from Virginia, and given the late hour she was grateful that Leslie had seen to every detail. The limo driver held Kate's door, and offered to take her bag, but Kate just tossed the duffle into the back and slid in alongside. The driver handed Kate a legal-sized envelope and closed the door. Kate recognized the logo, one of the firm's European partners, and she broke the seal. Inside was a handful of pages and forms, and the scanned image of a handwritten note.

My Dear Kate,

I contacted the American Embassy and Hotel de Crillon to alert them of your arrival. I'm assured of their discretion, and at the moment, Jake's identity has not been made public. It is my sincere hope that the media will not learn of your arrival or location, and it's helpful that you kept your maiden name.

The notes and forms in this envelope will help you navigate the issues related to an American citizen's death on French soil, but I feel compelled to warn you that investigators from the French Security Service may complicate matters. There will also be significant media attention and curiosity around Le American.

I'm sure you're exhausted and perhaps that will help you get some sleep. Tomorrow will come soon enough, and sadly, you will be one of many attempting to identify loved ones. Our European partner, Roche Fortier Avocats, prepared this package, and a representative of the firm will await your arrival at the IML, the Institut Medico-Legal de Paris. That is where Jake and the others were taken. Arnaud Fortier is a good friend, with significant political connections. His personal cell phone number is below. If you run into any difficulties, call him.

On a personal note, I'm devastated and can scarcely imagine how you're feeling. Your past is cloaked in shadows and mystery, but I know that you and Jake literally went through hell, and emerged the most loving and remarkable young couple I've ever known.

I should have said something long before now, but when the CIA placed you in the firm, I thought it was a mistake. I brought you in as a personal favor for a dear friend, but I realize now she did me the favor. You've been an extraordinary addition to the firm, and to my life. You pushed, inspired and challenged me, and I'm better for having known you. I'd like to think I've done the same for you.

I hope that you will return. There is still so much that we can learn from one another. But whatever the future brings, you will forever be in my heart.

All my love,

Leslie

What an extraordinary woman, Kate thought. She had grown close to Leslie without appreciating the depth of those feelings. *I will miss her.* And at that moment, Kate realized that whatever came next, she would not return to that life.

On the drive into Paris, Kate thought about Leslie's insights and guidance. *Stand your ground. Own your mistakes. Never let them see you cry.* Kate learned to seize the opportunity when men made the mistake of underestimating her strength, capabilities, or resolve. She couldn't imagine a better mentor or friend. It was Leslie who taught Kate to dress for the job you want and the respect you deserve. A sly smile crept on to her face and she recalled Jake's reaction to her growing collection of La Perla. Kate loved the power and confidence that came with attention to every layer of a woman's look, and that included where and how she concealed weapons.

The driver turned the corner and even at midnight the historic opulence of the Crillon was unmistakable. *Not a location Jake would choose*, she thought, but client proximity was a mission requirement and luxury accommodations were one of the few perks of the job. A dozen cars, parked at attention, stood guard over the hotel entrance. *Rolls. Lamborghini. Bugatti.*

The limo approached a set of gold stanchions, and stretched between them was a thick, black, theatrical rope that marked the Crillon's exclusive stretch of Place de la Concorde. *Oh crap*, Kate thought at the reality of her arrival. She looked down at what she was wearing, and again at the street scene developing in front of her. *What did Leslie call it,* she wondered. *Urban camouflage.* Exactly what Kate wanted. *Be inconspicuous. Invisible.* But she hadn't considered the big picture.

A young man, dark suit, white shirt, thin black tie, watched the limo's approach. Kate thought he might be a businessman waiting for a car until he stepped forward to open Kate's door.

"Bonsoir Madame," he said, and offered Kate his hand.

Kate accepted the help and stepped out of the limo. She slipped the messenger bag over her head and shoulder. When she reached back into the car to grab her travel bag, he offered to retrieve it, but Kate was too fast for him.

"I've got it. Thanks."

"Very good, Madame," he said. "This way, s'il vous plaît."

He escorted Kate past the black iron, gold-tipped railing, reminiscent of an honor guard of Roman spears, and toward the pair of massive glass doors. An impeccably dressed older gentleman met Kate the moment she passed through the entry. *Early eighties,* she thought. *Perhaps the GM, or one of Leslie's associates?*

The warmth of his greeting was startling, but the lingering pink in the whites of eyes, and the swelling that had almost subsided, revealed his story. There was an immediate bond of loss and grief. He kissed both cheeks, placed her hand in the crook of his arm, and guided Kate into a private salon. If the lobby was busy, she didn't notice. If anyone thought her clothes inappropriate, he didn't care, so neither did she.

"I am Thierry Boulleau, Managing Director," he said, and he took the chair next to Kate and cupped her hand in his.

"It is with great sadness that I welcome you to the Hotel de Crillon, but please know that we...that I am grateful for your husband's courage and sacrifice."

"Thank you," Kate said, but she knew his tears were for someone else. "You lost someone today?"

"Qui, madame. My niece worked at the cafe," he said, then looked away. He fought to keep his emotions bottled and continued. "But all of France grieves today. Thirty-six souls. And we pray for the wounded still fighting for their lives."

"I'm so sorry," Kate said, and squeezed his hand. Lost in her own grief, she hadn't grasped the magnitude of the tragedy or the scope of the suffering.

Thierry stiffened his back and sat up in his chair. "Many more would have perished without God's gift of your husband. For that, we are grateful beyond words."

"Have the authorities released Jake's name?"

"No, No. They haven't, and I have been asked to say nothing."

"How did you—"

"Know that your husband was *Le American?*" he asked. "I recognized him immediately. A man of your husband's stature and deportment is well, conspicuous. And of course, we were aware of the security detail that would accompany some of our guests."

"Are the guests still here?"

"Everyone attending the Global Economic Conference was moved as a safety precaution and most are already home or in the air."

"I'm sure that you are anxious to see your husband's room, and I have a key for you here," he said, and pulled the key from his coat pocket. "But might I offer you one of our suites?"

"That's very kind of you, but I'm sure Jake's room will be fine," she said. There was more, but she couldn't bring herself to say it out loud. *I want to be near him,* Kate thought. *I want to wrap myself in his clothes, curl up on his bed, hug his pillow and cry myself to sleep.*

"I understand, but should you change your mind, I have instructed my staff to assist you in any way they can."

"Do they know?"

"Some, like myself, recognized your husband, but we pride ourselves on our discretion. I can assure you that no member of Hotel de Crillon will divulge your husband's identity, or your presence here," he said. "And we have followed your attorney's instructions to the letter."

"My attorney?"

"I spoke with Ms Dodd personally," he said. "All authorized key cards were disabled and all house staff were barred from entry. Hotel security assures me that no one has successfully entered the room since your husband's... since your husband left the hotel this morning."

Kate appreciated the effort to be sensitive to her husband's departure, but she caught something more in Thierry's description of the lockdown.

"Successfully?" she asked.

"There was one attempt. When the key failed to open the door, the gentleman returned to the elevator. It's not unusual for guests to get off on the wrong floor and only discover the mistake when the door won't open."

"Was he a tall, trim, black man, roughly Jake's build?"

"Yes. Do you know him?"

"It was probably Marcus," she said. "He works, worked, with Jake, so I'm not surprised he had a key. I'm sure he was pleased to see you locked down the room. Tragedy is a magnet for thieves."

"I assure you that is not the case at L'Hotel de Crillon."

"No, of course not. It's just standard incident protocol to secure access. I'm sure you understand," she said, and changed the subject. "It's late. I won't disturb him tonight, but I would appreciate his room number. Last name, Jones. Marcus Jones."

"Right away," he said and stepped out of the room. He returned to Kate moments later and handed her a slip of paper. "Monsieur Jones is on the floor just below your husband's, but I'm told that he's not in. If you like, I can leave a message for him at the front desk."

"No, that won't be necessary," she said, and stood. He escorted Kate toward the elevator, but insisted she relinquish the duffle and a bellman fetched the bag.

Past midnight, Kate thought, and then realized she hadn't heard from Marcus since she left Richmond.

Thierry pressed his cheek against Kate's. Neither spoke, but Kate felt the tear that passed between them, and watched Thierry wipe his eyes when he walked away.

Kate stepped into the elevator, and the bellman followed. Her thoughts turned to Marcus. She had seen Jake grieve for a fallen brother, and pictured Marcus and the rest of the team. There would be rows of empty beer bottles and shot glasses. They would boast of legendary operations that grew in ferocity as the night wore on and the bottles drained.

With the GEC's regional meeting cut short, and the US delegation gone, the team will soon be headed home, she thought. The elevator passed Marcus's floor, and she checked the time. *Wherever he is, whatever he's doing, I hope he's OK*, she thought. Jake used to say 'tragedy begets tragedy' and he and I we're living proof.

The elevator opened. Kate stepped into the hall and turned to block the bellman.

"I can take it from here," she said, and before he could object, Kate slipped the young man a ten Euro note. She saw him smile and the elevator doors closed, and she turned toward Jake's room. Her heart raced, pounding with every step. *How many times did I think about surprising Jake? I should have*, she thought. *I should have just showed up. Maybe waiting for him in bed. He would have been so mad, but not for long.*

Kate stood at Jake's door, hands trembling. She fumbled with the keycard and dropped it. *Get a grip*, she thought. *Jake's gone, and with or without Marcus, come morning, you're going to get your husband and take him home. And then you're going to figure out what the hell happened, and make someone pay.*

Chapter 21

HOTEL DE CRILLON, PARIS, FRANCE

ON THE FLIGHT TO Paris, Kate had imagined this moment a dozen times. What if she opened the door and Jake was there, sound asleep? What if this was all a horrible mistake, a nightmare? A cruel trick. But the truth of the moment was inescapable. Kate swept the keycard over the door sensor, heard the click of the lock, and took her first step toward accepting a world without Jake.

His hotel room was exactly as she pictured. Jake was the neat one. He never left without making his bed. Sheets tucked tight in perfect forty-five-degree military corners. Clothes neatly folded, stacked and organized by function. *When he left this morning*, she thought. *He had no idea he wasn't coming back.*

"You were so damn precise," she said. "You had protocols and procedures for everything. Even how to make the bed. And none of it made any difference."

Kate grabbed and yanked the blankets, and the pillows flew across the room. She swept his clothes off the dresser and dumped his suitcase. All pretense of control was gone, but the rage caught her off guard. She sank to the floor, pulled Jake's clothes in tight and hugged them, hugged him.

"Damn it, Jake," she whispered. "You promised."

She held a T-shirt to her face. Felt the cotton caress her cheek and caught a hint of Jake's scent. For a moment, he was there. The anger faded, but the tears returned.

Kate peeled herself off the floor, surveyed the mess and made a half-hearted attempt to remake the bed. *Jake would not approve*, she thought. *But he never complained. Not once. He would just smile and fix it.* She undressed where she stood and looked down at the pile of clothes. *A puddle of Kate.* That's what Jake would call it whenever he stumbled, sometimes literally, on a spot where she had dissolved.

She hoped a shower would help, and for a few moments she closed her eyes and melted in the steam's warmth and the water's caress. But she was standing where Jake stood only hours ago. She could feel him. His arms wrapped around her. Strong, but gentle. Safe. Loved. His cheek pressed against hers, his breath on her neck. Chills ran down her arms and she tilted her head, inviting his kiss, but none came.

Kate opened her eyes and allowed her senses to grasp reality. It was only a memory. She was alone. Back pressed against the cold tile, she slid to the floor, pulled her knees in tight, wrapped her arms around them and sobbed. It was only when the water turned tepid that the tears subsided, the sobbing eased, and Kate stood.

Cocooned in the hotel's enormous bath sheet, Kate faced the mirror, swept her long auburn hair into a towel and wrapped it around her head. She removed the remnants of her morning makeup, but when she tossed a cotton ball into the wastebasket, something caught her eye. Kate reached in and retrieved the plastic retail packaging of a Moore Industries Quantum NanoVault. *That's odd*, she thought. *Why would Jake want one of these, and the Onyx is the most expensive model?*

Sitting just beneath the plastic was a folded sheet of paper. It was a page from a notepad, the Crillon's logo emblazoned at the top.

Le Cafe Pierre,
18 Rue de Tournon
Today, Noon

Kate read the note and darted into the bedroom. Lifting the notepad from Jake's nightstand, she titled it toward the light, ran a finger across the surface. *Perfectly smooth.* She spotted another pad near the phone on the desk, but it, too, was brand new. *The note wasn't written here,* she thought. *Someone gave it to him.*

She didn't recognize the handwriting, but Kate knew it wasn't Jake's. For all his strengths, Jake's idea of penmanship was barely legible printing. The note was cursive, fluid. *A woman's hand,* she wondered, but it was the message that ignited Kate's fury. *Whoever wrote this sent Jake to his death.*

CHAPTER 22

SATURDAY, APRIL 18
12:44 AM CEST

HOTEL DE CRILLON, PARIS, FRANCE

KATE FOCUSED ON THE note in her hand. It was just a slip of paper, but without it, Jake might still be alive. Perhaps a woman's handwriting, but that was just a guess. She sniffed the page. Was there a hint of perfume or cologne? Nothing. Careful not to handle the note any more than she already had, Kate set it on the dresser. It was evidence. Of what she didn't know, but she still had friends at the agency who might help.

Why was Jake at that cafe? Who sent him? Kate closed her eyes and imagined the video call. *Jake seated at the sidewalk table, sipping an espresso. He teased her with the promise of an anniversary present, then she heard Marcus. He was in a hurry, a little agitated. When Marcus realized I was on the phone, he relaxed. Marcus would always tease Jake that 'Every Church needs a Preacher', just to hear us groan, but not today. He needled Jake for being at the wrong cafe. But it wasn't a mistake. Jake was there for a reason. The note proves it. But why?*

Kate opened her eyes and scanned Jake's room. His laptop might have answers, but it was nowhere in sight. She dropped the towel where she stood and reached into the pile of Jake's clothes. She grabbed a T-shirt and slipped it on. Jake's XL shirt drooped off one shoulder and fit like a nightshirt. *The safe,* she thought. *He'd lock it up, along with...* She found the safe in the bedroom closet, and knew exactly what code Jake would use. Moments later, she surveyed the contents.

Laptop. Passport. A few hundred in Euros. Wedding band.

With the stack of items tucked under her left arm, Kate retrieved Jake's ring. A simple gold band they bought when they had nothing, but it was priceless. Jake never traveled without it, but when operating or on a mission, he kept it out of harm's way, and wore a silicon safety ring. Kate rolled it over in her fingertips. She glanced at the inscription inside, too small to read, but she knew it by heart. *If the angels ask...*

Kate slid the passport and the cash into her messenger bag and took the laptop to the bed. Sitting cross-legged, back pressed against the headboard, laptop cradled between her knees, Kate tried to log on. *That's strange,* she thought. *He changed the password.*

It was Kate's job to configure and maintain all of their devices, and she ensured they used military-grade encryption and secure communications. *Could he have been trying to hide something from me? Not a chance. As our system admin, Jake, would know, changing his password wouldn't even slow me down. He must have thought his password compromised, but why not say something?*

Kate logged on as the laptop's administrator and the screen filled with a familiar image. The laptop's wallpaper was a family photo, of sorts. Their family. Jake and Kate and the rescue dog that helped bring them together. Jake's cabin, nestled in the mountains of West Virginia, was visible in the corner of the photo and the lake was in the distance.

The smiling couple knelt just behind Mr Arthur Radley. Boo, as she preferred to call him, was an only child. The gray-faced black lab bore the scars of a tortured life before his rescue, and that just made him one of the family. For a moment, Kate was back in that world. The image, the memory, was pure joy frozen in time, but Boo was gone, and now so was Jake.

No more tears, she thought. *Maybe those two are together again. Jake's throwing sticks into a lake somewhere, and Boo's sprinting down the dock, launching off the end, and splashing into the water.*

It was the desktop folder named *Katherine Preacher* that drew her back into the moment. Jake rarely said 'Katherine' and never said 'Preacher' unless it was serious. *This is why he changed his password,* she thought. *He knew I would use the admin account and this would be the first thing I'd see.*

Her palms were clammy, and her heart raced. She took her hand off the touchpad and placed it on her chest as if she could will her heart to stop pounding. *Action dissipates fear - that's what Jake would say,* and she opened the folder.

Among a handful of documents, there was a single video recording.

In the event of my death.

Kate didn't realize she'd been holding her breath until her lungs ached for air. With a deep breath, and then another, she calmed and prepared herself. The video was only a day old. *Whatever he wanted me to know, he recorded it the night before he died... and he made sure no one else would see it.* She launched the video.

The jumbled first few seconds was a close-up of Jake's T-shirt and he carried the laptop and set it on the desk. The shirt she was now wearing was on the screen in front of her. Jake backed away from the camera and sat on the end of the bed. He looked into the camera for a minute, but didn't say a thing. With ruffled hair and dressed only in gym shorts and shirt, it looked like he'd been in bed for hours.

Kate watched Jake massage the sutured stump below his left knee. The skin was a blotchy red. *Must have walked a lot this week,* she thought. *For a guy with one leg, he doesn't let much slow him down, but I'll bet the pain woke him.*

He looked into the camera, and surprised Kate when he swept a knuckle across the corner of his eye to hide a tear. In five years of marriage, she could count on one hand the number of times she'd seen him cry.

"Hey Pal," he began, but his throat seized. He stopped to get a sip of water, and those two words echoed in her mind. *Hey Pal.* Her friends thought it odd, but she loved being Jake's best friend.

"I'm sorry," he continued. "You know I don't make promises lightly, and I prayed you'd never see this video, but watching it now means I'm gone."

Kate saw the anguish on Jake's face, heard the tremor in his voice, and she hit the pause button. *I don't know that I can watch this. Not right now,* she thought, and grabbed the box of tissue on the nightstand. She wiped away the tears and looked into the face on the screen. Whenever they struggled, whatever challenge they faced, Jake always came back to the same thought. *There's nothing we can't do together.*

She pressed play.

"I hope my death had meaning, but if it didn't, it's alright. My life had purpose, and you filled it with love. I think we probably lived and loved more in the last five years than most couples do in fifty, so whatever happened, please don't be angry."

I am angry, she thought. *But not with you.*

"When I asked you to marry me, I didn't have a future. There was no plan, and you didn't care. It didn't matter where we lived or what we did. Somehow you saw a life for us I couldn't even imagine, and I still don't know what I did to deserve you."

Maybe you didn't.

"I just knew I couldn't live without you, and you took a chance that an old door-kicker could change and could be something more."

Don't forget stubborn.

"For some mysterious reason, you agreed to marry this stubborn, one-legged, old door-kicker, and you had just one question."

"Love me?" she asked out loud.

"I didn't understand it. Not at first. I thought maybe I'd done something wrong. How could you not see how much I loved you? I wanted to spend the rest of my life with you, but I will never forget that moment, or the thousand times you've asked me since. Your face glowed when I pulled you in close. I looked into those sparkling eyes, all green and gold and flecks of brown, and I said I would always love you."

"You promised."

"We sealed that promise with a kiss, and that's when I realized what it meant. Most people don't know death the way we do. When everyone you've ever loved is taken, you swear you'll never hurt like that again. And then I met you. So I knew what you were asking because I wanted it too."

"I know."

"So I promised, whatever came next, we'd face it together. I would be there. And I prayed that was one promise I could keep. I wanted you to look back across thirty, forty, even fifty years or more, and know that I have always loved you."

You'd be here if you could, she thought.

"It breaks my heart to know I failed."

"Please, don't cry," she said, watching Jake struggle to regain his composure, wanting to reach out and wrap her arms around him.

Jake slipped off his wedding band, and for a moment he stared at it in the palm of his hand and then looked back at the camera.

"I know you remember," he said. "We were watching *City of Angels.*"

An angel was guiding a child into the afterlife.

"The angel asked that little girl what she liked best."

Right. Pajamas with feet.

"I looked at you and said, 'If the angels ask me what I liked best, I'd tell them every moment with you,' and you wondered what made me think I'd be heading that direction."

You said I was more devil than Preacher.

"So here I am. Thinking about my moment of truth. I have no idea if there's anything beyond this life, or what it might hold for me. Without you, there is no heaven, so it might as well be hell. Maybe I can strike a deal with the devil. I'd ask to stick around. Keep you safe. I know. I know. You don't need a bodyguard. That's just me hoping I can stay close."

I know you're here.

"I never told you," he said. "Never told anyone. But the moment I saw you, I knew I'd marry you. Believe me, marriage was the farthest thing from my mind. The teams were operating at an unbelievable pace. My entire world was my brothers, mission-first and front-sight focus. And there you were, ponytail, ball cap, jeans. Just this little thing tucked into the webbing of a C-130, and to me, you were the most beautiful woman I'd ever seen. Then your boss catches me staring and calls me over. God's honest truth. My heart skipped a beat."

Your hands were sweaty.

"What was her name? Margaret? No, something snobby, more East Coast... Yeah, Margot says to me. Can't have a dead analyst F-ing up my career, so get her a gun and teach her to shoot. Syria's a war zone, not Disney World, and now it's your job to keep her alive."

That was a tough job, and I didn't make it easy.

"Between your injuries and my deployments, I stopped dreaming. I knew I'd never see you again. But I wake up in a hospital bed and there you are, holding my hand, smiling down at me. And some scruffy old black lab hops up on my bed and starts licking my face. Nobody seems to notice the dog's laying across my cracked ribs, and I can barely breathe."

Oh. Sorry about that.

"When I saw you look at my leg, or what was left of it, I got angry. I told you to get Scarface off my chest and leave."

"I understood," Kate said. "When you saw me in the field hospital, I begged you to go. I couldn't bear to have you look at me. I couldn't look at myself. Not after what they did."

"But when you said, 'Come on Boo. We'll come back when Jake's feeling better' - it all came rushing back. I remembered quiet times and long conversations about our favorite books and movies. I realized Boo was the dog you stole from the old man's porch."

Hey, I think you mean rescued, and you helped.

"I asked you to come back tomorrow and bring Boo. And you said you'd be back every day, if I wanted, until the three of us walked, hopped or crawled out of that place. At the very moment I wondered if I could go on, you said to me.

'Legs don't make the man. All that matters is what we do with our time on this earth.' You gave me hope. You knew I would find my purpose. I was alive for a reason."

"Oh, Jake," Kate said, and the tears streamed down her cheeks. "I will miss you more than you could ever know, but I'm also so proud of you."

Jake, too, needed a moment before he could continue, and gulped the last of his water.

"The girl I met on her way to Syria, the girl I fell in love with, was full of passion and purpose and determined to change lives. Save lives. And God knows you did."

That girl's gone.

"I know you think she's gone, but you're wrong. You can't hide from the woman you were born to be, or the warrior I've seen you become. Not any more. The stakes are too high."

Now you're scaring me.

"I thought keeping you in the dark meant you'd be safe. I was wrong. No one is beyond their reach, but I can't say more on the video."

Jake tugged at the chain around his neck and fished out something from beneath his T-shirt. Kate saw the silver cross he always wore, his mother's cross, and the new NanoVault.

"It's all here," Jake said and held up the device. "Everything I know. And everything I don't."

He pressed his mother's cross to his lips, then slid the chain and NanoVault back under his shirt.

"Find this," he said. "And do *your* thing. See what everyone is missing. What I missed. Solve the puzzle. And take them down."

Take who down, Kate wondered, but she knew Jake wouldn't, couldn't, answer.

Jake composed himself and looked straight into the camera, straight into Kate's eyes.

"Kate, whatever happens to me, know that I loved you from the moment I saw you, and I will *always* love you."

CHAPTER 23

SATURDAY, APRIL 18
1:44 AM CEST

HOTEL DE CRILLON, PARIS, FRANCE

SLEEP NEVER CAME EASILY, and Kate knew tonight it was pointless to try. She set a wake-up alarm, just in case, but spent most of the night collecting, watching and organizing video of the Paris attack. Her analyst brain was now in charge, and she forced the grieving wife to take a back seat.

At the CIA, Kate learned to compartmentalize. It was the only way to stay sane in a job that required detailed analysis of the graphic imagery of war. She'd assess the impact of covert operations, study the twisted wreckage battlefield bombing, and count civilian causalities, trying to distinguish between children and adults.

Kate believed she could face the sheer volume of on-line video, photographs, and social media posts on the cafe attack. As part of the Agency task force that analyzed the 2015 Paris Bataclan Theater attack. She'd seen the face of terror before. Over one-hundred-thirty souls lost across all three coordinated target sites, and hundreds more injured. Kate thought she was prepared, but she was wrong.

This was different. The fleeting images of Jake charging the terrorists had captured the imagination of the news media, and catapulted *Le American* into worldwide headlines, but this was personal. This was her husband. Every image, every video, was a knife thrust into Kate's gut. And then she found a video of Marcus rushing to Jake's side, and struggling to save his life.

The young woman who recorded the video was crying, praying, her hands shaking. Blood was everywhere. Kate watched Marcus assess Jake's condition and collect the field trauma kits they both kept on their ankles. Marcus peeled off Jake's jacket, cut away the blood-soaked shirt, and then detached Jake's body armor.

Team protocol required everyone wear armor, but it wasn't enough. Kate knew something that the rest of the world wouldn't know for days. The sound that prompted her hack into the CIA's ballistic analysis system, the sound that echoed in Kate's mind, was a single shot from a sniper's rifle.

Kate watched Marcus search Jake's body for entry and exit wounds. He applied a pair of chest seals and stuffed blood-clotting combat gauze into another wound. Everything Marcus did was by the book. *The life you save might be your own,* Jake would say when he insisted Kate master the same field medic training the special forces teams receive. Knowing the outcome helped Kate watch with a detached precision. *I couldn't have done it better,* she thought. *No one could.*

The Halo chest seals Marcus used were effective. *Tourniquet the limbs, pack the junctions, and seal the box,* she thought. *Marcus did everything right.* Jake appeared stable, but only for a minute or two. Kate recognized the signs. She knew what Marcus needed to do, and she knew the risks. The three-inch decompression needle Marcus shoved into Jake's chest brought immediate relief. The labored breathing subsided, and Jake tried to talk.

Jake grabbed Marcus's jacket and pulled him closer. Jake whispered something, and Marcus froze, but there was too much background noise.

Pausing the video, rewinding, and watching again and again was useless. If the video caught what Jake said, she couldn't hear it. She let the video play on.

Jake's grip slipped, his hand hit the sidewalk. Marcus checked for a pulse, then swept his hand over Jake's eyes, and kissed his forehead. Kate couldn't hear what Marcus said, but Jake wasn't the first warfighter she'd seen fall. She knew Marcus would say goodbye as a brother and a warrior.

The video ended, and Kate was back in the moment. *What did Jake say? Marcus looked shook,* she thought. *I need to run the video through the forensic lab. I can strip out the audio, pass it through noise reduction filters, compress the voice, or I could ask a favor.* There was someone who could help, but it would mean crossing a bridge she burned when she left the agency. *Whatever it takes.*

There was nothing more she could do tonight, and her thoughts drifted to what the morning would bring. She imagined what it would be like to see Jake on a cold slab of steel. She wanted to stand alongside him, take his hand, run her fingers through his hair, but that's not how it's done. One common thread among the family members of the Bataclan victims was that the French identification process was cold, sterile, distant. They would present Jake's body from behind a wall of glass, unreachable, untouchable. Once she identified him, she could collect his things. *His things,* she thought. *That could be a problem.* She picked up the phone and dialed the front desk.

"Bonsoir, Madame. How may we be of service?"

"I'm sorry. I know it's late, but I was wondering if you might know where I could purchase a Quantum NanoVault, the Onyx model?"

"Of course. I will have another one sent up straight away."

"Another one?"

"Qui, Madame. Your husband requested one as well," he said. "They're very popular, and the market around the corner is open twenty-four hours."

Not long after, there was a knock at the door, and a young man handed Kate the same retail packaging she'd found in Jake's trash. *Perfect,* she thought, and she opened the package, noted the last few digits of the serial number, and tucked the device into her messenger bag.

Exhaustion swept over Kate, she curled up on the bed and wrapped her arms around Jake's pillow. The last of the day's tears slipped down her cheek, and sensing the battles that lay ahead, she whispered her own warrior's prayer, "Til Valhalla, my love. Til Valhalla."

CHAPTER 24

SATURDAY, APRIL 18
5:00 AM CEST

HOTEL DE CRILLON, PARIS, FRANCE

IT WAS 5:00AM WHEN Kate's wake-up alarm buzzed. She rolled over and spotted the flashing message light on the bedside phone. The automated system announced the message timestamp as 4:30 am and began playing.

"Kate, it's Marcus. I'm sorry I couldn't meet you at the hotel. We've been scrambling since the...".

There was a momentary pause, and then Marcus continued. "Everything's set. We'll meet at your room at 0600. Please, don't leave the room, and don't open the door until we arrive."

The recording continued for a few moments. Kate listened, but there was only silence. Marcus was the glib one in the group, she thought. He always knew what to say to lighten the mood, or to entice a woman to his bed, but without Jake, he was lost. Speechless.

The knock came precisely at 6:00 am. A quick look through the door's peephole confirmed it was Marcus, and he was not alone. Marcus stepped through the doorway, ushered Kate to the side, and wrapped his arms around her. They both tried hard not to cry, with limited success. Three others streamed in behind Marcus and spread out so quickly Kate didn't recognize them.

"Clear," said one of them.

"All Clear," said another, and they regrouped around Kate.

"You're here," she said, and wrapped her arms around and hugged each of the men she'd come to know and love as brothers. "I can't believe you're all here."

"Everyone's here," Marcus said. "The others are with the vehicles."

"I thought once the Global Economic Council delegates disbursed, you'd all head back to VA beach, or on to other assignments."

"Mission first," Marcus said. "You're family, and until you and Jake are home, we already have a mission."

"But I don't understand," Kate said. "What's with the full security detail?"

"You haven't heard," Marcus said. "Jake's identity is now public, and so is yours."

"That was just a matter of time," Kate said. "But what's the problem?"

"The jihadis Jake took down were linked to radical Imam Abu Walifa."

"Has he taken credit for the attack?" Kate asked.

"No, not yet. He issued a Fatwa calling for vengeance and Walifa's followers are calling Jake the murderer. We have to assume you're a viable target."

"Do they know where I am?"

"This location is secure, for now, but press and paparazzi are scouring every major hotel, and gathering along the route to the—"

"Marcus, it's OK," Kate said, and reached out to touch his arm. "I know where we're going, and the sooner I see Jake, the better. There's still a small part of me hoping I'll wake up from this nightmare."

There was another knock at the door. One of the team confirmed the identity of the new arrival, nodded at Marcus, and opened the door.

An attractive young woman, roughly Kate's height and build, stepped forward and introduced herself.

"We've never met. I'm Talya. Talya Aviram."

"Talya, of course. Jake always spoke so highly of you."

"Your husband was a remarkable man, a mentor and friend," Talya said. "And a gentleman in every sense of the word."

Kate saw what Talya's makeup couldn't conceal. She, too, had been crying. Jake had a way of helping his team discover their best selves, and they loved him. Kate tried to ease Talya's pain.

"I know Jake's only regret was that he didn't have more like you," Kate said, and then turned to the guys. "No offense boys."

Talya smiled. "Trust me, it takes a lot more than that to offend these guys." Talya reached into the small duffle bag that she was carrying and pulled out a pair of wigs, one chestnut the other auburn.

"As you've probably guessed, I'm your double," Talya said. "And you didn't make it easy. When I double for celebrities, their social media images give me everything I need and sometime more than I care to see. But you're practically invisible on the web, and these guys were useless."

Talya held the wigs near Kate's hair. "Looks like the auburn is the better match. You're taller than I am."

"Five-six," Kate said.

"Heels will take care of that, and we'll be moving fast, so no one is going to get a good look."

Talya headed off to the bathroom and returned a few minutes later, looking eerily like Kate dressed for work.

"Wow," Kate said. "You look great, and that's a little creepy."

"Your boss helped me with the clothing concepts — Diane Von Furstenberg, very nice."

"You spoke with Leslie?" Kate asked.

"She was very kind and happy to help," Talya said. "I opted for the slacks over the pencil skirt, but otherwise this ensemble is all Leslie's design, or should I say all Kate?"

"Right. I look great," Kate said, and they both smiled. "What are you wearing under the blouse?"

"Very observant," Talya said, and peeled back a layer of her silk wrap blouse. "This is HAVOK SharkSkin — lightweight, blade defense. It can't be cut and was literally developed to help divers deal with shark bites."

"Impressive," Kate said. "Let's hope you don't need it." Then she turned back to Marcus. "So, how is this going to work?"

"Alpha Team is Talya, flanked by Forest and Deon," Marcus said. "As soon as we're a go, Alpha will use the main elevator. Hotel staff is standing by to clear the path to the armored vehicles."

"So that's the show," Kate said.

"Exactly. Those are the vehicles we want the press and paparazzi to follow, and anyone else."

"Anyone else?" Kate asked.

"Given the fatwa, we have to assume Walifa's followers are a threat."

Talya isn't just a decoy, Kate thought. *She's bait.*

"Look, Marcus, it's not that I don't appreciate the effort, the sacrifice. I do. Really. But I couldn't handle any of you getting hurt."

Talya stepped forward, took both of Kate's hands and looked her in the eye.

"Please, let me do my job. For Jake. For you," Talya said. "I know what I'm doing, and we both learned from one of the best."

Kate wrapped her arms around Talya and gave her a hug. *Jake would be proud,* she thought. *And he would want the team to do everything they could to keep me safe.* Kate let go of Talya and turned back to Marcus. "Alright. Walk me through the rest."

"Bravo team is the three of us," Marcus said, signaling toward himself and the very large man standing behind him. "You and I are with Mike. While Alpha exits the front door, we'll be in the service elevator. Our exfil is the alley in a hardened van we've vinyl-wrapped as a mock catering truck."

"You arranged all this overnight?"

"It was a long night, but yes. The names Preacher, Church and *Le American* opened a lot of doors and we sourced everything we needed."

"What about the Forensic Institute? With dozens of victims, they'll have it locked down tight, just like they did after Bataclan," Kate said.

"That's right. There's just one way in past a barricade of identity screening stations, followed by rows of tents filled with grief counselors and psychological services," Marcus said. "And I wouldn't put you through that. Let's just say for plausible deniability, it's best you don't know the details."

Marcus turned his attention to his earpiece and listened as the vehicle teams reported their locations and status.

"It's go time," Marcus said. "The hotel and service elevators are in position. The drivers are standing by. Let's roll."

Alpha team was the first out the door and confirmed their arrival at the lobby.

"Our turn," Marcus said to Kate, and once Mike confirmed the hallway remained clear, Marcus notified the team they were on the move. "Scout is Oscar Mike."

Kate caught Marcus's arm before they stepped into the hall. "My mission code name is Scout?" she asked. "Was that your idea?"

"Nope. That's all Jake," Marcus said. "It got you out of Syria, so I figured it's good luck."

"And keeps Jake close. I like it."

Marcus and Kate stepped into the service elevator, and Mike took his position as a human shield just inside the doors. Kate noticed the young man with his hand on the elevator key looked terrified.

"What did you say to him?" Kate whispered to Marcus.

"He may be under the impression that his testicles would be severed from his body if he failed to hold the elevator."

Kate put a hand on the boy's shoulder. He twitched, but Kate said, "Thank you" and he relaxed.

"Bravo One. Come in," said Forest.

"Go ahead Alpha."

"The circus is in town. Police motorcycle escort. Press and civilians lined up behind sidewalk barricades."

"Copy that," Marcus said, and added, "Show time."

Forest and Deon sandwiched Talya between them and guided her toward the hotel's main doors. Several members of the Hotel Crillon's staff kept the lobby clear, and two more stood at the main doors.

When Alpha approached, the glass doors opened, and the crowd erupted. Cameras clicked and flashed. Press shouted questions, and the Paparazzi begged Talya to look their way.

The objective was straight ahead. A trio of identical Range Rovers waited at the end of the hotel's red carpet. Talya's transport vehicle directly ahead. A pair of Gendarmerie motorcycles sat at the front and rear of the motorcade, their bright blue handlebar lights flashing.

Alpha team moved in unison. All three scanned the crowd for threats, and Talya repeated Jake's mantra just loud enough for the team to hear.

"Slow is smooth. Smooth is fast," she said.

Most of the crowd was respectful, holding signs of gratitude and grief, but Talya's attention was pulled to the right.

"Three o'clock," she said to the team.

A hooded figure stood just behind the police barricade, his face partially hidden, but his eyes tracked Talya's path to the transport vehicle.

The protester's blood-red sign read, *Martyrs Never Die!* He waved it at Talya, striking the man standing alongside.

He yelled, *"Avenge the fallen,"* and climbed onto the barricade. Several people in the crowd tried to catch him, but he burst forward toward Alpha One.

Forest pivoted away from Talya, drove the man's face into the sidewalk, and blood spurted from the protester's shattered nose. Seconds later Forest had the man's hands locked inside zip-tie cuffs, but the team had broken formation.

Deon and Talya exchanged glances and scanned the barricades as they continued toward the car. Both knew the protester could be a setup, a diversion, and Deon slipped in behind Talya to cover her six.

They were steps from the Rover when a handsome young man, maybe seventeen, eighteen, smiled, ducked under the barricade, and approached Talya. She returned his smile and assessed the threat. Both of his hands cupped an enormous bouquet of red roses. No visible weapon, but Talya kept her hands in close to her body. With palms up, she graciously tried to decline the flowers.

"Contact Right," Talya yelled to the team when the knife appeared.

The roses fell to the ground, and the boy lunged forward. His left hand grabbed Talya's arm, and his right thrust the knife up toward her throat.

***

Marcus heard the contact call and shoved Kate into the catering van. He forced Kate down to the floor, and the second they were in, the driver punched the gas.

"What's going on?" Kate asked, but there wasn't time to answer.

"Alpha One. Report," Marcus called out, and waited.

***

Cameras flashed. A woman screamed. The crowd of onlookers edged forward, but Alpha team pushed ahead, swept past the chaos, and leaped into the waiting vehicles. The motorcycle sirens wailed, and the motorcade raced away.

The young man lay bleeding on the street. Talya's response was so fast, no one saw what happened. His throat flailed open, carotid pulsing, blood spurting between the fingers gripping his throat, and then he let go.

"Alpha Team. Status?"

"Secure," Deon replied.

"Injuries?" Marcus asked.

There was a brief pause as both Forest, and Deon checked on Talya. Her blouse was torn, but the SharkSkin barrier was untouched. There was some blood, but her quick thumbs up confirmed it wasn't hers.

"None," Deon replied.

"Tangos?"

Forest was the last one in the vehicle, so he responded, "Two. One secure. One DRT."

***

"CONFIRMED. ONE DRT. CHARLIE Mike," Marcus said, and added, "Scout en route to Bus Stop."

"Is Talya OK," Kate asked. "Is everyone OK?"

"Yes. They're good. Safe. And continuing with the mission."

"I caught the Charlie Mike, but I've never heard DRT."

"Ah...," Marcus said, and hesitated.

"Marcus," Kate asked again. "What is DRT?"

"Dead Right There," Marcus said. "Whoever came at Talya was coming for you and made a fatal mistake."

Chapter 25

FRIDAY, APRIL 17
11:10 PM EST

PERSONAL RESIDENCE, CIA DEPUTY DIRECTOR, LANGLEY FOREST, McLEAN, VA

MARGOT RYDER RETREATED TO the library of her grand estate home. She poured a generous shot of the Glenmorangie '97 saved for rare moments of celebration or contemplation.

Rest in peace, my friend, she thought, and raised the glass to the ghost in the room. At the first sign of tears, she downed the single malt, and poured another.

Her cell phone's encrypted call alert was an unwelcome intrusion into the solitude of the moment, and she snapped at the caller. "Do you know what time it is?"

"I apologize for calling so late," the young man began, "but we had a breach."

"That doesn't explain why you're calling me," she said. "We have protocols and calling the Deputy Director at home isn't one of them."

"I know, and I wouldn't have bothered you with this except..."

"Except what?"

"The credentials used to access the network belong to Katherine Preacher. The account's disabled, so we don't yet know how it was used, perhaps a backdoor buried somewhere in the code, but the Preacher file is flagged 'Classified: Eyes Only', and you're the only authorized recipient."

"I see."

"Are you monitoring the connection?"

"No. She was in and out in a matter of minutes, and somehow didn't trip any of the real-time sensors," he said. "A log analysis sweep caught the anomaly only after the event, but we've reconstructed the activity."

"What do we know?"

"She uploaded a small file to the ballistic audio analysis system."

"And?"

"338 Lapua Magnum."

"A sniper," Margot concluded. "What's the confidence level?"

"Ninety-eight."

"Send me a copy of the report," she said. "And—"

"Yes?"

"Monitor the account. If there are any further incursions, terminate the connection immediately, and no one, I repeat, no one, is told of this breach. Understood?"

"Yes, Ma'am."

"Oh, and don't waste your time trying to trace the source," she said and hung up the phone.

Ballistic analysis? Margot wondered. *Kate, whatever you're up to, I pray you're not about to kick another hornet's nest.*

Margot turned back to the cable news analysis of the Paris attack, the endless video of chaos and destruction, and highlights of the extraordinary actions of an unknown hero, the man the French press were calling simply *Le American.*

It won't be long now, she thought. She recognized Jake the moment video surfaced, but realized official acknowledgment took time. Margot knew the Navy would provide the French authorities with the unclassified details of Jake Preacher's distinguished military career, and nearly two decades of service in

Special Operations Command (SOCOM). She pictured the administration's PR machinery kicking into high gear to make the most of Jake's service, sacrifice and heroism and, of course, the US commitment to the global war on terror.

Another sip of the golden-brown nectar did little to help Margot swallow the grief and sparked a flood of images. Her first encounter with Jake was still vivid. Boarding the C-130 bound for Syria. Members of SEAL Team 10 laughing and sparring. And Preacher, the junior analyst she'd recruited. She pictured Kate. Brilliant. Resourceful. Naïve. And now a widow.

Margot consoled herself that no one could have predicted how the Syrian mission would unravel. She thought of the men who died, and the blood that united Jake and Kate. Margot thought too of the secret that propelled her career and of the pact she made with the devil. Without Mikhail Zhukov's intel, she wouldn't be Deputy Director. She liked to believe she'd done some important work, but she couldn't escape the guilt.

She polished off the whiskey and considered pouring another. *No,* she thought. *Kate may still need my help. If nothing else, to keep her out of jail.*

CHAPTER 26

UNDISCLOSED LOCATION

KEISHA WALKED TOWARD THE wall of monitors that floated above Nomad's workstation. Concerned that he hadn't eaten or rested, she was determined to interrupt his work and it wouldn't be the first time she faced his wrath.

"Good lord," Keisha said, when she realized what consumed Nomad's attention. "This morning I walk in to find you staring at your friend with a rope around his neck, and now you're glued to the news of that horrible tragedy."

"The entire world is watching."

"They may be, but you don't have to. Turn away. Don't fill your mind with such darkness."

"This darkness is my world."

"Your world?" Keisha asked. "Please tell me you had nothing to do with this."

"I had nothing to do with this."

"You could at least *try* to convince me."

"I'm sorry," he said. "I didn't see this coming, and there was nothing I could have done to prevent this one."

"You've prevented others?"

"Occasionally," he said. "I'm in a unique position. I hear things. See things. Some of what I know has been useful in the past, but this event was completely dark."

"That's unusual?"

"Yes, and devastating," he said, and paused the video.

Keisha looked at the face of *Le American* at the moment he's shot in the back.

"I don't know how you can bear to watch it," she said. "This video is everywhere."

"He's a hero, and everyone loves a hero, especially dead ones."

"Jesus Christ. Do you know how petty and bitter you sound?"

"I just wish it wasn't him, anyone but Jake."

"Jake? You know who this is?"

"That's Jake Church," he said. "Remember Katherine Preacher, the girl in the chess team photo?"

"Sure. The girl you had a crush on."

"I never said I had a crush on her."

"You didn't have to."

"It doesn't matter," Nomad said. "Jake's her husband."

"Oh, poor thing. She must be devastated."

"And she's probably already in Paris."

"What am I missing," Keisha asked. "You sound depressed."

"I'm running out of time," Nomad said. "I was thinking about reaching out to Kate."

"You lost one friend, isn't that enough?"

"I know. It's insane, but now it's out of the question. Even I can't ask a grieving widow for help."

"I'd like to think it was out of the question even before she lost her husband," Keisha said and glared at him. "You said the last time you two worked together you nearly got her killed. Let's not finish the job."

"You're right. I just need to think."

"And pray," Keisha added.

"That's your department, but I'll take all the help I can get."

"Then take my advice," she said, and with a hand on his chair's joystick, she took control. "Turn away from all of this and go get some sleep."

"When I close my eyes, all I see is Francois," he said, and turned the chair back toward the monitors. "I need to focus."

Keisha let out an audible sigh, knowing Nomad would just ignore her, but he recoiled when she reached across his chest and pointed at another monitor.

"Wait a minute," she said.

"What?"

"That one. That one there. Can you back it up? I think I saw something, someone," she said, and the video started again. "There! Is that..."

"Zhukov," Nomad said, turning his chair toward the monitor and uttering a few control commands to his system.

"The street camera must have picked this up minutes after Zhukov left Francois's apartment," Nomad said. "I didn't realize the Cafe was so close."

"So this guy walks away from a murder scene and goes to lunch?" Keisha asked. "That's one cold-hearted bastard."

They watch Zhukov approach the table. He's expected. The others smile, and the greetings are warm, friendly.

"Who's that guy?" Keisha asks, and Nomad paused the video where Zhukov is whispering in a man's ear.

"That would be Vitali Moshenski," Nomad said. "Zhukov's current employer and one of the richest men on the planet."

"No," Keisha said. "He may be paying the bills, but they look more like brothers."

"And they're leaving," Nomad said. "That's how I missed this. They leave just before the attack."

"Coincidence?"

"Not a chance. More likely, Francois's murder tripped alarms. Zhukov's lived this long by staying one step ahead of his enemies," Nomad said. "But he might have made a mistake. He's got Francois's laptop."

"I know. We watched him take it, and that scared the crap out of you."

"Not scared. Just concerned."

"I know scared when I see it."

"Forget that," Nomad said. "What's important is that the laptop might be the key. Zhukov will use it to try to find me, and there's a chance I can turn the tables."

"Only a chance? That's doesn't sound like you."

"This is different. Zhukov will have access to the best Russian hackers on the planet, and my life is on the line," Nomad said. "But somehow Zhukov knew about the Frenchman's work, our work. He was there for a reason. How did Zhukov learn about Francois? The answer to that question might be the key to getting back in."

"Back in?"

"There's only so much I can do from the outside," Nomad said. "To finish what I started, I need to get back inside Moore's network, and Zhukov could get me in the door."

"If he doesn't find you first."

Chapter 27

9TH ARRONDISSEMENT, PARIS, FRANCE

THE MOCK CATERING VAN navigated the roads behind the Hotel Crillon. No one noticed. No one followed, but Kate remained on the floor for several minutes. Marcus knelt alongside with one hand on her back, and the other steadying himself when the vehicle rocked.

"OK, we're clear," Marcus said, and offered Kate a hand.

Kate was happy to get off the floor, but the van's bench seat was only marginally better. She felt every bump, swayed with every turn, and she could hear a train nearby.

"Where are we?" Kate asked.

"We need to swap vehicles," Marcus replied. "Can't show up at the morgue in a catering van."

Marcus reached into his back pocket and pulled out a phone. "I meant to give this to you back at the hotel."

"Is that Jake's phone?"

"Yeah. Screen's cracked, and the battery's dead."

"But how did you —" Kate began, but then realized. "The man on the street, the businessman. He heard me calling out and picked up Jake's phone."

"Trust me. It's a moment I'll never forget. My best friend's dying in my arms, and some guy tells me my wife is on the phone. Then I realized it was Jake's phone, and you —"

Marcus couldn't finish the sentence. Kate slid in next to him on the bench and wrapped an arm around his back.

"It's OK," she said, and pulled him in tight. "I spent most of the night looking at video. You tried to save him."

"I've thought about it a hundred times. Could I have done —"

"Stop," Kate said. "You couldn't save him. No one could."

Kate stopped short of telling Marcus about hacking into the CIA's ballistic analysis site, or the sniper round she heard on the recording. *Jake's message was clear,* she thought. *Trust no one.* She trusted Marcus with her life, and knew Jake did too, but she also knew that intelligence analysis was a game of bits and pieces, like a puzzle scattered on the floor. She might be the only person on the planet that knew there was a sniper running overwatch during the attack. That was a vital piece of the puzzle, and she couldn't risk anything leaking before she knew more, before she got her hands on whatever Jake was hiding.

"Bravo, this Alpha," Forest said

"Go ahead, Alpha," Marcus replied.

"Checkpoint Diamond. Ten mikes from infil."

Marcus checked his watch and looked at Kate. "We're cutting it close."

"Alpha, maintain speed," Marcus said, and looking out the windshield, he added, "Scout at Bus Stop."

The driver pointed the van toward an aluminum roll-up door, which began rising when they approached and closed the moment they entered the warehouse.

Marcus exited the rear of the van. Kate grabbed her messenger bag and followed. They parked alongside an ambulance and Marcus popped the rear doors.

"So, this is the plan?" Kate asked. "We drive into the morgue in an ambulance?"

"Not quite," Marcus said. He reached inside and pulled out a pair of black body bags. "We're going in these."

"You've got to be kidding me," Kate asked. "Can you even breath in those things?"

Before Marcus could answer, the ambulance driver approached.

"Madame, I assure you that you are safe in my hands," he said. "My name is Jean-Paul. Jean-Paul Marsat, and I would drive you safely through the gates of hell and back if you so desired."

"Let's hope it doesn't come to that," Kate said. "But I'm a little confused, and frankly concerned. When our little ruse is discovered, and it will be, you'll be out of a job."

"That is of no concern," Jean-Paul said. "Over the last eighteen hours, I've made five trips to the L'institut médico-légal. I carried many directly from the cafe and a few that died at the hospital."

"I'm sure that was very difficult."

"Indeed. Very hard, but I am also most grateful my wife was not among them."

Marcus interrupted, "Jean-Paul's wife worked at the cafe."

"Qui, Madame. Janine, mon amour, was inside the cafe when the shooting began. She faced the door, saw a gunman approach, and made the sign of the cross," Jean-Paul said, and he did the same as he spoke. "Janine knew she would never see our children again, but the man didn't shoot."

"That's on Jake," Marcus said. "The crazy bastard drew that asshole away from the cafe and back into the street. God only knows how many more would be lying in the morgue."

"So," Jean-Paul said. "My job means nothing. Your husband was the answer to my wife's prayer."

Marcus pulled his sleeve back and checked the time. "Clock's ticking," he said and turned to Kate. "It's your call. We can still use the front door."

Kate pictured the building's entrance filled with grieving families, and the curious mob that flocked to tragedy, cell phones held high, capturing every moment of anguish. And there was the attack at the hotel to consider. *An entrance is always a choke point,* she thought. *Jake would call it a fatal funnel.*

"No, let's do this your way," Kate said.

Jean-Paul stepped forward, kissed Kate's cheeks, saying, "Merci. Merci. Merci," and the three of them climbed into the back of the ambulance.

Marcus crawled into his body bag. Jean-Paul zipped the bag shut and strapped it to the gurney. Kate laid back inside her bag, trying to push down the claustrophobia that was building, and she pulled the plastic across her face. *Just breathe,* she reminded herself. *Combat breathing. In-2-3-4, hold-2-3-4, out-2-3-4.* Concentrating on her breath was helping, until her zipper closed, and she felt Jean-Paul locking her down to the gurney.

With arms crossed over her chest, she reminded herself that she could cut her way out if it came to that. She slid her right hand in through the neckline of her shirt, and her fingers wrapped around the small, carbon-fiber knife and sheath clipped to her bra.

The knife was Jake's design, a birthday gift. She smiled and recalled the celebration. *Not exactly the most romantic gift,* she thought, but then she realized. *What's more romantic than saying do whatever it takes to come home to me?* The synthetic material was light-weight, and brutally sharp. Warm to the touch and absorbed body heat. And that was one reason the knife was virtually invisible to sensors and scanners. The size, shape and location also made pat-down detection a challenge for all but the most aggressive groping. Kate never left home without it.

Oh no, she thought. *The anniversary gift.* She pictured Jake on the video chat, gloating and tapping his coat pocket. *I hope they found it.* She thought too about the gift she had for him. The wrapped box sitting in her dresser drawer. It was a gamble. For a guy glued to his Garmin Tactix watch, she didn't know if he'd ever wear the dress watch she bought. But the Reverso was special and so was the custom art and engraving. Realizing now he would never wear it brought fresh tears. And as the minutes passed, she realized no one said how long the ride would take.

The ambulance started rolling and Kate felt the vehicle retrace the van's path across the warehouse ramp entrance and down the bumpy industrial roads, but then the road turned smooth. There were frequent stops and starts. *Traffic lights,* Kate imagined. After one stop, there was a brief conversation, too muffled to understand, and the rear doors opened. *This is it,* Kate thought, but the doors closed, and the ambulance drove on. *A checkpoint,* Kate thought. *That makes sense, and Jean-Paul knew exactly what to do, what to say.*

When the vehicle stopped again, Kate knew they had arrived. She heard Jean-Paul's voice. He unlocked and slid her gurney out of the ambulance. She felt the gurney's wheels pop free of the undercarriage and roll on the floor. The journey from the ambulance and into the building was brief, and so was the elevator ride to the lower level. Even in the bag, Kate could feel the change in temperature. *We're in the morgue, or very close,* Kate thought, and she lay waiting, listening. The silence was unnerving. *Maybe I should cut the bag. No. Stick with the plan.*

The zipper moved, Kate reached for the knife, but let go when Jean-Paul whispered.

"Madame," he said. "We have arrived, but please be very quiet." He helped Kate slip out of the bag, and then turned to Marcus. Jean-Paul gave the same warning, and then released Marcus from the heavy-duty vinyl coffin.

Marcus stood, shook out his arms, and whispered, "I will never, ever crawl inside another body bag. No sir," he said. "Not while I'm still breathing."

"But it worked," Kate said, and turned to Jean-Paul. "Now where?"

"This way."

Kate and Marcus followed Jean-Paul through a pair of automatic double doors and into the adjoining room. The stainless steel cadaver racks ran from floor to ceiling and wall to wall. Nearly full, the racks were a stark reminder of the magnitude of the attack and the staggering number of victims.

The scene took Kate's breath, her vision blurred, and Marcus grabbed her shoulders.

"You got this," he said, and she turned away from the racks.

"You're late," Kate heard someone say in French from the back of the room. A medical technician, wire-rimmed glasses, pristine white coat, drove a hydraulic cadaver lift toward her.

Kate stepped aside, and the lift glided past. The specialized morgue equipment was the medical equivalent of a forklift, and purpose-built to lift, place, and remove the cadaver trays.

Jean-Paul introduced Martin, but he ignored Kate and positioned the lift. Even as a fluent French speaker, Kate couldn't quite catch the exchange between the two men, but the tone was clear enough. Jean-Paul might not be worried about his job, but Martin wasn't happy about risking his.

Kate was thankful for the assistance. It was a gift she did not take lightly, and she understood her access, especially at a time when so many were suffering, was both unprecedented and risky for all involved. In French, she tried to assure Martin of her gratitude, but he remained focused on the task.

"Your husband is here," Martin said in English and the lift's forks reached beneath the tray. "We must hurry. Soon they will call to move the first group into the viewing rooms."

Martin might not have volunteered, but his expertise with the lift was unmistakable. He retrieved Jake's body tray with fluid grace and gentle care. *This is no warehouse jockey*, Kate thought. *He genuinely cares for those in his charge.*

Jake's tray floated onto the technician's prep table. Martin stepped away from the lift and approached the head of the table. Kate and Marcus followed. Jean-Paul stepped back and lowered his head. The only sound was the zipper as Martin opened the bag to reveal Jake's face, and then he, too, withdrew.

Kate froze. *Jake's gone*, she thought, grappling with the reality of seeing her husband's body. *But, I still feel him.*

No one spoke or moved until Marcus put his hands on Kate's shoulders.

"We'll leave you two alone," he said, and turned to the others. "Gentleman, if you'll come with me."

"How long do I have?" Kate asked.

"Not long," Martin said.

"Bravo One. Come in," said Forest.

"Go ahead Alpha."

"We're passing through the gates now."

"Copy that," Marcus said, and added Kate and Jake's code name status.

"Scout is with Atticus."

The double doors whooshed open, and the men left the room.

The ruse will be over soon, Kate thought. *I won't get this close again until I get him home.*

The name Atticus lingered in Kate's mind, and she stepped forward and studied Jake's face. *Pale. Serene. A warrior's peace at last*, she thought. *No more battles. No more nightmares.*

CHAPTER 28

CIA HEADQUARTERS, LANGLEY, VA

Margot Ryder, Deputy Director CIA National Clandestine Services, pushed through the security doors of the Special Activities Center, large black coffee in hand and surveyed the chaotic, late-night, scene. The buzz in the room was palpable and analysts grappled with the latest data feeds from the scene.

"Do we have footage?" she asked the room.

Ben was the first to speak up. "Yes, we're spinning it up now."

"Alright, let's have it," she said, and took another long, slow, sip of her coffee. It wasn't the first time she'd arrived in the middle of the night. *They call it the situation room for a reason*, she thought. The room's main screen lit up. "What am I looking at?"

"This is security camera video from the hotel's front entrance," Ben said. "The police barricades are holding the crowd back. Most of the crowd's signs appear supportive. The two-man security team exits first through the main doors. Preacher is close behind. She's sandwiched between the two men and they proceed toward the vehicles."

The room watches the scene unfold when a protester jumps the barricade, and is immediately subdued by a member of the security team.

"Decoy?" Margot asked.

"Almost certainly. He's in police custody." Ben said. "French citizen. So far, no intel on links to terror groups. Best guess is a paid protester. It's a lucrative business in Paris."

"It's lucrative everywhere," Margot said, and spots the young man with the bouquet. Decades of instinct prompt her to ask, "The flowers?"

"Yes," Ben replied, and they watched the teenager squeeze through the barricade near the vehicles.

What happened next was so fast that Ben had to stop, rewind, and advance frame by frame. The flowers fall, and the kid grabs Preacher's arm. A flash of light bounces off the eight-inch blade, thrusting toward Kate's throat. She deflects the knife and traps his arm and hand. Her pivot bends his elbow sending the blade slicing across his throat.

"Whoa," Ben said, and froze the frame. "That's bad ass."

"That's not Kate," Margot announced. She tried to hide the sense of relief and rephrase her statement.

"Katherine Preacher could pull off that move, but that's Talya Aviram, former Mossad, and a member of Trident Security."

There was a moment of silence mixed with curiosity and awe at the image on the screen, and then Ben spoke up.

"How would you like us to proceed?"

"What's the chatter?"

Another analyst chimed in. "It was all idle speculation immediately after the Cafe attack. No one's taken credit. Yet. But Imam Abu Walifa is rallying his followers. He's denounced the cafe attack as a CIA False Flag operation designed to stir Muslim hatred. He claims Jake was a part of the operation, and issued a Fatwa to avenge the fallen."

"And what are we hearing now?"

"Most are relieved that the American hero's wife was unharmed," the analyst replied. "But there's growing speculation that Katherine Preacher was CIA. And the boy bleeding out on the carpet was Muslim. That confirmation sparked a growing thread calling for the American widow's death."

"It could take Preacher days to claim her husband's body and in the meantime, this will escalate. The longer she stays in Paris, the more organized and sophisticated the effort to kill her or Americans in general," Margot said. "Let's get State to issue a warning. We need to put a lid on this thing. And, find me a way to get Preacher and her husband's body out of Paris."

Margot turned to leave the operation center, but Ben caught her at the door.

"There may be a way, but it will mean calling in some favors."

"I'm listening."

"Last night, Special Operations Group had an Al Shabab operation go sideways in Somalia. Two wounded, two KIA," Ben said.

"They're in the air right now, transporting the wounded to Germany. Then they'll escort their dead to Dover."

"Jake was Naval Special Warfare, DEVGRU," Margot said. "One of their own. If there's any way they can pick him up, they'll try. Let me see if I can twist a few arms to make it happen."

"It's not the most comfortable way to return."

"But it's the safest, and not the first time Preacher's strapped into a webbed seat."

CHAPTER 29

L'INSTITUT MÉDICO-LÉGAL (IML), PARIS, FRANCE

KATE WAS ALONE NOW, standing alongside Jake's body. She brushed back the hair that draped across his forehead and cradled his cheek in her hand. *How many times have I caressed this face*, she wondered. The answer brought tears. *Not enough.*

Just below Jake's left shoulder, Kate could see the top of his Bone Frog tattoo. Jake added this one following the mission where he lost his leg, and three members of the team lost their lives. She unzipped the body bag envelope down past his arm and peeled the plastic back far enough to expose the tattoo. She'd seen it for years, a reminder of brotherhood and loss, but today it was different. An exit wound shredded the lower half of the tattoo.

Kate reached into the bag and took Jake's hand. His left arm's sleeve tattoo was a story of service told in symbols and ink. Some she understood, some Jake never explained. Written in Arabic was the phrase, *I am the infidel your mother warned you about,* but her favorite, the one she often touched when they held hands, the one she outlined now with her finger, was the playing card etched just above his wrist. After Syria, Jake thought he'd lost Kate forever, but somehow he knew she would always be the Ace up his sleeve.

"I saw what you did," she said with the clarity and certainty that Jake could hear every word.

"I was up half the night. OK, all night. Watching videos," she added, and smiled. "For a one-legged old door-kicker, you move pretty fast."

"You did good," she said, resting a hand on his chest. "But don't think for one minute I forgive you. I'm still mad. Just because I'm proud doesn't mean I'm not angry."

"I know. I know. We talked about this," she said, imagining how the conversation might unfold. "We knew the risks, and I knew you wouldn't be happy doing anything else. You're a born guardian, and maybe every challenge, every tragedy, hammered the metal that forged this moment. I don't know. Is it fate? Was this place, this time, your destiny? There are wives in the arms of their husbands, children who still have parents, students who returned from school and lovers with a full life ahead of them because of you, because of *Le American*."

Kate drew in closer. She pressed Jake's hand against her chest.

"You're a hero, my love," she said. "My Atticus, born to do our unpleasant jobs for us. Your work's done, but I'm lost. What am I supposed to do without you by my side?"

Kate leaned in, kissed Jake's lips, then his forehead, as if kissing him goodnight and wishing him sweet dreams. She whispered into his ear. "I know that you're walking with the angels, and when it's my time, you'll come find me."

The sudden whoosh of the automatic doors was startling and Kate stood upright, still holding Jake's hand.

"Madame, who are you? How did you get in here? What are you doing?"

Kate swept away a tear and turned toward her inquisitor. "Would you like me to answer your questions in any particular order?"

The flustered Frenchman didn't quite know how to respond. "What? Yes. No. Wait..."

Kate interrupted in fluent French, which eased some of the man's tension.

"I'm Katherine Preacher. This is my husband, Jake Church. A private security firm believed my life was in danger and arranged for my entry, and I welcomed the opportunity to have a private moment with my husband."

"Impossible," he said. "I was informed, just moments ago, that Monsieur Church's widow had arrived. She is at this moment with Deputy Director Boucher."

"Yes, of course. I understand the confusion. That woman is my double," Kate said. "She's part of a decoy operation, orchestrated by the executive protection team. Perhaps you're aware there has already been one attempt on my, her, life."

"I am," he said. "We were shocked, but grateful she was unharmed."

"Then I'm sure you can appreciate the delicacy of the situation. We certainly meant no disrespect to you or your institution, but lives are at stake."

"Martin," he yelled. "Martin. Get in here."

Martin sidled in through the doors, eyes fixed on the floor. "Qui, Monsieur?"

"Is this your doing? No! Don't answer that. The less I know, the better. Just prepare the deceased for viewing," he said, and then he spotted Marcus. "Good Lord. Another unauthorized, unlicensed, interloper. This is too much. Too much."

Kate attempted to ease the man's concerns and introduce Marcus, but the man simply raised his hand and she stopped.

"Martin, do as I've asked," he said, and waving a finger at Kate and Marcus, added, "You two. Follow me. We'll let Security Services deal with you."

Chapter 30

UKRAINIAN EMBASSY, PARIS, FRANCE

Vitali Moshenski sat at his grandson's bedside and held his hand. They had given Stephan a mild sedative to help him sleep through the night, and Moshenski waited for him to wake. He was thankful the boy was alive and had seen enough video to know that was a miracle. Stephan's wounds weren't life-threatening, and those would heal, but the murder of his fiancée was a scar the boy would carry for the rest of his life. *Whatever their plans for the future,* Moshenski thought. *They are gone, and in that void, life might not seem worth living.* Moshenski knew the darkness that waited for the boy to wake.

The medical wing of the embassy was quiet except for a handful of staff that had gathered around the break room TV. Moshenski had no interest in the media coverage or the unending, plodding analysis of the events, but when the area erupted with gasps and profanities, Moshenski feared the worst. *Another attack,* he wondered. *A suicide bomber? Secondary attacks were all too common, but acting the following day was unusual. Unexpected. Perhaps that was the plan.*

When a nurse ran by his room, Moshenski called out to her, "What's happened? Another attack?"

"Someone just tried to kill the wife of Le American."

"Is she alright?"

"Qui," she said, and the nurse's eyes widened, eyebrows rose, and her voice cracked.

"Incroyable."

"Incredible. What?"

"She... she killed him."

Moshenski realized the outburst he heard was a moment of terror followed by amazement and relief. He reached for his phone. *It is not over*, he thought.

He turned on the TV in Stephan's room. The news crews covering the woman's exit from the Hotel de Crillon sent feeds to their networks. The morning shows broke from their normal programming, and warnings proceeded the graphic video. Moshenski knew such warnings only heightened viewer interest.

Without Le American, he thought. *Stephan would be dead. I am in his debt, and his wife won't be safe as long as she remains in Paris.* He was considering who to call, what forces to marshal to ensure her safety, when the broadcast cut to the video of the attack, and flashed the names Jake Church and Katherine Preacher across the bottom of the screen. He knew only that his grandson's savior was American, but the names changed everything.

Moshenski stood and approached the TV. He stared as the recording played. The woman's face remained in shadow when she stepped out of the hotel's double doors. Her security team were pros. They stayed in tight enough to block a potential sniper, and the woman's face lay hidden under a black, broad-brimmed, designer hat and large dark glasses. It was only at the moment of the attack that he was sure. *I have no idea who she is,* he thought. *But that is not Katherine Preacher.*

The first call he made went straight to voice mail. *Mikhail must still be in the air,* Moshenski thought.

"Call me the minute you get this," he said. "I have only just learned *Le American* is Jake Church, and Preacher is here, in Paris. She is safe. For now. I will do what I can. You, my friend, must remain focused on the task at hand. Much depends on your efforts to find Nomad while there's still time."

Moshenski's next call was to the private cell of the man he helped elect and as the dominoes tumbled, phones rang throughout the Palais Bourbon and the National Assembly.

CHAPTER 31

L'INSTITUT MÉDICO-LÉGAL (IML), PARIS, FRANCE

KATE AND MARCUS ENTERED the elevator. From the ID pinned to his starched white lab coat, Kate knew their escort was Doctor Marlier. His stiff back and hands stuffed deep into the coat's pockets told her that conversation was unnecessary and unwanted.

The IML's main floor housed the administrative offices, examination rooms and facilities for the forensic anthropology and pathology teams. Kate noted that it was a deceptively small building, given its importance. They passed Dr. Marlier's office and stopped in front of the door at the end of the hall. Kate noted the sign on the door.

DIRECTOR

DR. HENRI DUBOIS

INSTITUT MÉDICO-LÉGAL

Dr. Marlier knocked on the Director's door. When there was no immediate answer, he knocked again, louder and faster.

Dr. Dubois cracked the door, peered out and whispered, "Dr Marlier, what is it?"

Raised voices in the background told Kate her priority now was damage control.

"Dr. Dubois, pardon the interruption, but this is most urgent," Marlier said. Pushing past the Director, he ushered Kate and Marcus into the office, and addressed his comments to the man standing behind the desk. "This woman claims she's Katherine Preacher."

"I am Katherine Preacher," Kate said, and glanced at Talya and the other members of Jake's team. "I'd like to apologize—" Kate began, but was cut off.

"Madame! I am Deputy Director Boucher of the Direction Générale de la Sécurité Intérieure. You have no comprehension of the damage you have done to this institution and my investigation," he said. "At your security detail's request, our Protection Division provided armored vehicles, physical barriers, traffic control and motorcycle escorts, but it was all a ploy. Theater. And if I learn your team used my officers to lure potential threats, the consequences will be severe."

Kate glanced at Marcus, who shook his head. That was all the assurance she needed.

"Deputy Director, with all due respect, this is a highly experienced team of executive protection operators with a stellar international reputation. They put their lives on the line to ensure my safe arrival and they succeeded," Kate said, and pointing at Talya. "She could have been killed, so let me assure you, no one on this team revealed my location."

"Perhaps not, but the fact remains. I have a protester in custody, another body on the way in for identification, and the media hounding me for answers. Greeting your surrogate made me look the fool."

"You know what they say..." Marcus said.

Kate interrupted and glared at Marcus. "Please, just go stand with the others."

The Director of the IML had been hovering in the corner of his office and stepped forward. He took Doctor Marlier's elbow and directed him toward the door. Kate saw the look of disappointment on Marlier's face. No doubt he was hoping to stay and watch the show, she thought.

"Deputy Director, as my office isn't suited to a gathering of this size, Doctor Marlier and I will leave you to proceed unencumbered. With so many victims, we're needed elsewhere."

"Yes. Yes. Go," Boucher said with a wave of his hand.

"Before I leave," the Dr. Dubois said, turning to Kate. "I know from experience there is nothing I can say to ease your pain, but please accept my deepest sympathies." He kissed both of her cheeks, and added, "And my eternal gratitude for your husband's unwavering courage."

Kate fought to maintain her composure, but her throat tightened and she looked at the Director and just uttered, "Merci."

Dr. Dubois nodded toward Boucher and whispered in Kate's ear, "His bark is worse than his bite," and closed the door behind them.

Kate seized the opportunity to continue the conversation in French, and avoid Marcus, or any of the team, saying something that might complicate an already difficult situation.

"Deputy Director Boucher," Kate said. "Let me begin by offering my sincere thanks for the police escort, and my apologies for the deception employed to assure my safety."

Kate's gentle tone and French fluency caught Boucher off guard, precisely as she had hoped. While the rest of the team watched, Kate approached Boucher. With the exception of an occasional name or a glance in their direction, Kate knew the conversation would fly over their heads.

"Might I suggest you satisfy the media's attention by taking responsibility for the use of a decoy, and your reception as the vehicles arrived was an essential part of selling the plan?"

"You think me so vain that I would take credit?"

"Not vain. Practical," Kate said. "Neither of us benefits from the appearance of friction between the French Security Services and the widow of the man the press has hailed as a hero. No doubt your superiors, even the Director of the

DGSI, are facing media pressure. Taking credit for the plan to ensure my safety serves everyone's interests. I believe we share a common problem and goal."

Kate could see that Boucher was uncomfortable, but he agreed. His reticence was a surprise. She imagined that someone in his position was a skilled political player, but she realized he was a professional investigator who had earned this role and knew it was deadly serious.

With the immediate problem resolved, and assurances that the security team would face no repercussions or prosecution, Kate turned her attention to the matter of her husband's remains.

"As I have already seen my husband, I'm sure you'd agree there's no need for a formal viewing," she said. "I would like to proceed with the paperwork to have Jake and his belongings released, and I understand an avocats-conseils from Roche Fortier is here to assist."

"Yes, your avocat is here," Boucher said. "He is waiting to speak with you, but I have already informed him we can't release your husband or the items in his possession until my investigation resolves some troubling questions."

"What questions?"

"For example, why was your husband at the cafe..." he began, but Kate interrupted.

"You can't be serious. Will you be questioning the families of every victim at or near the Cafe?"

"Please, allow me to finish," Boucher said, and from behind the desk he produced a couple of large, plastic evidence bags. The words Le American appeared across the top of each bag and just below was the name Jake Church.

"We recovered several items at the scene that we believe are your husband's, and that raise questions we need answered. Do you recognize this bag?" he asked.

Kate could see the bag held a Maxpedition brand black shoulder bag.

"Jake has one like it, but that doesn't make it his," she said. "It's a very popular brand."

"Surveillance video has your husband carrying this bag..."

"Or one like it," Kate said.

"Very well," Boucher said. "The video shows your husband carrying a similar bag and placing it on the chair to his left. Do you recognize these items?"

Kate scooped up the small evidence bag and flipped it over and back a few times to be sure.

"As you already know, they removed these from Jake's body. That's his watch, wallet and silicone wedding band," she said, and she fondled the remaining items. "This is the silver cross and chain his mother gave him on her deathbed, and his NanoVault."

Boucher retrieved three more small bags and laid them out on the desk. "And these three items?"

"I'm unfamiliar with the rest of these things."

"Come now, Ms. Preacher. There's no need to be coy," he said. "Your State Department was kind enough to provide comprehensive dossiers on your husband and yourself. As an Intelligence Officer myself, I suspect your position with the State Department was a cover, but no matter, your established area of expertise is digital forensics. Surely, you are familiar with this equipment."

"Monsieur Boucher," she replied, echoing his formality. "Perhaps unfamiliar was a poor choice of words. Would you mind if I had a closer look?" And without waiting for an answer, Kate leaned over Boucher's desk and sorted the evidence bags. The bag with Jake's personal items, she swept to one side. Boucher's eyes followed Kate's hands, examining the individually bagged electronics.

"This is an Israeli Phantom cell phone jammer," she said, and continued. "This one may be a Femtocell or perhaps Macrocel. I couldn't be sure without my equipment but these emulate cell towers, and that's a cell phone SIM cloner."

"I appreciate your honesty," he said. "As you're no doubt aware, all three of these devices are illegal, and in combination, it's my understanding they pose a significant security threat."

"They can momentarily disrupt cell phone service and capture cell phone traffic, but that's hardly a significant threat."

"Given the proximity of the shoulder bag to your husband's known location, I think it is likely we will match this equipment to your husband," Boucher said. "And with your husband's SEAL training and intelligence expertise, I must return to my original inquiry. What was your husband's true purpose at the cafe? What was his role in the attack?"

Kate's first thought was to punch Boucher in the throat, and drop him where he stood, but she opted to slap his face.

Boucher's glasses launched into the air, snot flew from his nose, his head wrenched left, and his shoulders twisted away. Kate slid a hand into the evidence bag she had staged on the edge of the desk. She palmed Jake's NanoVault, deposited the blank one, and reset the bag's zip-lock seal.

A knock on the door sent Boucher scrambling for his glasses and his composure.

"I asked not to be disturbed," he said, but the intruder knocked again, louder than before.

"What is it?" he asked.

A young woman opened the door, and peered in, and said, "Monsieur Boucher," she said. "You have a phone call on line two."

"Whoever the hell it is, take a message."

"But Monsieur," she said, and glanced at the others. Hesitant to speak, but unable to leave.

"What?"

"It's the Ministre des Armées."

Boucher turned to the phone and punched line two.

"Bonjour, Boucher à l'appareil, sous-directeur de la division antiterroriste de la DGSI."

Boucher's tone and formality were a surprise. Kate expected a more submissive tone with the Minister of Defense, given she reports directly to the Prime Minister. *He's confident,* she thought. *He must believe he has the full support of his superiors, and a free hand in this investigation.*

He turned his back on Kate and the others, and Boucher's side of the conversation was sporadic and muffled. Kate heard a few mumbled words of

al1hRelentless 143
4.xggm

protest, but Boucher was cut off at every turn, and never managed a complete sentence.

Boucher's distraction was an opportunity Kate could not resist. She fished a tiny USB dongle from a pocket in her messenger bag and pressed into the back of Boucher's laptop. *One-thousand-one, One-thousand-two, One-thousand-three*, she thought, and yanked the device. Three seconds was all Kate needed to plant the malware seed. If it worked, she'd be able to monitor his investigation and gain access to security footage and evidence far outside her reach.

Boucher hung up the phone. His face flush. White specs of saliva were visible in the corners of his mouth. There was complete silence while he surveyed Kate and the others.

"You four," he said, pointing at Marcus and the rest of the team. "You are free to go."

Boucher was visibly struggling to continue and convey the rest of the message.

"The French government thanks you for your assistance executing the DGSI's plan to ensure Ms. Preacher's safe arrival at the IML."

"I, we," Marcus said. "Appreciate your thanks, but the mission's not over. Kate is still in danger."

"On that we agree, Monsieur, but Ms. Preacher's safety is now out of your hands, and mine."

"Then who's in charge?" Marcus asked. "What's the plan?"

"Our Ministère des Armées is working with your government."

Marcus raised his eyebrows and glanced at Kate.

"Think Department of Defense," she said to help Marcus keep up. "And what about my husband?"

"As we speak, an American C-130 Hercules is approaching Villacoublay. They diverted a flight from Germany to accommodate both you and your husband's remains."

Kate and Marcus exchanged looks. He shrugged his shoulders and shook his head. Neither had heard of anything like this before, and Boucher punctuated their confusion.

"All I know is that you have powerful allies, or a guardian angel."

"Perhaps both," Kate said. "How do I get there?"

"This facility links to the Pitié-Salpêtrière Hospital through a tunnel. A military escort will be here shortly, and a medevac helicopter is waiting at the hospital to take you directly to the airport."

"And the others?"

"Kate, don't worry about us," Marcus said. "We're good, and I need to tie up some loose ends in Paris before I can return. Just take Jake home."

"And my husband's things?"

"Everything from the hotel will be on board the helicopter."

"No, I mean these things," Kate said, pointing at the items on the desk.

"I will keep the crime scene evidence until my investigation is complete."

Kate knew Boucher was clinging to the one area where he remained in total control, and she needed to tread lightly.

"I understand, and in your position, I would do exactly the same," she said. "But my husband's cross was a gift from his late mother. He never took it off. I can't imagine that it has any investigative value, and it would mean the world to me if he was wearing it when —"

Kate couldn't finish the sentence, and the question must have served as a reminder to everyone in the room that whatever Boucher suspected, whatever the aim of his investigation, Kate was a widow who just wanted to bury her husband.

Boucher didn't say a word. He retrieved the silver chain and cross from the evidence bag. Kate extended a hand, and he lowered the cross into her palm and closed her fingers around it. The tenderness caught Kate by surprise. *I just slapped the man*, Kate thought. *But this gesture. So soft, and kind.* And then she understood, and she knew why this job was so important. *He lost someone. Not here. Not now. But he knows my pain because it's his too.*

The knock at the door was a welcome interruption. Two men entered the room, dressed in black from helmets to boots. The body armor, tactical vests and automatic weapons brought everyone back into the moment, and the mission at hand, escorting Kate safely to the helicopter and ultimately out of France.

"I just need a minute," Kate said to the new arrivals. She slipped Jake's chain over her head, tucked the cross into her shirt, then turned to the team.

She hugged Talya. "I don't know how to thank you," Kate said. "I might not be here, if it weren't for you."

"You would have taken him down," Talya said, and smiled. "But thanks for letting me cover for you."

Kate held on to Talya and lowered her voice.

"Before I go," Kate said. "Do you still have contacts in Mossad? People you trust?"

"Yes, of course," Talya said. "If there's something you need, just let me know."

"I will. Thanks."

Kate let go of Talya and turned to Forest and Deon.

"Jake loved you guys," she said and wrapped an arm around each in a group hug. "He would be so proud."

Neither of them could speak, and Kate saw they were trying hard not to cry.

"When you see the rest of the team, please thank them for me. I know you won't pass along a hug, so just raise a glass. I'm safe and Jake's going home. Mission accomplished."

"Not yet," Forest said. "We know you can't... won't rest until that analyst brain of yours has answers."

"I'm that predictable?"

"Yep, and we've got your back. Anytime. Anywhere. Whatever you need."

Kate smiled and hugged them again. "I know where to find you."

Marcus stepped forward and took Kate's elbow before she could say anything to him.

"Not yet, Kate," he said. "I'm coming with you. It's not goodbye until I see you board the medevac."

"Then do me a favor."

"Anything."

"Call me Preacher," she said. "I've known you too long to change now."

The pair of soldiers led the way out of the medical director's office and down the hall. Kate and Marcus followed, but Marcus held Kate back just far enough to talk without being overheard.

"Alright, Preacher," Marcus said. "I saw what you did."

"What?" Kate asked.

"That little sleight of hand with the NanoVault," he said. "What's on it?"

"Honestly, no idea," she said, and retrieved the device from the front pocket of her slacks. "Until last night, I didn't even know Jake owned one of these things."

"Last night?"

"It's a long story, but Boucher was right about one thing. There are questions that need answers. Someone planned the attack. Someone paid for it, and what was Jake doing with that equipment?" she asked. "I need to know why my husband is dead."

Kate fished around in the messenger bag. Among the many digital forensic tools she kept within reach, a Faraday bag was essential. "Can't be too careful," she said, and sealed the device so nothing could get in or out. "This thing might have answers, or at least clues."

"And what about Boucher's laptop? What was that about?"

"That was instinct. Impulse," Kate said. "I don't know that I'll even try to access his laptop, but now I can try."

"What do you hope to find?"

"I don't know," she said. "But whatever Boucher knows, I'll know, and that's a start."

"Kate, I mean Preacher, you just lost your husband, the love of your life. Don't you think it would be best to let yourself grieve?" Marcus asked. "Let Boucher handle the investigation. He may be an asshole, but he strikes me as competent, and you know the FBI and the CIA will be with him every step of the way."

"And while I'm grieving, the trail goes cold."

"What trail?"

"Exactly. Whatever trail there is will disappear while I'm curled up in a little ball and the three-letter agencies squabble over jurisdiction and compete for headlines."

"I will remind you that you're not an analyst any more, and you left the agency for a reason. Betrayed, captured, tortured. I'd say you left for a damn good reason," Marcus said. "Let someone else handle this. Someone who's not personally involved, or emotionally compromised."

"I'm not compromised. I'm focused."

"What about your job and the people that need you?" Marcus asked. "Jake said you just helped some single mother stay out of jail and got her kid into a special needs program. That sounds like important work."

"Yeah, that was a good day, but those days are rare," Kate said. "Most days, I use my finely honed skills to track down men cheating on their wives or dodging alimony payments. I help politicians hide payoffs to their mistresses. And I convince sexual harassment victims it's better to take a settlement than be confronted with every photo and comment they've ever posted online. I may be good at it, but its crushing my soul. Jake knew I was hiding, and he never said a word. He just hoped I'd find my way, find my purpose, again."

"What are you saying?" Marcus asked. "Are you going back to the agency?"

"No. Maybe. I don't know. The agency offers access and resources, but I can do things on the outside that even the most off-book operators wouldn't touch."

"And get yourself arrested," he said. "Or killed."

Kate and Marcus followed the two soldiers into the elevator and fell quiet. The four of them stepped out at the heliport. The Medevac chopper's blades were spinning up, and they felt the air pushing against them.

"I love you too," she said, and wrapped her arms around Marcus before turning to board the helicopter. She watched him while the Medevac lifted, his clothes billowed in the rotor blast. Marcus shielded his face, but never took his eyes off her, and she blew him a kiss.

CHAPTER 32

VÉLIZY-VILLACOUBLAY AIR BASE, PARIS, FRANCE

AIDED BY THE MEDEVAC helicopter's high speed, maneuverability and pre-flight clearances, Kate's trip from Pitié-Salpêtrière Hospital to Villacoublay Air Base was a matter of minutes. The joint military and civilian airport was the closest to Paris that could handle the C-130, and Kate saw the enormous aircraft parked near several other military planes.

The helicopter touched down near the Hercules. She climbed out the chopper and the Commander of the Joint Special Operations Command (JSOC) marched toward her. She guessed the Commander was about Jake's age, maybe a little older, but he and Jake shared the same hammered steel look. *Jake would say, It's not the years, it's the missions.*

"Mrs. Preacher, I'm Commander Lewis, JSOC," he said, extended a hand and grasped her with both hands. "I was devastated to hear about the Senior Chief. I'm so sorry."

"You knew Jake?"

"I did. We served together in Iraq, and crossed paths a few times at SOCOM," he said. "We lost touch after his injury, but the minute I saw the video, I knew it was him. Church was one bad ass mother... oh sorry."

"It's alright, Commander," she said. "And for the record, I agree."

"The Chief's transport should be here any minute. Would you like to board and settle in?"

"No. Thanks, Commander. I'd like to wait," she said. "I'll board when Jake boards."

"Good call. This bird's configured for team deployment, and is full of gear, that leaves mostly web seating. It's going to be a long flight. Eight, maybe nine hours, depending on the weather."

"Not my first rodeo," she said, but winced when she pictured the long trip home.

"Right. Of course not."

"I just want to thank you for the ride. You have no idea what this means to me."

"It wasn't my call, but it is my honor," he said. "Jake may have retired, but he's still a brother."

"Whose call was it?"

"Great question. All I can tell you is we were in the air, and the next thing I know we have new orders and the French have cleared us to land," he said. "I'll tell you this. It took somebody with serious juice, both in DC and here in France, or maybe multiple players, but whatever levers they pulled, it worked. We'll get the Chief home and keep you safe."

"I'm guessing you heard about the attack?"

"Saw it."

"That wasn't me."

"We know, and that was a smart play," he said. "But there are a few team guys hoping your friend's single."

"I'll let Talya know," Kate said, and smiled. *Feels good to smile*, she thought. "Did any of these guys serve with Jake?"

"No. Most are too young to have known the Senior Chief personally," he said. "But you know how the teams are. Stories spread. Legends are born."

"Legends?" Kate asked.

"Let's just say that gambit in Syria turned a lot of heads, and the more classified the op, the wilder the speculation," he said. "So, everyone thinks they know the Preacher and Church mission."

Kate's attention shifted to the approaching vehicle.

"Here he comes," the Commander said, and they both watched the military ambulance driving up the edge of the airfield's taxiway.

The Commander's SEAL team disembarked. Most of the men lined the ramp into the Hercules, eyes fixed forward, hands at their sides, silent. Four members of the team stood ready and approached the back of the ambulance. The truck's rear doors opened. Each of the men grabbed a corner, and they rolled the coffin out of the ambulance.

The aluminum box glistened in the sun, and beams of light flashed across Kate's face while the men marched toward the aircraft ramp. The SEAL team in front of the ramp snapped to attention and saluted as Jake passed. Kate and the Commander followed up the ramp. The team remained outside.

The transfer team locked Jake's coffin into the cargo hold alongside two others. Commander Lewis and the four members of the dignified transfer team saluted and stepped aside. The rest of the SEAL team members boarded in silence. They entered single file, and one by one, they laid a hand on all three coffins. This gentle touch, a symbol of unity, respect and brotherhood.

Kate looked on at the row of coffins, and when the transfer formalities were complete, she approached Commander Lewis.

"I'm sorry, Commander," she said. "I didn't realize."

"Thank you," he said. "All good men. Bad intel."

"I understand," Kate said.

"I know you do."

Kate settled into the rear cargo area and took the webbed seat closest to Jake's coffin. They invited her to go forward, where this bird had a few rows of passenger seats, but she preferred to leave those seats to the SEAL team and the mission staff. She was happy to sacrifice comfort for solitude and she had work to do.

Her only company in the cargo area was Chief Petty Officer, Donoghue, the Casualty Assistance Officer. Donoghue's mission was to shepherd the two fallen SEALs back home to their families, and he got the call to expand his mission scope to include Jake as well.

"Ma'am," Donoghue began. "I know you'll be more comfortable up front, and you have my word. Your husband will never be alone."

"Thank you, Chief," Kate said. "I appreciate everything you've done for Jake and me, but this isn't my first time in the cheap seats. I'll be fine, and this gives me a chance to collect my thoughts and do a little work. It's been a rough couple of days."

"I'll leave you to it," he said. "But if you would like something to eat or drink, or if you'd like to talk about anything, I'm a good listener."

Kate nodded and smiled, and the chief headed for a seat that would afford Kate some privacy. She watched him pull a small, leather-bound book from a canvas tote, and flip open to a bookmark. *Looks like a Bible,* she thought, and the embossed cross on the cover confirmed it.

The plane's engines whined during takeoff, but settled into a steady rumble when they reached altitude. Kate's seat was cold and hard, little more than a thin layer of foam on a bar stool. The canvas rigging that wrapped around her held the odor of men. *Beer, sweat and cheap aftershave,* Kate thought, and she reached out to touch her man.

That's enough, she thought. *No more tears. Get to work.* And with that command, Kate swung her messenger bag around to her lap, retrieved her laptop, and grabbed the Faraday bag that held Jake's NanoVault.

Kate powered up her laptop, reached into the Faraday bag and grabbed Jake's device. It was wet, sticky.

"Oh no," she said. "No. No. No."

Donoghue rushed over, saw the black fluid on Kate's fingers, and retrieved some paper towels.

"Are you alright?" he asked and handed Kate the towels.

"No. Dear God. Please no," she said and dabbed at the thick, black, gunk leaking from the device.

"What is that?"

"Bad news," she said, and dug into her messenger bag. Kate donned a pair of latex gloves and grabbed a small magnifying glass. She examined every millimeter of the device until she found it.

"There it is," she said. "A hairline crack. The bullet might have nicked it."

"Bullet?" Donoghue asked. "Was that your husband's?"

Kate set the device on the paper towels and looked up. She had been so focused on the device, Donoghue's presence and questions didn't register.

"I'm sorry," Kate said. "What did you say, Chief?"

"It's not important. Can I get you some more towels?"

"Yes, please. I need to get this open as fast as possible, and it might get messy."

Donoghue returned with a full roll of paper towels, some plastic sheeting and a crate Kate could use as a makeshift table.

"I didn't know what you might need, so I just grabbed a few things I thought might help."

"This is great," Kate said, and just stared at the device like it might explode.

"Is that dangerous? Should I alert the Commander?"

"No. Nothing like that," Kate said. "These devices use a chemical power system. They can run for years without recharging."

"Is that what's leaking?"

"Yes. It's relatively harmless to us," she said. "But it can damage, even destroy, everything inside. The chemicals not only power the device, they protect it."

"I don't understand."

"It's a brilliant model. Try to force your way in, or reverse engineer the device, and the contents, even the entire core architecture, just disintegrates."

"Is that what's happening?"

"Honestly. I don't know," she said. "They built these devices to take some serious abuse, and it was just a nick. The altitude and the pressurization may be helping."

"I can see you need to concentrate," Donoghue said. "But I'm here if you need anything."

Before Kate could even attempt to examine the NanoVault's contents, she had to unlock it. *Jake, what's the combination*, she wondered. She stared at the popular device. Eight rings wrapped around the memory core. Each ring has a different set of letters and numbers, and there's only one way in. *Nearly three trillion possible combinations,* she thought. *But you knew I could open it. You set it to something I would know, and others couldn't guess.*

She rotated the dials into sequences of dates, names and places that held meaning. The effort to unlock the NanoVault was both frustrating and painful and it forced Kate to relive pivotal moments in their relationship. Hours disappeared. Donoghue brought Kate some snacks, water, and coffee. She gulped the coffee without saying a word and ignored the rest.

I missed something, she thought. *Jake was confident I could open it.*

Kate leaned over the desk, her head in her hands, eyes closed, and let out a deep, anguished cry. Tears streamed down her face and onto the laptop. All the pain and struggle of the past few days had caught up to her, and she was overwhelmed. *I'll never learn what Jake was doing, and what he wanted me to know,* she thought. *I'll never see that face again, never hear his voice.*

Donoghue came over, sat alongside, and put an arm around Kate's shoulder. She sobbed even harder, but it was comforting to have a shoulder to cry on.

Minutes passed before Kate could pull away, and when she did, she realized she was holding Jake's cross. Kate slipped it on when she and Marcus left the Director's office, but she'd forgotten it until this moment. She looked down at the small silver cross in her fingertips and kissed it. Kate took a deep breath and ran her fingers across the intricate surface. She couldn't escape the sense that this small object was a bridge connecting her and Jake, and it was comforting to hold.

"Would you like me to pray with you?" Donoghue asked.

Kate looked up at the stranger sitting alongside, with consoling eyes and a gentle spirit. She knew he meant well, but he misunderstood.

"No, thank you, Chief," she said, and touched his hand. She looked down at the cross. "This belonged to Jake's mother. She died when he was very young. Cancer. But he wore this every day from the moment she passed, and believed it kept him safe."

"May I see it?" Donoghue asked, and Kate held it out for him to have a closer look. "It's beautiful. Fine craftsmanship. European, I suspect," he said, and glanced at the back for a maker's mark. "That's odd."

"What?" Kate asked, and she examined the back side.

"They made this in the Holy City, just as I thought, but there's something else. Something scratched into the silver."

Donoghue peered closer, squinting. "It's a number. Could be twenty-something. I don't recognize that symbol."

"I do," Kate said, and smiled. She leaned forward and kissed Donoghue's forehead. "Thank you, my friend. You are truly heaven sent."

Kate ran her fingers over the back of Jake's silver cross. *Two, Zero, Dash.* The symbol etched into the back was a message, a reminder. No one but Kate would understand, and that was the point. Jake needed to ensure that no-one else could open his NanoVault, and he knew if they tried to force it open, the information he collected would vanish.

She closed her eyes and was flooded with images of Syria. The blinding sun, and blistering heat. Her right hand pressed against her chest. *Relax*, she thought, and tried to slow her breathing. *It's over. History.* But her linen shirt did little to obscure the raised scar tissue that criss-crossed her chest.

More images flashed. Dark. Painful. The dim light of the interrogation room reflected off the blade of the knife. Damascus steel forged into a mesmerizing mosaic of dark and light swirling patterns, and honed to razor-sharp perfection. The hand that wielded the blade was calloused and weathered. The Syrian's wrist bore the same Al-Shammar tribal symbols that were carved into the ancient knife's curved handle.

Stop, she thought, and opened her eyes. *None of that is important. Focus.* Jake's message was clear, and she just needed to map what she knew to the dials on the device. The rescue, the injured, the dead. She saw every detail of the event in slow motion, and somewhere in that memory was the key. *The date, location, people. And two units O negative, that was the difference between life and death.*

Kate began turning the dials. With a renewed sense of hope, she tested a few combinations and heard the click. *Got it*, she thought, and exposed the core device. More of the black, sticky fluid oozed out of the access port. Her heart sank. Was the core exposed the entire time? Did she take too long to solve the puzzle? The answer didn't matter. All that mattered now was to see if anything remained.

She turned to the laptop and connected to Jake's device. *Good*, she thought. *I can connect. That's a start.* There were dozens of folders and hundreds of file names. Timestamps ran back almost a year. *Jake was collecting data on something for over a year, and he kept me in the dark,* she thought. She pushed down the anger and focused on the work.

The core file system was damaged. The contents appeared intact, but she couldn't open or copy anything. She hoped the folders and file names would give her some clue, but most were just dates and cities. Some of the folders mapped to locations where she knew Jake and the team had contracts. *These are probably mission plans, and maybe after-action reports.* But there were countries and cities Jake had never been. *Or had he,* she wondered. *What was Jake hiding?*

With a tap on her shoulder, Commander Lewis startled Kate back into the moment. "Mrs. Preacher, please follow me."

The two of them walked forward, dodging hammocks slung in every direction, and men snoring. When they neared the cockpit, she found several team members huddled around laptops and the SOCOM communication terminals.

"It just went crazy, sir," one man said. "I've never seen anything like it, and I can't stop it."

Kate took one look at the laptop screens and shouted, "Shut them down! Shut everything down. Anything and everything connected to the network needs to be turned off."

"Do it," Commander Lewis shouted. "Do it now!"

Kate sprinted back to her seat and grabbed Jake's NanoVault. She shoved the device back into the Faraday bag, sealed it, and shut down her laptop. When she turned around, Commander Lewis was standing right behind her.

"What just happened?" he asked.

"I can't be sure," Kate said. "At least, not without a forensic investigation, but I think some kind of virus or worm just ripped through these systems."

"What does that mean?"

"It means that everything on board, every laptop, cell phone, tablet, anything connected to the aircraft's internal network needs to be quarantined and turned over to NCIS as soon as we land."

"Could your work back here have something to do with this?" the Commander asked. "You were in a hurry to get back to it."

"Not a chance," Kate lied. "As you might imagine, in my line of work, my systems have multiple layers of protection, but I didn't want to risk losing anything. Better safe than sorry."

"I won't pretend to understand what just happened," he said. "But under the circumstances I must insist, for the safety of the crew and the aircraft, that you cease all electronic activity."

"Yes. Of course," Kate said, and she made a show of closing up everything and putting it away, and the Commander returned to the front.

Kate took her seat, her mind spinning with questions and possibilities. *Was Jake's device infected*, she wondered. *What was it trying to do? Did Jake know? I don't dare expose the device again until I'm back at the office lab, and I pray that whatever Jake wanted me to see is still there.*

The forensic lab Kate built at *Frank, Burman and Dodd* was impressive, but it was still just a law firm and far short of what she had at her fingertips with the Agency. She considered some Langley contacts she could approach, a few favors she could call in. *No. I can't. It's not safe,* she thought. *Whatever Jake was doing, whatever he was hiding, he warned me not to trust anyone and I still don't know why.*

But what if I can't do it? What if I lose my one shot at Jake's files? I know there's something waiting for me. I can feel it. A message, a video. Whatever it is. I need to find it. I have to know.

There was someone who could help. Someone with the skills and the resources, and who she trusted once, years ago. *I don't even know if I can reach him,* she thought. *And between his clients and his enemies, what are the odds Nomad's even still breathing?*

CHAPTER 33

SATURDAY, APRIL 18
11:30 AM EDT

JFK INTERNATIONAL AIRPORT, NEW YORK, NY

Mikhail Zhukov's Ukrainian Diplomatic Passport, one perk of his relationship with Vitali Moshenski, sped his entry through JFK and he headed straight for the taxi stand. He feigned reception of an important call and waved a few others ahead. He never took the first cab, randomly selected another in line, and always paid cash. Zhukov knew his protocols weren't foolproof, but if someone wanted to track him, he would make them work for it.

"The Overwatch Nexus," he said, and was pleased the driver was familiar with the Lower East Side destination.

"You don't strike me as a gamer," the cabbie said. "Overwatch tends to attract a younger crowd. I'm more old-school. You know. The classics. Conan the Barbarian. World of WarCraft."

Zhukov said nothing and fixed his gaze on the rear-view mirror. When the cabbie looked back, the meaning was clear.

"I'm cool, man," the cabbie said. "None of my business. It's all good."

The hour-long drive was quiet. Zhukov played the voice message several times, and with each pass, he listened for anything that might suggest he was needed. He concluded that Vitali was right. There was no reason to return, nothing he could do. *Vitali has powerful friends, in every level of government, who depend on his generosity and support,* he thought. *To stay in his good graces, and ensure the money keeps flowing, they will do whatever he asks.*

The driver stopped, and Zhukov looked down the alley. The Lower East Side neighborhood was a mix of older industrial buildings and an eclectic art scene. The pavement was cracked and littered with discarded bottles and cigarette butts, and the walls of the alley were covered in layers upon layers of colorful graffiti tags and obscenities.

"Wait for me," Zhukov said. "Fifteen minutes." And before the cabbie could object, Zhukov handed him a pair of hundred-dollar bills.

"Take your time," the cabbie said. "I'll be here."

Zhukov's destination was the red door at the end of the alley. Scrawled across the door's peeling paint were two words. *Overwatch Nexus.* He braced himself and entered. Zhukov was immediately engulfed in the chaos of night-club style lighting, and visual effects, and the glare of hundreds of computer screens. The frenzied clicking and tapping on keyboards merged with the background of thundering bass and electric guitars. It was an assault on the senses that echoed like a battlefield.

Despite the warehouse scale of the space, every corner had stacks of computer equipment and gamers crammed in tight, their faces lit by the glow of monitors. The walls were covered in posters, and the air was thick with the scent of sweat and fast food.

The man guarding the elevator was the only clue that the Overwatch Nexus was anything more than a 24/7 gamers' paradise. The Maori was the size of a sumo wrestler, with tribal markings across his face and shaved head. The black suit, shirt unbuttoned at the collar, gave him a professional look, but the earpiece wire coiling down his neck revealed his connection to something beyond the gaming floor.

When Zhukov approached, the Maori nodded and stepped aside. The short ride to the basement was a welcome relief from the onslaught above. The lower level's acoustic insulation rendered the room nearly silent. *If I shoot him,* Zhukov thought. *No one would hear.*

The server room consumed a third of the massive space. Walls of glass surrounded and protected banks of computers stacked in neat rows and columns. Larger machines flanked every row, each one a black monolith peppered with blinking lights and switches. A faint hum radiated from the climate-controlled enclosure, and bundles of cables reached for the ceiling and cascaded down on a central server. Zhukov knew the main floor's heavy power consumption and conspicuous bandwidth was the perfect cover for the massive network below.

Zhukov's footsteps echoed on the concrete floor. He approached the lone man in the room, but the man kept his eyes fixed on the monitor, his fingers flying over the keyboard. Zhukov was close enough to see what the man was watching and typing, but the blur of letters and numbers streaming across the screen was meaningless.

"Alexei?" Zhukov said, expecting the man to stop and face him.

"Did you retrieve the device?" Alexei asked over his shoulder, but continued typing.

"No."

"I warned you there wasn't much time," Alexei said. "And the Frenchman?"

"Dead."

Alexei stopped. His hands hung in the air for a moment, and then settled in his lap. He turned toward Zhukov and removed a pair of augmented reality glasses that made his eyes look more extraterrestrial than human.

"So, it's over?"

"I have the Frenchman's laptop," Zhukov said, and he handed it to Alexei.

"Don't get your hopes up," he said. "I'll have a look, but I've been tracking Nomad for years. So has every intelligence agency on the planet. No one's even gotten close."

"What makes him different?"

"For one thing, he's never in one place long. You trace his activity to Cairo, and he shows up in Bali. I've tracked him all over the planet."

"Maybe Nomad is just a cover for a team."

"Teams have quirks. Idiosyncrasies that reveal individual skills and style. No matter how hard they try to look alike, they can't do it. No, this is one man, or woman. No one knows."

"How much time do you need?"

"A day, maybe two. This is either going to lead somewhere or not, but I need to move slow," Alexei said. "If he sees me coming, I'm screwed."

"Every day you sound more like an American."

"Thanks."

"It was not a compliment," Zhukov said. "Time to stop chasing him around the globe. Use the laptop as bait, and he will come to you. Oh, and one more thing," he said, and pulled a folded photograph from his jacket pocket and flattened it out on Alexei's desk. "I need you to identify everyone in this photo. Who are they? Where are they now?"

Zhukov pointed to the young Frenchman in the photo. "The Professor we know, and the girl is of no consequence, but the others may be important."

"That's easy," Alexei said. He scanned the image into his system and handed the photo back to Zhukov.

The photo appeared on Alexei's monitor, and Zhukov watched selection boxes appear around the heads in the photo.

"Your people could handle this," Alexei said. "Why ask me?"

"You are easier to kill," Zhukov said and reached for a pen and paper. He wrote down the number of his burner phone. "Text me when you have what I want."

The audible ding of an image search result brought both men's attention to the monitor, and the screen filled with a grid of high probability matches.

"That was fast," Alexei said, and he clicked on one of the thumbnail images. "Whoa. Devin Moore. I'm guessing you already know who that is."

"Yes," Zhukov said, "And I know where to find him. Find the rest."

CHAPTER 34

DOVER AIR FORCE BASE, DOVER, DE

KATE WOKE TO THE thud of the C-130's wheels striking the runway. The webbed airframe seat did little to cushion the impact, but at least the lap belt kept her from flying into the cargo hold. The first thing she saw were the three transport coffins draped in red, white and blue.

It surprised Kate that she fell asleep, but once she locked down Jake's NanoVault and secured the aircraft's network, sheer exhaustion consumed her. If she dreamt, there were no lingering images, and she was grateful. The video analysis of the Paris attack was burned into her brain. She relived Jake's death countless times; the mindless brutality of the attack, Jake's relentless pursuit of the killers, and the single sniper shot that rang out.

Trouble sleeping comes with the territory, Kate thought. She and Jake worked hard to heal their scars and free their ghosts. But there was no escape, only the lingering fear that anytime you closed your eyes, the demons might return. *Maybe I should be happy for Jake, at least now he's free.*

"I'm glad you got some sleep," Donoghue said.

Kate rubbed her eyes and fought to focus on the man's voice. *Who? Oh Right. Donoghue,* she thought, and she wrapped her mind around the plane's arrival.

"Chief, how long was I out?"

"Not long," he said. "I think an hour, two at most."

Kate yawned and stretched. She could hear the others up front, whispering and shuffling gear.

"They're getting ready," Donoghue said.

"Ready?" she asked, without thinking, and then added, "Of course, thank you."

The Hercules turned at the end of the runway and began the long journey back along the tarmac. She sensed that even the aircraft's approach was part of the dignity and respect shown to the fallen, and the captain handled the big bird with grace and precision. When the aircraft came to a full stop, the sound of marching boots echoed through the plane. Commander Lewis accompanied the SEAL Team Leader, and the Team assembled in front of the coffins.

Some of the Team members had obvious injuries and visible bandages, but they all stood firm, backs straight, eyes locked forward, hands at their sides. They all committed to the cause and to the creed. *Jake was proud to be a SEAL,* Kate thought. *He would be grateful they brought us home.*

The hydraulic ramp dropped, and in the early morning light, Kate saw the families flown in to receive the two fallen SEALs. An older couple stood together. The tall gray-haired man wrapped his arms around his wife's shoulders, but the sight of the three coffins sparked a fresh wave of tears. He pulled her in tight, but she turned away, buried her face in his chest and sobbed.

A young woman rushed toward the ramp, and clicking cameras raced to catch her. "No," she yelled at the press photographers, and they lowered their lenses.

Chief Donoghue caught her when she reached the ramp, but he didn't try to stop her. He helped her climb the ramp and navigate the hold. Kate saw Donoghue was every bit the gentleman and gentle man that he'd been when she came on board.

"Mrs. Sanders," Donoghue said, directing her to the coffin on the right. "This is Chief Petty Officer Sanders."

The young woman knelt beside her husband's coffin, laid her head down on the flag, and draped an arm across the top. That's when Kate saw the woman's other hand resting on the baby bump.

Oh my God, Kate thought. *She's pregnant.* Kate stifled the gasp, but not the tears. She looked away to hide her face and wipe her eyes. On the tarmac she saw a little girl, flowery dress, pigtails. *So young,* she thought. *Maybe four or five.* The girl was in grandpa's arms, resting her head on his shoulder.

Kate's father died in action when she was three, too young to remember more than fragments. But she was seven when she lost her mother. She could still see her mother's smile, hear her singing, and recall the language games they played on the way to school.

Looking at the little girl, Kate knew. *She's old enough,* Kate thought. *She knows her dad's not coming home. Not this time. He'll never lift her into the sky or swing her between his legs.* Kate thought about the baby on the way, losing a father's love, and the gaps in her own memory. *What's it like to be wrapped in a father's arms, to know you're loved and to feel his strength?*

Donoghue helped Mrs. Sanders stand and prepare to walk back to her family. The two women locked eyes for a moment. There was nothing Kate could say or needed to say. Both widowed, the bond of grief they shared was written on their faces and reflected in their eyes.

The base commander approached Kate. "Mrs. Preacher," he said. "If you'll come with me, please," and he extended an arm to assist her down the ramp.

"I'm sorry Sir," she said. "I'd like to stay with my husband."

"Of course."

The commander and the chaplain saluted the fallen, turned, and walked down the ramp. They took positions near the families and the dignified transfer process continued.

Six men marched, two by two, toward the ramp. A seventh man followed. All wore dress blues and white gloves. The carry team stood alongside Chief Sander's coffin, and bent low to grab the handles. As the coffin rose from the deck, the SEAL Team saluted. The carriers turned in unison, and with precision steps, began the long, measured descent down the ramp and toward the transport van. All military personnel present saluted while civilians and family pressed a hand on their heart.

Senior Chief Rossi was the next to be transferred. His parents found the strength to face their son's coffin and watch its descent from the aircraft. The father's crisp salute revealed he was former military. His wife stood stoically at his side when the coffin approached the van. The carry team lifted the coffin into the air and placed it on the loading shelf. The bearers released the handles and peeled away as they pressed the coffin into the van. When loaded, the seventh man stood at the rear and led the others in a final salute.

The carry team marched to the aircraft one last time. Jake's coffin floated into the air and the honor guard saluted. Kate looked at the gathering of SEALs standing at attention, saluting her husband. One or two knew Jake personally, but they all knew him by reputation. And all shared an unshakable bond of brotherhood.

Jake's coffin descended the ramp, and Kate followed. She placed a hand on the coffin and walked in unison with the carry team. The press photographer's cameras erupted, but she couldn't hear or didn't care and her eyes never wavered. Section by section, the men released their grip on the handles, and Jake's coffin slid into the back of the van, and then they were gone.

Kate was alone, her hand clutching the field of deep blue and bright white stars, and she couldn't let go, wouldn't let go. It was only when her knees buckled and she released the flag that she realized Donoghue was standing alongside. He caught her and signaled to the others to stand back.

It took a moment, but Kate summoned the will to stand strong on her own. "Thanks, Chief."

He snapped to attention. Saluted the three men in the van and offered Kate his arm.

"Ma'am, it's time."

Kate looked into his eyes. They were an intense blue, focused and purposeful, but with a vulnerability he couldn't hide. There was a shimmer, a glistening, of a man fighting to keep his emotions in check. *He feels our pain,* she thought. *And still he takes on one of the hardest jobs in the military. That's true courage.*

Kate placed her arm in the Chief's, and he led her toward the waiting limousine.

CHAPTER 35

WILLARD INTERCONTINENTAL, WASHINGTON, D.C.

MANUEL ROJAS STRODE INTO the lobby of The Willard and entered a bygone era of luxury and elegance. The marble floors, high ceilings and grand chandeliers made him feel small, out of place, and amongst this opulence, he was invisible. *Just another suit with a briefcase,* he thought. *Perfect.*

Rojas entered one of the lobby seating areas. At the end of a side table, tucked just behind a large blue vase, he found a folded copy of the Wall Street Journal. He scanned the room, but it wasn't clear who left the paper. The chairs and couches were abuzz with the Washington DC cadre of deal makers and lobbyists hunched over laptops. He swept up the Journal and headed for the elevators. Tucked in the paper's centerfold was the keycard he needed to reach the top floor.

Dressed in a charcoal gray suit, black shirt, and matching charcoal tie, Rojas was the epitome of the gray man — inconspicuous, invisible. He kept his eyes down, his fedora slanted toward the hotel's hallway cameras, and strolled past Cahill's suite. The advance team reserved the adjoining suite, and Rojas suspected this was how they bugged and monitored Cahill's extra-curricular activities. *Politics is a dirty business*, he thought. *But why kill him? They own this guy. Whatever game they're playing, Cahill must be worth more dead than alive.*

Rojas opened the briefcase and put on the full body environmental suit, shoe covers, and headgear that would eliminate any chance of DNA contamination and conceal his identity from the room's hidden cameras. He looked around his room. *They're probably watching me right now, recording everything,* he thought. *But what's the point? I've already sold my soul, and the contract is do or die.*

While the hotel's hallway doors employed sophisticated electronic locks, the interior door to the adjoining suite, the Senator's suite, was a simple deadbolt. Within seconds, Rojas picked the lock and entered the Senator's suite. He found Cahill's drugs, completed phase one of the plan, and returned to his room. *It won't be long now,* he thought, and glanced at the time on the burner phone.

A few minutes later, the phone buzzed. He received an alert on the BountyHunt app. The cartel's Magic Touch cleaning van had arrived. *The Senator won't be far behind,* he thought, and he clicked on the message's embedded link. A real-time video feed showed the interior of the Senator's suite.

The delivery team, dressed in their mock cleaning crew uniforms, rolled the utility cart into the room. They confirmed the suite was empty, removed the shackled girl from the cart, and disappeared from view. Rojas was staring at the girl's back, half-leaning, half-kneeling at the foot of the bed. Ropes stretched her arms out wide and bound her to the bed's metal frame.

Jesus, Rojas thought. *They're capturing this live and broadcasting it on the app.* He wondered who, or how many, would watch him work, and he was thankful that the environmental suit kept his identity secure.

Senator Cahill's arrival brought the mission back into focus. If the audio was being captured, it wasn't being broadcast, so he didn't know what Cahill said to the girl, but she squirmed and pulled against the ropes.

Cahill laughed at the girl's distress, and piece by piece, he removed and placed his clothes on a chair. When he was down to his bulging Harvard crimson-logo boxers, he removed a small black box from a dresser drawer, and prepared to enhance the experience.

He pulled a small, polished mirror from the case and set it on the dresser. With practiced precession he shaved, crushed and prepared the bright white powder. When he had two lines of equal length and girth, he placed a short wide straw up his nose and, alternating nostrils, inhaled both lines.

Cahill stepped out of his boxers, placed his hands on the girl's hips, and crashed to the floor. Rojas watched the Senator's lips turn blue. He'd seen enough fentanyl overdoses to know it would be over in a few minutes. *Sometimes they vomit,* he thought. *That can be noisy.* But Rojas knew nobody would report strange sounds coming from the Senator's room. *I bet he craps his pants. They all do, and they're too sedated to even know. It's the sedation that kills. They forget to breathe.*

Rojas checked the time. *Ten minutes. He's gone,* he thought, and opened the deadbolt to reenter the Senator's suite. When the girl heard the door open, she squirmed and pulled against the ropes. She tried to speak but, with the ball gag in her mouth, the best she could manage were gurgling grunts and nasal whines. He approached the girl so that she could see him and put a finger to his mouth. *I must look like an alien,* he thought, and she fought the restraints even harder.

He was right about Cahill's condition and stepped around the urine and feces. He didn't want to risk contaminating the scene, or tracking trace evidence into the adjoining room, but he needed to check. He needed to confirm the kill.

Rojas pressed two nitrile-gloved fingers into Cahill's carotid. "Good," he said, and regretted. *That was stupid,* he thought, and tried to minimize the risk. *A voice sample that small would be nearly impossible to match. Just finish this and leave.*

He opened a Velcro flap on the environmental suit and removed a portable syringe case. The girl's eyes widened and bulged. Tears flowed, snot dripped, and flecks went flying when she fought the restraints and shook her head. Rojas stretched a thin blue elastic strap tight around the girl's right bicep. He tapped the back of her hand, pressed and probed. A usable vein firmed up. The ropes held her still enough for the needle to find its mark. He drew back on the syringe. A puff of red seeped in and swirled, mixing with a precision heroin and fentanyl cocktail.

Rojas released the tourniquet to let the drugs flow, but the girl was already floating. The terror subsided. Soon she would feel nothing at all. He nestled her hand in his. For the camera, he feigned monitoring her pulse, and nodded to the camera when it was over. He followed Cahill's pattern and stripped off the girl's clothes. The puzzle needed one last piece. Rojas wrapped the Senator's fingers around the body of the syringe with the thumb on the plunger, laid the syringe near the other drugs, and surveyed the scene.

The stage was set. Cahill's last drug-fueled party, he thought. *Two dead. Both naked. Visible drugs and paraphernalia. Tragic overdose.*

Rojas returned to his room, locked the deadbolt into the Senator's suite, waited and watched the real-time feed of the stage he created.

Right on cue, he thought, and checked the time. The live feed of the Senator's bedroom captured the photographer recording the scene. What the news outlets would make of the story was anyone's guess. Some might refuse to run the graphic photos, but he was certain they would leak, maybe even the Senator's video recordings. Whatever legacy the Senator had was gone, and a nameless, faceless child paid the price.

The photographer had one last job. Rojas watched him pull a USB key from his pocket and approach the TV. Seconds later, the video feed went black. *It's done. They got what they needed and are covering their tracks.*

The moment Rojas was certain the photographer was gone, he returned to the Senator's room, and shoved the Narcan nasal spray into the girl's right nostril. Her lips were already an ominous shade of blue. He checked the time. It took too long to get back in here, he thought, and prepped a second dose. Don't you die on me. Rojas lifted her chin. Please, God, don't let her die. She didn't ask for this. In a moment of pure desperation and hope, he administered a second Narcan dose into her left nostril.

Seconds felt like an eternity as he waited for a response. Then a gasp, and a sudden desperate inhale. Her eyes fluttered, and the color began to return. Rojas sent a one-word text message to a room down the hall, *NOW.*

Rojas answered the knock at the door. A man and a woman in janitorial uniforms rolled a utility cart into the room, cut the girl loose and wrapped her in an emergency mylar blanket.

"How much did you give her?" the woman asked.

"Enough to be convincing," Rojas said. "She'll be out for a while."

"I don't want to know what this shit is," she said, looking at the body on the floor and Rojas dressed in an environmental suit. "But we're even. Don't ever call me again."

"Is she OK?" Rojas asked.

"She may never be OK," the woman said. "But she's alive, and she's got a chance. I'll get her as far away from D.C. as I can, and away from this life."

Returning to his room, Rojas locked the deadbolt into the Senator's suite, and then bagged and sealed the environmental suit.

The phone call was not a surprise, but it was startling and shattered the quiet reflection of the moment.

"Well done," Riley said. "Precisely as planned."

Rojas recognized the voice. Calm. Professional. Annoying. *But he doesn't know,* he thought. *Not yet.*

"You'll find the balance of the contract is already in your account," Riley added. "Celebrate. You're now a man of means. Book a luxurious hotel suite somewhere. Not here, of course," he said, and laughed. "Get yourself a hooker. Make it two. You can afford it."

"Not my style."

"No matter," Riley said. "I do have news about your daughter."

"I warned you to leave my daughter out of this."

"Come. Come. You know that's not how this works. She's part of the family now. We look after family. I just thought you'd like to know she aced her final exams. That's one smart kid. Bright future."

Rojas knew better than to say what he was thinking, and Riley continued. "Oh, and don't worry about the kid bullying your daughter."

"What bully?" Rojas asked. "Is Angela OK?"

"She's fine," Riley said. "Sorry. Thought you knew. Figured your ex would say something, but then I guess you two aren't really talking, not since, well, you know."

"Riley, what the hell did you do?"

"Tragic really. Hit and run. Very sad."

"You killed some kid?"

"No. No," Riley said. "Nothing so dramatic. After all, he's just a kid. But he'll be in the hospital for a while, and his skateboard days are over."

Chapter 36

CHARLES C. CARSON CENTER FOR MORTUARY AFFAIRS, DOVER AFB, DE

ALONE IN THE BACK of the limo, she stared out at the airfield. Rows of C-17 Globemaster and C-130 Hercules aircraft stood ready to respond to a global emergency, or critical mission deployment. *How many times had Jake answered the call,* she wondered. She had a general idea, but other than scheduled deployments, most of Jake's life was classified. And, given her role with the Agency, they both understood and accepted that their pasts were locked away.

The drive to the Center for the Families of the Fallen seemed to stretch out forever. Kate sat in silence, her mind racing with questions she feared might never be answered. She couldn't, and wouldn't, imagine a life without Jake. It wasn't real. Not yet.

She felt the car slow to a stop. The driver opened her door and extended a hand. Kate slid out and managed a thin smile for the woman in Dress Blues and white gloves.

"Mrs. Preacher," she said. "I'm Major Bennett, the base Casualty Assistance Officer," and she extended a hand.

Major Bennett shook Kate's hand, but held it for a moment. "Before we head in, I just want to say how truly sorry I am. I know how little value words have at this moment, but I want you to know that I once stood where you are standing now. Long before I took this post, I walked these halls as a widow."

Kate felt the genuine empathy of the Major's admission, one that she suspected few others would be told. That kind of honesty is just not protocol, and Kate was prepared to hear a well-rehearsed speech. Something about the United States Department of Defense's deepest condolences, and on and on.

"Thank you, Major," Kate said. Without warning, the tears returned, and the Major wrapped her arms around Kate.

"This is how it will be," the Major whispered in Kate's ear. "It springs from deep inside, and often when you least expect it, but my husband always said *tears cleanse the soul*."

"Let's head inside where we can sit and talk," the Major said. "And please, call me Rachel. We're going to be together for the next several hours, and ranks and last names are cumbersome. May I call you Katherine?"

"Thanks, Rachel," Kate said. "And please call me Kate."

"Alright, Kate, my office is this way."

The two women entered the Family Center, passing through large glass doors into the main hall and atrium. A marble wall captured the mission of the place with the words "Dignity, Honor and Respect" engraved across the top. Skylights bathed the memorial for the fallen in a warm, yellow glow.

The atrium had a raised garden with a lush carpet of moss and ferns, and a Japanese maple, its branches gracefully twisted and reaching for the light above. Plush couches, chairs and floor cushions surround a meditation pavilion. A small fountain burbled in the corner. Water cascaded down the rocks, flowing from pool to pool, and shimmering sunlight danced on the walls.

On the way to her office, Rachel pointed out a few of the meeting rooms and private family gathering areas. In one room, Kate spotted the young girl she'd seen earlier. Grandpa was balancing himself on a bean-bag chair, while the girl drew a pink, stick-figure dog on a large chalkboard.

"What's that?" Kate asked.

"This is the children's area. The kids come in here to play with the toys, and roll around on the floor, but the major attraction is the chalk wall. We encourage the kids to draw or write something for the person they've lost."

Kate read the words written in all caps across the top of the board, "Our hero for always."

"We erase the board periodically," Rachel said. "Always leaving a few things, like a flower, or a phrase."

There was a subtle break in Rachel's voice. *The children must be the hardest part of the job*, Kate thought.

"We don't know who wrote the phrase up top," Rachel added, "but none of us can reach it."

Kate knew that was an excuse. No one would want to erase that message, and so it stayed.

Rachel furnished her office with multiple seating areas to accommodate the range of family sizes and ages that she counseled, and Kate selected one of the leather chairs directly across from the desk. Kate scanned the room and noticed it was attractive and functional, but not personal.

"Wondering why no photos of my husband?" Rachel asked.

"Actually, I am."

"That part of my life. Our wedding photos. Robert looking sharp in his uniform. Vacations, and... and his burial flag are at home," Rachel said. "I find it easier to help others with their loss when I'm not focused on my own."

"I understand."

"You will," Rachel said. "We all find our way to cope. Shall we get started?"

"Yes, please."

"To begin, the Senior Chief is...," Rachel began, but Kate interrupted.

"Would you mind if we dropped the Senior Chief?"

"Of course. Whatever you prefer."

"Jake is fine."

"So, Jake is currently with our medical examiner for official identification."

"Identification?"

"This is just a legal formality and may already be complete. As I'm sure you can imagine, there are situations where identification is a critical part of our medical services," Rachel said.

I don't need to imagine it, Kate thought, recalling the graphic imagery the Agency often required her to analyze and assess. *I lived it.*

"From the Medical Examiner's office, Jake will go into Mortuary Services. While you and I review Jake's wishes, his body will be prepared for burial."

They trained Rachel to tread lightly and choose her words carefully, and Kate appreciated it. She didn't need to hear the details, and had seen enough death to know what was happening.

"I have Jake's last deployment file outlining his wishes, but given his medical discharge and subsequent marriage, we defer to the spouse in these matters."

"I've seen Jake's Death File," Kate said. "And nothing has changed. I would like to proceed with his wishes exactly as specified. Jake wants to be buried at Arlington with his team, the brothers he lost in Afghanistan."

"Then we will use his instructions, as our guide. If there's anything we can't do or handle in a timely manner, you and I can discuss options."

"Is there something you're concerned about?" Kate asked.

"No, not concerned. But you should know that Arlington burial arrangements can take up to three months. Faced with that reality, and seeking closure, some families elect a home state burial."

"I had no idea," Kate said. "But Jake's wishes aren't negotiable."

"Then let's get on the schedule," Rachel said, and started typing. "Hmm, that's odd."

"What?"

"Oh sorry," Rachel said. "I need to make a call."

"Should I step outside?"

"No, you're fine. Stay right there," Rachel said, and picked up the phone.

"This is Major Bennett, Casualty Assistance..."

"Yes. I can hold."

"Regarding Senior Chief Church..."

"I'm staring at his file right now..."

"No. I wasn't notified, and neither was his wife."

"Of course I'm sure. She's sitting in my office."

"Hang on."

Rachel muted the call and set the receiver down.

"Kate, I don't know what happened or when, but Jake's scheduled for burial a week from today."

"How is that even possible? You thought it could take months."

"And it usually does," Rachel said. "My best guess is that someone cashed in a big favor. But this timing is take it or leave it."

"Take it!"

Rachel picked up the phone. "We'll take it. Send me the confirmation, and we'll have Senior Chief Church transferred as soon as he's ready."

"So what happens now?"

"Jake had specific requests for pallbearers, and I will reach out to them immediately. Per Jake's instructions, anyone we can't reach or who cannot attend, we'll replace with other SEALs. I will coordinate with DEVGRU, and make arrangements for substitutes, if needed," Rachel said. "Given your husband's reputation among the Teams, and the whole world witnessing his heroism, I know the list of volunteers will be substantial."

"Thank you," Kate said. "I don't think that I could talk to any of them right now."

"That's why I'm here. Let me do all the legwork, and we'll give the Senior Chief... we'll give Jake the service he wanted and deserves."

Rachel glanced at a pop-up message on her monitor.

"They're almost ready for you."

"Ready for me?"

"I'm so sorry," Rachel said. "I never got to finish explaining the sequence of events today. They fitted Jake's final uniform. You'll be able to see him soon."

***

KATE FACED THE DOOR into the private viewing area. She touched the sign on the wall. *Senior Chief Jake Church. I can feel him,* she thought. The analyst in her said she was just imagining it, but her heart knew better.

She summoned the strength to enter. A dark blue aluminum casket rested on a table in the center of the room. An American flag draped across the lower half. Jake was in full dress uniform, dark navy blue coat, gold buttons, a narrow black tie on a starched white shirt. He was lying on a bed of blue velvet. *So handsome,* she thought, walking toward him. *So dignified and proud.*

The tears welled up again, and Kate was thankful tissues were within easy reach. Standing alongside, she looked down on the love of her life, smiled and caressed his cheek. *How many times have I seen him nap, just like this,* she thought, and she would wake him with a gentle touch or a kiss. *Not this time.*

She reached in and placed a comforting hand on his chest. "Everything's being arranged," she assured him, as if he could hear her, and believing he could. "It will be just what you wanted. You'll soon be back with your team," she said. "But you already know, don't you? I'll bet the guys saw you coming and had a beer in hand."

Kate brushed back a lock of Jake's hair. "Is your mom there too? I hope so. I hope she's been watching all this time and knows what an extraordinary man you became. Good and kind. Courageous."

"Oh here, you should have this back," she said, and lifted the silver chain over her head, wrapped it around his hands, and laid the silver cross on top. "By the way, using the cross was brilliant. I have to admit I didn't think I'd figure it out, at least not in time. I was a wreck, and when I opened my eyes, the cross was in my hands. I'm guessing you had something to do with that."

There were several chairs in the room, and a cushioned bench running the length of the coffin. Kate took a seat on the bench. "We need to talk."

"I'm still angry," she said. "And confused. I don't know what you were doing, or why you were hiding it from me, and I'm scared. It's not like you. I thought we didn't have secrets. Well, not this kind, and there's a problem."

"If you're watching," she said, addressing the room. "Then you already know. Your NanoVault's damaged. The data's corrupted. How bad? I don't know."

She stared at the floor, cradled her head in her hands, and fought to hold back the tears. "I know you think I'll find a way. I always do. But what if I can't? What if I never know?"

Kate cleared her throat, dried her eyes, and stood up tall. She looked into the face of the man she loved and saw the warrior. Above Jake's left pocket, the golden SEAL Trident, set ablaze by light streaming in from above. Below the Trident, rows of colorful ribbon racks cataloged two decades of service and achievement.

Hanging from a ribbon of red, white and blue was Jake's Silver Star. Kate slipped her fingers under the five-pointed star, and her thumb caressed the laurel wreath that surrounded the center star. She flashed on the mission, and the blood and destruction that bound them both to that star.

Your actions in the face of grave danger have not only saved a valued member of our intelligence community, but have also prevented potential catastrophic harm to innocent lives. In recognition of your remarkable performance under the most challenging circumstances, it is with great pride that we award you the Silver Star for Gallantry.

"I never lost hope," Kate said. "I knew you would find me. And even when everyone believed it was a trap, I knew you would come."

She laid the star back down and patted his chest.

"I need to go," Kate said. "You're home now, and I have work to do. I will try to recover whatever intel and evidence you collected, but with or without it I'm going to track down the people who took you from me, every single one, and send them straight to hell."

CHAPTER 37

MOORE TOWER, MANHATTAN, NY

MOORE TOWER WAS A monument to Devin Moore's brilliance and audacity. Superstorm Sandy devastated the Metropolitan Tower's once-elegant grand entrance, flooded the lower floors and salt-water destroyed the building's core power grid and mechanical systems. Devin Moore seized the opportunity to purchase the abandoned building for pennies on the dollar, and a few years later, the city welcomed Moore's new luxury hotel, and celebrated the building's abundant cultural spaces.

The Tower's combination of luxury suites, boutique shops, art galleries and intimate theaters entertained the hotel's wealthy guests and seduced the building's elite residents. The Tower also provided Moore with his first glimpse into the power that came from the volume of sensitive data that flowed in and out of the building every minute of every day. From that insight, the concept for the Quantum NanoVault was born.

Devin Moore's luxury penthouse residence occupied the top two of the seventy-two story structure. The blend of incubator, startup and production businesses that comprised Moore Technologies occupied another three floors. Moore would joke with the business media that he had the shortest commute in New York, and his only lament was the building's 1960s roof-top heliport was unusable.

Moore's private office entrance was as intimidating as the man himself. The double mahogany doors stood at an impressive 10 feet tall. The appearance was unyielding and impenetrable. He was on the phone when the intercom light flashed, and he put the call on hold.

"Yes?" he asked.

"Mr. Zhukov has arrived."

"Good, send him in," Moore replied, and he pressed one of the office control buttons embedded into the underside of his desk. The custom-made Martin Goeble Noir desk was a six-figure work of art, crafted from Macassar ebony and polished aluminum. The desk, while visually striking and ergonomically designed, was also Moore's command center.

The automatic doors into Moore's office opened, and Zhukov crossed the gauntlet. Moore returned to his phone call and, with a grand wave of the hand, motioned for Zhukov to have a seat anywhere. Plush Italian leather furnishings occupied the area directly in front of Moore's desk, but there were designer couches, chairs and tables spread throughout the cavernous space.

Moore's eyes followed Zhukov when he turned toward the library. Two massive bookshelves, standing twenty feet tall, occupied the corner of the office. A rolling ladder curved from one wall to the other. A chess board of polished ebony and rosewood sat on a coffee table. Captured pieces lined the board's edges, the remaining pieces clustered together. Moore watched Zhukov admire the set. *I wonder if he plays,* Moore thought. *He's Russian. Of course, he plays. And he's not admiring the craftsmanship, he's studying the board.*

The call ended, and Moore joined Zhukov.

"Can I offer you something to drink?" Moore asked, pretending Zhukov was a guest. "We have everything."

Zhukov shook his head and examined a section of the library that caught his attention.

"You found my favorite collection," Moore said. "I'm not surprised. I have everything from Machiavelli to Churchill and from Sun Tzu to Patton."

"Have you read these?"

"I have," Moore said. "And hundreds more. The library upstairs has thousands of books. Centuries of accumulated human history and wisdom."

Taking Sun Tzu's book off the shelf, Zhukov asked, "Do you think war is art?"

"No, not literally," Moore said. "But it's my belief that if we're ever to find peace, we should study the methods, proponents and politics of war."

Zhukov replaced the book and said, "You won't find peace in a book."

"Then where do we find it?" Moore asked.

"In the grave," Zhukov said, and he pointed at the chessboard. "Are you playing white?"

"I am."

"You will lose."

"I beg to differ," Moore said. "Sadly, I will never know. My opponent recently passed. Suicide. I wish I had known he was suffering. Perhaps I could have helped, but for now I can't bear to reset the board. In my mind, the game's still not over."

Moore's intercom buzzed again. He glanced at his watch, returned to the desk, and pressed the speaker button.

"Is everything set?" Moore asked.

"Yes, sir."

"Very good. We'll be right down," Moore said, and looked at Zhukov. "Time to go."

"Where are we going?"

"Anywhere. Nowhere. That's not important."

"I don't understand."

"You'll see," Moore said. "We just need the right look, and you, my chiseled Russian friend, are perfect."

Zhukov headed for Moore's private elevator, the direct route to the underground garage and the building's most secure exit, but Moore stopped him.

"Not today," he said. "Today we need to be seen, so we'll be using the front door."

A member of Moore's security team stood near the office's main elevator.

"One moment, sir."

Moore waited. The guard placed a finger on the device in his right ear, and then confirmed. "They're ready for you, sir."

"Who is ready?" Zhukov asked.

"Patience, Mikhail. You'll see."

Moore and Zhukov entered the elevator, and Moore pushed the lobby button. He smiled when Zhukov stepped in front to shield the door. Moore's total control of the building automation ensured the elevator would not stop before it reached the lobby, but Zhukov had no way of knowing and prepared to prevent anyone else from entering.

On the way down, Moore seized the opportunity to question Zhukov.

"I know you've just arrived from Paris, but have you heard about Senator Cahill?"

"Yes," Zhukov replied. "Remarkable how rapidly your media exploits tragedy."

"You know what they say, if it bleeds, it leads," Moore replied. "And our friend. Do you know if Vitali has seen the news?"

"He has and remains concerned."

The elevator doors opened, and Zhukov led the way. The lobby security team kept the area clear, so there was no immediate danger, but just beyond the entrance was the objective. Moore leaked he was leaving for an important meeting, and his limo and driver were waiting at the curb.

The horde of reporters, paparazzi, and camera crews swarmed Moore when he emerged from the imposing glass tower. He took a moment to adjust his tie, compose himself, and put on a polite smile before approaching the cluster of microphones and cameras.

"Mr. Moore! Mr. Moore! Can you comment on Senator Cahill's death and the allegations of his involvement with a minor?" one reporter shouted.

Devin raised an eyebrow and responded, "I am deeply saddened by the news of Senator Cahill's death. It is a tragedy for his family, friends, and the country. As for the circumstances of his death, I cannot speculate. That is a matter for the authorities to investigate."

Another reporter stepped forward. "There are reports that Senator Cahill was investigating Moore Technologies and the NanoVault as a threat to national security. Can you speak to those allegations?"

Devin took a measured breath, carefully choosing his words. "Our company has always operated within the bounds of the law, and we stand by the integrity of our product. The Quantum NanoVault is simply a tool for individuals to protect their privacy and security in an increasingly digital world where literally everyone and everything is spying on them."

Another reporter shouted and caught the crowd's hushed attention. "Mr. Moore. Sexually explicit photos and videos are flooding social media, filling the tabloids, and fueling speculation that the source of this material was Senator Cahill's personal NanoVault. Is there any truth to the rumor that a hacker breached the NanoVault's encryption and released the senator's files?"

Devin's smile disappeared, and he responded with a hint of annoyance, "I don't comment on rumors and baseless accusations, nor will I comment on the Senator's alleged activities. What I can tell you is that the NanoVault undergoes rigorous, continuous, testing, and the quantum key encryption surpasses the capabilities of even military-grade security," Moore said, and smiling again, he added. "And as you all know, the bounty for cracking the device remains unclaimed. At this moment, the Bitcoin value of the bounty is well over fifty-million-dollars. The world's leading mathematicians, cryptographers and, of course, infamous hackers, have all tried and failed."

A female reporter chimed in, "Mr. Moore, the young girl, photographed bound and naked, in the Senator's suite is believed to have been trafficked into the US by the Quimera Cartel, and her body has yet to be recovered. Care to comment?"

"I haven't seen the photos," Devin said. "And, honestly, I don't want those images in my head. It's all very tragic and macabre."

"But isn't it true that Quimera uses your NanoVaults to hide their illicit activities and doesn't that make you complicit in the girl's death?"

Devin's expression turned to one of disgust. "I find those insinuations offensive and completely unfounded. I have no knowledge of or connection to any illegal activities or individuals, and I certainly do not condone or participate in any form of human trafficking or drug trade."

The crowd of reporters continued to hurl questions at Devin, but he glanced at his watch, stepped back from the microphones, and waved to the crowd. The security detail cleared a path to the limo, and Moore and Zhukov slid into the car.

"What do you think?" Moore asked. Zhukov was slow to respond, so Moore answered for him. "Trust me. That went very well," he said. "The American media is carnivorous, and they'll be feasting on Cahill's carcass for days."

"Cahill was your contract?"

"Let's just say I won't be shedding any tears," Moore said. "The guy was a scumbag, and when I refused to fund his reelection campaign, he came after me. That was a mistake."

"That was not sanctioned."

"I'm aware," Moore said, "But it was an opportunity to remove an obstacle and provide the Coalition with a demonstration. The data we leaked on the good senator was only the most salacious of what his NanoVault collected. I have National Security briefings, committee meetings, and the always amusing lobbyist lunches and back-room deals."

"And what of the data breach?" Zhukov asked. "If you can not secure the data you are collecting, you put us all at risk."

"As I told Vitali personally, we located the source and eliminated the problem." *A half-truth is better than a lie*, Moore thought. *And everything's under control.* "We prevented anything from being exposed, and in the meantime, deployment and collection is exceeding our projections. The GEC will get everything I promised."

CHAPTER 38

UNDISCLOSED LOCATION

NOMAD HAD NO IDEA where in the world the Frenchman's laptop might surface, so he scanned the globe using every zombie computer he had at his disposal. It had taken years to build his botnet, but time and patience were resources Nomad had in abundance. Now, thousands of compromised computers would do his bidding with a simple wake up command.

Given Zhukov's Russian Military background and Moshenski's underworld connections, Nomad expected the laptop would surface in Eastern Europe. With some of the brightest minds and skilled hackers on the planet, that seemed a safe bet. Wherever the laptop was now, the moment they powered it on Nomad's embedded code would seek a way to reach out and send up a virtual flare.

"You've been staring at those screens for hours," Keisha said, and came up alongside Nomad's chair.

"What's your point?" he asked.

"My point is that you need a break," she said. "At least eat something. I warmed some bone broth. You can sip on it and stare at the same time."

"It's in New York," Nomad blurted out. His chair's electric motors hummed. The chair spun around, and Keisha pulled the cup back just in time.

"The laptop's in New York," he said, oblivious to Keisha's quick save. "That means Zhukov's in New York."

"Are you sure?" she asked. "Maybe he's doing that trick of yours. You know where it looks like you're in one place, only to be somewhere completely different."

"I'm going to pretend you didn't just insult me," Nomad said. "But I don't dare nail down the laptop's exact location. Not yet."

"I thought this is what you wanted? Isn't this why I couldn't tear you away from those screens?"

"Yes, and yes," Nomad said. "But it's also a ploy. That blip on the radar is just a pawn. An opening move to test my reaction."

"What's your move?"

"My move is to wait. I'll give them some time and wait for a mistake."

"I thought we didn't have much time," Keisha said. "I thought it wouldn't be long before Moore, or Zhukov, or God knows who else, figures out where we are."

"My opponent doesn't know that," Nomad said. "When I don't take the bait, they'll be forced to be more aggressive. Zhukov will be paying them for results, and that makes them eager, vulnerable. They put a toe in the water. Next it will be a leg, then they'll go swimming."

"And you just sit and watch?"

"Imagine I'm a Great White shark circling their boat, only they don't know that I'm lurking beneath the surface. When the prize is worth the risk, I'll bite."

"I saw that movie," she said. "It doesn't end well for the shark."

"Look, it's a risk, I know," Nomad said, and turned his chair to face Keisha. "And it's one I must take. I need to finish this, but you don't have to stay."

"We've had this discussion," she said. Keisha placed the bone broth in his chair's cup holder and positioned the straw.

"If, when, they do come, we'll see them coming," he said, and nodded at the security cameras. "You'll have time to get into the safe room."

"What about you? Couldn't you just hide in there with me?"

"I'm the one they want, and once they have me or kill me, they won't look any further," Nomad said. "But if they can't find me —"

"I get it. They'll tear this place apart," Keisha said. "Now, drink up."

CHAPTER 39

MOORE TOWER, MANHATTAN, NY

MIKHAIL ZHUKOV WONDERED WHERE he and Moore were going. But as soon as the limo was well beyond the news crews, and certain they weren't being followed, the driver worked his way back to Moore's private entrance. In the retrofit of the Tower, Moore moved all the critical infrastructure above the flood level, and turned the lower levels into resident and valet parking. His entrance, automated, monitored and guarded like an embassy, led to a separate parking wing for himself, the occasional invited guest, and his private army of former special forces operators.

Moore and Zhukov took the private express elevator to Moore's office. The elevator could reach the penthouse as well, but entry into Moore's personal life was reserved for a select few, and controlled by Moore himself. The women who made it to the penthouse wore it like a badge of honor, and far more claimed it than achieved it.

Zhukov followed Moore into the office and watched Moore's hand disappear beneath the desk. With whisper-quiet precision, Zhukov heard the hydraulic pressure engaging the steel bolts of the massive doors. *Like a bank vault*, Zhukov thought. *Or a prison.* A moment later Moore's bookshelves swung open and the two men stepped inside Moore's data center control room.

"You know Dilbert," Moore said, and pointed at the rotund, bespectacled man sitting in the center of the room.

"Hello Drew," Zhukov said, ignoring Moore's attempt to demean the man.

"Welcome back, Mr. Zhukov," Drew said, and smiled.

Zhukov had toured the control room once before with Vitali, but it remained an impressive sight. He thought the room would be like the war room in Moscow, or how he imagined NORAD might look. But what he saw was more science fiction than bomb shelter, like something you'd find on the bridge of a starship.

The room was ringed on three sides by massive screens, each monitoring distinct parts of the globe. Smaller monitors filled and flashed with pictures, videos, and documents. A classical soundtrack was just audible in the background, and the only other sound was Drew tapping on the keyboard. At a glance, it was difficult to grasp what was happening, but Zhukov knew Moore's system was capturing, cataloging, and correlating massive, almost incalculable amounts of personal data.

"Is that Barber's Adagio for Strings?" Zhukov asked.

"Why yes," Drew said. "It is."

Zhukov noted the surprise in Drew's response, and the look on Moore's face. "My wife was a concert violinist," he said. "Why she married me over many others, I will never know."

"Mr. Zhukov, please forgive my surprise. It's a recognizable piece, but most people don't know the name," Drew said. "Most find it sad, but I find it comforting. It helps me concentrate, and anything is better than the live track."

"What is the live track?"

Drew glanced at Moore, and he nodded. "It's OK. Show him."

A moment later, the room exploded in sound. Tens of thousands of voices echoing off the walls. Every imaginable language and tone. At first, indecipherable. Then laughter. Giggling girls. A woman screaming. Zhukov's brain struggled to comprehend what he was hearing. Snippets of sound would surface and register. A baby crying. Gunshots. The 911 operator. Zhukov crooked his neck, closed his eyes and listened. A man asking for directions.

"What is this?"

"Life," Moore replied. "Every second of every day, from all over the world. Under the right conditions, the NanoVault has a capture radius of up to twenty feet."

"Astonishing."

Zhukov suspected the device's capabilities exceeded the Council's expectations, and Moore's audio surveillance demonstration confirmed his suspicions.

"That's enough," Moore said, and Drew muted the live feed. "But isn't it fascinating how noise slowly becomes information? The brain is truly remarkable, but when the AI comes online, we'll capture, correlate and discern the speaker's intent in real-time."

"But the AI is still learning, growing?"

"Yes," Moore said. "But it won't be long now. We'll soon be fully operational."

Vitali was *right*, Zhukov thought. *In Moore's vision of the future, every utterance would be ammunition to control and manipulate, but there may still be time.*

The two men approached an area of the control room where Drew appeared dressed for surgery. The meticulously organized workstation was an electronically sterile environment. Bright LED panels bathed the desk in light and illuminated the object of interest like a precious jewel.

Diagnostic tools, all foreign to Zhukov, surrounded the Onyx version of a Quantum NanoVault. The enigmatic device, no larger than a ChapStick tube, was secured within a specialized gyroscopic vise and appeared to defy gravity. But the centerpiece of the workstation was a high-powered digital microscope mounted on an articulating arm. The microscope's real-time image analysis was visible on the monitor and it scanned every millimeter of the device.

"Where was it found?" Zhukov asked, pretending he didn't know the answer.

"Paris."

"How is it you recovered the device so quickly?"

"Fate, my friend," Moore said, and smiled. "Or perhaps divine intervention. Ronin was in Paris. Literally blocks away."

"And the owner?"

"Once Ronin collected the device, he concluded the owner was of no value."

Zhukov pictured the Frenchman's body hanging from the ceiling beam, still swaying when he arrived. *Had I arrived a few minutes sooner,* Zhukov thought. *The Frenchman would still be alive, and Ronin would be dead.*

"Alright, Dilbert," Moore said. "Show us what you've found."

Zhukov saw the sweat on Drew's brow, hands trembling.

"I haven't found anything," Drew said. "I've run every conceivable diagnostic. There's nothing special about this device. It's identical to factory new in every way."

"Then how the hell did it breach the network?"

"Honestly, I have no idea. What I do know is that it can't happen again."

"How can you be sure?" Zhukov asked. "You do not even know how it works."

"We know where it connected," Moore interrupted. "And that door's locked down tight and continuously monitored. I assure you, it can't happen again, so there's nothing to worry about."

"There was something odd," Drew said, and Zhukov spotted the look on Moore's face. *Whatever Drew was about to say made Moore nervous.*

"Go on." Zhukov said, encouraging Drew to talk freely.

"It's probably nothing," Drew said, and glanced at Moore.

"Do not worry," Zhukov said, and he moved next to Moore. "Just tell us what happened, and let us decide if it is important."

"It was just a matter of minutes. Two. Maybe three. Tops," Drew began. "The tripwires I set for this device went off, but the connection was different."

"Different how?" Moore asked.

"The Frenchman's device tunneled straight into the network. Like it knew exactly where to go," Drew said. "But the signal that tripped the alarms was different. Random. It looked like normal NanoVault data. You know, the kind you see on the screens all around us, only..." Drew hesitated.

"What?" Zhukov asked.

"It was in the clear," Drew said.

"I do not understand," Zhukov said, and turned to Moore.

"Our data stream is covert," Moore said. "It's masked to look like background noise. To anyone monitoring, we're virtually invisible."

"If the connection hadn't tripped my alarm," Drew added. "I would never have known."

"Tell me you traced the source," Moore said.

Moore's tone captured Zhukov's attention. *Moore's afraid,* Zhukov thought. *He's vulnerable.*

"I was able to tri... tri... triangulate a location," Drew struggled to say. "Bu... but it wasn't much help."

"Just spit it out."

"The North Atlantic Ocean," Drew said. "One minute it was there. The next it was gone."

CHAPTER 40

THE OVERWATCH NEXUS, MANHATTAN, NY

ALEXEI SUMAROV DOWNED THE last dregs of a cold cup of coffee, and choked on the cigarette butt he'd drowned an hour earlier. *I knew this was a dead end*, he thought. But when Zhukov said to use the laptop as bait, it wasn't a suggestion.

He spent hours scrubbing the Frenchman's laptop for any trace of how Francois and Nomad communicated, but when nothing brought him any closer to Nomad's location, there was no choice. He mounted his defenses, shielded the laptop as best he could, and connected a network cable.

Zhukov was confident Nomad would be watching and take the bait. Alexei was doubtful, but ready. If Nomad connected to the laptop, he would be traceable, vulnerable to a hack-back. But there were risks. Alexei's gut told him that going head-to-head with Nomad was a mistake. But when Zhukov gives you a task, he doesn't ask twice, and defiance is deadly.

Adrenaline flowed. Heart pounded. Right knee bounced. With his hands hovering over the keyboard, fingers ready to fly, Alexei war-gamed attack and counter-attack moves. But nothing happened. He glanced at the wall clock. Minutes passed, then hours. He checked the flow monitors. Nothing but normal network traffic. *Zhukov was wrong,* he thought. *Nomad's not watching, or he knows it's a trap. Either way, we're not going to find him this way. But I can say I tried.*

Alexei was just killing time. Stalling. He needed to send Zhukov an update. *Something is better and safer than saying nothing,* he thought, but he hesitated. *There's still a chance. Nomad could make a mistake.* Alexei's exhaustion was nearing a dream state. *Imagine if I did catch him.* He tweaked a few network settings, just the slightest of changes to expose more access to the laptop. *Maybe now Nomad won't be able to resist.*

Another hour had passed, and Alexei accepted defeat. It was time to focus elsewhere and summarize what he'd learned from the photo Zhukov asked him to analyze. As he predicted, the task was trivial, and again he wondered why Zhukov didn't have his people do the research. *There's something here,* Alexei thought. *Zhukov wants to keep to himself. Whatever it is could be valuable — or get me killed.*

The image search discovered Zhukov's photo also appeared with the caption that read, *MIT Chess Team Wins PanAm Tournament.* The photo captured the four members of the team, and a man Alexei assumed was their coach, holding the PanAm Intercollegiate Team Chess Championship trophy.

He didn't have the names, not at first, but the facial recognition results filled in the blanks and Alexei was able to track down everyone in the photo.

- Dr. Francois LeGrande, Directeur de Recherches, Institut des Hautes Études Scientifiques

- Devin Moore, Founder and CEO, Moore Technologies Inc.

- Andrew Freeman, Director of Artificial Intelligence, Moore Technologies Inc.

- Katherine Preacher, Digital Forensic Analyst, Frank, Burman and Dodd

- Julian Pryce, Deceased

The only adult at the time the photo was taken was Francois, and Zhukov wasn't interested, but Alexei was curious. He considered himself a decent chess player, and was impressed to learn that the Frenchman's highest FIDE rating was 2200. *He was a master in his prime,* Alexei thought. *No wonder the team invited him to coach and then went undefeated.*

It was no surprise that the boy holding the trophy was team captain, Devin Moore. They took the photo Moore's senior year, and he was clearly the oldest member of a young team. *Even then, he had that smile. Like he knows something everyone else missed.*

The geek in the middle of the photo was Andrew Freeman. *On Facebook he calls himself Drew, but he hasn't changed much. Dorky tee-shirt. Glasses. Nearly bald now. Still eats way too much pizza. Looks like the guys gaming upstairs,* Alexei thought, picturing his Overwatch-addicted clientele. *Graduated with honors and Moore hired him straight away. Interesting. He stuck with Moore, even through the failures. The guy's probably worth a small fortune now.*

The girl in the photo was Katherine Preacher, and she was nearly invisible online, with virtually no social media footprint. *Not your typical nerd,* Alexei thought. *Worked in the State Department for a few years. Lives in Richmond, VA. Employed at a law firm. Boring.*

The shortest and youngest in the photo was Julian Pryce. Not much on Pryce, either, but it didn't take long to learn why. He died at fourteen. The chess team photo was the only photograph, and newspaper details of Pryce's death were sketchy. *Brilliant mind* and *tragic loss* was the theme surrounding the boy's death, but nothing about where or how he died except to classify his death as an accident. *The kid must have been something special,* Alexei thought. *MIT at fourteen? What a shame.*

Alexei sent a text message to Zhukov's burner phone. The summary of the people in the photo was brief and to the point. Whatever Zhukov was hoping to find, Alexei suspected he would be disappointed. To buy some time and stave off Zhukov's wrath, Alexei added he was still working on the laptop. *That wasn't a lie,* he thought. *Just not exactly the truth.*

CHAPTER 41

SATURDAY, APRIL 18
7:00 PM EDT

METROPOLITAN MUSEUM. MANHATTAN, NY

DEVIN MOORE ARRIVED AT the Met Gala in a black Rolls Royce. His twin companions, super-models Adriana and Natalia Petrov, wore Versace and Fendi couture gowns of silk and feathers with side slits almost to the waist. Adriana went strapless. Natalia opted for a deep, plunging neckline. Neither gown left much to the imagination, and both chests were the perfect stage for exquisite diamond necklaces. Moore, in a classic black tuxedo, framed with a stunning beauty on each arm, owned the walkway and the threesome basked in the shower of flashing cameras.

The marketing plan was simple, elegant. The publicity photos from the gala would help promote Moore's upcoming product release, the Diamond NanoVault, a designer line of wearable, functional art. His lapel pin, featured in all the photos, was a prototype of the production device. But promotion was only the beginning. Moore's Diamond NanoVault provided a live feed of every conversation and infiltrated every electronic device within range. The miniature earwig tucked deep in his right ear kept him connected to the data center and the progress of his experiment.

The crowd of attendees, press, and photographers appeared to part and make way for the threesome. Their entrance elicited a wave of whispers and stares, and everyone gazed upon the young, handsome, wealthy bachelor. Given his global standing and bachelor status, the smiling beauties were no surprise.

Devin helped the women climb the stairs until they reached a plateau where an entry queue had collected. Heads turned to look when they passed, and he nodded politely at the friendly faces around him. From his position in line, he could see the celebrities already walking the carpet, accompanied by their own entourages. Actresses, actors, and models, all wearing designer labels, dripping in jewels, striking practiced poses for the cameras.

The crowd welcomed Devin's turn to walk the red carpet with an enormous round of applause. He strolled onto the carpet, arm in arm with the two women. Cameras flashed and captured every step, move, and expression.

"I see New York's most eligible bachelor," said Vanessa Unger, the host of the Vogue live stream. "And sorry ladies, he has not one but two super-model bodyguards this evening. Devin. Over here. Come, say hello."

Devin smiled, waved and headed for the microphone.

"Good evening Vanessa. You look spectacular," he said. "Is that Chanel?"

"Why yes," she said. "I didn't realize you had an eye for fashion."

"An eye for fashion and beauty," he said with a broad smile, and turned to face another array of photographers. Devin slipped his arms around the slender waists of his companions, drawing them in close with a delicate touch. Their bodies pressed against his, their heads tilted toward him, as if they shared a secret. The cameras exploded.

Vanessa faced the broadcast cameras and captioned the threesome for her audience.

"I'm joined now by the legendary Devin Moore, and supermodels extraordinaire, the Petrov twins, Adriana and Natalia. Ladies, you two are an absolute Met Gala showstopper, and Devin, those necklaces are blinding."

The models smiled and posed while Devin fielded the interview. "These are bespoke Bulgari pieces I commissioned for the show, but Adriana and Natalia make them sparkle."

"They're stunning. Both the necklaces, and the ladies," Vanessa said. "Are these diamond-studded creations replicas of your wildly successful NanoVault?"

"They're not replicas. These are fully operational NanoVaults," Devin said. "We'll just have to imagine what secrets these two stunning beauties need to protect."

"Devin, you naughty boy. Don't be scandalous."

"Their secrets are safe with me," he said, and winked. "But the night is young."

Vanessa turned to the cameras. "The incomparable and incorrigible, Devin Moore." She faced Devin for the wrap-up shot. "Thanks for coming over and chatting. I know you three will have an incredible evening."

Devin smiled and waved to the adoring press and fans, and the group continued their climb to the top of the carpet. At the entrance to the Metropolitan Museum, they stopped again for a few moments. Photographers shouted for their attention and they turned, posed and smiled as requested. Devin knew a few extra seconds would help ensure the photographers captured a shot they could post online or run in the press, and everything about this evening was product positioning and business development.

Moore scooped a glass of champagne off a server's tray and checked in with Drew.

"Dilbert," Moore said, and took a sip of the Dom Pérignon.

"You know I hate that name."

"I'm just teasing, but I promise I'll try to be more considerate," Moore said. "So Drew, how do we look?"

"The Met's no cell phones policy is a bust," he said. "There are dozens of phones popping up on your data feed, and we have contacts, messages, photos, and more streaming in fast."

"Excellent."

"Whoa," Drew said.

"What?"

"Um..."

"Dilbert. I mean Drew, don't leave me hanging. What do you see?"

"Ah, some of the photos coming in from the guests phones are rather... Um... sexually explicit."

"That's no surprise. You should see what some of these women are wearing, or more accurately, not wearing."

Devin took another sip of the champagne, smiled, nodded and wandered. "Where are the Petrov's?"

Drew checked the GPS transmitters on the NanoVault necklaces the models were wearing. "They're in the women's room, about forty feet west of your location."

"Got it. Thanks," Moore said and headed in that direction. It was almost time to take seats for dinner.

"Can I ask you a question?"

"You can ask," Moore said. "But I may decline to answer. What's on your mind?"

"Well, both women are famous and gorgeous and nearly identical."

"Yes, go on."

"Which one will you take to the Penthouse?"

"Oh, Drew. That's precious."

"I don't understand."

"No, apparently you don't."

CHAPTER 42

UNDISCLOSED LOCATION

THIS NETWORK WAS A worthy opponent, Nomad thought. *Solid security. High-end equipment.* Nomad already knew the laptop was in New York, and now he knew who Zhukov tasked with finding him. When his passive vulnerability scans were complete, Nomad realized the laptop was hiding in plain sight. *The Overwatch Nexus. Alexei Sumarov. No wonder this reminds me of hacking the GRU.*

Nomad predicted his opponent would grow bolder with time. He counted on his adversary being tired, frustrated, and making a mistake. He was right and completed his takeover of the Nexus network.

Judging from the segmentation of the network, Alexei had isolated the Overwatch players, but he used their traffic to mask his activities. And Nomad used them to hide his attack. *Let's see what he's been up to,* Nomad thought. With access to the heart of Alexei's network, Nomad hoped he could discover how Zhukov learned about Francois.

Like Nomad, Alexei conducted most of his business on the dark web. They were both service providers. For hackers, that meant brokering information, providing access, disrupting target businesses and, on occasion, complete system destruction. In-person clients, like Zhukov, were rare. Nomad had a simple rule. Stay invisible. If they can't find you, they can't put a bullet in your brain.

Some of Alexei's clients were familiar aliases. A few were Nomad's clients too, others he was too busy to take on, and a few he had refused. One alias stood out. Grandmaster. *That's the name of the client that ordered Francois killed,* Nomad thought. *Coincidence? Not likely, but what's the connection?*

Nomad pulled on the thread and dug deeper into the network. *There has to be a communications trail. Follow the money,* he thought. He only knew Alexei by reputation. *Did he want the device for himself? Did he have the resources and connections to hire a contract killer?*

Nomad was determined to find the connection between the Grandmaster and the Frenchman, and possibly Zhukov. And he did.

Nomad's howling anguished cry, like the wail of a wounded animal, brought Keisha running, Mossberg 500 Cruiser in hand.

"Damn you," she said. "Nearly gave me a heart attack."

"I'm going to burn down that mother—"

"Whoa. Whoa. Whoa," Keisha yelled. "What the hell is going on?"

Fighting to focus, Nomad took a few deep breaths. Keisha set the shotgun down on the desk, grabbed a tissue, and dabbed at the tears that welled up in the corners of Nomad's eyes.

"I'm guessing the laptop thing worked," Keisha said. "And you found something. Something serious."

"I know the hacker Zhukov hired to find me," Nomad said, and his voice cracked. "His front is a gaming center on the Lower East Side."

"That's good, right?" Keisha asked. "Now, you can use this guy to get back into Moore's system. Right?"

"No," he said, and his head dropped. "That's over. There's no way in now."

Nomad lifted his head, turned back to his console. Within minutes, thousands of zombie computers were waking on the Internet.

"What are you doing?"

"Going to war."

"Hang on," she said. "Let's think this through."

"There's nothing to think about," Nomad said. "Francois's dead, and Alexei set him up. I'm going to destroy him."

"I don't understand," Keisha said. "You told me the guy who murdered Francois was hired by some character calling himself the *Grandmaster*. Are you saying that's Alexei?"

"No, I'm sure the Grandmaster is Moore," Nomad said. "Fits Moore's ego, and the circumstances of Francois's death. But I thought Francois approached Moore directly. It was all Alexei. He put them together. I see it now. When Moore realized Francois had the device, he played on their MIT relationship and the professor's ego. He probably sold the meeting as a chance for Francois to join Moore Technologies in some esteemed capacity."

"But what about Zhukov?" Keisha asked. "How did he know where to go?"

"Alexei. It's all here," Nomad said. "Encrypted correspondence. Digital payments. Everything. He sold his intel to both the Grandmaster and Zhukov."

"So that's it? It's over," Keisha said. "You'll burn this guy, and Moore or this Grandmaster or whoever gets away with killing Francois?"

"What do you want me to do?"

"Stay in the fight, damn it," Keisha said. "I've watched you play chess hundreds of times. Maybe thousands. I've seen you lose, but I've never seen you quit."

"Sure I have," Nomad said. "When you're out of moves, you resign. Tip over the king. Walk away."

"But you're not out of moves," she said. "What about the girl in the photo? If she's half the woman you think she is, she'll help. You'll see. But you have to ask."

"I can't," Nomad said. "I mean. How could I? Not after —"

"Oh, stop whining," Keisha said. "If there's one thing you've taught me, it's that you need to assess the board. The entire board. Look at what you have. You now know that Alexei cashed in on both Zhukov and Moore. Brother, that's gold. On the streets, that kind of double-dealing gets you killed. And I wouldn't want that big Russian coming after me. And I'm guessing Moore won't be too happy to hear that Zhukov tried to beat him to the device. And now you own Alexei's network. Right?

"I do."

"Then don't piss it away. Use it. Stay out of sight. Capture everything he does. Track everyone in his world. Who knows where that might lead?" she said. "But if you take him down now, you'll just tip off both Zhukov and Moore."

"You're right," Nomad said. "And a little scary."

"Damn straight I'm right, and you *should* be scared. I've lost track of the last time you slept, so button this up for now, back away and get to bed," she said. "You've got work to do, and you need to be sharp."

Chapter 43

UNDISCLOSED LOCATION

NOMAD IGNORED KEISHA'S WARNING to get some sleep. Long hours and minimal sleep were part of the game, but he appreciated her igniting his determination. He continued to monitor the Overwatch Nexus network for information or activity that might help his cause. He caught the summary Alexei sent Zhukov and smiled. *They have no idea where I am,* Nomad thought. *And Alexei has no idea I own his network.*

With Alexei under control, Nomad turned his attention to Katherine Preacher. Keisha was right, he thought. I need to give Kate a chance. I need to ask for her help, and make my case, but first...

Nomad sent a flurry of commands, and security camera feeds popped up one by one on a matrix of monitors.

"What are you doing?" Keisha asked. "Whose building is that?"

"That's the Richmond Pinnacle, home to the Richmond Federal Reserve Bank."

"You hacked the Federal Reserve?"

"No," he said. "Just their office building."

"Oh, OK. Just the building. That's a relief," she said. "But you're still going to jail if they catch you."

"Relax. I've been lurking in this network for years."

"At the risk of asking a stupid question, why?"

"Frank, Burman and Dodd."

"Sounds like a mortuary or a law firm."

"Law firm, and that's where..."

"Oh my God," Keisha interrupted. "That's where she works. Isn't it? The girl. You've been spying on her for years."

"I wouldn't call it spying."

"Then how about stalking?"

"I get it," he said. "On the surface, this might look kind of creepy."

"On the surface, underneath and all the way around. It's creepy."

"Well, then, let's just keep this between you and me."

"Who the hell would I tell?"

"Good. Now, can I get back to work?"

"On what? Exactly?" Keisha asked.

"I need Kate's help, but I can't just blurt out what's happening and what's at stake. She'll never believe me. No one would."

"So, your plan is to stalk her?"

"My plan is to do a little reconnaissance. See what she's working on. Maybe I can help, and that would be a way to reconnect."

"You're going about this all wrong."

"What makes you the expert?"

"I'm a woman."

"Fine. I don't know anything about women, but I know this will work," he said.

"I have a bad feeling about this."

"Trust me. It'll work," Nomad said. "I've helped her before. She just didn't know I was pulling strings and opening doors. Besides, I don't even know if she'll go to the office. She may just go home."

"Please tell me you haven't hacked her home."

"Kate locked the house down tight," he said. "She's that good."

"That's not an answer."

CHAPTER 44

SATURDAY, APRIL 18
8:30 PM EDT

RICHMOND JET CENTER, RICHMOND, VA

THE CESSNA CITATION TOUCHED down on runway 2/20 at the Richmond International Airport, and taxied toward the Atlantic Aviation FBO. Kate collected her things and checked the time.

With her single-minded focus on getting Jake to Dover, Kate hadn't thought about how she'd get home. The private jet, courtesy of the Department of Defense, was a surprise and a subtle reminder that Kate was still in the spotlight. *The widow of Le American,* she thought. *By now, millions have seen the Paris attack video, and watched my husband die.*

Kate scanned the tarmac as the jet pivoted and stopped. A town car parked just inside the jet center gate, and the driver stepped out and buttoned his coat. *All clear,* she thought. *No one leaked my arrival to the press, but I have to assume they're camped out at the house.*

With her messenger bag over her shoulder and the small travel duffle in hand, Kate headed for the town car. The driver offered to assist, but Kate waved him off and slid into the back seat. A half-folded newspaper sat on the driver's seat, which he folded and shoved aside, but not before it caught Kate's attention.

"What was that?" she asked.

"Oh, nothing. Sorry, Ma'am."

"It's alright. I'd like to see it."

He handed Kate the newspaper and splashed across the front page was the photo of Jake's coffin and Kate gripping the flag.

"Mrs. Preacher," the driver said. "I'm so sorry for your loss. We all are."

"Thank you."

The driver proceeded through the jet center gates and stopped.

"Would you like me to drive you home? Or perhaps a hotel?"

Kate smiled. *That's kind*, she thought. *They briefed him that home might be difficult.*

"I'm sorry," she said. "I didn't catch your name."

"James, Ma'am."

"James, I need a favor."

"Of course. Anything."

"Let's start with the main terminal parking garage," she said. "I'll show you where to go once we get inside."

Kate directed the driver to the area where Jake parked when flying. They cruised by a few cars until she spotted Jake's Rubicon, and James pulled up in front. Jake always backed the Jeep in tight against the structure's cement wall. *He had a protocol for everything*, she thought. She squeezed in between the wall and the Jeep, crouched down by the trailer hitch safe, and dialed the combination. Out popped the hitch drawer with a spare key and several hundred-dollar bills.

As soon as Kate was sure the Jeep would start, she turned back to James.

"Nice rig," he said, admiring Jake's setup. "Oh, sorry, Ma'am."

"It's alright, James. I swear if there was a pretty girl standing alongside, you boys would stare at the Jeep, and I get it," Kate said. "She's black, bold and beautiful, and there's nowhere she can't go."

Kate pulled her bags from the town car and tossed them on the passenger seat.

"Since she's good to go, I'm fine on my own now. But here's what I'd like you to do," Kate said. "I'd like you to swing by my house. The press is likely to be waiting, and I'd just like you tell them to go home. They will hound and grill you, and for that I'm sorry, but please don't say anything more. Not where you dropped me, and not what I'm driving."

"No problem," he said. "I've got this."

Kate offered him one of the hundred-dollar bills, but he refused.

"No, Mam. I can't take your money, but you can count on me," he said, and offered to shake on it.

"I know I can," she said, and stepped in and gave him a hug.

James drove off on his mission, and Kate climbed up into the front seat. She pulled the Jeep forward about three feet and stopped. *That should be enough,* she thought, and headed for the back. *It would have been nice to swing by the house, take a shower and grab some clothes, but this will have to do.*

Kate thought about what will happen when James shows up, and he was kind to take it on. *The minute he pulls up, they'll go crazy. I hope that when they realize I'm not coming. They'll leave. Fingers crossed.*

Kate lifted the rear glass and swung out the tire carrier and tailgate. Strapped just inside the rear were two small tactical backpacks. One for Jake, the other for Kate. She didn't need the emergency supplies, and she could shower at the office, but a clean set of clothes would help her reboot and focus. She knew trying to recover Jake's data would take all night.

The Jeep's cargo bed held Jake's custom TruckVault. The storage vault spanned the full width of the interior and stood about eight inches high. Kate punched in the combination and slid out the drawer. The EVA foam-lined interior wrapped around an array of Jake's personal defense and executive protection equipment. He had configured the Jeep as a covert mobile armory, and tactical E&E (escape and evasion) vehicle.

The envelope sitting inside was out of place. It had her name on it, but she couldn't imagine why Jake would hide a note.

FARGO

Remember this word!

You'll know when to use it.

There's nothing in here that needs a code, Kate thought. *But Jake knew if I opened the drawer, I'd see it. Makes my head hurt, but easy enough to remember.* She set the envelope aside and dug into the drawer.

Among Jake's firearms, burner phones, communication earwigs, and smoke grenades, Kate found the items she had staged. After a quick scan around the vacant parking floor, Kate grabbed her Glock 43x, checked the chamber, checked the mag, and tucked the appendix holster into her waistband. The IFAK (individual first aid kit) wrapped around her right ankle, and she slipped the rest of her everyday gear into pockets - flashlight, knives, spare mags.

She had geared up this way many times before when training with Jake and the team, but the image of the boy lunging at Talya was haunting. *Would I have seen it coming,* she wondered. *If I was on that carpet, would I be standing here now?* Somewhere deep inside, she was confident the answer was yes.

Kate's evolution from desk-bound CIA Analyst and digital forensics expert toward Skilled Operator was an ongoing journey. The first thing she learned was training never ends, but it began when Jake was released from the hospital. At his grandfather's cabin, deep in the West Virgina mountains, Jake rebuilt his body and wrapped his mind around life with one leg. In the process, he trained and drilled Kate like a SEAL. She loved the challenge and discovered Jake's path to recovery and rehab was hers, too. She learned to accept her scars and face her demons. Kate would never be a victim, not again.

She wasn't tested in Paris, but Kate couldn't shake the feeling that Paris was just the beginning, and she needed to be ready. *Whatever Jake was doing, whatever he found, he thought it might get him killed. He thought it was safer to keep me in the dark.* Kate closed and locked the TruckVault. *He was wrong. So, it's my mission now, and I will do whatever it takes. Starting with his NanoVault and the puzzle he asked me to solve.*

CHAPTER 45

SATURDAY, APRIL 18
8:55 PM EDT

RICHMOND PINNACLE BUILDING, RICHMOND, VA

KATE EXPECTED THE PINNACLE building would be empty, but wasn't sure until she pulled into the parking lot. She often worked on the weekends and evenings, especially when Jake was traveling. She was friendly with a few of the other night owls in the building, and thankful she wouldn't see them tonight.

She backed the Jeep into a visitor parking spot directly in front of the main doors. *Always back in*, she thought, and considered possible exits. *Leave enough room to back up and ram my way out, or reverse over the edge and down through the landscaping.* After a while, Jake's protocols just came naturally. He had a method and a reason for everything, and now they were second nature, but with Jake gone, she found the little things he taught her comforting. *Jake would be proud.*

The security guard monitored the vehicle's approach, realized it was Kate and greeted her at the door.

"Thanks, Pete," she said. He held the door as she stepped inside, then locked it behind her.

"Oh Kate," he said. "Broke our hearts to hear about Jake. How are you holding up?"

"Honestly, Pete, I don't know. Right now it's just one foot in front of the other."

"When Jake would come by, he always took time to say hello and ask how I was doing. And asked like he really wanted to know. And my how you two glowed. Like me and the Mrs."

"Linda's well?"

"She's better, but sad," he said. "We all are. It's all over the news, of course, Jake being a hero and all, but I can't bring myself to watch."

Kate knew that Pete, a retired Marine, wrestled with his own demons, and the last thing he needed was to be thrust back into the middle of an urban war zone.

"Don't," Kate said. "There's nothing to be gained," and they hugged.

Pete reached for a handkerchief and dabbed at his nose. "Didn't expect I'd see you here. Not for a while. And thought, maybe never."

"I wondered the same thing," Kate said. "But I have some unfinished business, and not much time. It could be a long night."

"If you need anything, you let me know."

"I do need a favor. I came straight from the airport, and don't have my keycard. Would you mind scanning me in and unlocking the elevator?"

"Sure thing," he said, and waved his badge across the entry turnstile. "There you go."

The two of them headed for the elevators. Kate pressed the up-arrow, the doors opened, and Pete reached inside. Several of the floors were access controlled, and the law firm was one of them. With a wave of his badge, the top floor lit up. But Kate held the door for a moment.

"Is anyone up there?"

"This time of night?" Pete asked. "Just me 'til 3:00. Otherwise, the building's all yours. Again, I'm real sorry, Kate."

"Thanks, Pete. Please, give my love to Linda."

Chapter 46

SATURDAY, APRIL 18
9:10 PM EDT

RICHMOND PINNACLE BUILDING, RICHMOND, VA

KATE'S RETURN TO THE offices of Frank, Burman and Dodd was more difficult than she imagined. The last time she had stepped off the elevator, she and Leslie Dodd were celebrating a major victory. Kate forced a crook to resign. They would soon reunite an innocent woman with her son. And Jake was about to call from Paris.

The office was dark except for pathway and exit lighting. Kate stepped behind the reception desk and logged into the office automation system. Moments later, lights flashed in the lobby, along the hallway, and in the common rooms. *That's better*, she thought, and headed for the break-room. *Brew some coffee, take a shower, recover Jake's files.*

The shower helped, and Kate knew the coffee would do its part, but entering her office was a leap back in time. Papers and photos from her desk littered the floor. In a flash she was in that moment, screaming Jake's name, her arms flailing, the desktop items flying in every direction. In the center of the room lay a pile of her office clothes, and that's where she began. She collected the skirt and blouse, and recalled Leslie's face. *I'm not sure what Leslie found most shocking,* Kate thought. *My scars or my holster.*

Gathering the papers was easy. Nothing from before held any importance now, so she just scooped them up. She avoided looking at the photos, and just slid them out of the way, and she didn't think twice about the desk calendar until it was in her hand. She filled the page on top with nearly two weeks of crossed-out dates marking Jake's departure and tracking his progress toward the day circled in red.

Oh my God, she thought. *April 24th. I'm burying my husband on our anniversary.*

When Major Carter said Arlington was ready for Jake, it was just a week from today. Just a day, not a date. Kate sat on the floor, pulled the calendar to her chest and wept. Carter warned her, *'this is how it is'* she said. *'It springs up from deep inside, and often when you least expect.'*

She hugged the calendar, closed her eyes and rocked back and forth. An image formed in her mind. She was at her desk when Jake's video chat rang through on her tablet. *He's relaxed. Smiling. Espresso in hand. He's meeting Marcus for lunch, and joking about being home for our anniversary. I reminded him of the score. If he made it, that would be two out of five.*

"Enough." She stood, wiped her eyes, and addressed the ghost in the room. "I know what you'd say. Stay in the fight. Work the problem."

Kate's forensic workstation sprang to life, and she retrieved the Faraday bag. Holding the small, black envelope, she pictured the device inside. *Jake's NanoVault. Bought the night before he...*

"Jake, what the hell were you working on? Why did you keep me in the dark?" She didn't expect a response, but still she waited.

"Fine. I'm sick of nothing but questions. Time to get some answers," she said. "Given what happened on the flight, I need to put a leash on this thing. If this device was responsible, I can't risk it corrupting my lab, or worse, the firm's network."

It took time to enable all the safeguards, but she needed to be confident there was no way out. She couldn't be sure Jake's device could transmit, but she didn't believe in coincidence and the timing was hard to ignore. Now, with guardrails in place, if the NanoVault tried to connect or transmit beyond her lab, she was ready to trap the signal and record the data.

Kate pulled the device from the electronic isolation of the Faraday bag and rolled it over in her fingertips. *There's a little residue, but nothing fresh,* she thought. *Let's hope that's the end of it, and I can still connect.*

She played Jake's video in her mind. She saw the chain around his neck, the NanoVault and the silver cross together in his hand. *"Find this,"* he said. *"Do your thing. See what I missed. Work the problem. Solve the puzzle. And take them down."*

"OK, you little bastard," she said, talking directly to Jake's NanoVault. "Let's do this."

The device instantly paired with her workstation.

"You're in my world now. Nowhere to run. Nowhere to hide. If you've got something to say, let's hear it."

CHAPTER 47

SATURDAY, APRIL 18
9:30 PM EDT

UNDISCLOSED LOCATION

NOMAD FEARED HIS PURSUERS were gaining ground, and over Keisha's objections, he pushed his mind and body well beyond their limits. Exhausted, he slumped over in his chair. The physical restraints kept him from crashing to the floor, and there he slept.

The system monitors tracking activity at Richmond Pinnacle sounded the alarm and brought Keisha into the control room. Nomad was out cold. He woke to the chirping sound of the alarm and Keisha's stethoscope pressed against his chest.

"What are you doing?" he asked.

"Thinking about what I'm gonna do when you're dead."

"What?" Nomad asked and fought his way back to consciousness.

"You fell asleep in your chair. Again," she said. "But when I couldn't wake you, I got scared."

Nomad spotted the drop of dried blood on his fingertip.

"You poked me?"

"I did, and you didn't move a muscle. Your blood sugar's fine, by the way, but I thought for sure you crashed. Now, will you please silence that incessant noise while I get some aspirin?"

"I don't need any aspirin."

"I'm the one with the headache," Keisha said. "That damn alarm's been ringing for the last ten minutes."

Nomad silenced the alarm and checked the Richmond Pinnacle building logs. The elevator went to the top floor, Kate's floor, and that's what triggered his alarm. He grabbed the elevator camera feed.

"Let's have a look."

Keisha peered over his shoulder. In the live feed, the elevator was empty, so he rolled the timeline back about twenty minutes, and saw Kate heading up.

"That's odd," he said. "It's Kate."

"This is good, right?" Keisha asked. "She's there."

"Yes, but how did she enter the building?"

"What difference does it make? She's there."

"That's obvious," Nomad said. "But how did she get in without tripping my alerts? The second she used her keycard, I should have known."

Nomad pulled up the lobby security camera. The guard was sitting behind his station, feet up, munching on a sandwich. He focused on something below the counter, possibly the security monitors, but given his expression and rapt attention, Nomad suspected some sporting event.

With the timeline slider, Nomad drilled back about twenty-five minutes and watched. He saw the guard get up from his desk, approach the front door, and Kate stepped into view.

"Here she comes," Keisha said.

Kate and the guard talked for a few minutes, then hugged. The guard used his badge to walk Kate through the entry turnstile, and then to the elevators. Nomad watched the guard hold the elevator door with one hand while the other reached in.

"Kate, what are you up to?"

"So she forgot her card or badge or whatever," Keisha said. "What's the big deal?"

"Something's up," Nomad said. "Kate doesn't want anyone to know she's in the building."

"The old guy knows."

"No one on the *outside*, and now there's no digital record of her entering the building."

Nomad returned to the live feed of the security cameras and created a matrix of views of the lobby, elevators, and Kate's floor.

She must already be in her office, he thought, and activated her PC's video conference camera. Kate's face filled one of Nomad's monitors.

"She showered and changed," Keisha said

"She did?"

"Seriously?" Keisha asked. "She's wearing different clothes. Her hair's wet and slicked back into a ponytail. And she's been crying."

"I can see that."

"Oh good. I never know with you," Keisha said, packed her medical bag and turned to leave. "Whatever you do now, please try not to creep her out. The poor thing's been through enough."

Nomad's virtual world sprang to life. Monitors filled with code and streamed past in a blur. He pivoted his chair from station to station and tracked the system's responses to his commands.

Kate took a long, slow sip from a chipped BlackHat conference mug. *Wow, she still has it,* he thought. *No. Can't be the same one. That was ten years ago.* He gazed into Kate's eyes. Even he could feel the sadness, but there was something else. *I know that look. I've faced it,* he thought, recalling a brutal chess match beating. *That's Kate's battle face. Someone is going down.*

Nomad's system hijack code lay dormant, undetectable, waiting. He executed the last of his wake-up commands and gained complete control of Kate's office lab. Another monitor lit up with a mirror image of Kate's desktop. Everything on her screen, every mouse movement or key press reflected on Nomad's monitor.

He launched a scan for any other devices he could intercept and control. Kate's iPad connected to the office network. *Got it.* Her phone was next. *I'm in.* Nomad was now in complete control. Whatever happened now, whatever Kate was working on, he would soon know.

Alright, Kate. Let's see it. What are you hiding?

CHAPTER 48

UNDISCLOSED LOCATION

FOR OVER AN HOUR, Nomad sat in silence watching Kate make meticulous network configuration changes. She launched a variety of standard network traffic monitors and recorders, but the SIGINT (signals intelligence tools) spooked him.

Could she know I'm monitoring, he wondered. *That's some serious tech she's running, some of which she must have liberated from the Agency.*

Nomad remained confident his presence would remain undetected, but this configuration was way outside Kate's normal work flow. *I missed something*, he thought. *Let's have a look.* He flipped the video back to where Kate appeared to begin working and watched in slow motion. Kate was typing, then reached for something. A small black envelope was visible in the frame's corner, so small it didn't catch his eye in the real-time feed.

"Hello there," he said. "What do we have here?"

"You're talking to yourself again," Keisha said.

"You don't have to listen," he said and returned to the video and began voicing commands. "Pause. Crop. Lower right quadrant."

The screen filled with an image of Kate's hand and a corner of the black envelope.

"Play. One quarter speed."

The video started again, and he watched Kate remove something from the bag.

"Pause."

"Is that one of those devices?" Keisha asked.

"Isn't there something on TV you could watch?"

"Well, let's see. There's a new show about a brainiac geek hunted by a psychopath or two. His old flame is grieving for her dead husband, and the geek's gorgeous private nurse is standing guard with a shotgun. That sounds interesting."

"Gorgeous?"

"Geez. That's the part you're hung up on?" Keisha asked. "Just go back to work."

"Well," he said. "You're right. It's a Quantum NanoVault, an Onyx model."

"Zoom. One-hundred-fifty. Pan. Right. Hmm."

"What?" she asked.

"It might be damaged. See that black stuff?"

"Oh, I recognize it," Keisha said. "All the devices you destroyed made quite the mess. Thank you very much."

"That's bad," he said. "There's probably nothing left on it, but Kate seems determined to have a look."

"What if it's his?"

"Whose?"

"Her husband's, you dolt. You may be a genius, but sometimes I wonder about you."

He caught the look Keisha threw at him. "My husband's been dead twenty years, but if I thought there was a chance, I could see his face or hear his voice…"

Nomad heard the crack in Keisha's voice. She never talked about her husband, and he realized he never asked.

Keisha took a minute, cleared her throat, and said, "I'm just saying. If it's his, it's precious."

"It's likely to be wiped clean," he said, and issued another system command. "Live feed."

All the monitors linked to Kate's office refreshed with the real-time video stream.

"She's working hard on something," Keisha said, and they could hear Kate's fingers dancing on the keyboard.

Nomad scanned all the data sources in Kate's office. Her workstation was the only device linked to the NanoVault, and moments later, the file directory popped up on Kate's screen.

"That's surprising," Nomad said. "She might have a chance. The directory's corrupt, but it's not a total loss. There's obvious damage, but the data may still be accessible."

"Is it his?"

"I can't tell for sure. Most of the filenames are cryptic. Just dates. Places," he said. They both watched Kate scroll through the list of folders, then stop.

"It's his," Keisha said, staring at the folder Kate selected. The name was corrupted but was still obvious.

K%@e

Kate tried, but it wouldn't open. She closed the error screen and launched a suite of file recovery tools.

"Can you help her?" Keisha asked.

"Not yet. She's doing everything I would do, and she's the forensic expert. But if this fails, I'll have something to offer, and we can help each other."

"Like you and Francois?"

"Yes."

"Will you tell her?"

"Oh sure," he said. "Hey, Kate. You remember Francois, our chess team mentor? We found something that could help you get Jake's files, but using it, got Francois killed."

"Be serious."

"I am. It's different this time. I promise," Nomad said. "I can protect her."

"I think you believe that," Keisha said. "I just hope it's true."

"But one thing still bothers me."

"Only one?"

"You said something this important would be precious."

"Absolutely."

"So why did Kate spend over an hour configuring network monitoring tools before she even tried to read it?"

"How long has it been?" Keisha asked.

"One hour, thirty-seven minutes, and 42 seconds."

"Don't get smart with me. I'm just checking on you and her."

"I'm good," he said.

"And Kate? Is she making any progress?"

"No. But it's stunning to watch her work. Brilliant mind," he said. "I still have no idea why all the precautions or what she thought might happen. Literally zero network activity worth capturing."

"If she's as smart as you say, she has a reason, so stay sharp."

"*Carpe noctem*," he said and smiled. "The night is when I do my best work, but it's late. If you're going to pester me in the morning, you better get some sleep, but do me a favor."

"What?"

"Don't sleep with that shotgun."

Keisha marched off in a huff and mumbled something under her breath. Nomad was still grinning when he turned back to the monitors, and his smile vanished. All he could see was the top of Kate's head, but she was crying and the mic captured a few voice fragments between the tears.

"I'm sorry, Jake," she said, and sobbed. "I've tried everything. Nothing worked. I can't open the files. I have no idea what you were doing, why you thought it was dangerous, or what puzzle you hoped I could solve."

Nomad listened to Kate talking to Jake, trying to explain, while struggling with renewed grief. Another devastating loss. The catalyst for the tears was staring Nomad in the face. He could see the NanoVault's directory structure had degraded even further. The folder names that were readable when Kate started were now random gibberish.

He didn't know what she meant when she said 'dangerous' or 'puzzle' — like Keisha, Nomad assumed recovering the NanoVault's contents was personal, one last chance to connect with Jake. *It's something more,* he thought. *Much more. That's why she covered her tracks, hid her arrival at the building, and wrapped the device in layers of security. She knows something or suspects it.*

"There's nothing more I can do," Kate said, but the crying stopped as suddenly as it began.

Kate lifted her head and started typing. *She has an idea,* he thought, and watched her work with a hint of envy. He hadn't been able to move that fast in so long he'd forgotten the exhilaration that comes with that mind-body connection.

Nomad watched Kate jump from her Windows desktop to a whonix virtual machine, and with her anonymity ensured, she launched the Tor browser. "Could she be..." he wondered out loud, afraid to finish the sentence. *Wait for it,* he thought. *We'll know soon enough.*

Kate was browsing deep within the Darknet. The obscure world frightened most, and for good reason. But it was clearly second-nature to Kate. The Darknet was Nomad's world and home to an eclectic mix of personalities and personas, and every facet of human existence, from the most noble to the most malevolent. Everyone was anonymous as they entered, and if you knew what you were doing, you could stay that way.

Nomad held his breath as Kate typed in the onion domain of his private service. She authenticated using the persona she'd created years ago.

The solid black screen had a single, flashing prompt.

Mockingbird>_

"Come on Kate," Nomad said. "Say something. Anything."

Kate began to type.

Mockingbird>Nomad, are you there?

"Good. Now, just hit enter."

She deleted the question.

"No. No. No," he said, but she started typing again.

Mockingbird>I'm sorry about how things ended, but after Syria, I...

Nomad waited and hoped, but Kate stopped typing. *I've lost her.*

CHAPTER 49

RICHMOND PINNACLE BUILDING, RICHMOND VA

KATE'S HANDS TREMBLED AND floated just above the keyboard.

Mockingbird>I'm sorry about how things ended, but after Syria, I...

She stared at the prompt on the screen and struggled to collect her thoughts and finish the message, but she couldn't. Nomad, the asset Kate recruited for the Agency, was at the center of unimaginable suffering. The memories she tried not to face came crashing in on her. Kate pressed a hand against the raised scar tissue that criss-crossed her neck, breasts and abdomen.

Kate closed her eyes, and she was back in Syria. She saw the face of the sweet young woman, the interpreter, who lured her away from the CIA compound.

There was sorrow and guilt in the woman's eyes. *They have my children. And promised you would not be harmed.*

Assad's men, from the ruthless Al-Shammar tribe, slit the woman's throat. Kate was forced to watch, and at that moment, she knew the woman's children were already dead. The interpreter was just a pawn. Expendable.

The hood over her face and the rifle-butt strike to the side of her head left Kate dazed and drowning in a world of black. She woke on the floor of a vehicle moving at high speed. Her hands and feet bound, and she struck the floor again and again as the vehicle bounced over ruts in the desert road. And the kidnapping was only the beginning.

Kate jumped when her network alarms sounded. The tools she'd configured as a safety precaution flooded her screen with pop-up alerts, beeps and whistles. She silenced the alarms, closed the connection to the Dark Web, and focused all of her attention on Jake's NanoVault.

"So it was you," she said, glancing at the device. "Been playing dead all this time?"

She'd been working for hours, and there was no sign the NanoVault had any kind of communication capabilities beyond pairing with her computer. That illusion lay shattered, and Kate tracked and recorded the transmission.

It's like a rat stuck in a maze, she thought, watching the traffic monitors. *It's smashing into every roadblock I set, then it morphs and tries another route.* Kate watched in amazement. *I've never seen anything like it. The signal is polymorphic and determined to escape. No wonder it crashed into everything on the flight from Paris.*

Confident she had the burst contained, Kate investigated the transmission packets. *Looks like a single encrypted message repeated in every packet,* she thought. *And given the state of the device, the message might be damaged.*

Kate extracted the repeating characters from the data stream and pasted the string into her suite of decryption protocols. *I won't hold my breath,* she thought. *This could take days, and that's only IF the message isn't corrupt.*

With her world quiet again, Kate thought about returning to the Darknet. *I still need help,* she thought. *And the broadcast is a sign. The NanoVault has power, and there's enough of the OS still intact that it woke up and tried to communicate. And if anyone can resurrect this thing, it's Nomad.*

Kate was about to reconnect with Nomad's server, when a single word kicked out from the decryption software. She stared at the screen. *What the hell? That can't be right. Not that fast,* she thought. *It must have grabbed something from system memory.* She closed the application and tried again. Moments later. Same result. One Word.

The decryption tool cranked on in the background, pegging Kate's processor as it struggled to reveal more of the message, but she couldn't take her eyes off the screen. Sitting in the decryption result window was the word:

Kate's

With the success of the first word, Kate hoped the rest of the message wouldn't be far behind, and she stayed glued to the screen. The longer it took, the more she worried the message was damaged, and what she had was too little to draw any kind of conclusion, but she could speculate. Her gift for languages, a skill she attributes to her birth-mother's childhood lessons, proved to be useful to the Agency. And linguistic pattern analysis could reveal intent and motive. When you're tracking terrorists, every clue matters.

Kate considered what she knew. This single word revealed one thing, the apostrophe was possessive. *It's Jake's device, so it's reasonable to assume I'm the subject of the message,* Kate thought. *So, it's about something I have or something I am.*

CHAPTER 50

UNDISCLOSED LOCATION

THE SOUND OF NETWORK alarms sent Nomad scrambling to capture everything appearing on Kate's workstation. Kate struggled to contain and understand what she was seeing, but Nomad knew exactly what happened. While analysts, academics and hackers tackled the NanoVault head-on, Nomad took an entirely unique path toward securing Moore's Bitcoin bounty.

He failed, but what Nomad discovered was far more valuable and insidious. He discovered the NanoVault's firmware core used worm code he wrote years ago, at MIT. And with his code, everything the devices were meant to safeguard was being transmitted to Devin Moore and archived at Moore Technologies.

Nomad was speechless. If he hadn't seen it, he would never have believed. But there it was. Kate's device had an open communications channel. A direct link into Moore's data collection architecture. He and Francois worked for months, and destroyed hundreds of NanoVaults trying to breach the device's nearly imperceptible covert communication channel. Their success was fleeting.

Francois was dead, and the method they discovered was so challenging that Nomad couldn't repeat it, not alone.

When Nomad couldn't contain his wonder any longer, he called out to Keisha.

"You've got to come see this," he yelled down the hall. *She'd hasn't been gone that long,* he thought. *She can't be asleep.*

Keisha came down the hall, her flip-flops smacking the cement floor. The old vertical parking structure was an ideal environment for Nomad's chair-bound world. The nondescript structure offered smooth mobility between floors, privacy and security, but the cold, hard floors were unforgiving.

"Did she recover Jake's files?" Keisha asked, and rubbed her eyes.

"Better," Nomad said. "She opened a channel."

"That thing you and Francois did?"

"Exactly. I don't know how, but I'm staring right at it. This one's different, but that's good. Moore may not have seen it."

"I doubt Kate will share your enthusiasm."

"That's only because she doesn't know what's at stake," he said. "If she did, she'd understand. She had her pick of six-figure jobs, but she chose the CIA. You don't join the CIA if you don't care."

"That was then. This is now. And right now, her husband's memories are the only thing she cares about," Keisha said. "Will this channel-thing help you get them back for her?"

"No. Well, maybe, but probably not," he said.

I can't risk it, he thought. *I won't have much time, and I'll only have one shot...if I'm lucky.*

"What's she doing now?"

"She's capturing the data. That's smart. She doesn't know what's happening or why, and it really doesn't matter," Nomad said. "All she knows is that it's coming from Jake's device, and that makes it important. That makes it hers."

"But it's all gobbledygook."

"It's encrypted and could be corrupt."

"Will she be able to read it?"

"Some of it, given enough time and processing power."

"And you could help with that, right?"

"I can, and it may even prompt her to reach back out," he said. "She was just about to contact me when her system alarms went crazy."

"Now you tell me?" Keisha asked. "That's huge."

"It didn't happen, so it wasn't worth mentioning."

"Still, that had to feel pretty good. She needs help, and in spite of whatever happened in the past, she thought of you."

Keisha was right. Nomad imagined reconnecting with Kate. He could reveal his identity, express his sorrow and regret for what happened in Syria, and hope for her forgiveness. He carved out a lucrative life in the digital world, but it was still a prison.

Nomad dodged Keisha's efforts to get him to open up and focused on the task at hand.

"I need to concentrate now," he said.

"Alright. I know that's code for go back to bed," she said. "I'll be praying you both find some peace."

Nomad injected the first slice of his code into Jake's data and waited for the delivery confirmation. He needed to be sure it reached Moore's network.

Nothing. She's got it locked down too tight, he thought. *For this to work, I need to change that.*

With his stealth-mode access and control over Kate's lab, he began making network configuration changes. She might detect the modifications, so it forced him to crawl through the process.

"Done, and gone!" he said. The first slice of his code was on its way into Moore's system. Once all the code was in place, he'd assemble and execute, and it would be over. Everything Moore collected would be gone, irretrievable. *Including Jake's files*, he thought. *But there's no choice.*

Again, Nomad waited, but the confirmation never came. *It's blocked. Moore must have spotted the anomaly and blocked it. So what now?*

It was pointless to try again. It wasn't an error, but between hopelessness and desperation, he hit send and waited.

"Are you freaking kidding?" he said out loud when he saw the delivery confirmation. "I don't know what just happened, but it's game on. Let's go."

Nomad seized the moment. He packaged, inserted, and sent the rest of his code, slice by slice, over the next twenty minutes. With each transmission, he waited. Each confirmation brought higher expectations. *If this works, I won't need to involve Kate.* Then nothing. He sent again, and again, but it was pointless. The window was closed. He failed. Again.

He fought back tears. The roller-coaster of emotions from Francois's death to another defeat was exhausting. He was running out of time, energy, and options.

I'm sorry, Kate, Nomad thought. *I hoped it wouldn't come to this, but I can't do it alone. Not with these hands. If I'm going to stop Moore, you'll need to take Francois's place. I know you can do it, and you're the only one I trust with my life.*

CHAPTER 51

SATURDAY, APRIL 18
11:12 PM EDT

MOORE TOWER, MANHATTAN, NY

ANDREW FREEMAN WOKE TO a high-pitched wailing that echoed through his bedroom, and he jumped out of bed like his condo was on fire. In the darkness, he fumbled for his phone and knocked it to the floor. *It's back,* he thought. *And Moore will be pissed if I don't catch it this time.*

The NanoVault he tracked over the North Atlantic ocean was back online and tripped his alarms. He hoped it would stay on line long enough this time for him to nail down the location and capture the transmission. *I don't dare tell Moore until I know for sure.*

Drew pressed his feet into a pair of UGG slippers and headed for the door. Dressed in gray sweatpants and a vintage MIT T-shirt, he dashed out the door and down the hallway. The reverberations of the alarm still echoed in his ears, the soles of his slippers smacked against the tile floor.

At the elevator, he jammed the up button again and again. "Come on. Come on. Let's go." After what felt like an eternity, the doors opened, and he waved his access card over the sensor pad, and headed up to the Moore Technologies main floor. Devin had a private entrance hidden in his office, but Drew's entrance was on the floor below. The data center and control room sat behind a six-inch-thick vault door, equipped with both retinal and palm scanners. Drew thought the security excessive at first, but as he built out Moore's vision, he grew to enjoy the power at his fingertips and appreciate the absolute need for secrecy.

He cleared the system alarm and confirmed it was the same NanoVault device ID. The first hit on the location scan came back in moments later. North America. *Good*, he thought. *It's on land.* The more specific the location, the longer it would take, and he thought about alerting Moore. He considered tracking Moore's location or even eavesdropping on the Diamond NanoVault he was wearing, but knew the boss would have his head if he found out. *The Petrov twins! I can do a GPS ping. And at least see where they are.*

A quick check on the GPS coordinates turned up The Standard Hotel. The Top of The Standard, known to most as The Boom Boom Room, was the hot spot for invite-only events. Drew pictured Moore and the twins, laughing, drinking, and dancing among the stars. Now it was even more tempting to listen in, but his curiosity would have to wait. He would satisfy his voyeurism much later when he would have time to edit the logs and hide his tracks.

Signals from the mystery device were sporadic but narrowed down along state lines. He was confident the origin was somewhere in Virginia. *Time to call. I think.* But Drew hesitated. *He won't be happy. But waiting will only make it worse.*

CHAPTER 52

SATURDAY, APRIL 18
11:37 PM EDT

THE BOOM BOOM ROOM, THE STANDARD HOTEL,
MANHATTAN, NY

DEVIN MOORE WAS HOLDING court from a plush, white booth that hugged the back wall of The Boom. He let his bow tie hang loose around his neck and looked even more the brash, charismatic figure. The Petrov twins sat alongside, each vying for Devin's attention between celebrity visitors that stopped to chat.

Adriana's hand moved to Devin's chest. Her fingers traced the crisp edge of the shirt's placket, then with a subtle, teasing gesture, she slipped a finger in the narrow gap between the overlapping fabric.

Natalia's fingers curled around Devin's knee with an affectionate squeeze. Her touch ventured upward and veered toward his inner thigh.

"Can I interest you ladies in a nightcap?" Devin asked, and their coy smiles answered, but before he could stand, Drew was whispering into the earwig tucked deep in Moore's ear.

"I'm sorry, Mr. Moore, but I knew you would want to know right away," Drew began. "It's back."

"What's back?" Devin asked. "And speak up. It's hard to hear you over the music."

"The device broadcasting in the clear," Drew said. "The NanoVault I tracked over the North Atlantic. It's back online and trying to connect."

Moore stood, knocking Adriana to the floor, and cell phones sprang into action.

"You're sure?" Moore asked, but he already knew the answer. *Dilbert wouldn't dare call*, he thought. *If he wasn't absolutely certain.*

"Do you have a location this time?"

"Yes. Virginia," Drew said. "I'm still narrowing down the exact coordinates."

"What's taking so long?"

"The device must be damaged. Whatever's wrong is messing with the signal, or it's partially shielded."

"Shielded? If that's true, we have a bigger problem."

"I don't understand."

"Just get me an exact location. I'm on my way."

Devin reached into his jacket lapel pocket, found the quarter-size disk clipped to the fabric and squeezed. Two tall, lean men with close cropped haircuts appeared within seconds. In bespoke suits, they could easily be mistaken for guests, but both were part of Moore's personal security detail.

"You. Have the Rolls take the Petrov sisters wherever they want to go, and with whomever they choose, at my expense. But stay close and collect those necklaces in the morning."

"Yes, sir," he replied and he ushered the twins away, shielding Devin from the Petrov's flurry of Russian curses.

"And you," Devin said, addressing the remaining guard. "Alert the team we're leaving. Now."

"Destination, sir?"

"Straight back to the Tower," he said, and headed for the elevators. "And get a team on the way to Virginia."

"Mission scope, sir?"

"Recovery and sanitation," Moore said. "Location and objectives provided en route."

CHAPTER 53

MOORE TOWER, MANHATTAN, NY

DEVIN MOORE ENTERED THE control room and found Drew hard at work. Noting Drew's choice of sleepwear, he was confident Drew was alone when the alarm sounded.

"Perfect timing," Drew said. "I have an address. Richmond Pinnacle, Richmond, Virginia."

"I know it," Moore said. "Something like twenty floors of offices, and the Federal Reserve."

"I'll have the exact floor and business in a minute."

"What changed?" Devin asked. "You thought the intermittent connection was blocking the GPS data."

"I think it was shielded, and now it's not," Drew said. "That's the only explanation that makes sense."

"You're confident that whoever has the device is aware the device is broadcasting."

"Makes sense. Otherwise, why try to block it?" Drew said. "Bingo! The device is on the eighteenth floor, a law firm. Frank —"

"Frank, Burman and Dodd."

"You know them?"

"Yes, I'm a client," Devin said. "And now I know who has the device."

Devin grabbed his phone and launched the BountyHunt app. He connected with a thumb print scan, selected a game already in progress and began typing commands. With a team already on the way to Virginia, he just needed to pass along the address for the Richmond Pinnacle and update the mission parameters.

This was a Recovery and Sanitize protocol mission. Devin described the Onyx Series NanoVault to be recovered and added instructions to secure and seal the device in a Faraday bag. Then he described his former MIT Chess Teammate, Katherine Preacher, five-foot-six, auburn hair, hazel eyes, one-hundred-twenty pounds. On target acquisition, silence and sanitize the location.

"So, who works there?" Drew asked.

"Do you remember Katherine Preacher?"

"She's hard to forget," Drew said. "I know she's the reason we won the PamAm trophy, but playing against her was brutal. I mean, checkmate in ten moves. I've never been so embarrassed."

"Preacher does the digital forensic work for the firm and has for several years now. Don't ask me why," Devin said. "We've crossed paths a few times, but when I couldn't lure her away, I stopped trying."

"You think she knows —"

"She might," Devin interrupted. "And I can't take any chances. Not now. Not when we're so close."

"I remember she and Pryce were joined at the hip," Drew said, recalling his former roommate and their freshman year at MIT. "Well, until the accident. Then she pretty much just kept to herself."

"Focus on the device, and let me know if it disconnects," Moore said, and he checked the time. "It won't be long now."

"Long for what?"

"Just let me know if anything changes."

"I almost forgot. I captured the body of the transmission."

"You did? How?"

"I cleared a path through to the scrubbers."

"You let it in?"

"Yeah, but —"

"Shut it down. Shut it down. Now!"

Drew scrambled to change the network parameters as fast as possible, and the faster he typed, the more mistakes he made, until finally he stopped and threw his hands in the air.

"Done," Drew said. "But I don't know why you're alarmed. The scrubbers examine every byte flowing in, and there was absolutely nothing malicious."

"Would you bet your life on it?" Devin asked. "Because you just bet mine."

"I was only trying to help," Drew said, looking and sounding like a scolded puppy. "Earlier today you asked if I captured any of the message, and seemed disappointed that I hadn't. I thought this is what you wanted."

"You're right, Drew," Devin said. "But the situation has changed. The stakes are higher, and until I'm certain Nomad is out of the picture, we're vulnerable. Any progress on Nomad's location?"

"I'm still peeling the onion. One layer at a time," Drew said. "But there's no way to know how deep the rabbit hole goes."

"And Zhukov?"

"Mr. Moshenski's jet will be arriving soon, and Mr. Zhukov will be meeting the flight."

"Good. That will keep both of them out of my hair for a few hours. Long enough to make this disappear," Devin said. "And Drew, this never happened. Not a word. To anyone. Ever. Understood?"

"Absolutely," Drew said. "My lips are sealed."

Devin watched Drew pretend to lock his mouth and toss the key. *What a paradox,* he thought. *Brilliant in so many ways. A complete idiot in others, but the NanoVault wouldn't exist without Drew's code.* An alert on Moore's phone captured his attention. Mission ETA 10 minutes.

He slipped his tuxedo jacket over the back of a workstation chair. The custom Recaro Sportster seat looked like it belonged in the cockpit of a fighter jet. Moore sank into the deep bucket shape and placed his left hand on the scanner. A pale green light passed from top to bottom. Multiple monitors ignited in front of him. He slipped an ear piece and mic over his right ear, and with a voice print authorization, he was in. Unlimited access to the central brain of his entire operation was now at his fingertips.

"Inquiry," he said "Richmond Pinnacle building, Richmond, Virgina"

With a single command, the monitors filled with a high-level overview of the building. Photos. Schematics. Occupants. He could take subsequent inquiries in any direction he desired. Everything within his grasp was sourced from his NanoVaults and the networks, computers, phones, and tablets his devices had infiltrated.

Moore navigated through the maze of data until he found his targets, the building's security camera service contractor, and building's head of IT. With detailed dossiers populating the monitors, it took less than a minute to log into the building's security cameras and configure one of his monitors with a direct feed of the lobby camera. *A single aging guard, probably half-asleep. I trust that won't be much of a problem.*

A few minutes later, he was digging through the profile of Mark Wilson, the building's head of IT. The cameras were trivial to access. Vendors often use the same credentials for every client, and all the service techs have them. It only took one careless tech to capture the password, but Wilson was a bit more scrupulous in his security procedures. *Alright Mark,* Devin thought. *Everyone makes mistakes. Where's yours? Ding. Ding. Ding. We have a winner. Thanks for playing.*

With Mark's credentials in hand, Devin logged in remotely to the building's automation, and did a quick review of what was within his reach. Thermostats. Phones. Lighting. Elevators.

Won't be long now, Devin thought. *I'll just sit back and watch the show.*

Chapter 54

UNDISCLOSED LOCATION

Keisha was right, Nomad thought. *I am a stalker. Watching Kate work, listening to conversations with Jake. Wondering what my life could have been if I hadn't been so stupid.*

Nomad watched Kate push the keyboard back on her desk, cross her arms like a pillow, and rest her head. There was nothing she could do now but wait. Her decryption algorithms were grinding in the background, trying to decipher the rest of Jake's message, and Nomad wrestled with how to make contact.

He knew Kate would be furious if she discovered he was already in her system, watching everything she did. Even he realized that was an unforgivable breach of trust and personal space, but there was no turning back the clock. The only chance he had of keeping that secret was for Kate to contact him. *I could help decrypt Jake's message*, he thought. *And even suggest that I might be able to retrieve the files from his device. That's not a lie. Just not likely. Then I'd ask for her help too. That could work. It seems plausible, but she needs to get back on the server and send that message.*

Kate stirred, lifted her head off the desk, and yawned. She checked for anything from the decryption process, but there was still just the one word. Nomad prayed this was the moment. *Come on Kate. You need my help. Please, just ask for it.*

Nomad glanced at the matrix of Richmond Pinnacle security camera feeds. The security guard was sitting at his station, and somehow stayed awake through the long, boring night. But the guard sat up straight and stared out the front of the building. Another camera feed caught a black SUV pull up and stop in front of the main entrance, parking along the red, fire-lane, curb.

Two businessmen exited the vehicle's front seats and approached the main entrance. *Who the hell is this?* Nomad wondered. *It's after midnight.* He flipped the camera matrix to split-screen the exterior entrance and lobby feeds and cranked up the audio. *Let's hear what they have to say.*

The guard approached the entrance and stood just inside the interior set of glass doors. The man that exited the passenger seat was tall, slender, close-cropped blond hair, black suit, white shirt. He was carrying a large manila envelope. The driver was short, stocky, shaved head, same black suit. His hands were empty. Both men moved in unison with a determination that had Nomad suspecting they were Feds, and in the still night air he could hear the men's shoes squeak on the building's decorative cement. *Odd. Look like dress shoes, sound like tennis shoes.*

The guard pressed an intercom button and was the first to speak.

"I'm sorry, Gentleman. The building's closed."

The driver responded. "We understand, and we wouldn't be here if it wasn't important," he said. "We have some papers for Katherine Preacher."

"For Kate?"

"Yes, sir. Kate asked us to bring these as soon as possible, and we drove straight down from the New York office."

Nomad knew that was a lie. He'd been with Kate all night. If she asked for anything, he'd have seen it.

"So you're with the firm?"

"We are."

"They're lying!" Nomad yelled at the screen.

"I can't let you in, but I can see she gets them."

Again, Nomad yelled at the guard. "No, don't. It's a trap. They'll kill you, then Kate."

"That would be great. We've got a long drive back."

The guard punched in an alarm code and reached for the keys clipped to his belt. Just before he unlocked the door, he hesitated.

"I think I better check with Kate. Just give me a minute."

"Yes, of course. We understand," the driver said, and took two steps back.

When the guard turned his back, the man with the envelope stepped forward. He tossed the envelope aside, produced a suppressed MAC-10 and opened fire. The first quick burst from the 45 caliber automatic shattered the glass doors. The second caught the guard when he tried to turn and draw his pistol.

The two men strode across the crackling glass, into the lobby, and stood over the guard. Nomad saw the blood bubbling and oozing from the guard's mouth, and more pooling beneath his body. The driver swept back his suit jacket, drew his weapon, and shot the guard in the head.

"Not again," Nomad said. "First Francois, and now Kate. Dial Katherine Preacher," he commanded and his system responded with an anonymous Internet call to Kate's cell phone.

He watched Kate reach for the phone, glance at the Unknown Caller ID and hang up. He tried again, but this time he added a spoofed caller ID. *Please don't hate me. Just answer the phone.*

Kate's phone rang again. A smiling face appeared above the contact profile for Jake Church. Kate answered the call and started yelling into the phone.

"I don't know who the hell you think you are, but using my husband's caller ID is cruel and I hope you burn —"

"Kate. Don't hang up. It's Nomad."

"Nomad?"

"I don't have time to explain. You're in danger," he said. "A two-man team just breached your building and killed the guard. They're coming for you and the NanoVault."

"Is this some kind of sick joke?" Kate asked. "Why on earth would I believe you're Nomad? You could have picked up that name anywhere."

"I gave you the Syrian intel that almost got you killed. Now, can we focus?" he said. "Two heavily armed men are headed your way and are about to enter the elevator. I can slow them down, but you need to —"

"That's total BS," she said. "I'm hanging up and calling the guard station."

Before Kate could even reach for her office phone, Nomad's text hit Kate's cell with a video clip of the assault team. She watched them blast their way through the glass doors, then execute Pete. Her reaction wasn't quite what Nomad expected. Kate stood, lifted her shirt, and drew a weapon. *She's going after them.*

He called back, and she took the call on her AirPods.

"Stop!" he said. "Please, just listen. I know what you're thinking, but you're out-gunned. I can help you find out what's on Jake's device, but it won't matter if you're dead."

"How do you know about Jake's device?"

"Just listen. I have control of the building," Nomad said. "I can't lock the elevator, but I've triggered elevator calls on every floor. That should give you eight to ten minutes. Now bag the NanoVault and take the East stairs to the lobby."

Kate shoved the NanoVault back into the Faraday bag, sealed it, and slipped it into her messenger bag. With her bag slung around behind her back, she ran for the emergency exit door, pushed through the door, and started running down the stairs.

"Someone just cleared my elevator settings."

"What does that mean?"

"I'm not alone in the system, and they'll hit eighteen in about thirty seconds."

"I need two minutes," Kate said. "You've got to keep them occupied on eighteen. Lights. Video. Music. Whatever you can control. Just distract them long enough for me to reach the lobby."

Chapter 55

RICHMOND PINNACLE BUILDING, RICHMOND, VA

KATE HAD HIKED UP and run down her office building's stairs many times. Her best time jogging down was three minutes, ten seconds. She needed to beat that time. Kate holstered her gun and ran like her life depended on it.

When she hit the bottom floor, she pushed through the stairwell exit door, and landed in the lobby.

"Grab the guard's keys," Nomad said into her earpiece.

"What?" she asked and struggled to catch her breath.

"The keys. Grab his keys," Nomad said. "The fire control panel at the guard station will recall the elevators."

Kate found it hard to approach Pete. Hours earlier, he was sharing Kate's grief and talking about his wife. With one hand, she closed his eyes, and with the other, lifted the keys off his belt.

"Where are they?" Kate asked, afraid the men might already be on the way down.

"We're good, for the moment," he said. "They're clearing room by room, but hurry. Once he sees you on the lobby cameras, he'll send them down."

"Once *who* sees me?" Kate asked, fumbling through Pete's key ring, searching for the elevator key.

"I'll explain everything later. Once you're safe."

"Got it," Kate said, and turned the elevator control key.

"It worked," Nomad said. "They're locked out, and heading for the stairs. Go."

Glass crunched beneath Kate's shoes as she burst through the shattered main doors, but she stopped at the SUV.

"Don't even think about," Nomad said when he saw Kate open the driver door. "You don't have time for this."

Kate didn't answer, and Jake's training echoed in her head. *A retreat is still an opportunity to gain an advantage.* She swung the messenger bag around in front and fished out the OBD scanner, about the size of a cell phone. With her back on the floorboard, she reached up under the dash and connected to the SUV's Onboard Diagnostic port. Seconds later, she had the data.

"How much time do I have?"

"Two, maybe three minutes, but that's pushing it."

"That'll work. Can't have them following me."

Kate started the Jeep and went around to the back. She unlocked Jake's truck vault and grabbed a red can about the size of a soda can.

Standing next to the SUV, she asked, "Can you see me?"

"Yes."

"Good. Then whoever *he* is can see me, too."

Kate pulled the pin and set the canister in the center of the SUV's hood. The thermite incendiary grenade ignited with a spray of bright white sparks and a wave of intense heat. In seconds, the glowing red fireball burned through the hood, and started consuming the engine. The smell of burning rubber and oil filled the air. The heat and light pushed Kate even farther away, and she turned to the front entrance camera and offered a one-finger salute.

"Kate, you gotta go," Nomad begged. "Please. Go."

She climbed into the front seat, shoved the Jeep into reverse, and floored it. The rear end jumped over the parking lot berm and plowed backward through the flowers and bushes that lined the lot. Kate skidded to a stop on the sidewalk and then took off.

"Go to ground," Nomad said. "When you're safe, you'll find me where the shadows meet."

The call ended, but not the intensity. Kate's heart was pounding. She'd caught her breath, but her head was spinning. Images from the video were still fresh in her mind. Pete laying in a pool of blood. Executed. And for what? Jake's NanoVault? If Nomad hadn't called, would she be dead? Was that really Nomad? Who else would tell her to find him where the shadows meet? The Darknet. That was the only way they communicated. It had to be Nomad, but how did he know so much? The answer was obvious and infuriating. *He was already in the system, watching the cameras, watching me.*

Go to ground, she thought. *He's right. I can't go to the police. Not yet. Not until I know what Jake was doing, and who might be involved. And cops have rules. They can't go where I can go, and won't do what I will.*

Where would Jake go? And the minute she asked, she had the answer. *His grandfather's cabin. Nothing electronic links them to the property. That's perfect.* The plan took shape in her head. She would stick to the neighborhood roads and wind her way out of town, avoiding the cameras at major intersections and freeways. *Anyone capable of hacking Richmond Pinnacle has serious skill. Best to stay as far off the grid as possible.*

Once Kate was clear of downtown, and out of the path of anyone responding to the fire she set, she hunted for a place to stop. The empty parking lot of an abandoned grocery store was perfect. *Minimal lighting. No cameras. No residents close enough to care.* Her phone had to go in the Faraday bag along with Jake's NanoVault, but there was something she needed to do before she locked it away. The video she received was evidence, and Kate moved a copy to a private Tor server where it could stay hidden. Then she saved a copy where it could be seen, but only if you had the link.

She went back into the truck vault, and this time she fished out a pair of Jake's old-school flip phones. These burner phones were back to basics, just the essentials, Wi-Fi capable, plain text messaging, no GPS. The Jeep's trickle charge kept them primed and ready.

Kate crafted a message that contained nothing but plain text, mimicking the link to the video. While her phone had no idea what she was sending, a smart phone would see the structure and convert it to a hot link. The minute the message was delivered, she pulled and snapped the SIM card, then smashed the phone. *One and done. That's the rule.*

The second phone she used to make a call that went straight to voicemail.

"Marcus, it's Preacher," she said. "Red smoke rising. Watch the video and call this number."

CHAPTER 56

SUNDAY, APRIL 19
12:22 AM EDT

MOORE TOWER, MANHATTAN, NY

DREW WATCHED KATHERINE PREACHER destroy the SUV with some kind of explosive, then raise a hand and flip off the camera before disappearing out of view. He could hear a vehicle in the parking lot and the engine revved. There was the sound of scraping and crunching, tires screeching, and then the sound faded away.

Damn, Drew thought. *I don't how, but she made it.*

Moore leapt out of his chair and sent it flying. He threw his headset at the monitor, and it crashed to the floor. He turned his back on the workstation and looked straight at Drew.

Uh-oh, he thought. *This is going to get ugly.*

"Drew, post another bounty," Moore said. "I need that device, and I want Preacher stopped."

"Are you sure you want to go outside on this?" Drew asked. "You have people you trust."

"There isn't time," Moore said. "And this can't wait."

"Like Paris?"

"Exactly. Look how nicely that worked out."

"I don't know," Drew said, and shook his head. "The Ronin player looked like he might be a problem. Can we risk another rogue?"

"Why are you stalling?" Moore asked. "Is it Preacher? Did you two ever—"

"Me? No. Never."

"Then get on with it."

Drew logged in to the app using his phone's facial recognition. Once inside, he activated the New Bounty interface and added Kate's physical description under a Jane Doe. He took a screen grab photo from her exiting Richmond Pinnacle and smirked at the image of her giving Moore the finger. He added details on the NanoVault as well, and its probable location in the target's messenger bag, and included another photo.

"Alright," Drew said. "I've created the bounty. Mission Scope, Object Recovery and Target Capture."

"Or kill," Moore said, and Drew could hear the venom, and knew the result Moore preferred.

"OK. Mission Scope, Object Recovery and Target Capture or Kill. What parameters?"

"Ten-thousand, confirmed target sighting with photo and precise location."

Moore paced the room a bit and then turned back to Drew. "One-hundred-thousand. Capture or kill. Paid only on recovery of the NanoVault in her possession."

Drew entered Moore's parameters, and there was only one piece left. The player level that would receive the New Bounty alert.

"I assume you want to offer this to Level Five again, like Paris?"

"No. Wide Open. Entire East coast region," Moore said.

"Wide open? You want everyone to have a crack at this?" Drew asked. "Some of the players are just kids."

"Yes, everyone," Moore said. "We'll have eyes everywhere. There won't be anywhere she can run and nowhere to hide. Somebody will take her out, and the sooner the better."

***

DEVIN MOORE RETURNED TO his workstation. He picked the headset up off the floor and grabbed the chair. With the new bounty out for Preacher and the device, he turned his attention to Richmond Pinnacle and the mess his team made. He had two stranded operators and a dead guard. The fire department would be the first to arrive, but once they saw the body in the lobby, the police would be right behind.

The best he could do at this point was to get his people out of there and wipe the video. That would leave the police with a crime they couldn't explain and would never solve. Even the burnt-out vehicle, registered to an offshore company with a fleet of such vehicles, would link back to a stolen vehicle report. Just another dead end.

Devin instructed the operators to secure transportation, but remain in the area. The minute a BountyHunt player got a location on Preacher, they would be sent to pursue and collect the device.

When Devin attempted to access the Pinnacle's security recordings, they were already gone, and he realized whoever helped Preacher escape was still in the system. He flagged down Drew and had him start a packet trace of everything into and out of the building. Then he reached out to engage his competitor.

"Might this be the great, the one and only, Nomad?" Devin said, trying to goad Nomad into responding. He knew he risked Nomad just killing the connection, but he hoped ego would be his edge.

"That depends," Nomad said. "Who's asking?"

"Oh, come now. Is the masquerade really necessary? We've been dancing for so long now, I feel like we're old friends."

When Nomad didn't answer, Devin relented.

"Very well, if you insist. I am the Grandmaster. At your service," Devin said. "I believe congratulations are in order. It was a narrow victory, but a victory nonetheless."

"And to the victor go the spoils."

"Yes, of course, but to what end? And now you've roped an innocent woman into your scheme. Katherine Preacher is innocent, isn't she? Does she know what you're planning, what you really want? Will she be the next to die for you?"

"Don't pretend you care about her. You sent a team to kill her."

"And that wouldn't have been necessary if you and I had could come to a mutually beneficial arrangement, and now look, another body, and Preacher running for her life. She'll be dead before morning."

"I know what you're doing," Nomad said. "I will stop you."

"Forget what you think you know. You can't begin to fathom what's at stake, and as for stopping me, you're already too late."

Drew signaled Devin to keep going.

"You know, I'm told Francois tried to shield you, but everyone breaks eventually. Ah, but that's right, you were there. Weren't you? Watching. You saw it all, and still you did nothing," Devin said. "It's dangerous to be your friend, but you can still end this. No one else needs to die."

The connection dropped.

"Did we get it?" Moore shouted at Drew.

"No, but this will help. I can overlay these routes to what we already have. The correlation just might be the key."

"Don't even think about leaving this room until you have Nomad's location."

CHAPTER 57

BRASSERIE D'AUMONT, HOTEL DE CRILLON, PARIS, FRANCE

MARCUS JONES WAS IN the hotel's open-air brasserie, reviewing his schedule for the day and sipping an espresso, when a cryptic text message hit his phone. He didn't recognize the number, and while it had a Virginia area code, there was no way he was going to click on the embedded link. He deleted the message.

His phone rang two minutes later. A different number, but it too had a Virginia area code. Marcus never answered calls unless the caller was already in his contact list. He would just let the call go to voicemail, and if it was legitimate, the caller could leave a message. Kate did.

"Marcus, it's Preacher. Red smoke rising. Watch the video and call this number."

Marcus retrieved the deleted text message and clicked the link.

"What the hell," he asked out loud, and an older American couple turned to look his direction. He tossed some Euros on the table, walked away and returned the missed call.

"Preacher, what's going on?" Marcus asked. "Are you alright?"

"I'm fine. For now," she said. "But that was close."

"So, you're saying the team that took out the guard was coming for you?"

"Yes. That's where I work. The video only shows their entry. The next stop was my floor, my office."

"Christ. What is going on?"

"I wish I knew."

"Well, whoever they are, they're pros. Moved like operators."

"Agreed."

"And probably ghosts."

"What makes you say that?"

"Brass everywhere. Faces captured on video. And they didn't care. They knew it didn't matter. How the hell did you get out?"

"I had a little inside help."

"I'd ask what that means, but this is an open line," Marcus said. "Are you sure you weren't followed?"

"Yeah. I'm sure."

"I'm glad you're alright," he said. "I couldn't bear to lose you, too."

"That's why I'm calling. I'm going dark, and I didn't want you or the team to worry. You won't be able to reach me, but if I need help, I'll reach you."

"Hang on," Marcus said. "Isn't there someone in DC, or even Langley, that can help?"

"It may come to that," Kate said. "But not until I know who I'm dealing with, and what they want?"

"And how do you expect to do that by yourself?" Marcus asked. "Wait. You have help, don't you?"

"Maybe," she said. "We'll see."

"Is this someone you trust?"

Kate was silent for a moment.

"Preacher? You still there?"

"I'm here."

"Sounds like you might have second thoughts."

"No. I trust him," she said. "We have a past, but he just saved my life. That counts for something."

"Well, trust your gut," Marcus said. "Jake called you his shaman for a reason, so pay attention to that little voice in your head."

The call ended and Marcus deleted the voice mail and text messages from his phone. He knew Kate would follow protocol and destroy the burner, so it was pointless to keep the number. Whatever she did next, Kate was on her own.

I hope you're watching, buddy, he thought. Marcus didn't believe there was anything beyond this life, but figured it was worth a shot. *Preacher may need you.*

CHAPTER 58

SUNDAY, APRIL 19
12:30 AM EDT

KIMPTON HOTEL MONACO, WASHINGTON, D.C.

AFTER SENATOR CAHILL'S DEATH, Manuel Rojas checked out of the Ritz and into the Kimpton. It was comfortable, even stylish, but without the ultra-luxury price tag that can attract attention. Rojas knew that amateurs spent their windfalls, and professionals kept a low profile. Patience is more than a virtue, it's a skill that's honed like any other.

He wondered about the girl. *She's alive*, he thought. *That much I know, and it's best that's all I know.* But sleep eluded him while the prospect of his betrayal loomed, and he wrestled with his decision. *Was his daughter safe?*

The New Bounty alert was an unexpected distraction and piqued his interest. *Last known location Richmond, Virginia. Believed to be heading west. The drive would do me some good*, he thought. *Get me out of my head for a while. Get me out of DC. Headed west? That makes sense.*

He'd done some hiking and fishing in the West Virginia mountains, and knew if you wanted to get lost, the area offered a lot of opportunities. If the target headed that direction, he had some ideas on how to get a leg up on the competition.

Jumping into the car was a gamble. There was no guarantee the target would ever be within his reach, and he didn't care. It was something to do. *If it doesn't pan out, I'll grab some gear and go fishing,* he thought. *Make a little vacation out of it.*

The drive from DC to West Virgina would take a few hours and give him time to think. On the drive, he tried to pretend it didn't matter who the target was, but he recognized the photo. He knew what her husband had done in Paris, but all that mattered was the contract. Someone wanted the NanoVault in her possession, and she was expendable. *It's just a job, and if not me, it'll be somebody else,* he thought. *But man, that guy was a true warrior. Not me. I'd have found cover. Or run as far and as fast as I could.*

The realization he was a coward was unnerving, and Rojas tried to rationalize it as survival thinking, but the shoe fit, and he knew it. He consoled himself with the terms of the bounty, capture or kill, and committed to trying to keep her alive. But even that was a lie. His life wasn't the only one on the line. If a choice had to be made, if his daughter's life was at stake, he'd kill without a moment's hesitation.

The encrypted call from the app caught him by surprise. Rojas looked for a turnout and pulled off the road.

"What did you do with the body?" Riley asked.

Timing's about right, Rojas thought. This was the call he was dreading. "What body?"

"The girl's body. What did you do?"

"Riley, I have no idea what you're talking about," Rojas lied. "When I left, she was tied to the bed. And the whole world has seen the photos."

"Yes. Yes. We've all seen the photos, but the client is furious. The morgue only has Cahill's body, and now there's a firestorm of speculation about her."

"You're sure she's dead?" Riley asked. "Both our lives depend on it."

"Hell yes. I gave her enough heroin to kill a horse."

"Then what happened? Where's her body?"

"My money's on the cartel."

"I don't understand?" Riley asked.

"Look, it's bad for business to have their property exposed to the public, especially a sex-trafficked child," Rojas said. "I think they got to somebody, maybe even the coroner, but if I'm right, that's one body you're never going to find."

"That's good," Riley said. "I can work with that."

The call ended, and Rojas took a deep breath. *It's over. He bought it, and the girl's safe,* he thought. *And his daughter's still safe. I'll look before I leap next time. No kids.*

CHAPTER 59

SUNDAY, APRIL 19
5:00 AM EDT

PERSONAL RESIDENCE, CIA DEPUTY DIRECTOR, LANGLEY FOREST, McLEAN, VA

It was 5:00AM and Margot Ryder was sitting on the edge of her bed. She woke early every day, even on weekends. As the Deputy Director of CIA's National Clandestine services, she found the early morning hours the most peaceful of the entire day. In a job that had no weekends and no days off, she relished the time to herself. It was an unwritten rule that she was not to be disturbed, and few dared break that rule, but today was an exception.

She answered the call, and warned, "This better be important."

"Yes, Ma'am. It is."

"Well go on," she said. "Let's have it."

"We just received a copy of an NSA intercept with a person of interest, and they unmasked the U.S. recipient."

"And?"

"It's Katherine Preacher."

"Good Lord. What has she done now?"

"It's not that," he said. "There appears to have been another attempt on her life?"

"On U.S. soil?"

"Yes, Ma'am."

"But she's alright?"

"Yes, Ma'am. They linked the intercept to a video of the incident. Both the video and a transcript of the call are in your in-box, but given the circumstances, I thought you would want to know right away."

"You were right," she said. "Do we have her location?"

"No. Her phone is offline, and she hasn't been home since — since her husband was killed."

"Where was the attack?"

"Richmond Pinnacle, the building where she's employed. There were two assailants, and one fatality. A security guard."

"Have we ID'd the assailants?"

"We're running facial now, but so far, nothing."

"Did the NSA identify the person they were surveilling?"

"Yes. Marcus Jones. Also a US Citizen, currently in Paris."

"I know Jones. He's a member of Trident Security, Church's team. Former MARSOC, I think."

"Yes, that's correct."

"Did they say why Jones was under surveillance?"

"No. There was nothing in the report."

"I'll see what I can find out, but Preacher's location is the priority."

"Yes, Ma'am."

"It's unlikely you'll find her until she wants to be found, but don't stop looking."

Margot ended the call. With her robe and slippers on, she headed for her library office. Buried among her daily deluge of incoming email was the encrypted NSA intercept and video. She watched the clip and read the transcript. Neither gave her any insight into why Kate was targeted, but one thing was certain. These were not jihadis bent on revenge. That made her job easier and gave her some political cover if the news picked it up.

And Margot had a hunch where Kate might go. She needed to make a call and retrieved a black phone from her safe. This phone, developed in Israel, was the only one used at the highest executive, intelligence and political levels. It was the only phone she trusted with her secret, and the one phone number Margot knew Zhukov would answer, day or night, anywhere in the world.

He answered the call with one question. "What is wrong?"

"A few hours ago, someone tried to kill her at her office. Two men. Professionals. I'll send you the video."

"Where is she now?"

"We're looking, but no-one knows for sure."

"But you do?"

"I have a hunch, that's all. I could be wrong," she said, and described the location. "You won't find it on a map. I'll send you the coordinates. Where are you?"

"New York."

"Good. You're close," Margot said. "What will you need?"

"Two men. A breacher and a sniper. And a Little Bird for a night op insertion. She can't know we're coming."

"The bird I can get you," she said. "The operators need to be off-book. That could take some time."

"We go tonight," Zhukov said. "Call when you have it. And tell the men they do exactly what I say. Nothing more. Nothing less."

"Alright. I'll make it happen, but you need to keep a lid on this."

"I will handle it."

"What are you going to do?"

"Better you do not know."

"Look, if our arrangement goes public, my career's over."

The line went dead. *Russian bastard,* she thought. *I made a pact with the devil.*

Chapter 60

RUBY'S CORNER, WEST VIRGINIA MOUNTAINS, WV

KATE WOUND HER WAY from the Richmond Pinnacle building and across the state line into West Virginia. Avoiding the larger towns and toll road cameras tripled the drive time, but she needed to keep the Jeep off the radar. She made a simple and safe assumption. *Anyone who has a couple of killers on speed dial, and can hack the Pinnacle, can also track her movements,* she thought. *Never underestimate your opponent.*

Jake always kept the Jeep's Rotopax spare gas cans full, and there were four strapped to the rack, but she wanted to keep those in reserve. If her destination wasn't safe, she could push the Jeep even deeper into the Appalachian Mountains, and she needed to prepare. Kate considered where to stop for gas and groceries that would be open at first light and secluded enough to go unnoticed.

Ruby's Corner would work. Ruby was long gone, but the store remained unchanged in the last fifty years. It was still the most convenient location for bait and tackle, and had a decent selection of groceries and local farm-fresh produce. Kate hoped modern necessities, like security cameras, had bypassed the store and she was right.

She parked alongside one of the two gas pumps and filled up. With no other patrons in sight, Kate opted to leave the Jeep where it was and head into the store. An old brass bell rang as she entered. The scruff marked floors creaked beneath her feet. She took a few steps in and looked around. She was alone.

There was a counter to her left, and a long aisle stretched out ahead. To her right was an old refrigerator. She could feel the chill from where she stood, and saw it stocked with beer. *No craft beer or microbrews,* she thought, and smiled. *These folks keep it simple.*

The air was musty and still, thick with the scent of spices and old wood. She saw ancient jars and cans on the shelves, labels browned with age. There were boxes and barrels of various shapes and sizes, their contents long forgotten. Locals ignored all of this, but for the few tourists who happened along, it was country chic.

At the far end of the aisle, she spotted the produce section. It was small and unassuming, but the items were fresh, the produce marked with a handwritten sign and a list of prices. Nothing too exotic, but enough to get by. She chose a few apples, some corn and potatoes, and a head of lettuce. She grabbed a jar of homemade pickles and a can of beans. The bread wasn't fresh but it would do, and the eggs were only a day old.

Kate made her way to the counter and hit the bell. The ring was barely audible, but a few moments later, a woman appeared from the back room. She was short, with gray hair and a friendly face. Kate smiled at her and put the basket on the counter.

The woman surveyed the items, looked up at Kate, and said, "That'll be six dollars and fifty-five cents."

Kate handed the woman a ten. "I'll be right back," the woman said and disappeared into the back room.

She must think it's safer to keep the register in back, Kate thought, but she couldn't imagine the little store had much to worry about. The pickup truck that screeched to a stop had Kate thinking she might be wrong. Everything about the Ram Heavy Duty truck hit Kate's tripwires. The stereo blasting, the roaring Cummin's diesel engine, and the four occupants.

The woman returned with Kate's change, and the look on her face told Kate she was right to be concerned. Four boys. Late teens to early twenties, Kate thought, in a split-second assessment. Baggy jeans and hoodies. None were obviously armed, but that clothing was a risky combination.

"Best you stay here with me," the woman said. "Those boys are trouble. Just like their daddy."

Three-inch lift. High-end rims. Off-road tires. Kate thought. *Whatever daddy does, he's making good money, and the boys look like they've been out all night. Might even still be drunk.*

Kate watched the boys circle the Jeep. That wasn't unusual. Jake's rig was something special. He tried to tell Kate she had more jewelry, but they both knew that was a lie. She liked to tease him that the Jeep was his "other wife."

"I better go have a chat with them," Kate said.

"Oh, I wouldn't do that. The big one's Billy. A real piece of work, that one. The others follow him like sheep."

"I'll be fine, but do me a favor."

"You want me to call the sheriff?"

"Actually, no," Kate said. "Whatever happens, please don't call the sheriff."

"Alright. If you say so, Missy," the woman said. "I sure hope you know what you're doing."

"I've got this. I'll be back for the groceries."

Kate strode out toward the Jeep, stopped about halfway and said, "She's a beauty, isn't she?"

"This rig yours?" Billy asked.

When he turned toward Kate, she watched his body language, hand gestures and scanned again for weapons. *He's right-handed. Pocket knife clipped to the front right pocket.*

"It's my husband's."

"Where's he?"

"Oh, he'll be out in a minute," Kate bluffed. "But I gotta tell you, he's a former Navy SEAL with a nasty temper. You know. PTSD. Might be best for you guys to be on your way. If he sees you leaning on his baby, he might get upset. I swear he loves that Jeep more than he loves me. But trust me, you don't want to see him upset."

"We're not scared," Billy said. "And besides, we're just looking."

"Have it your way, but don't say I didn't warn you."

Kate could see she spooked the younger boys, and they just wanted to finish gassing up the truck and leave. A little psychological warfare had shaken their resolve and broken the pack's unity.

"Come on, Billy. Let's go," said the youngest.

"We're not going anywhere," Billy said. "I want to see this guy."

"You know Billy. If you really want to meet him, you could just go inside."

"Billy, let's go. Dad's gonna kill us if we don't get the truck back before work."

Go on, Billy, Kate thought. *Your brother's offering you a lifeline. You should take it.*

"Fine. We're outta here."

Billy climbed into the driver's seat, and the kid called shotgun. The other two crawled up into the truck bed. The engine roared, and a cloud of thick black diesel smoke floated toward Kate. *What an ass,* Kate thought. *The shopkeeper was right, but at least they're leaving.*

When the brake lights flashed and the truck skidded to a stop, Kate's alarm bells sounded. Something changed. She'd lost control of the situation, and every fiber was telling her it was about to get ugly.

The truck whipped around and stopped a few feet in front of the Jeep. All four jumped out. Billy was holding a cell phone. He looked at Kate and back at the phone.

"You were right," Billy said to the kid half his size. "She's the one they want, and she ain't no Jane Doe."

Billy gave the phone back to the kid and took a step forward. "Nice try, lady. I know who you are. And I know your husband's dead."

"Yes. My husband is dead. And a few hours ago, a friend of mine was murdered," Kate said. "I'm tired, hungry and unbelievably angry, and I don't have time for this... whatever *this* is."

Kate's left hand was up chest high, palm facing the boys. The gesture's message was simple. Stop where you are. Her right elbow pressed against her hip to lock down the orientation of her hand to her gun. Muscle memory would do the rest. *Take the hint, boys, and climb back into the truck.* She still hoped to disengage without drawing her weapon, but her gut was telling her something different.

She visualized the worst case scenario in her head, scanned for cover, and began to set the stage. *What brought them back*, she wondered. *Something on that phone.*

"We just got a bounty alert on a Jane Doe," the youngest said. "And I knew it was you."

"Excuse me?" Kate asked, and she drifted left. "You got what?"

The kid held up his phone, and even at twenty feet, Kate recognized her picture.

"A bounty," he said. "You're worth a whopping ten grand just for a confirmed sighting." And smiling large, he took Kate's photo.

"What the hell is that?"

"It's a game called BountyHunt. Starts off like a scavenger hunt," the kid said. "You find things people want, and you get paid. No questions asked. But you can move up and make some real money. If a bounty gets posted in your area, they pay you if you're first to register a sighting, and more, a lot more if you can —"

"Capture," Billy said. "Or kill."

Billy's right leg and right hip canted back slightly. *He is carrying*, Kate realized. The others had squared off and faced her directly.

"So you boys think you won the lottery? All you have to do is turn me in and collect?" Kate said and meandered closer to the gas pump. "Guys, this is some kind of demented scam or con. Anyone can post a picture of someone in the news. That doesn't make it real. Let me ask you, did you pay to join? Do they have your credit card?"

"Oh, it's real, alright," Billy said. "My dad's a level three."

"Billy, shut up," the kid said. "He'll whip you bloody."

"Who's *she* gonna tell? A little thing like her won't be no trouble." Billy said. "Why, I think we might all have a little fun first in the back of my truck." He grabbed the scruff of his little brother's neck and teased him. "You might even get a go this time, if you can get it up."

Kate's CIA training and experience gave her a keen sense of body language and intent. She could spot a lie, and what she saw sent a chill up her spine. *I wouldn't be the first girl these boys brutalized. She knew the look. She'd seen it up close.*

Images of Syria flared up like the adrenaline pumping through Kate's veins. Beaten, tortured and raped. Her chest carved up for the sadistic pleasure of watching her bleed. And for what? Questions she couldn't answer.

Kate's focus and demeanor changed. One of the boys even took a half-step back, but she knew they all saw it. *No one is laying a hand on me,* she thought. She gave them one last chance to leave, but knew they wouldn't take it.

"Playtime's over," Kate said. "Jump back into daddy's truck and drive away."

"Or what?" Billy asked.

"Or you're going to the hospital or the morgue," she said. "And I don't care which."

Billy swept his right hand back to grab his gun. Kate's first move was to step behind the gas pump. Her left hand ripped up the front of her shirt and her right wrapped around the Glock tucked in her waist. Billy's gun came swinging around his hip, but all he could see was the blur of Kate ducking behind cover.

He stepped into the open, gun up, arms locked out, eyes searching. Kate lowered her body, leaned out just enough to put her red dot upper center mass. Billy pivoted toward her. She pressed the trigger, eased it back out to catch the reset, and pressed again. From draw to fire. Two rounds. Two seconds. Kate looked over the top of the slide at Billy, stepped out from behind the cover, and scanned the others. Billy's legs buckled. He collapsed where he stood, staring straight up into the sky.

The youngest ran to his brother's side. "Help him," he screamed. "Somebody help him." The boys were frozen. No one moved. No one spoke. Billy's vacant eyes said it all. He was gone.

Billy's gun lay nearby. Kate saw the kid look at it, and flinch.

"Don't even think about," she said. "Or your dad will be burying you both. Now, just stand up and kick it over here."

The kid did as he was told, and Kate kept her gun in tight to her chest, low ready. Jake would say, *Stay sharp. You don't get to say when the fight's over. He was right.*

The two that rushed her must have figured she couldn't shoot them both. They were wrong. The second they moved, Kate's gun was up and on target. They froze. Hands flew straight up.

"Don't shoot, lady," one said. "Please. Don't shoot." The other just started sobbing.

"Get in the back of the truck, and keep your hands where I can see them," Kate said, and turned to the kid still hovering over Billy. "Can you drive?"

"Yes," he whimpered, and wiped the tears and snot on his shirtsleeve.

"Bring me your phone," she said. "Show me the game."

He unlocked the phone and clicked on BountyHunt. It looked like every other kids' game, all bright colors, and flashing animation. Then he opened level one.

"How did you get to that level?"

"You get an invite and fill out a questionnaire. If you're approved, you can see the bounties for your level. As you complete missions, you build reputation points. Then you can move up in rank and standing."

"You're only a level one," Kate noted. "Why did I show up?"

"I don't know," he said, still choking back tears. "Some kind of all levels broadcast. Open to anyone on the East Coast."

"Why hasn't this thing been shut down?"

"If you talk, someone you care about gets hurt, or they disappear and you get body parts in the mail. They call it collateral, but they can't hurt me now," he said, and wiped his face. "Billy was my collateral."

Kate took his phone and forced a system wipe and reset. When she was certain her photo and everything was gone, she gave it back to him. "Don't grow up to be Billy. Now, go."

Kate watched the truck drive away. She took the opportunity for a quick tactical reload and replaced the partial mag in the Glock before holstering and straightening her shirt. Then she picked up and pocketed the two spent shell casings. *Always police your brass.*

The shop keeper came out carrying a double-barreled shotgun. Kate thought about reaching for her gun, but the woman lowered the shotgun.

"Relax. If I wanted you dead, you'd be dead. Your husband teach you that stuff?" she asked, but didn't wait for an answer. "Mine was a Marine, Force Recon, back in the day."

"You know who I am?"

"Course I do, missy. We may live in the sticks, but we still get the news. Brave man, your husband," she said, and looking at Billy's body, and in Kate's eyes, added, "This isn't your first, is it?"

"No," Kate said, and she could still recall the face of the first man she killed. Jake helped her put it in perspective, and when they got married, it became the cornerstone of her training. *When your life is on the line, what's the goal? Get home to you. And what do you do? Whatever it takes. How do we feel about that? Victorious.*

The shop keeper walked over to Billy, pointed the shotgun, and pulled the trigger. She unloaded both rounds into his chest. "That's for my husband, you son of a bitch."

"He killed your husband?" Kate asked.

"Never could prove it, but he'd rob me blind and warn me to keep my mouth shut or I'd end up like my John. The devil can have this one," she said, and spit on him. "Good riddance."

The woman turned back to Kate and said, "I'll tell the Sheriff he tried to rob me for the last time, and the boys he was with drove off before I could get a good look."

"Will the Sheriff buy that?" Kate asked, and she pocketed the two spent shell casings.

"Hell yes. Been friends twenty years. He'll buy it with a smile on his face," she said. "This boy's been dancing with the devil for years. Rape. Robbery. Assault.

You name it, but they couldn't make nuthin' stick. Folks were just too afraid of what might happen if they spoke up."

"What about the others?"

"They can say what they like. No one is going to believe those two meth-heads. And if I catch wind they're mouthing off, I'll let them know you're coming for 'em. Why, I think they just might crap their pants."

The two women headed back into the store.

"I need to get back on the road, but more will be coming. They'll want to know which way I went."

"What do you want me to say?"

"South. Tell them South."

"I'm guessing that's a lie."

"Nope. If they believe you, they won't hurt you."

Kate grabbed one of Jake's emergency hundred-dollar bills and borrowed a pen. She printed a few words in large block letters, folded the bill in half and handed it to her.

"Hand this to whoever comes looking," Kate said. "And feel free to suggest they go home."

CHAPTER 61

RUBY'S CORNER, WEST VIRGINIA MOUNTAINS, WV

MOORE'S PAIR OF OPERATORS were the first to reach Ruby's corner, Kate's last known location. The coroner's wagon passed them on the road, and now they knew why. Yellow crime scene tape wrapped a twenty-foot square around the store's gas pumps. By big city crime standards, there wasn't much to see. Blood stained the cement in front of the gas pump island. A couple of vehicles slowed down and stopped, and some kids on bikes were gawking and laughing from the street.

The sheriff was gone, but a deputy was still on the scene to keep folks from getting too close. The store was open, so the operators found a place to park and wandered in.

The driver glanced at the blood and the splatter. *That's a lot of blood*, he thought. But apparently not enough to close the store.

The two men entered the store. Joe, short, stocky and bald, hung back by the door, while the tall, lean one walked straight down the aisle, looked around and shook his head.

OK, we're alone, Joe thought and approached the counter. "What happened out there?" he asked, nodding out the window.

"Young fella tried to rob me," she said. "Ended up on the business end of my shotgun."

"You don't mess around, do you?"

"No sir. I don't," she said. "Now, what can I do for you boys?"

"We'd just like to ask a couple of questions."

"I figured you weren't here to shop."

"Did the suits give us away?" he asked and smiled.

"Well, that and the SIG on your belt."

He straightened his jacket and looked over his shoulder at the county sheriff's deputy.

"Just ignore him," she said. "He's just a kid and he won't bother us none. Kate said someone would come looking for her. I imagine that's you two."

"What else did she say?"

"Said to tell you she's heading South."

"South, huh? Did you see her drive off?"

"I did."

"Which way did she go?"

"Like I said, she went south. If it were up to me, I'd have said north, but she wanted me to tell you the truth."

"What's she driving?"

"Can't say exactly. It was early. Still dark."

"Two-door. Four-door. Car. Truck. SUV?"

"No, not a truck. More like an SUV."

"What color?"

"Black. Maybe dark gray. And she asked me to give you this," she said and handed him the hundred-dollar bill.

He unfolded the bill and read Kate's message.

His partner walked over and asked, "What's it say?"

"I'll tell you on the way."

They turned to leave, but the shopkeeper asked, "You boys mind if I hang on to that bill?"

"Sure," he said, looking around the shop, and handed it back. "Looks like you could use it."

"Oh, it's not that," she said, and slipped the bill back into her pocket.

"Then what?"

"You're the first to ask about her, but I expect there will be others," she said. "They should see it. Maybe they'll think twice. Maybe *you* should think twice."

He smiled. "We'll be fine."

"Suit yourself," she said. "But that's what he thought." And she nodded toward the crime scene tape.

"She did that?" he asked, but the shopkeeper just smiled and winked.

The two men headed out the door, past the yellow tape and around the corner to their car.

The tall one stood at the open passenger door and called across the top of the car. "Hey Joe, what did she write?"

"I am the storm."

"That's it?" he asked. "What's that supposed to mean?"

"Carter, are you serious?" Joe asked. "You've never heard that phrase? It's a warning."

They climbed in. Joe started the engine and pointed the car south. He could see Carter fidgeting and guessed he was wrestling with Kate's message. *Not exactly the brightest bulb in the box,* he thought. *But he does what he's told.*

When Joe couldn't stand the toe-tapping a minute longer, he snapped, "You tap that foot one more time and I'll put a bullet in it."

"Oh, sorry."

"What's your problem? You're usually cool as ice."

"I keep thinking about it," Carter said. "What she wrote, I mean. Is that supposed to scare me? She's all of five-foot-six and just a little slip of a thing. What am I missing?"

"Let me know when you're done rambling on about this," Joe said. "And I'll tell you what you're missing."

"Fine. I'm done."

"It's a warrior's creed and goes something like this. Fate whispers to the warrior, 'You cannot withstand the storm.' And the warrior whispers back, 'I am the storm.'"

"Now do you get it?" Joe asked. He glanced over, but his partner's silence and blank stare said he was afraid to speak. *Maybe he thinks I'll shoot him,* Joe thought. "It *means* she'll be waiting for us. And judging by whatever happened at that store, she's not afraid to spill a little blood."

Chapter 62

RUBY'S CORNER, WEST VIRGINIA MOUNTAINS, WV

MANUEL ROJAS SMILED WHEN the BountyHunt Location Update hit his phone. He smacked the steering wheel and laughed. "Called it!" he said. "West Virginia Mountains. Damn, I'm good."

He'd reach the target's last known location in about three hours. *Plenty of daylight,* he thought. *I shouldn't have any trouble rounding up what I need before dark.* He knew that others in the area might have a head start, but he remained convinced that his approach would work.

By late afternoon, the scene at Ruby's corner had changed. The crime scene tape was gone. They removed the body and documented the scene, so there wasn't much use in securing the scene. As the shopkeeper predicted, it was an open and shut case. Local hoodlum pushed his luck a little too far, and got more than he bargained for.

When Rojas arrived, a teenager with a bucket and push broom was scrubbing a stain. The rust-colored water looked like an old radiator overheated. Rojas paid no attention, parked his car and headed in. He hadn't eaten much on the drive down, and looked over his options. He grabbed an apple and took a bite. Rojas found a small basket and finished the apple while he loaded some chips, cookies and a couple of Red Bulls.

"I hope that's not dinner," she said, and Rojas turned to see a petite, silver-haired woman standing behind the counter. *She wasn't there when I arrived*, he thought. *Must have come out of the back, but I'm slipping. I didn't hear a thing.*

"No, Ma'am. I sure hope not," he said. "But you know how road trips can be. Best to have a few items in the car."

"Where you headed?" she asked.

"Nowhere in particular," he said. "Spent some time in these mountains a few years back. Thought I might just poke around again, maybe do some fishing."

"Well, there's fishing and there's catching."

"Ain't that the truth," he said, and smiled. "I'd rather do some catching."

"Either way, if you decide you want to drop a line in somewhere, come on back. I can set you up. License. Bait. Whatever you need."

"Thank you," he said. "I might just take you up on that, but you know, my car's not going to make it into the areas I remember. The best spots were four-wheel only. Is there somewhere I can rent an ATV?"

"Up the road. Can't miss it," she said, and looked over his basket. "That'll be four eighty, including the apple."

He gave her a five and started to leave.

"You want your change?" she asked and caught him at the door.

"No, that's OK."

"Then how about a little advice?"

He turned and stepped back inside. "You know a good fishing spot?"

"Not exactly," she said. "But something tells me the fishing isn't what brought you down here."

"That's true enough," he said. "The fishing was an afterthought. It's been a rough couple of days, and more than anything, I needed to get away from it all."

"That explains the big-city-clothes," she said. "Not many strangers come this way, and nobody goes fishing in a sports coat and wingtips. But maybe fish isn't what you're hoping to catch."

The shopkeeper pulled out the hundred-dollar bill from her apron and held it out.

"What's this?"

"A young woman was in here first thing this morning, another stranger like you, and she wrote this down. Thought it might mean something to you," she said and opened the bill.

Rojas read Kate's note. "Nope. Doesn't ring a bell."

"Well, you enjoy your trip," she said, and pocketed the bill. "And if you decide to head up into those mountains, you be careful. Never know when a storm might strike."

CHAPTER 63

SUNDAY, APRIL 19
3:17 PM EDT

**PERSONAL RESIDENCE, CIA DEPUTY DIRECTOR, LANGLEY
FOREST, McLEAN, VA**

MARGOT RYDER RETURNED HOME to make the call. She opened the safe,
retrieved the black phone, and dialed. This phone had just the one contact, and
he answered on the first ring.

"Is everything arranged?" Zhukov asked.

"Yes," she said. "Get over to Teterboro Airport. There's a jet waiting for you.
I'll text the details."

"Destination?"

"Virginia. Shenandoah Regional Airport. From wheels up, you'll be there in
an hour. The jet will hold there until you return or cut them loose."

"And the Little Bird?"

"The bird and the crew are already in Virginia," she said. "It's a public airport,
so the team, equipment, everything stays dark until you get to a staging area.
Understood?"

"Understood," Zhukov said. "And you were right. She was seen on the state line heading into West Virginia."

"Where did you get that intel?"

"You have your sources. I have mine."

"Do you trust the source?"

"With my life."

"Alright," she said. "I've kept my end of the deal. Your end is to keep my involvement quiet and the intel flowing. Are we good?"

The line went dead. Margot held her tongue and swallowed the first word that popped into her head. *It's like talking to a brick wall,* she thought. *For all the good that's come from this deal, I know when I'm being played. What is Zhukov's end game? If Preacher survives, maybe I'll finally find out.*

Chapter 64

APPALACHIAN MOUNTAINS, WV

KATE'S LONG DRIVE UP the mountain was slow going in four-wheel-drive. Navigating the incline, rolling over or around fallen branches and the road's deep ruts tested her off-road skills. The driving challenge helped distract her from images of the man she killed.

Jake had a way of handling his darkest memories, and after nearly two decades in special forces, he had more than his share. He tried to help Kate get a handle on hers. *Put them in a shoe box,* he would say, *and then high on a shelf somewhere in your head.* Now and then, a box fell off that shelf, spilled all over the floor, and they worked together to pick up the pieces. *Jake can't help me now,* she thought. *I need to box this one up all by myself.*

The closer she got to the cabin, the more memories she encountered. Jake driving, she's smiling and humming along with the radio. Hum noises, that's what Jake called them. Boo's in the back seat, bouncing from window to window, scouting for squirrels and barking every time he saw one. The time the three of them spent up in these mountains was some of the most peaceful she'd ever known. The cabin was a sanctuary, an escape.

Kate stopped the Jeep and walked about twenty yards into the forest. She stood at the foot of a massive white oak tree, six feet wide and a hundred feet tall. A small stone tablet lay against the base of the tree, and a tear rolled down her cheek when she knelt and cleared away the dry grass and leaves. "Arthur 'Boo' Radley. Beloved friend and guardian. Forever in our hearts. Until we meet again." Kate sat down and sobbed.

The day Boo disappeared was frightening. She and Jake searched the woods for hours, and it was getting dark. Boo never strayed far, and would always come the moment he was called. Kate knew something was wrong. She'd known for days, but couldn't bear to think about it or tell Jake what she was feeling. *It wasn't real, just fear,* she thought. She always knew the day would come, and when it did, it would be too soon. Kate felt drawn to the old white oak. Boo was laying at the base of the tree, his breath shallow, his eyes opened just a slit when she approached.

Kate screamed for Jake, but they were too far apart. She looked for blood or any sign of injury. Boo whimpered when she tried to examine him, and then she knew. Boo had wandered off alone to take one last nap by his favorite tree. Kate laid down alongside and wrapped her arms around him. She heard Jake come up behind her and she knew he would understand. Neither of them said a word. Kate just stroked Boo's head and whispered in his ear. "Goodbye, my friend. I will always love you." And he was gone.

Jake scooped Kate up in his arms and pulled her in tight. She felt the tears that streamed down his face. She kissed his cheek and then nestled into the warmth and strength of his embrace. This old, sweet, tortured-soul of a dog brought them together, and for that she would be eternally grateful.

Kate stood, wiped away the tears and walked back to the Jeep. Her legs were heavy, the grief she carried a weight on her shoulders. *I'm alone,* she thought. *There's nothing here now but pain and sorrow. Nothing but memories of an extraordinary man, and the love that gave me strength. Memories of a dog, horribly beaten and scarred, who proved that love conquers all. All but death.*

She drove on, passing the rifle and pistol ranges Jake carved into the mountainside. Overgrown practice bays filled with grass and weeds three feet high, and steel targets looking like the Tin Man, rusted and frozen. Kate had no idea how many hours they spent training. *These are perishable skills,* she thought. But Jake made every lesson a competition, and she loved to win.

Just around the corner was the cabin, set in the center of two hundred acres of woodland privacy. The sun had set, and an array of solar walkway and safety lighting glowed around the cabin and outbuildings. The dojo they built together held a special memory and was a pivotal moment in Jake's recovery. Resembling a Japanese teahouse, the open frame design welcomed fresh mountain air and offered spectacular views of the valley below.

Kate was on her own for sunrise yoga, while Jake watched her move and sipped his espresso. The hours spent grappling on the tatami mats were painful. Don't you quit on me. Don't you dare, she recalled driving past. That was the challenge one-legged Jake needed. The mats rekindled Jake's confidence and sparked the dream to build his team, an elite executive protection team, under the Trident banner. When the sessions were their most intense, their secluded dojo became an oasis. Two glistening, muscular bodies entwined in a flurry of energy, passion, and ecstasy.

The cinderblock shop was Jake's domain, and a source of pride. Every brick and timber he set himself. Kate ventured in occasionally to bring him lunch or a beer, and she'd find him covered in grease. In Jake's shop, every tool had its purpose and its place. He kept the equipment ready to run, just like his grandfather had taught him, and heaven help you if you borrowed something and didn't put it back where you found it.

Kate pulled up to the cabin and backed into the spot where Jake always parked. *Protocols,* she thought. *I will never escape Jake's protocols.* But there was comfort in the thought and even the hint of a smile.

She fired up the propane generator and headed inside with the few groceries she'd collected. The cabin had been in Jake's family for generations. The fresh water and remote location made for a great moonshine setup back in the day, and there was an overlook rise nearby where you could see anyone approaching a mile away. Jake added the solar-powered game cameras to catch any two-legged critters that might stray too close.

Jake and his grandfather did most of the work, bringing the cabin into the twenty-first century. There was always work to be done, but it was a warm and comfortable home.

"I'm back," she said, stepping through the door. It felt like she was just out running errands. The weight was lifting. This space was so much more than memories and loss. Kate had always been sensitive to things she couldn't see or explain, but she knew how things felt. And this felt like home. She felt safe.

Kate looked over the groceries and passed. She unlocked the wine cellar door, and down the steps, dug eight feet below ground, was a large root cellar. Jake found it amusing to call it the wine cellar, and the name stuck. There were no wine racks, just a few cases of wine and beer, and all the other food and supplies that lasted forever in the constant cool of the room.

Armed with a bottle of Pinot Noir, a jar of popcorn, and a can of preserved Red Feather butter, she was ready for dinner. Kate sipped while the corn popped and she melted the butter. She sat crossed legged on the couch with an enormous bowl of popcorn cradled in her lap. *Boo loved popcorn*, she thought. *Almost as much as I do.* She pictured him laying perfectly still at her feet, eyes glued on her hands. With every piece that went into Kate's mouth, he seemed to wonder. *Is that one mine? What about this one?* And every so often Kate would toss one that Boo caught on the fly.

She finished the popcorn and ran her fingers over the remnants of the butter and salt. She poured another glass and took it to her workstation. Jake reluctantly setup a satellite link for Kate, and she launched into a series of system checks and configuration steps. *The office was a close call*, she thought. *Whatever went wrong cost Pete his life.*

Kate retrieved the Faraday bag and set it on the desk. *I have what you want, you bastard,* she thought. *Whoever the hell you are. I will figure out why you would kill to get it. And I'll retrieve Jake's files, someway, somehow.*

She feared it was more wishful thinking than strategy. She needed a plan, and given the narrow escape at Richmond Pinnacle, the obvious first step was to contact Nomad.

CHAPTER 65

SHENANDOAH VALLEY REGIONAL AIRPORT, WEYERS CAVE, VIRGINIA

MIKHAIL ZHUKOV LOWERED HIS head and jogged out to the helicopter. The MH-6, Little Bird, was ready for takeoff. The rapid thumping of the rotor blades grew more intense, and the wind whipped his face. Standing at the open bay of the passenger compartment, he could feel the heat of the engine's exhaust. The two men he requested occupied the passenger seats, and each gave him a quick thumbs up. He nodded, tossed in a heavy black kit bag, and the men dragged it in and strapped it down.

Zhukov circled around the front of the bird and climbed into the co-pilot's seat. He clipped the three-point harness and grabbed the aviation headset hanging just above his head. With the headset on and the boom mic in position, he gave the pilot the OK, and the tower cleared them for takeoff.

"How long to the staging zone?" Zhukov asked the pilot.

"Fifteen mics."

"Alright. Listen up. I am Zulu-One. Breacher, you are Zulu-Two. Sniper..."

"Zulu-Three. Got it."

"Interrupt me again," Zhukov said. "And it will be the last thing you do."

"Yes, Sir. Sorry, Sir."

There was complete silence for the rest of the fifteen-minute flight. An MH-6 is small, highly maneuverable, and can easily land on streets and rooftops, making the Little Bird ideal for special forces insertion, and the roof of a deserted warehouse was the perfect spot for a low profile landing. The height of the warehouse provided cover, and the distance from the road below kept the bird and the team out of view.

Zhukov and the two operators grabbed their gear bags. Gun belts, tactical vests and body armor plate carriers went on first, followed by helmets and NODS, their night vision gear. They extracted their sidearms from transport cases, inserted magazines and racked the slides. The breacher's kit included a combination of explosive charges and detonators. Zhukov knew that without a specific mission plan, Zulu Two had to guess what he might need, and that would have to do.

With all the gear in place, and the kit bags stowed, they did a comms check. Then Zhukov gave a short briefing.

"Flight time from here is twenty mics," Zhukov began. "We drop two clicks from the target and proceed on foot. The HVI is a woman believed to be hiding in a rural cabin. Consider the target armed and dangerous. Once we are in position, Zulu-Three will take overwatch. Three will monitor vehicles approaching our location, but take no action without authorization. Understood?"

"Yes, Sir."

"Zulu-Two. You are with me. We'll confirm the HVI is inside and alone. Nothing more until I assess the situation. Understood?"

"Yes, Sir."

"Questions?"

"What are the rules of engagement?"

"The HVI is not to be engaged under any circumstances," Zhukov said. "The target has intel we must collect. Elimination protocols apply to any hostiles we encounter."

The men nodded their understanding. All three men clipped into the retention harnesses on the side of the Little Bird, their feet resting on the skids. They'd proceed to the drop zone in the open air, the rotor blast and cool night air slapping their faces.

The darkness of a moonless night was a gift. The chopper made a fast, low approach and hovered. Harnesses popped, and boots hit the ground. The trio assumed low defensive positions, and the Bird lifted, skimmed the trees and headed back to the staging area.

"On me." Zhukov said, and the three men began the climb toward the coordinates Margot gave him.

Zhukov couldn't risk a daylight approach, and they got here as fast they could, but he couldn't help wondering if she made it to the cabin. *Or is she already dead?*

CHAPTER 66

SUNDAY, APRIL 19
4:48 PM EDT

UNDISCLOSED LOCATION

WITH NO WAY TO reach Kate directly, Nomad watched and waited, and thought about the past. While Kate was at Langley, her Darknet activity drew his attention. He let Kate believe she was recruiting an asset, but Nomad sought her out. She grew to trust him and his intel. Their intelligence collection intercepted arms sales, shutdown terrorist funding, and exposed a chemical weapons cache. Through it all, they used Nomad's Darknet services to communicate. Kate had no idea where in the world Nomad operated. She never saw his face, and he never revealed his true identity.

After Syria, everything changed. Kate broke off all contact and left the Agency. When she landed at the law firm, Nomad followed. His connection to her lab was a lifeline. Nomad imagined himself as more guardian angel than stalker, but the truth lay somewhere in between. He kept their private channel open on the Darknet, hoping she might reach out again someday, but he never imagined his life might depend on it.

"You want me to watch for a while?" Keisha asked. "I wouldn't have to do anything, right? Just let you know if the screen changes?"

"Yeah, it's pretty boring, but I can't seem to focus on anything else," Nomad said. "And it's been hours, so I'm hoping it will be any time now."

"Did you get any sleep?"

"It may surprise you, but yes, I did. I suspected it would be hours before she could get somewhere safe. She knows the game. Wherever she's headed, she'd avoid major towns and roads, and that will slow her down."

"Didn't think of that."

"She would."

"Smart girl," Keisha said. "Any idea where she'll go?"

"No clue," he said. "Kate's social media and online presence is pristine, and that's prefect."

"So Moore won't know where to look?"

"Exactly. For once, we're on a level playing field. He doesn't know anything more than I do."

"I must be good luck," Keisha said.

"Why do you say that?"

"Have a look."

Nomad turned his chair back to the monitor and there it was. Mockingbird was logging in. *She's safe,* he thought. *Thank God.*

Once Kate authenticated on the server, she sent a quick message.

Mockingbird>Are you there?

Nomad>I am. Are you OK? Secure location?

Mockingbird>Yes and yes. Now, tell me what the hell is happening. Who was on line? Why do they want Jake's NanoVault?

Nomad>I can answer your questions, but you may not believe the answers.

Mockingbird>Try me.

Nomad>There are things you need to see.

Mockingbird>Tox?

Nomad>Yes.

Using the Tox video chat client, they'd have solid end-to-end encryption, and none of the risks of mega-corporation products like Skype or Zoom snooping on the conversation. A few seconds later, Nomad answered Kate's call.

"I can't see you," Kate said. "Can you see me?"

"Yes," he said. "It's not an issue with your client. While there's some video I need to share, I still need to protect my identity. In my world, remaining hidden is my only protection."

"Fine. Whatever," she said. "Let's just get on with it."

"Jake's NanoVault is damaged."

"I know that."

"What you don't know is the damage exposed something that Moore's trying to keep hidden."

"Hold on. Are you seriously suggesting Devin Moore, billionaire, philanthropist, sent those goons to my office? Somehow. Moore's responsible for Pete's death?"

"Yes, and I said you wouldn't believe me."

"Well, you were right. That's absurd. I know Devin. We were at MIT together. And he is one of the firm's biggest clients."

"Yes, I know."

"Look, he may be a misogynistic narcissist, but he's no killer."

"Let's just table that for now," Nomad said. "Before you connected to Jake's NanoVault, you took some extraordinary steps to secure your communications channels. Why?"

"Wait, a minute. How could you possibly know that?" Kate asked. "You hacked my lab."

"I did, and it saved your life."

"How long have you been spying on me?"

"It's not important," Nomad said. "And we don't have a lot of time. Can we focus on the issue?"

"How long?"

"From your first day on the job?"

"Jesus Christ," she said. "You bastard."

"I know how it must look."

"No. You don't," she said. "I don't think you have any idea how violated I feel right now."

"After everything that happened, I wanted to know you were OK. And then I thought I could help."

"Help me? How could you help me?"

"Like the Smiley embezzlement case you were working," he said.

"What could you have possibly done on the Smiley case?"

"You were running out of time —"

"You opened the port."

"Those Cayman Islands banks are hard nuts to crack," he said. "And you were so close."

"That explains it," she said. "I figured some newb in IT screwed up a firmware update, and suddenly I'm in. That was you?"

"Everything else was all you," he said. "You found what you needed, moved the money, saved the day, and now Smiley's history."

"What do you mean Smiley's history?"

"You haven't heard?" he asked. "Sorry, I just assumed, but with Jake and Paris, I guess you missed it."

"Missed what?"

"Smiley's dead. Same day the resignation news broke, he committed suicide."

Kate walked away from the camera, and there was complete silence. *I've lost her,* Nomad thought. *I'm just a stalker creep, and now she'll never trust me. It's over.*

She sat back down and looked into the camera. "OK. What's done is done," she said. "You asked why I locked down my lab. On the flight from Paris, I wanted to see if I could access Jake's NanoVault. He left me a clue to the pass-phrase, and I unlocked it. The damage was obvious, but I hoped I'd be able to read at least some data. It's important. And not just because it's Jake."

"Were you able to read the data?"

"The damage was bad. Not as bad as it is now, but what I could see wasn't much help. I couldn't open or copy any of the file folders."

"Then what happened?"

"Everything connected to the plane's network went crazy. We shut everything down, and I bagged the device. I wasn't sure the NanoVault was the source, but I didn't want to take any chances. I thought I had my lab locked up tight, and nothing happened for hours. Just when I thought Jake's device had nothing to do with the flight home, it happened again."

"I saw it."

"Right. You were in my network, spying on me," she said. "And you saw it, but what was it?"

"Moore's covert communications channel."

"Stop saying Moore."

"I'll try," he said. "Every Quantum NanoVault has a covert communications channel."

"There was nothing covert about what I saw."

"Exactly! That's the problem. Jake's device is broadcasting in the clear. The message is encrypted, but the transmission and the signal propagation affects everything within reach."

"Are you telling me that the NanoVaults are some kind of huge mesh network?"

"No. It's much more than that."

"Then what? What are they doing?"

"Moore..." he began. "Excuse me. Someone is using the NanoVaults as the world's largest, most sophisticated intelligence collection network."

"And you're the only one that knows about it?"

"There was one other," he said. "I had a partner, but he's dead."

"I suppose Moore killed him."

"He hired the man who did."

"Oh, of course he did," she said. "I don't think you have any idea how crazy this all sounds. And if you had any hard evidence, anything at all that backed up this fantasy, you could just leak it to the press and they'd eat him alive. They love nothing more than to see the mighty fall."

"Look, you wanted to know why two professional killers stormed your building, killed a man and came hunting for you. Now you know. Believe me or don't, that's up to you. But if you want to know what's on Jake's NanoVault, we need to work together. And we need to start now."

CHAPTER 67

APPALACHIAN MOUNTAINS, WEST VIRGINIA

KATE WRESTLED WITH NOMAD's offer. She needed to know what was on Jake's NanoVault, and she knew the window to recover anything would soon close, if it hadn't already. But she was also convinced Nomad was delusional, paranoid and obsessed with her. The smart choice was to kill the connection and walk away.

"Alright," she said. "Where do we start?"

"Everything you did at the lab was perfect, so start there."

"If it was perfect, Pete wouldn't be dead," she said, and began taking the same network hardening steps she did at the office. "But if they show up at my door, I'm not running. Not again."

"It won't come to that, but I need a favor."

"Let me guess. You want me to hand over control."

"It's not that you can't do the work," he said. "It's just that I'll be able to work a lot faster—"

"Stop. I get it," she said, and seconds later, she handed Nomad complete control of the cabin's network and her workstation.

"I'll let you know when I'm ready for the NanoVault."

"Fine. I'm going to see what I can pull from the vehicle data I collected."

"You had me scared," Nomad said. "I hope it was worth the risk."

"We'll see."

While Nomad prepared Kate's machine, she grabbed a laptop and the Onboard Diagnostic scanner from her bag. The OBD device was an essential part of Kate's digital forensic work. Perception might feel like reality, but armed with the data, Kate knew the truth. Vehicle speed, braking, lights, turn-signals. It's all in there. Navigation systems are the car's nanny cams, exposing bar hopping drivers. And smart phone integration took vehicle digital forensics to an entirely new level, with contacts, calls, text messages, and even play lists.

Let's start with navigation, she thought. *Where did you guys come from?* Kate didn't recognize the street address, but they came from New York. *Can't say I'm surprised. New York's been an underworld haven for decades.* She mapped the address. *Moore Tower. So they parked the car at the Tower. There are probably hundreds of cars parked there right now.*

Kate explored the navigation history. While the vehicle traveled extensively in and around New York, it always returned to Moore Tower. *There are dozens of businesses and shops, and God knows how many residents and employees.* She continued exploring, and the connection to Moore Tower was inescapable. *But nothing in the navigation system connected the car specifically to Moore Technologies.*

She retrieved the car's VIN and tracked down the registration. A Wyoming LLC owned the vehicle and a dozen more, just like it. *Probably a private car service,* she thought. *Basing the service at Moore Tower was a smart business decision, nothing more.*

Let's check the contacts and call log, Kate thought. *Assuming the occupants were stupid enough to link a cell phone.* Contacts were blank. *Probably a burner.* But a handful of numbers appeared in the call log. She sorted by frequency and began searching for the associated listings. The most frequently dialed numbers mapped to New York restaurants. *Pizza, Chinese, Deli. Probably all takeout.* But one number caught her by surprise.

That's the main office number, she thought. *Someone in the car called Moore Technologies every few days.* That was a connection Kate could not ignore, but refused to accept Nomad's conclusion. *This doesn't mean they're connected to Devin,* she thought. *He has hundreds of employees. Any one of them could be involved.* But there was no denying a possible connection between the assailants and Moore Technologies. *Did someone in Moore's world direct the assault on the Richmond Pinnacle building?*

"Kate?" Nomad asked.

She tapped the AirPod in her ear and unmuted the mic. "Ready for it?"

"Yep. It's time."

Kate pulled the Faraday pouch out of her messenger bag and removed Jake's NanoVault. She set the device near the workstation, and Nomad completed the connection.

"It still connects," he said. "That's something. Now, let's see what we've got."

The directory display was not encouraging, and Kate's heart sank.

"Don't panic," Nomad said. "We've got a long way to go, and we're just starting."

"What's the plan?"

"I'll throw everything I've got at the device, and salvage whatever I can, but—"

"Don't get my hopes up."

"That's not what I was going to say, but yes, this doesn't look good."

"What were you going to say?"

"I'm hoping for another broadcast wave, like the one on the plane and in your office."

"That didn't show up for hours."

"And there's no way to know how long it might take tonight, or if it will even happen, but if it does, I'm ready."

"Ready for what?"

"OK. This is going to sound crazy."

"Crazier than before?"

"Yeah. Definitely," he said. "If we get another wave, I can seed the broadcast with my code and surf straight into Moore's network."

Kate didn't stop him from saying Moore this time. She still didn't believe Moore was a killer, but the device did broadcast a message. She saw it, even decrypted part of it before she ran for her life. *Some part of that message was her name,* she thought. *Whatever the message, it wasn't supposed to be broadcast. People buy these devices to guard their secrets and mask their identities. What if that is a lie?*

"Let's say you get inside, and for the record, I think that's a long shot, but then what?"

"I'll get in," he said. "This will be lucky number three."

"So, once you're in, you'll have control?"

"I wish," he said. "No, this is a massive system. But I will have access and that's a start. I can assemble my code and search for proof."

"You'll never be able to use it," she said. "Trust me. I've walked this line before with some creative data collection, and nothing you find will be admissible."

"Believe me, I know, and Moore would never let anything go to court. He owns the DAs and the judges."

"You could leak it to the press."

"Like the Cahill video? No thanks," he said. "Besides, I don't want to destroy the NanoVault or the company. Moore's scripted and rehearsed stories of the NanoVault spurring entrepreneurship are actually true. I've seen it. The NanoVault is, or could be, a secure way to sell your services, collect payment, and pay your bills. The device's foundation is solid, and ordinary people, all over the globe, would suffer significant losses if the whole thing went down."

"You lost me. You want back in to find proof, but for who?"

"For you," he said. "I need you to believe me."

"Why?"

"Because I can stop the data collection. And wipe clean everything he has, but I can't do it alone."

"What about Jake's data?"

"I promise," Nomad said. "I will do everything I can, but you're not the only one they're hunting. If they find me, it's checkmate."

Checkmate? That makes Nomad the king, she thought. *And my job now is to keep him safe.*

"I'm not saying I believe you," she said. "For Christ's sake, I don't even know your name, your real name, and all of this talk is absolutely insane, but I want the truth. If someone has hijacked these devices, they need to be stopped."

Kate stepped away from the workstation and tried to stifle a yawn.

"If you don't need me, I'm going to take a quick power nap. Twenty-minutes, tops. I'll be right here on the couch, and you're in my ear," she said, tapping the AirPod, "So if you need me, just say so."

"Before you go," Nomad said. "Did the vehicle data show anything?"

"Nothing useful," she lied.

CHAPTER 68

MOORE TOWER, MANHATTAN

ANDREW FREEMAN HIT A dead end. Kate's social media presence was virtually nonexistent. A couple of accounts, but no friends or followers. She scrubbed the few photos that existed - no GPS tags, or any source data. *Why did she even bother to post,* he wondered.

He hoped the BountyHunt sighting at Ruby's Corner would provide a clue, but other than general travel direction, it was another dead end. There were reports that Ruby's was the site of a shooting early this morning, one dead. It seemed an unlikely coincidence, given the time on the sighting, but they wrote it up as a robbery.

Jake's social media was a bit more robust, no doubt a requirement of his business, but here too every photo of Jake, his team, and occasionally Kate, were all sanitized. At least Jake had friends and followers, and Drew followed every path down every rabbit hole.

A gray-faced black lab showed up in some of the older photos, but nothing in the last year. Old scars criss-crossed the dog's face, some raised and thick, others deep like dry creek beds. But in every photo there was joy in everyone around and a gleam in the dog's eyes.

The Rainbow Bridge, he thought. *They loved this dog. Probably rescued from some place horrible, and he found his forever family.* Drew searched back through Jake's posts. *Got ya. Boo. That's the old boy's name.*

Drew's hunch paid off. Jake's message on the Rainbow Bridge was a moving tribute to a dog that changed their lives and would be in their hearts forever. A family photo of Jake, Kate and Boo, near a small lake, captured their love and their location.

The photo's geotag gave Drew a starting point, and a satellite search turned up one cabin and a few outbuildings just a couple of miles from the lake. The coordinates placed the cabin in the Appalachian Mountains of West Virginia and aligned with Kate passing through Ruby's Corner.

This has to be it, he thought, and he called Moore.

"Did you find Nomad?" Moore asked.

"No, but I have a high probability location on Preacher," Drew said. "A remote cabin in West Virginia."

"Why didn't this show up on the property searches? We should have seen this hours ago."

"It's in a state park, and there's no digital record of a deed." Drew said. "Best guess is the property was recorded a hundred years ago, passed down as a legacy, and now looks like it's inside a state park."

"That's where you'll find her," Moore said. "Is anyone close?"

"I just ran the location checks. We have the two from Richmond Pinnacle. They're ours, and that would let us keep this in house."

"Anyone else?"

"Yes. Red's getting close."

"That's interesting," Moore said. "Red took Cahill's contract, right?"

"Yes, that's right," Drew said, and pulled up the profile. "Real name, Manuel Rojas. Former DEA."

"I'm still pissed about the missing girl, but let him play. He might redeem himself," Moore said. "But close the open bid. We can't have amateurs rushing in now. Not when we're this close. What's the ETA?"

"It's rough mountain road terrain, so it will be slow going. From their current locations, I'd estimate two hours, three at most," Drew said. "Now, this is interesting," Drew added.

"What is it?"

"Ronin just checked in and wants to join the hunt. His locater has him at JFK. He must have just landed and saw the alert," Drew said. "But we don't need him, and he's nowhere near the target."

"What's the harm? He's quite resourceful. And Paris shook his confidence in the system, it wouldn't hurt to buy a little good will. Let him play."

"Alright. He's in."

"Excellent. One way or another, we should be able to wrap this up before breakfast."

Chapter 69

APPALACHIAN MOUNTAINS, WEST VIRGINIA

KATE STRETCHED OUT ON the couch, tucked one of the accent pillows under her head, and pulled a throw blanket down on top of her. *How long had it been since she slept*, she wondered, but before she could do the math, she was gone.

Jake was in the kitchen doing dishes. Boo was lying on the carpet right below her. She reached down and ran her fingers along his back until she reached his head. His ears were frayed and calloused, but she swore he purred when she rubbed them just right.

She sat up and stretched. "That was a delicious nap," she said. "Come sit down."

Before Jake could find a seat, Boo jumped up, taking half the couch, and lay across her legs.

"Sorry, Pal," Kate said, pointing at Boo's command of the couch. "You weren't fast enough."

"I'll make it work," Jake said, and he wiggled in between Kate and the arm of the couch. He wrapped an arm around her and she nestled into his shoulder. "I'm glad you slept."

"I guess I needed it."

"I'm afraid you did," Jake said. "Boo and I have been keeping an eye on you. You've been running pretty hard since..."

"Don't say it," she said. "I can't think about that. Not right now. I just want to enjoy the moment. The three of us together."

She looked up at his face, and into his beautiful brown eyes, warm and welcoming. Her sanctuary. She placed a hand on his cheek and felt the slight roughness of his stubble and the scar along his jawline. His eyes deepened as he looked into hers, the way he did when he was looking into her soul.

"I'm OK," she said.

"You will be."

"Love me?"

"Always."

Kate stirred, and the dream faded. But wrapped in the blanket's warmth and the glow of sweet memories, she soon faded off again. Kate slept longer and deeper this time, her body seizing the opportunity to regroup and recharge.

"Hey, Pal," Jake said, and kissed her forehead.

Kate smiled, knowing Jake was trying to wake her. "Five more minutes."

"You said that five minutes ago."

Boo joined in, licked her face, and barked.

"Alright. I get it. I'm up. I'm up."

"You need to get ready," Jake said.

"Ready for what?"

"They're coming."

"Who's coming?" she asked, but he was gone.

She called out after him. "Jake, who's coming?"

"Kate, are you awake?" Nomad asked.

"Is everything OK?"

"Yes, sorry to wake you."

"What time is it?" Kate asked, still half-asleep.

"About 8:30."

"It's been *three* hours?" Kate asked. ""Are you sure everything's alright?"

"Yeah, we're good. Better than good. I got back in."

"Did you find Jake's files?"

"No," he said. "Not yet. But I found something you need to see."

Kate rolled off the couch and sat down at the workstation.

"OK, let's see it," she said. "What the hell?"

"Sorry, I didn't mean to leave that on the screen."

"Are you seriously surfing porn?"

"No. No. That's not. It's —"

"Take a breath," Kate said. "Just tell me what's going on."

"This is Senator Cahill... with the girl."

"So it's true," Kate said. "She's so young. I had no idea."

"Trust me. There's stuff here you do not want to see," Nomad said. "And I found it all sitting inside Moore's network. Everything that was leaked to the media. And more. Much more. The public hasn't seen. At least, not yet."

"So one of Moore's political hacks is sitting on a pile of Cahill's dirty laundry," she said. "It's no secret they hated each other, but all this proves is that Moore and his people are ruthless. That won't surprise anyone."

"Agreed, but you're missing the point."

"Which is?"

"Where or how did they get all this material? I can tell you this is some very up close and personal media, email and texts. Everything digital in Cahill's world had to be compromised to collect all this."

"I'll give you that, but I've seen the same level of data collection on the CIA's high value targets."

"But what if Cahill wasn't a surveillance target? Not explicitly. What if all he and those around him had to do was buy a NanoVault? When this material showed up on the web, there was speculation it came from Cahill's vault, and Moore exploded when asked."

"So you think the conspiracy nuts were right?"

"Half right. I believe some of this material was definitely Cahill's — his personal trophy recordings of he and the girl."

"That's disgusting."

"I agree, so you won't catch me crying for him. But there's more that couldn't possibly have come from his personal NanoVault," he said. "There's something I'd like you to see, but I have to warn you. Cahill's death was no accidental overdose. He and the girl were murdered, and someone recorded the whole thing."

Kate flashed on the images she'd seen over the years at Langley, and the brutality of the Paris attack. But if this was the evidence Nomad claimed he could find, she needed to see it.

"I'm ready."

A man, dressed in an environmental suit, entered a hotel room, located a stash of drugs and swapped them for a similar packet of white powder.

"You're looking at Senator Cahill's suite, and that was the setup," Nomad said. "For both our sakes, I'll fast forward now, but you can see the girl being smuggled into the room and tied to the bed frame, and then Cahill arrives."

Nomad switched to fast forward again and sped through Cahill disrobing, snorting and dropping dead, then back to normal speed. The man in the environmental suit, returned to the Senator's suite, confirmed Cahill was dead, and injected the girl.

"We need to go to the police." Kate said.

"With what? A video I stole from a data center that doesn't exist. We have nothing. Not really. Plus, we're nobody. Moore is one of the richest, most respected people on the planet, and his legal team would crush any investigation. Anything actionable would vanish before they could issue a subpoena, and that's assuming they found a judge that Moore doesn't already own or couldn't intimidate."

"That's a pretty cynical view of our justice system."

"Not cynical. Practical," he said. "Imagine millions of NanoVaults distributed worldwide. All spying on their owners. Every secret a vulnerability, leverage for manipulation. And if someone resists, or they're no longer useful, they get the Cahill treatment."

"That's my point," she said. "Whatever our feelings about the man, a United States Senator was murdered. We have to do *something*. I still have contacts in the CIA, people I trust. And a friend at the NSA."

"First, we *are* doing something. Something important, and the window to stop Moore could close any minute," Nomad said. "And second, your contacts can't bring Cahill back. At best they could open an investigation, and more gridlock. They can't stop the next murder, but we can."

"If all of this depends on us, I need to see the data for myself," she said. "I need to know, beyond any doubt, that there's no evidence of file manipulation or insertion. If you're right about the NanoVaults, whether or not you're right about Moore, I'll know."

Kate took control of the link into Moore's network. She found herself with root access on a Linux server and began exploring. Kate knew that if Nomad was right, data collection on that scale would call for massive storage and Big Data analytical tools. She found both. Searching the data directly could trigger security alerts, but no one sets tripwires on event logs, and she dug in.

"Oh, no!" Kate yelled.

"What is it? What did you find?"

"Jake was right," she muttered, recalling the dream, and the warning. *Get ready. They're coming.* "Moore knows where I am," Kate said. "My location is in the logs. I don't know how, but he knows."

"You need to leave. Now. Grab the device and go."

"Go where?" she asked. "Moore has data streaming in from everywhere. Nowhere's safe."

"New York," Nomad said. "The encrypted file I just texted has my address. The password is Planck's Constant to six places. Find me and together we'll finish this."

"No."

"What do you mean, no?"

"They'll just follow, and I'll lead them straight to you," she said. "This ends here. Tonight."

"Kate, think about what Jake would want…"

"I am," she said. "Jake told me get ready. And that's what I'm going to do. You wanted a link back into Moore's network. Use it. Do whatever you set out to do, but make it quick. With a system this sophisticated, they will find your connection and shut it down. You may not get another chance, so make it count."

Chapter 70

SUNDAY, APRIL 19
8:22 PM EDT

APPALACHIAN MOUNTAINS, WEST VIRGINIA

MIKHAIL ZHUKOV AND HIS operators hiked toward the target coordinates. Their helmet-mounted NODs, night observation devices, allowed them to climb like they were hiking in daylight, but they stopped several times to maneuver around the infrared game cameras that monitored the hillside.

When they neared the top, the three men took up initial positions on the rise just below the cabin. Zhukov used a hand-held thermal scanner to assess the cabin's interior and signaled confirmation of a single occupant. Switching to white phosphor mode revealed additional detail, and given the height and shape of the image, Zhukov was confident this was his target.

As a precaution, Zhukov continued to limit comms and used hand signals to show that Zulu-Two should follow him, and Zulu-Three, the team's designated sniper, would seek higher ground and establish an overwatch position.

All three retreated far enough down the hill to minimize the chance of detection and then circled around into optimal locations. Zulu-Three set up a sniper hide with a field of fire concentrated on the gravel road that approached the cabin. At the higher elevation, the canopy of trees faded away, providing a clear view of the road. The road, carved into the side of the mountain, made a long sweeping turn, climbing steadily toward the cabin. If authorized to shoot, Zulu-Three would ensure nothing made it up the road. With three fast clicks on the mic button, Zulu-Three confirmed he was in position.

Zhukov and Zulu-Two took cover just below the stone retaining wall that corralled the large, flat driveway. With a clear view of the front door and main floor windows, they watched and waited.

Kate stormed out the front door and headed for Jake's shop.

"Should we grab her now?" Zulu-Two asked.

Zhukov shook his head, removed a vehicle GPS tracker from his tactical vest and gave it to Zulu-Two. When Kate entered the shop, Two worked his way around to the Jeep, and planted the small black device inside the rear passenger wheel well.

Mikhail checked the receiver and confirmed the signal strength. *Now, she can lead us to Nomad.*

CHAPTER 71

APPALACHIAN MOUNTAINS, WEST VIRGINIA

8:47 PM KATE UNLOCKED Jake's shop, marched inside, and hit the lights. While there was a gun safe in the house, the equipment she wanted was in the armory, behind a four-inch-thick vault door, and surrounded by six inches of steel-reinforced concrete.

From a key rack on the wall, she grabbed the ATV key and smiled when it started right up. That's my boy, she thought. *Always prepared.* Jake kept the utility vehicles on a trickle charge, and each had the same trauma kits they kept in the cars, and wilderness emergency gear, flares, snacks, and water that he refreshed periodically.

She spun the mechanical combination dial, zero-seven-six-two. Then turned the vault's stainless steel spindle to retract the bolts, and pulled the door wide open. Kate stepped inside, turned off the alarm, and faced the camera. She blew Jake a kiss, like she'd done a hundred times, knowing Jake would see the entry alert and the video feed. *Wherever you are, my love. I know you're watching.*

Kate had been in the armory many times, and while she knew exactly where to look, it all felt new. Somehow, different. This was his world. His things. Built from the ground up to meet his exact specifications. *Jake could have been an architect or engineer*, she thought. *But after nine-eleven, the world changed, and we changed with it.*

Along the twenty-four-foot length of floor to ceiling slatwall, the rifles hung by caliber and function. Next to each rifle was a rack of loaded magazines or a shoulder sling of loose rounds. Kate lifted the AXMC off the rack and pulled back the bolt, which slid out like butter. *The chamber was clear, of course, but rules are rules, and Jake wouldn't have it any other way.*

The Accuracy International rifle chambered in .300 Winchester Magnum was one of Kate's favorites. The one she pulled down was configured for night operations an INOD thermal weapon sight clipped on in front of the Nightforce scope. In the right hands, this weapon was true to its moniker, Advanced Extreme Long Range. Kate attached a SureFire SOCOM suppressor and cased the rifle. She secured the case to the ATV and went back inside to grab the rest of her tactical gear.

She pulled her tactical vest off the wall rack, slipped it over her head, and secured the Velcro straps on the open side. In the chest magazine pouches, she stuffed four 10 round mags. The last piece was the Ops-Core helmet and NODs. While she didn't need the helmet's ballistic protection, the night vision would allow her to run the ATV without running lights and weave through the trees and up to Jake's sniper hide.

Kate secured the armory and the shop, pointed the ATV toward an adjacent hill, and started climbing.

***

9:00 PM ETHAN STONE, former USMC Scout Sniper, was part of a small group of independent contractors that Margot Ryder kept in her little black book. If an op needed plausible deniability, or called for domestic action, Stone was on the short list.

Designated Zulu-Three for a mission he didn't understand, Stone established an overwatch position, creating a makeshift sniper hide among the scrub brush and trees. A McMillan TAC-338 was his weapon of choice, and given the rush to meet this operation's timetable, and the lack of target intel, Stone wanted to be prepared to engage at longer distances. He also assumed a night op profile configured the weapon with an ADUNS thermal sight and image intensifier.

Zhukov broke comms silence and said, "HVI vehicle approaching your position. Take cover."

An ATV passed within fifty feet of Stone's location and continued climbing up and out of sight. He could see the driver was wearing night vision, and spotted the rifle case strapped to the rig. *What the hell is going on*, he wondered. *Who is this woman?*

"Zulu-One. Be advised. HVI wearing NODs. Armed with a long gun."

"Confirmed," Zhukov responded.

"Rules of engagement?"

"Zulu-Three. Do not engage."

***

9:05 PM KATE CONTINUED climbing until she reached Jake's sniper hide. The hide was nearly invisible, even from the air, but it wasn't built for comfort. Kate rolled out the shooter's mat, which offered some padding and insulation from the cold, hard ground. She flipped up the NODS, crawled in and setup the rifle's bi-pod and a sand-filled rear bag. From a push-up position over the stock, she lowered straight behind the gun, kicked her legs wide and rolled her feet out.

Wider. That's better, she thought, because that's what Jake would say. When they would hike up here, he'd tell her stories. *I was just a boy when my grandfather brought me up here. I thought you could see the entire world from here. Well, my world anyway. When my grandfather was a boy, he would come here to keep watch in case the sheriff came calling. Those were the moonshine days, and great-granddad made some of the best. Kept the family fed when times were tough.* Kate loved Jake's stories. She'd heard them all a dozen times, maybe more, but his face would light up when he talked about his grandfather, and she loved the sound of his voice.

Kate spent a few minutes on the glass familiarizing herself with the terrain and getting reacquainted with the weapon platform. The night vision device was nothing short of phenomenal, and far exceeded the capabilities of civilian gear. Kate had no idea how Jake came by the equipment and assumed it was one of the unspoken perks of his service and active duty SOF connections, but she knew it was the NVD of choice among the nation's elite snipers.

She pulled the Kestrel 5700x from her tac vest and ran through the ballistic calculations for the current temperature and wind. Jake's laminated range card was tacked just to the right of where she was setup. The card listed prominent landscape features along with the distances Jake had lazed with a range finder. The edge of the ravine at twelve o'clock, giant pine at the bend in the road, granite boulder.

Her plan was to keep it simple. Catch the vehicle when it made the turn, and faced directly at her. Depending on the vehicle's speed, the engagement window was three to five seconds. With a glance at the range card, she knew what to dial. *Engage at 930 meters,* she thought, and pictured training with Jake from this exact spot. They'd drive down the hill, set a row of melons along the road, then go back and settle in behind the rifle.

Picture ten football fields stacked end to end, Jake would say, to help her visualize the distance, and all that did was make her nervous. *How the hell was she going to hit something that small at that distance?* But he insisted that with the right equipment and a solid grasp of the ballistics, he could teach anyone to shoot at this distance, and he did. Kate ran the calcs, and dialed in the elevation. *Wind's minimal. I'll hold for the wind if needed.*

Kate wondered how long before trouble arrived. From the log files in Moore's network, her location was compromised about two hours earlier. *This location should have been secure,* she thought. *Zero digital footprint. I missed something.* She had no way to know the precise drive time, but the Ruby's Corner mess gave her a starting point. *Might be another hour,* she thought. *Maybe sooner.*

Headlights flickering through the forest canopy changed her mind. *Looks like sooner.*

She snugged in behind the gun and pulled back the bolt. Running the bolt forward, she chambered a round. *Now breathe*, Jake would say. *Slow your heart rate down. That's it. In, two, three, four. Hold, two, three, four. Release, two, three, four.* Kate felt the tension drifting away. She watched the illuminated reticle's crosshairs float, and she prepared to engage.

An SUV, very much like the one she destroyed in Richmond, exited the thickest part of the forest and began the long, sweeping drive along the mountain road. Her interdiction plan was simple enough. *Trap them between the mountain and the ravine. There's no cover on either side. What about a high-speed reverse,* she wondered. *At night, on a gravel road, with the turn right behind them? They'll go flying off the edge, roll to the bottom of the ravine and their bodies may never be found. They could speed up. That brings them into my field of fire, and they'll never make the turn. No, the smart move is to bail out. I'll empty the magazine into the engine, and they'll be walking. If they're in decent shape, take 'em a couple of hours to reach the cabin, and I'll be long gone.*

***

9:14 PM STONE WAS on his rifle, monitoring the road up to the cabin. His Flir night vision gear gave him man-sized target clarity well past the 1,000 meter range. He watched in silence until he spotted vehicle lights in the distance. The approaching vehicle maneuvered the winding road, its lights alternating between hugging the mountain road and darting out over the ravine.

"Zulu-One. We have contact. Single vehicle. Three clicks."

"Any identification?"

"Negative, One," he said. "Civilian SUV."

"Occupants?"

"Two Tangos. Both male. Permission to engage?"

"Do not engage."

Stone locked in tight behind his rifle, flipped the safety off, trigger finger indexed and prepared to engage if ordered. He watched the vehicle navigate a narrow turn and begin to face him. He held his reticle along the vehicle's path. With surgical precision, he anticipated a point of aim that would place the point of impact on the driver's chest.

"I have the shot."

***

9:19 PM Kate pressed the safety lever forward and eased her finger onto the trigger. The vehicle lights flared out into the night, and they began the turn toward her. Her point of aim was well below the front bumper. At this distance and from the elevated position, that would put her rounds through the grill and into the engine block. With no wind worth considering, she exhaled, held her breath, and confirmed the point of aim. She pressed the trigger to the rear and all the way through the shot.

She heard the suppressed pop when the round exited. She cycled the bolt and fired again. In the one-point-two-seconds it took the first bullet to reach the vehicle, Kate was back on target and ready to fire a third shot. She assessed the first shot. The engine impact was a near perfect center hit. The second shot broke a little left, but both were solid grill and engine strikes. The driver slammed the brakes, both men lurched forward, and then bailed out. Kate sent a third and then fourth round into the stationary vehicle. *They won't be going anywhere,* she thought. The two occupants cowered behind the open doors. *I could punch through those doors like paper, but that's not the plan.*

***

9:20 PM STONE HEARD the pop of a suppressed rifle. He swept his optics across the vehicle and assessed the damage.

"Zulu-One. HVI has engaged. Vehicle stopped. Tangos uninjured."

"Did the shooter miss?"

Stone considered what he was seeing through his scope, and the shot pattern.

"Negative. Vehicle disabled."

"Continue to monitor and advise, but do not engage," Zhukov said. "Mission success requires HVI remain unaware of our presence. Understood?"

"Copy that."

***

9:20 PM KATE STUDIED the scene and readied a follow-up shot. *I should empty the magazine into the engine*, Kate thought. *Just to be sure those two will be walking.* But the visible damage to the grill and hood, combined with the steam and smoke confirmed additional shots weren't required. *Up hill or down, doesn't matter. Either way, they're stranded in the dead zone. No cell coverage for miles. No one's coming to help, and now the vehicle's blocking the road for me. Perfect.*

But she hesitated. An image flashed in her mind. A moment of recognition. *What was it,* Kate wondered. *What did I see?* She swept her scope back over the scene. The vehicle's interior lights were on and, for a moment, painted the area with a bright white LED glow. The driver's head popped up, framed in the door's window, then he turned and sprinted for the rear. Kate's mind filled with images. *Automatic gunfire shattering the building's glass doors. Bullets ripping through the security guard's body. Pete laying in a pool of blood, eyes fixed and pleading with the bald man standing over him. The execution.*

That's him. Bald. Stocky, Kate thought. *And the passenger. Tall. Thin. That's the other one.* Kate's face flushed, heart raced and adrenaline surged. *These two killed Pete and tried to kill me. And they're back to try again. OK. New plan.*

The lift back of the SUV flipped up. Another interior light flashed on, then off. Kate saw movement, but no clear target. She snugged her finger up against the trigger, but resisted the urge to fire. *If I start blindly pumping rounds into the back of the car, I might get lucky,* she thought. *But I could also push them out of my field of fire, or even down into the ravine. I need to think.*

***

9:21 PM STONE WATCHED the two men sprint to the rear of the vehicle, and collect some gear.

"Zulu-One. Vehicle's occupants are now wearing plate carriers and ballistic helmets."

"Weapons?"

"Stand by."

He saw one man crawl along the far side of the SUV, and tuck behind the engine block for cover. A long gun barrel popped up over the hood.

"Long gun," he said, and then he spotted the barrel's distinctive muzzle break.

"Barrett. Fifty-cal."

"What is your assessment?"

"The fifty has no identifiable target. Tangos have minimal cover, but are now much smaller targets."

"What is the shot?"

"Six inch head shot at a thousand meters," he said, and added. "I have the shot, but HVI would hear it. My location would be blown."

There was a moment of silence, and then Zhukov asked, "If she shoots, can you follow her shot?"

"Zulu-One. Say again."

"Can you hold on target and shoot only if she does?"

That's nuts, Stone thought. *But just crazy enough to work. My shot would sound like an echo. If I can pull off the timing. I don't know who this woman is, but clearly my job is to keep her alive.*

"Affirmative," he said, and took aim.

***

9:28 PM KATE SAW the two men hunt for cover. The SUV traveled farther than she hoped, and at that angle, it offered some protection. The driver appeared to hunker down behind the rear wheel. She knew the steel around the wheel and axle could absorb hits that would slide right through most of the vehicle.

The tall one dragged something toward the engine block, and when the barrel popped over the hood, she recognized it. *Barrett fifty-cal*, she thought.

Jake had a fifty, and they'd taken it out a few times. Neither of them cared for it. At one time it was considered the pinnacle of vehicle interdiction, but it's heavy, loud and kicks like a mule. She was happy with her choice, and no one could argue it wasn't effective.

Kate's thermal vision optic painted the scene well enough for her to know the situation just became way more complicated. She spotted ballistic helmets, chest rigs, and suspected plate carriers. The barrel of the fifty-cal was draped across the hood of the SUV, and the shooter tucked behind the engine block. *My target just got a helluva lot smaller*, she thought. *Maybe I should just go. Put a few rounds downrange to keep them guessing and leave. After all, that was the goal.*

Kate weighed her options. *Other than general direction, the fifty-cal doesn't have a target. Tucked inside Jake's hide, I'm invisible. But if I shoot again, the men could see a flash. The suppressor's good, but nothing's perfect.* She ran through what she had within reach that could stack the odds. *Ah...the ATV has flares. A distraction might just work. If it doesn't, I'll leave.*

She crawled out of the sniper hide and hiked back to the ATV. Kate grabbed what she needed, worked her way back up the hide, and tucked in behind the gun. She checked her point of aim, and the wind. *Good. Still no need to hold for wind.*

Kate unscrewed the end-cap on the MK8 rocket flare and the launch pull cord dangled. It would take two hands to launch the flare, but flight time would let her get back on the gun before the flare ignited. With a few deep breaths to slow her heart rate and clear her mind, she was ready. *Let's light em up.*

She yanked the launch cord. The flare launched with a whoosh and arced toward the SUV. *One thousand one. One thousand two.* Kate counted and waited. Flight time was roughly six seconds to reach an altitude of about a thousand feet, and that gave Kate time to hold steady on the shot.

***

9:35 PM NOTHING COULD distract Ethan Stone. Tested under countless battlefield conditions, he knew lives depended on maintaining focus and staying on target, no matter what was happening around him.

Stone held his aim tight on the stock of the Barrett Fifty-Cal. He estimated where the shooter's head would have to appear if the Tango reached for the gun. The fifty was not a weapon you took lightly. To control the shot and recover from the recoil, the fifty required solid footing and weight behind the gun.

The pop of the flare was unexpected, but Stone didn't flinch. The flare ignited with an explosion of sparks and a sharp crack that echoed in the ravine. A bright red ball glowed and swayed beneath the parachute trailing smoke on its long, slow descent. Stone waited.

***

9:36 PM KATE WAS on target when the barrel of the fifty-cal swung left and the shooter came up behind it, his head following the flare. *He's hunting for the launch point,* Kate thought. *Shooter Ready? Ready. Send it.*

Kate pressed the trigger, cycled the bolt, and in less than a second was right back on target. The bullet's impact, just above the ear, left no doubt in her mind. *One down, one to go.*

Where are you going, she wondered, watching the driver wriggling on his belly. *Like the snake you are,* she thought. *With his partner dead, he's going for the ravine. That's smart.* Kate didn't have the shot, but she put a couple of rounds into the car just so the sound would put the fear of God into him. *Don't look back you bastard, the devil's waiting for you.*

Kate counted, collected and pocketed her brass, then backed out of the hide. She was careful to sweep away tracks and footprints, as she exited and strapped her gear back on the ATV.

I need to get to New York, she thought, and the minute she did she knew Jake would not be happy. He viewed the once great City of New York as one of the highest risk destinations for his clients. Thanks to some very well connected clients, Jake was licensed to carry in New York, but he knew if he ever drew his weapon, he'd be going to jail. His personal safety rule for Kate's business travel was simple. *Don't go anywhere, you can't go armed. But if you have no choice, remember, you're the weapon.*

***

9:36 PM STONE HEARD the muffled report of Kate's rifle and followed her shot with his. There was a distinct double-tap-pop between the two suppressed rifle sounds. *Nailed it,* he thought. *Sounded like an echo in the ravine. No reason for the HVI to suspect anything.*

The blood and brains on the hood of the SUV confirmed the kill, and Stone hunted for the second target. He spotted a man crawling toward the ravine. *She doesn't have the angle,* he thought, and then heard two more shots. *She's just rattling his cage.*

"Zulu-One. Tango One is down. Tango Two headed for the ravine."

"Do you have a shot?"

"Affirmative."

Three minutes later, Stone heard the ATV motor starting and revving, followed by the exhaust sound of the ATV heading back to the cabin. He knew it would mask his follow-up shot.

Stone got back on comms. "Zulu-One. HVI returning to the cabin. Permission to engage Tango-Two."

"Send it."

Stone watched his target move, body pressed low against the ground, arms and elbows inching forward. His knees flared out wide, ankles flat against the gravel road. The target moved forward in a methodical, controlled manner, relying on the ballistic helmet and ceramic body armor for protection. Stone shattered that illusion when his bullet tore through the target's exposed neck and shoulder. He didn't need a second shot. *See ya, dirtbag.*

"Zulu-One. Come in."

"Go ahead."

"Tango-Two is down."

CHAPTER 72

SUNDAY, APRIL 19
9:40 PM EDT

APPALACHIAN MOUNTAINS, WEST VIRGINIA

MANUEL ROJAS HAD SECURED everything he needed, so when the alert hit his phone, he was ready. He fed the BountyHunt's target GPS coordinates into Gaia GPS, and studied the map. Rojas had hunted enough traffickers through the mountains that he appreciated Gaia's topological maps with trails, forestry and fire roads that most didn't even know existed.

He followed the roads as far as he could, towing the flatbed and ATV he'd rented. He gambled that a cabin deep in the West Virginia mountains might have more than one approach, and he was right. It was slow going along the fire trail. The ATV crawled over fallen branches and stones and rocked through erosion ruts.

It took over an hour to get close, but Rojas was confident the winding road and thick vegetation was a natural sound block. To be safe, he stopped about a half-mile from the cabin's coordinates, threw on a backpack, and started off on foot.

It took Rojas another thirty minutes to walk the fire road up to the cabin. He heard an engine and thought it might come down the road. He drew his handgun and waited. *So much for taking her alive,* he thought, imagining that he had no choice now but to stop her escape. When the sound faded, he continued up the road.

He reached the cabin, saw lights on inside, and a Jeep parked near the front door. *She backed in,* he thought. *She's ready to run, and I'll bet the keys are in it.* He considered taking the keys. *No, too risky. I'd have my back to the door, and if she heard something, I'd be dead.*

He picked a secluded spot where he could observe both the front door and the vehicle. *If she heads for the Jeep, she'll never see me coming. If she heads back inside. I'll wait until she's asleep.*

CHAPTER 73

APPALACHIAN MOUNTAINS, WEST VIRGINIA

KATE DROVE THE ATV back into Jake's shop and opened the armory. She released the rifle's magazine, cleared the chamber and laid it on Jake's maintenance table. She removed her tactical helmet and put it back on the shelf, then slipped off the tactical vest. Kate set the vest on a vacant wall hook, but the hook tilted, the vest slipped off and it hit the floor.

She bent over to pick up the vest and noticed a section of the wall popped out. She pressed, and it snapped back into place. *That's odd,* she thought. She pulled on the hook again and the panel popped. *It's a lever.* This time, she caught the edge of the panel and pulled. It swung away from the wall. Overhead, lights kicked on, revealing steps down to a landing and then turning back under the armory.

Whoa, there's another level, directly below this one.

Kate looked over her shoulder at the security camera. "Seriously?" she muttered. "Another secret? Now, you're scaring me."

The vault door at the bottom of the stairs was identical to the one above, and the combination was the same.

Well, that's a surprise, she thought. *If you're going through this much trouble to keep a secret, at least change the combination. Didn't you learn anything from me?*

The vault door upstairs swung out, but this one pushed in. Kate peered inside. The room was dark, and the air cold. She could see papers and photos lining the walls. *It's not weapons storage,* she thought. *Looks more like an office.*

Kate stepped inside and searched for the light switch. Lights flashed on, and the door slammed shut.

"OK. Jake, that's creepy. Just saying."

She pulled on the door's spindle and then tried turning.

Locked? Are you kidding me?

The exterior had a mechanical combination, but the interior had a keypad. She punched in the same numbers she used to enter. A red light flashed twice, and the pad beeped.

"Not that one. Fine, there are others."

She tried a few account pins and combinations they've used. None worked. Kate rested her forehead on the cold steel door and tapped it twice. Come on now. Think.

Kate stepped away from the door to take in the entire wall. That's when she saw the digital clock. Mounted just above the vault's steel door frame. Two minutes and dropping.

"Don't panic," she said. "Just work the problem. There's still plenty of time, and you know Jake better than Jake knows himself. Look around. There are probably clues."

She scanned the room. Jake plastered the walls with photos, printouts, and post-it notes. Colored string connected one image to another. *Looks like a detective's corkboard murder wall,* she thought. *Really Not helpful. Just concentrate. What's that?*

In every corner, Jake rigged ceiling-mounted claymore directional mines. Staring Kate in the face were the words FRONT TOWARD ENEMY.

"Oh, hell!" she said. "Now you can panic."

Kate grabbed an office chair and climbed up to examine the claymores. *They're real, and wired into the alarm system.* She climbed down and went back to the door.

"Wow. You really did not want anyone coming in here," she said, and checked the clock.

OK. Thirty seconds. What do we know? Jake would never hurt me. Remember the cardinal rules of password management. Something we are. Something we know. Something we have. Jesus. Jake's Jeep. His note!

Kate looked at the clock. Fifteen seconds.

"You said I'd know when to use," she said. "God, I hope you're right, or I'll be seeing you sooner than expected."

She typed FARGO on the keypad, pressing 32746, but the clock kept running. 5-4-3.

Hit enter, you idiot. Hit the pound key.

She did.

With a loud thud, the door shook, and the bolts retracted. Kate pulled, the door swung in, and the clock reset to three minutes.

Kate sat on the floor, her back pressed against the open door. The back of her shirt was wet, and she wiped the sweat off her forehead. From the floor, she stared up at Jake's "wall of crazy" — that's what they called them at Langley when mapping random bits of data in search of a pattern.

She saw a collage of newspaper clippings, photographs, and scrawled notes, all intricately linked by a colorful web of strings. However, the scarlet threads all radiated from a central image—a classic black and white illustration of a masked Samurai wielding a sword. Beneath the sketch, in bold letters, read a single word: RONIN.

Kate's heart began racing, and she struggled to breathe. *I need to get out of here,* she thought. *Now.* She jumped to her feet, closed the vault behind her and ran to the top of the stairs. Then, back inside the armory, she set the alarm.

Back inside the large open shop, and the cool night air, she leaned over and set her hands on knees. *What just happened,* she wondered. She rested in that position for a minute. Her heart slowed down, breathing settled, and she stood up straight. *Was that a panic attack? Claustrophobia? Whatever the hell it was, I've never felt anything like it.*

Kate locked up the shop, but couldn't stop thinking about what she saw, what she felt. *Now that I know how to get in and out of Jake's 'hidden office' I have to go back,* she thought, and a chill rippled down her arms. She'd faced fear before, but this was different. *Am I afraid of the room? Or what I might find? I thought I knew Jake. Was I wrong? And who is Ronin?*

The crackling snap of dry leaves pulled Kate's attention to the woods. She scanned, waited, listened. Nothing. *I need to keep moving,* she thought, and returned to the cabin.

Mikhail Zhukov and Zulu-Two watched Kate drive the ATV into the shop. It surprised Zhukov how long she stayed in the shop, and when she left, there was an intensity and urgency in her movements. She slammed the shop's large service bay door, secured the padlock, and bolted for the cabin. About half-way, she stopped and stared in their direction. Whatever she heard or felt, it passed, and she continued inside.

"Something spooked her," Zhukov said. "And she knows it is not safe to stay. She will leave soon."

CHAPTER 74

UNDISCLOSED LOCATION

NOMAD WANTED TO BE sure Kate could grab the device and leave as soon as she returned, so he worked fast. That was a mistake. It raised the suspicious activity profile on Moore's network, and his connection ended.

"Thank God," he said, when Kate walked through the door.

Kate picked up the AirPod she left behind and pressed it into her ear.

"Are you OK?" he asked.

"I need a minute," Kate said. "But I'll be fine."

"Were you able to slow them down?"

"They won't be following me," she said. "I'll spare you the details, but these were the same guys that killed Pete, the security guard at the Pinnacle."

"Then you know what that means?"

"I know what you want me to say," Kate said. "It's Moore Technologies. I know. I accept that, but Devin? For now, let's just focus on the task. How did you do?"

"It *was* moving along pretty well, but…"

"They locked you out."

"I know. I know. You were right."

"It was only a matter of time," she said. "But now what?"

"With your help, there's still a chance," Nomad said. "You have my address. Remember the key —"

"Planck's Constant — six places," Kate said. "Got it."

"Then get to New York as quickly as you can. Moore, or whoever is behind this, will wait to hear from his men. That buys you a little time. But when they realize the men failed, the hunt will intensify."

"I just need to change, and grab a few things."

"Hurry," Nomad pleaded. "And Kate?"

"Yes?"

"My life is in your hands now."

"I know," she said. "I got this. Your location's safe with me."

Prioritize the King's Security, she thought, and visualized a chessboard in the life and death game she was thrust into playing. She pictured Nomad's advancing adversaries and knew protecting the king was now the key. *Anyone coming for Nomad will have to go through me.*

Chapter 75

APPALACHIAN MOUNTAINS, WEST VIRGINIA

MIKHAIL ZHUKOV AND ZULU-TWO watched the cabin's front door. It wasn't long before Kate made a trip out to the Jeep and tossed a duffle bag into the back.

"Looks like you were right," Two said.

She headed back inside, turned off the lights, and locked the front door.

Kate opened the Jeep's door, and had one foot on the rock slider, when an arm wrapped around her throat and pulled her back. His timing was perfect. A second earlier, Kate might have seen something in the side-view mirror, and with one foot heading up into the Jeep, she lost her balance.

Zulu-Two moved to intercept, but Zhukov yanked him back into position and gestured to bring up the rifle. Zhukov knew with a single tap on the shoulder, a headshot would take out the intruder, but it would also kill his mission. *She has ten, maybe twenty seconds,* he thought. *But he is not trying to kill her. She may yet prevail.*

Kate's attacker dwarfed her slight frame. His right arm wrapped around her throat, and locked on to the massive biceps of his left. Her head was pushed down and to the side. Kate knew it was a perfectly executed blood choke, and with a knee in her back, her own body added to the intensity of the hold. She wrestled with the arm tucked beneath her chin, tried to break the headlock, but she was no match for the muscle compressing her carotid arteries.

The man with his arm locked around Kate's throat kept dragging her back. She tried again and again to plant her feet. Precious seconds evaporated in the fruitless struggle. They were near the house now, and motion lights lit the scene like a prize fight. Kate's head was pounding, her vision blurred. She could breathe, but her blood-starved brain was shutting down. Ten seconds were gone. In another five, she wouldn't have the strength to fight. At twenty seconds, she'd be unconscious.

Her primitive survival instincts surged with one word commands. *Fight. Eyes.* Kate's fingers spread like pitch forks and she thrust both hands up over her head, praying for contact. He was so much taller, and with the back of Kate's head pressed down, his mouth and nose were as far as she could reach. She drew blood. He flinched. His grip loosened. Not enough for her to break free, but a surge of blood to the brain bought a few seconds.

The man stopped dragging her, but she felt his grip reset and tighten. Her arms fell limp at her sides. Her vision narrowed, then went black. That's when she saw Jake and she yelled. *Don't just stand there.*

"*You sure wasted a lot of time,*" Jake said. "*Trust your training. Shooter ready?*"

Ready, Kate thought, recalling her draw and fire speed drills. She imagined the shot timer's BEEP!

Completely blind, she yanked up the bottom edge of her shirt. Right hand gripped the Glock and ripped it from the appendix holster. She shoved the barrel into the elbow wrapped below her chin and pulled the trigger. The shot rang in her ears. The bullet shredded bone and muscle and nerve, spraying blood across her face.

A primal roar erupted, like a wounded bear, angry, ferocious, frightening. But Kate bought more time, and a chance to turn and face him. With fresh blood and oxygen feeding her brain, some blurred vision returned, but she was weak and struggled to find her balance. She saw his right arm dangling bloody and limp. Kate tried to get the gun back in the fight, but he swept Kate's arm away and then trapped it under his left arm.

The massive hand on the back of Kate's head yanked her in close and he drove his head into the side of her face. The headbutt sent shockwaves of pain through Kate's body, igniting bright white sparks in her left eye. *Stay in the fight,* she thought, but she struggled to stay conscious.

She launched a knee into his groin, but he deflected it. *I'm too close.* But the blood brought renewed strength and clarity. The hand on the back of her neck tightened. *Another headbutt,* she thought. *I don't know that I could take the hit. Do something. Quick.*

Kate struggled to free her right arm, but his arm lock kept the gun out of the fight. His head rocked back for another strike, but Kate grabbed his groin and squeezed with every ounce of strength she could summon. The effect was immediate and devastating. She felt his testicles rupture and heard the deafening scream that erupted in her ear. She pulled her right hand free and tried to push him away.

She was swinging the gun up toward his chest when he lunged to block it. Kate fired, leapt back, and trained the gun on his chest. Her attacker fell to his knees, clutching his groin, and collapsed on to his side. In the bright porch lighting, Kate saw his eyes shut tight, tears streaming, and blood pooling beneath his waist.

The bright red, pulsating spurts of arterial blood were unmistakable. Kate maintained her distance, gun trained on him, eyes watching for any sudden movement. *I hit the femoral,* she thought. *That gives him three, maybe four minutes. I can wait.*

"Don't let me die," he begged through the pain and tears. "Not yet."

He'll bleed out without a tourniquet, she thought. *But I'm not going anywhere near him. He's probably armed. God knows why didn't he just shoot me and collect the bounty? Maybe he had other plans.*

"You're going to bleed out," Kate said. "Unless..."

"What?"

"Unless you can set a tourniquet, and you'd need to move fast."

"I can try."

Given the pain written on his face and in his eyes and the angst in his voice, Kate didn't think he would even try to live. She expected he would let death roll over him like a warm blanket, and welcome the relief. *He's got something, or someone, to fight for.*

Kate pulled the tourniquet from her ankle trauma kit and took it apart, so he could slide the band under the wounded leg. With her right hand, she kept the Glock pointed at his chest.

"Here you go," she said, and tossed him the tourniquet. "But it you reach for a gun, I will shoot."

She watched his bloody hands, ready for any movement that even hinted he was reaching for a weapon. What she saw was a man struggling and fumbling with one good hand, but he was fighting for his life. *He's not going to make it. And even if he got it on, he's never going to get it tight enough.*

"Lay back," she said. "Slide your arms up above your head. If you move, you're dead. Got it?"

The man just nodded and did the best he could to raise both arms. Everything Kate knew about tactics and defense screamed this was a huge mistake, but the voice in her head said it would be OK. She'd learned to listen. She trusted the voice, and this moment was no exception.

Kate knelt alongside him, pulled the SIG he had on his right hip, and slid it over to the Jeep. She set the tourniquet as high and tight as she could and that movement alone had him gritting his teeth. *If that hurt, this next part is going to be excruciating.*

"This is going to hurt," she said. "I know you're already in a lot of pain. This is going to be worse, but don't move."

Kate turned the windlass on the tourniquet, and gentle wasn't an option. He'd already lost a lot of blood, so she cranked it fast, with one eye on his hands, and the other on the blood. His screams echoed down the mountain and into the ravine until he passed out.

Did he lose too much blood, Kate wondered. *Or was it the pain?* Whatever the reason, the unconscious man presented Kate with an opportunity. She checked his pockets and pulled his phone, wallet, keys, and a Benchmade Claymore knife. *He could have killed me with this,* she thought. *With the jump he got on me, I'd have never seen it coming.*

She continued digging. *Oh, great. Why am I not surprised?* Kate found a NanoVault and took it over to the jeep. She picked his gun off the deck and set it inside the Jeep. Her messenger bag was on the front seat, and she added his device to the Faraday bag. *I'm not taking any chances with these things.*

Standing at the side of the Jeep, Kate fished through his wallet. *Nothing personal.* There was a license and a few credit cards. The names all matched. *Manuel Rojas. Probably fake.* Home address in Arizona. *You're a long way from home.* But it was his phone that Kate wanted most. She used his thumb to unlock the phone and then disabled the security.

"Let's see what we have here," she said. "Yep, there it is. BountyHunt."

Kate needed the man's thumb again, but then she was in. *I see they call you Red,* she thought. *Well, Mr. Red, what have you been up to? Ah, no history. That's smart. But here I am, Jane Doe, and my location.* Kate examined her profile. *Interesting. They didn't want you to know my name. And that's not a good picture.*

"Welcome back," she said, when Red stirred and moaned. "No, this sure isn't heaven, but I'll bet it feels like hell."

"Thank you," he said.

Not the first words I expected from a man I just shot, Kate thought. *But I'll take it.*

"So, is it Rojas, or would you prefer Red?"

"Rojas," he said. "Where did you hear Red?"

"Your BountyHunt profile," she said, and his eyes widened. "Yeah, I know what it is, why you came, and how you got my location. What I don't know is why you didn't shoot? Why go for a choke out?"

"I would have killed you," he said. "If you gave me no choice."

"You came pretty close," she said, and felt a warm trickle of blood from the cut above her eye.

"Do you also know about collateral?" Rojas asked.

"I've heard of it."

"My daughter is my collateral," he said.

"Why the hell would you do that?"

"I didn't know," he said. "I had nothing when they invited me to play. My wife, daughter and career. All gone. Somehow, these people know things. Know everything. Former Marine and DEA, I've killed with no regrets. I guess I fit their profile, but I would never have risked my daughter's life."

"Are you saying they'll kill her because you failed?"

"They'll kill her if I live. There's no quitting the game. No arrests. No hospitals. No chance I might talk. Only my death can set her free."

"Then why did you fight so hard to stay alive? Dying is easy."

"I want my daughter," he said, and winced. "I want Daniela to have my NanoVault."

"Did you just ask me for a favor?"

"I know. I have no right to ask," he said. "Look, I don't know who wants you or why, but you could have let me die, and you didn't." He coughed and spit out blood. "I've made many mistakes. But my daughter's not one of them. There's no reason she should suffer. I don't expect you to help me. I don't deserve it. But would you do it for her?"

"What's on the device?"

"There are letters I wrote, but could never bring myself to send. They tell her things she should know, but I never had the courage to say. There's some Bitcoin. Enough to get her into a decent college, or start a business, whatever she wants."

"You want to give your daughter your blood money?"

"They paid me to kill an evil man who did vile things to children, and soon, I will join him in hell," he said. "But money has no soul. Let some good come of it."

The guy fights to live, only to turn around and ask me to let him die, she thought. *This day can not get any more bizarre.*

"What's the combination?"

"Her birthday," he said. "She's sixteen years old today. And her mother's address is in the NanoVault."

"I'll try," Kate said. "Assuming I live long enough. So, what happens now?"

"When you go, I will say a prayer, ask God for the forgiveness I don't deserve, and loosen the tourniquet," he said. "But the game...they need to know I'm dead. I can't just disappear. If they think I'm running, they will hurt her, so someone has to find my body."

"OK. Here," Kate said, and tucked his wallet back into his pants. "I'll make sure someone finds you. I just need to be long gone when that happens."

Kate climbed into the Jeep and headed for the fire trail road Rojas used to sneak up on her. The porch lights washed across his face, and Kate could see him, eyes closed. The motion sensor timed out, and the driveway was black. *It won't be long now,* she thought. *He'll be facing whatever judgment waits for us all.*

Chapter 76

APPALACHIAN MOUNTAINS, WEST VIRGINIA

THE MINUTE KATE'S JEEP was out of sight, Zhukov raced forward, tightened the intruder's tourniquet, and checked for a pulse. "He is still alive."

"Shouldn't we just let him die?" Zulu-Two asked. "We took out two others. Why save this one?"

"A man willing to die for his daughter is a man worth trying to save," Zhukov said. "Now, call the Little Bird, and tell Zulu-Three to come down. We are leaving."

There was more to saving the man than Zhukov would admit. He too had a daughter, once. The metal plate in Mikhail's head was a cold, hard reminder that he too would risk his life to save her, and do it again if he thought the outcome might change.

Zulu-Two made the call to the chopper and added that they were "one heavy, requiring medical assistance." Then he turned back to Zhukov. "What about that whole collateral speech? Do you believe it?"

"It is true," Zhukov said, and pulled the intruder's wallet. "If he survives, I will give them a body his own mother wouldn't recognize, and make sure they recover his ID." Zhukov glanced at the man's license. "Mr. Rojas will be marked deceased."

Standing over the wounded and unconscious Rojas, Zhukov was surprised Kate didn't kill him. Still, he admired her determination to fight and her obvious skill. *He taught her well,* Mikhail thought, picturing Kate's husband. *But she was born with a warrior's soul.*

Mikhail walked up to Kate's porch and peered in through the windows. It reminded him of simpler times, warm and comfortable. A place where family gathered just to enjoy each other's company. He imagined sitting on the couch, his arm wrapped around his wife, her head on his shoulder. His daughter sound asleep, her head on his lap. He stroked the crown of her head and caressed the long, curly brown hair. And when it was time for bed, he scooped her up in his arms, and she melted into his chest.

"See something?" Zulu-Three asked when he arrived.

Zhukov turned away from the window. "No. Nothing of interest."

"I have to ask," Zulu-Three began. "Who the hell is this woman?"

"She's no-one," Zhukov said, and walked off to collect his gear.

"Oh, she's somebody alright," Zulu-Two whispered. "I mean, check out this dude. Twice her size. He had her in a solid blood-choke, and she was going down hard. But he's lying here, and she's gone."

"Did she kill him?"

"He's unconscious, and lost a lot of blood. I'm not sure he's gonna make it, but he's coming with us," Zulu-Two said. "That's Zulu-One's deal. Don't ask."

Zulu-Three approached Zhukov. "When the clean-up crew comes to collect the bodies and the vehicle, I'd like to see the report on the guy behind the fifty-cal."

"You think she made the shot?"

"I can't be certain," Three said. "I was concentrating on my shot, but, yes, I think she did."

The rotors of the Little Bird could be heard approaching, and they dragged Rojas clear of the bird's driveway landing site. Once they were all airborne,

Zhukov checked the tracker on Kate's Jeep. *Good. Strong signal*, he thought. *As soon as she leads us to Nomad, we can move.*

CHAPTER 77

SHENANDOAH VALLEY REGIONAL AIRPORT, WEYERS CAVE, VA

THE HELICOPTER PILOT SET the Little Bird down and an ambulance rushed up alongside. The paramedic crew transferred Rojas to a stretcher, began monitoring his vitals, and started an IV.

Mikhail Zhukov and his two associates exited the chopper, looking like business executives wrapping up a hunting trip. All carried duffle bags and headed toward the waiting cars. The two younger men nodded and climbed into the Escalade. No one said a word, and minutes later, they were gone.

Mikhail surveyed the man in the dark suit standing near his limo. *This will be one of Ryder's spooks,* he thought, and he was right.

"Mr. Zhukov," the man began. "All the medical arrangements have been made. The paramedics will take it from here, and the team waiting at the hospital will ensure his anonymity. If you have the gentleman's identification, we'll have the death certificate prepared and locate a suitable cadaver."

Mikhail handed him Rojas's wallet. "And the tracker?" Zhukov asked.

"She's headed North-East."

"New York," Zhukov said. "Hiding in plain sight."

"If that's her destination, she'll be on the road for several hours."

"That is her destination. Let's go."

"Very good," he said. "The jet is waiting at the general aviation terminal."

Chapter 78

MOORE TOWER, MANHATTAN, NY

Devin Moore burst into the network control room and confronted Drew. "We should have heard something long before now," he said. "They've had Preacher's location for over five hours."

"The area is a designated wilderness," Drew said. "There isn't a cell tower within a hundred miles. But both Rojas and the Richmond Pinnacle team were approaching the area when I lost them."

"When did you lose contact?"

"Let's see…Rojas dropped off about four hours ago. The other two have been dark for a little over three."

"Did you estimate the drive time to the target?"

"No," Drew said. "In those roads, it would just be a guess."

"Then guess."

"The Richmond Team was on a marked gravel road. It looks like they could have reached the coordinates about an hour ago, give or take."

"What about Rojas?"

"His route is a mystery," Drew said. "I suspect he found an old logging road or some other way up the mountain."

"They're dead," Moore said. "And she's gone by now."

"We don't know that. Not yet, anyway."

"You need to think worst case," Moore said. "If we don't hear from them in the next hour, they're captured or dead, and for their sake, they better be dead."

"What have you got on Nomad's location?"

"He's definitely in the continental US," Drew said. "I would have bet on Eastern Europe, but he's here. The Richmond building's remote connection gave me what I needed to narrow things down, and there's a pattern. He's using proxy servers in every major hub from coast to coast, anywhere that has enough traffic to mask his activity."

"Show me the list."

Drew sent the list to one of the enormous central monitors.

1. San Francisco, California

2. Seattle, Washington

3. Los Angeles, California

4. Austin, Texas

5. Chicago, Illinois

6. Boston, Massachusetts

7. Atlanta, Georgia

8. New York City, New York

9. Washington, D.C.

10. Dallas, Texas

11. Denver, Colorado

12. Raleigh, North Carolina

13. Minneapolis, Minnesota

14. Portland, Oregon

15. Houston, Texas

Moore walked into the center of the control room and studied the list. "Sort it by proxy volume. Show me where he hides most of his traffic."

1. Seattle, Washington

2. San Francisco, California

3. Los Angeles, California

4. Portland, Oregon

5. Denver, Colorado

6. Austin, Texas

7. Dallas, Texas

8. Houston, Texas

9. Minneapolis, Minnesota

10. Chicago, Illinois

11. Atlanta, Georgia

12. Raleigh, North Carolina

13. Washington, D.C.

14. New York City, New York

15. Boston, Massachusetts

"What do you see, Drew?"

"He prefers the West coast."

"Yes, but not for the weather," Moore said. "Concentrate your search on New York. I'll bet he's been right in front of us this whole time."

"I don't understand."

"Misdirection, Drew. And miscalculation," Moore said. "Look at this list. I'm willing to bet the one place he doesn't want you to look is one of the places he used the least."

"What about Boston?"

"Boston is a decoy," Moore said. "If you want to hide, New York is the place, but he couldn't ignore it. Not completely. That would have been too obvious. But bottom of the list? Not a chance. That was a strategic mistake. No, he's here."

It won't be long now, he thought, and imagined the triumphant end of the hunt for Nomad. *This is my city, and I will find you.*

Moore walked around the control room, surveying the magnitude of the data collection stream and the progress of his AI's final data assimilation stage. The massive screens that surrounded the room flashed with the most intimate and valuable data of millions of duped Quantum NanoVault owners. The screens' vibrant colors, illuminated text, and streaming visuals cast a mosaic of light on Moore's face, like a living van Gogh canvas swirling with vivid blues, radiant yellows.

The AI's spaceship-like console occupied the very center of Moore's control room. Of the dozen monitors that spanned the console's one-hundred-eighty degree interface, only one had activity. Moore glanced at the screen and assessed the progress. *Soon. Very soon,* he thought. *The cognitive incubation phase is almost complete. When she's activated, there won't be any secret, desire, or vulnerability that can hide from us.*

"Drew. Concentrate everything you have on New York. Find me the needle in the haystack. Find Nomad."

Chapter 79

MONDAY, APRIL 20
7:30 AM EDT

NOMAD'S FORTRESS, MANHATTAN, NY

KATE'S DRIVE TO NEW York was long but uneventful, and for that, she was grateful. It also gave her time to think. *Did Devin Moore try to have me killed,* she thought. *Twice. The Devin I know has a laundry list of character flaws, but a murderer?*

She struggled to imagine Devin at the heart of everything that had happened to her, Francois and Pete. But she couldn't shake the feeling that Nomad was right. *What would Devin do to protect his empire,* Kate wondered, and the voice in her head said, *Anything.*

Her mind was also spinning with questions about Jake. *What was he investigating? Why did he hide it from me? What else don't I know about the man I married?* That was the thought that scared her most, and she fought to push it from her mind.

While still a few miles from her destination, she made several random turns, and parked along the side of the road to let cars flow past. Her stops were followed by U-turns to break the flow of any vehicle surveillance teams. When she was confident no one was following, she drove on to Nomad's address.

When she arrived, she double-checked the number. *Is this it,* she wondered. *Not much to look at, but I guess that's the idea.*

The four-story building was an old parking garage, covered in graffiti, and surrounded by litter. A narrow cement drive led to a metal roll-up door. Three black and yellow striped vehicle barriers blocked entry beyond the keypad mounted to a black steel post.

Kate pulled up alongside the keypad and saw several discrete high-end security cameras. *Yep, anti-ram barriers, and cameras, this is the place.*

Kate pushed the call button, and she heard it ringing.

"Hi, I'm..."

A woman interrupted.

"I know who you are," she said. "Were you followed?"

"No"

"Are you sure?"

"Yes," Kate said. "I'm sure."

"Drive straight in and follow the ramp up to the third floor. You can park next to the van and walk the rest of the way up the ramp."

The call ended as abruptly as it began, and the vehicle barriers retracted until they were flush with the cement entry. The roll-up door shook, and the motors whined under the load. When Kate passed through the entry, the door banged back down with a clang that echoed throughout.

It's a parking garage, Kate thought. *And something of a fortress, too.* She wound her way up to the third floor and spotted the van. *No handicap plate, but it's equipped with a chairlift.* Kate backed the Jeep in against the wall, climbed out, and slipped the messenger bag over her shoulder.

The fourth floor was furnished, and as she walked up the ramp, more of it became visible. Office partitions segmented the open space. In the far corner, there was a kitchen. Another section appeared to be a kind of living room with a designer-quality, over-stuffed couch and a massive Sony, flat-screen TV. *Nomad turned a solid cement parking garage into a home,* she thought. *Now, that's a new one.*

A tall, black woman walked toward her.

"Nomad?" Kate asked

"Lord no," she said, and laughed. "I'm Keisha. I...I work with Nomad."

Keisha extended a hand. Kate shook it, and asked, "Is he here?"

"Oh yes. He never leaves," Keisha said. "Give him a minute. He'll be along. In the meantime, can I get you something to eat or drink?"

"No," Kate said, and remembering her manners, added. "No, thank you. I'm fine.

"The bruises on your neck look fresh and the cut above your eye is swelling," Keisha said. "I'm a nurse, or I was, but we've got Arnica, ice, or maybe some aspirin. What do you think?"

"I may take you up on that a little later, but nothing right now. Thanks."

"If you change your mind, just let me know."

Kate turned around at the sound of electric motors whirring, and wheels clinging to the cement floor.

"Hello Kate."

"Julian?" Kate asked.

"In the flesh, or what's left of it," he said, and managed a mock hand wave over the body strapped to the chair. "I realize this comes as a shock —," he began.

Kate wrapped her arms around him, hugged and cried, then stood and slapped his face.

"I guess I deserved that."

"Damn straight you do," Kate said. "I thought you were dead. We all did. Christ, I went to your funeral. For three years, I visited your grave just to be near my best friend, and tell you about life at MIT."

The wave of emotion caught Kate off guard, and she reached for a chair. *Julian's alive,* she thought, and wrestled with the reality of it. She sat, dipped her head and pressed her fists into her eyes. *And Julian is Nomad!* That image brought on a wave of anger, and she could feel her face flush. *Alive all this time. And spying on me for years.*

"I can explain."

"I seriously doubt that," Kate said. "But start talking before I start walking."

"The night of the frat party, Devin invites me over."

"I remember," she said. "I told you not to go."

"But this was my chance," Julian said. "A chance for Devin to see me as a peer, as an intellectual equal."

"Julian, he was never going to see you as a peer. I tried to tell you," she said. "Devin came from old money and New York society. You and me, we're nobody from nowhere. And for the record, Devin is brilliant, but he was never *your* intellectual equal. You didn't see it, but trust me, he knew."

"I don't remember the accident," Julian said. "They kept me in a medically induced coma for almost two months."

"I know," she said. "I was there. Every day."

"No one thought I would survive, and if by some miracle I did, I would have profound neurological impairment and physical disabilities," Julian said. "And that's when the devil showed up and made my parents a deal they couldn't refuse."

"The Devil? What are you talking about?"

"Metaphorically, of course. Devin's father, the esteemed legal luminary, Jonathan Moore. The most feared legal foe in the country, and perhaps the most misunderstood."

"What was the deal?"

"Simple, really. I needed to die."

"Excuse me?"

"Jonathan Moore would do anything, pay anything, to protect his son, the fraternity president. They had already swept away the truth of what happened. There was no party, or alcohol, or invitation. Falling off the balcony was a tragic accident, and a comatose boy wouldn't change that. But one that could talk was a problem."

"And your parents went along with this?"

"What choice did they have? They had little to begin with, and they were drowning in medical bills, facing multiple surgeries, and years of rehab."

"So they faked your death?"

"It wasn't all that hard. When you're the hotshot lawyer that bailed the hospital out of some troublesome lawsuits, you know where the skeletons are buried, and they were happy to do him a favor. At least, that's what I suspect. They released me to hospice care, and from there it was a quick hop to the grave. The End."

"What really happened?"

"The man I thought was the devil turned out to be my guardian angel. He set up the trust that paid for everything. Every surgery, all lucky thirteen of them, and the years of rehab that followed. I lived in a beautiful medical care facility in upstate New York. Jonathan would visit from time to time. We'd play chess. He was an average player, but enthusiastic, so I'd drag the game out for the company. Jonathan was a good man, and he hoped Devin would grow to be the same. Someday."

"So Devin never knew?"

"Not a clue. Even after his father passed and they settled the estate. I looked like one of the many charities his father supported, and the inheritance gave me a start."

"And your parents?"

"They died within a year of the deal, and just months apart. I know my choices took years off their lives, and I will always regret that. But I've accepted my situation," he said, nodding at his chair. "My consequences are my own."

"But when you're a kid, you don't think about the price others pay."

Kate came alongside Julian's chair, and he flinched.

"Relax," she said. "I won't hit you again unless you give me a reason."

She leaned in and pecked his cheek.

"I'm glad you're alive," she said. "I missed you." Kate grabbed an office chair. "But we can catch up later." *If we survive,* she thought. "Tell me what you need me to do."

CHAPTER 80

MONDAY, APRIL 20
7:55 AM EDT

NOMAD'S FORTRESS, MANHATTAN, NY

KATE TUCKED HER CHAIR in next to Julian and he walked her through what he'd been able to accomplish and the challenge ahead.

"I've been inside Moore's system three times now," he said. "Once on my own, and I'll walk you through that in a minute, and twice with Jake's miracle key. I honestly don't know what else to call it. I wouldn't be anywhere near this close without it."

"Is there any chance we can recover Jake's files?"

"We might find them in Moore's data, but nothing's recoverable from the device," he said. "I tried every tool I had, anything with even the slightest chance of success, and nothing worked. I did record the broadcast from Jake's device. It seems to be stuck in a loop, just repeating the same code over and over."

"Yeah, I caught it too," Kate said. "Managed to decrypt one word, my name, before all hell broke loose."

"That's interesting."

"Which part? My name or all hell breaking loose?"

"Your name," he said. "You know I was there for the rest. It's interesting that you recovered text. The broadcast I recorded is an encrypted audio file. I suppose the audio file could have included the text as a transcription."

"Anyway, the audio file is cranking away over there," he said, and pointed at a machine running a series of decryption algorithms. "If it's intact, we should be able to play it."

"I think you really should put something on that," Keisha said, studying the lump above Kate's eye.

It was tender to the touch, and Kate agreed. "Yes. Thanks. Ice would be great."

After Keisha left, Kate said, "She seems nice. And she's cool with the whole Nomad persona thing, and that you hack for a living?"

"Remarkable as it seems, she is. I'm lucky to have her."

"Have you told her that?"

"Well... no... not in so many words."

"With any words?"

"Let's just focus on the work. There's something you need to see," Julian said, and he launched a compiler. The screen filled with color-coded source code. "Do you recognize this?"

"Move over," Kate said. She slid her chair over and scrolled through the code.

"No. I can't say I've ever seen anything like it," she said. "I suspect it would take days, maybe weeks, to wrap my head around this, but I'll go out on a limb and say it's a polymorphic worm. I assume this is your work?"

"Yes and no," he said. "It's my code alright, but it's sitting on every Quantum NanoVault.

"Is this—"

"The worm that ripped through MIT?" Julian said and smiled.

"That wasn't funny," Kate said. "You ruined my freshman year's Mystery Hunt. In a matter of minutes, this thing locked up every connected device on campus. Nothing was immune."

"It was three minutes, eleven seconds, to be precise, and all anyone had to do was solve the puzzle."

"But no one could."

"Almost no one," Julian said. "Professor LeGrande solved it and if he hadn't, I would have stepped in."

"Yeah, but that took hours. In the meantime, there was total chaos and paranoia. No one knew who was responsible, and Devin was the prime suspect," Kate said. "He never admitted it, but I think he loved the attention."

"This is how the NanoVault propagates and communicates, and why no one else has detected it. To anyone else, it's just noise."

"That's why he's chasing you, I mean Nomad," she said. "He has no idea how Nomad breached his system, because the only person who had a chance is dead."

"Exactly. What could be safer than using a dead man's code?"

"I know where this is going," she said. "If you hijack this code, your code, you could connect to every NanoVault on the planet. You could nuke Moore's spyware and close the comm channel. The devices would become nothing more than what people believe they are."

"I knew you'd see it."

"Yeah, I see it. But this could take days, maybe weeks. I'm guessing we don't have that kind of time."

"No, we don't," he said, and smiled.

"Why the grin?" Kate asked. "You've already done it, haven't you?"

"I did. Days ago. This turned out to be the simple part. After all, it was my code."

"What's the distribution?"

"I'm at roughly seventy percent worldwide. The mesh network architecture Moore stole from me is doing all the work, and spreading peer-to-peer. Think *World War Z*."

"Zombies consuming everything in their path, spawning more zombies. Got it," Kate said. "But how exactly *did* you get inside?"

"The puzzle. It's still there," Julian said. "Moore may have tried to remove it, but the code won't compile without it, and I'm guessing he never did fully grasp how it all worked. In the end, he probably figured it was harmless."

Keisha returned with a bag of frozen peas.

"Here you go, honey," Keisha said, and handed Kate the bag. "Have you told her about Francois?"

"Professor LeGrande?" Kate asked.

"Yes, he and I played online periodically. He only ever knew me as Nomad, but names didn't matter. He loved chess, and I appreciated the challenge."

"That's code for the Frenchman beat him," Keisha said. "Now get to it. She needs to know."

"Give me a minute," Julian said, and Keisha stood at the side of his chair and waited.

"Like I said, when I recognized the code, I knew the puzzle had to be there, and I found it. But I couldn't solve it."

"Did Moore change something?"

"He made a few modifications, but that wasn't the problem," Julian said. "I just couldn't physically do it."

Kate saw Julian struggled to explain, and his face flushed.

"The puzzle is speed chess, a three-minute blitz game," he said. "I can't move fast enough anymore. When I wrote it, I never imagined this would be my life, my body."

"Then how did you get in?"

"I shared my discovery with Francois and asked for his help."

"Did he realize who you were?"

"Yes, I think so. He said as much the last time we spoke, right before—"

Whatever Julian was struggling to say, Kate saw he was losing the battle, and his eyes filled with tears.

"Right before what?"

"They killed him."

"Tried to make it look like a suicide," Keisha said, and she helped Julian wipe his nose and blot the tears.

"I saw everything. Heard every word," Julian said, and he stiffened in his chair, trying to compose himself.

"I saw Francois teetering on the edge of a chair, a rope stretching his neck so tight he could hardly breathe, and he never said my name," Julian said. "I begged his killer to let him go."

"You spoke with the killer?" Kate asked.

"I tried to tell him Francois didn't know anything, and couldn't help, but the killer just laughed. 'Mission First,' he said and kicked the chair."

Kate stood and paced the room. "Did you record it?"

"Yes, I had control of Francois's laptop, and recorded everything."

"I'll need a copy of that recording."

"It's hard to watch, and the killer dressed in black from head to toe, including a ski mask. I don't imagine you could find anything that would identify him."

"I'm sure you're right, and that's not the priority right now, but I'd like to have it, just in case," Kate said. "I spent years analyzing intelligence. There might be something you wouldn't think is important."

"Now, tell her about the big Russian," Keisha said.

Kate saw the look Julian gave Keisha. *Whatever it is,* Kate thought. *He didn't want me to know, and wasn't planning on telling me.*

"Come on Julian," Kate said. "No more secrets."

"I was still connected to the laptop when he arrived. Francois's body hanging in the middle of the room, and he brushed past like it was a piece of furniture. The moment I saw his face, I knew it was him."

Kate sat down, her head in her hands. Julian didn't need to say the name. The fact that he didn't, couldn't, say the name was enough.

"Zhukov," she said, her voice trembling.

Wherever Zhukov goes, death follows, Kate thought. *That's what I wrote in my briefing. Zhukov was in Syria to help Assad with a chemical weapons cache. An attack might follow. I had credible intelligence from a reliable source, and Nomad was the source.*

"It's OK," Kate said, and lifted her head. She looked into Julian's eyes. "I'm OK, and I don't blame you. It wasn't your fault. None of it was your fault."

"But I could have passed that intel to someone else, anyone else," Julian said. "But I gave it to you—"

"I know why you gave it to me," Kate said. "And it's alright. Yes, Syria was hell, and if I saw my captors today, I'd kill them on the spot. But we saved hundreds, maybe thousands, and I met the love of my life. I don't believe in fate, but if you hadn't told me where to find Zhukov, I would have missed the most incredible love and life any woman could dream."

Always, Kate thought, and wrapped herself in Jake's memory like a warm blanket.

"See, I told you," Keisha said, and patted Julian's shoulder. "I told him if you were half the woman he thinks you are, you could handle it. Better to have it all on the table."

"You're right Keisha. We have work to do," Kate said. "So you expose the puzzle. I beat the three-minute game clock, and you're in. Then what?"

"Jake's NanoVault helped me sprinkle code inside the core, but I need to pull the pieces back together. When I launch it, NanoVaults all over the globe will start dropping offline. Moore will see them as a cascading system failure, but he'll be locked out. Just like that day on campus."

"What about the data he's already collected? That has to be massive."

"It is, but once I have a beachhead, a single system, the same mesh network model will spread destruction to the rest."

"Zombies."

"Actually, the analogy is more apt than you might think. In a matter of minutes, the entire storage array will be brain dead."

"Alright. The clock's running. Moore's honing in on this location, and Zhukov's after something. Whatever it is, he won't be far behind. Once you're in, how much time do you need?"

"I need to find and move the Omega code into one directory. This is where I need to be careful. I can't risk detection."

"Omega code?" Kate asked.

"I thought it deserved a name. *The Code* is so boring, and what better name than one that suggests a mythological end? Catastrophic and irreversible destruction."

"How long?"

"An hour, maybe less."

"What's next?"

"I compile. That's two minutes, tops," he said. "But when the Omega's ready, the decision to execute is yours."

"Mine?" Kate asked. "Why mine?"

"I'd given up hope," he said. "I thought Francois died for nothing, and I was responsible. But you and Jake changed everything. You've given us a chance, but when we execute, Jake's data will disappear, along with all the rest. Whatever he wanted you to know will vanish forever."

"Will we have time to search?"

"I hope so," Julian said. "And as long as we have a connection, we can hunt for Jake's files and still launch Omega, but if we get cut off..."

"Checkmate," Kate said. "Moore will be the last one standing, armed with a treasure trove of data and a global reconnaissance network."

"There's still the public option," Julian said. "Take what we know, and promote it anywhere we can. We can try to educate the public, and confront Moore Technologies. That might at least stop people from using the device."

"But that doesn't change the outcome," Kate said. "With the data he's already collected, Moore probably has tentacles wrapped around the throats of global political, judicial, media, corporate and banking figures. Going public now would just add us to the ranks of conspiracy nuts who died under suspicious circumstances or simply disappeared."

"Let's hope it doesn't come to that," Julian said.

"Let's get started," Kate said. "So, who is my opponent? Am I playing against fourteen-year-old Julian?"

"Remember when I said Moore made a few modifications?"

"Yeah," Kate said. "But now that sounds like a problem."

"You'll be playing against Moore's AI."

"You expect me to beat an AI?"

"It's not fully operational. Not yet. He's still training the system, feeding it everything he's collecting."

"This just gets better and better," she said. "If the AI goes live, he'll have the most sophisticated data mining capability on the planet, and if I know Devin, he's already lined up customers."

"There may only be one," Julian said. "Moore's reportedly very cozy with the Global Economic Council."

"That's disturbing. The terrorist attack in Paris forced the GEC to cancel the remainder of their conference," she said. "And Jake's team was protecting some members of a US corporate delegation. He mentioned there was resistance to some of the GEC agenda. I don't know what, but now I wonder—"

"If Jake heard or saw something, he wasn't supposed to know?"

"I don't believe in coincidence. If Jake suspected something, he may have been at that cafe to collect the evidence. He had cell phone jamming and cloning equipment, and I don't even know where he got it."

"So you think whatever evidence he collected, it's on his NanoVault?"

"I need to find out," Kate said. "So, is this AI any good? I mean, as a chess player?"

"All I can say is that Francois burned through fifty-six NanoVaults trying."

"What does that mean?"

"It means every game is do or die. If you lose, the NanoVault's destroyed, and we try again. But don't worry, we still have plenty," he said. "Besides, it's three-minute speed chess, so mistakes and blunders are part of the game. And you're much younger and faster than Francois."

"Thanks for the pep talk," Kate said. "Alright. I'm ready."

CHAPTER 81

MONDAY, APRIL 20
8:20 AM EDT

NOMAD'S FORTRESS, MANHATTAN, NY

KATE LOST THE FIRST ten games and watched Keisha collect the NanoVault trash. While the AI was no doubt learning from Kate, absorbing her technique, capturing her patterns, Kate studied the machine. She mentally cataloged moves and reactions, compared the machine's strategy and style to players she'd encountered and games she'd studied.

"How many more of those have we got?" Kate asked, pointing at the blackened oozing pile of NanoVaults.

"Enough," Julian said. "Don't worry about it. You're doing great. You pushed that last game out to two minutes, twenty-four, so your time management is spot on."

"I can't seem to find my rhythm."

"You're just warming up."

"Can I get you anything?" Keisha asked.

"Yes. A double espresso," Kate said. "No, make that a quad. I may be at this a while."

By game thirty-seven, Kate was feeling the pressure. There was no obvious weakness in the machine's play. It didn't matter if she drew white and set the pace, or was following as black. Every move she made was followed by a consistent counter or advance, but the timing of the AI's moves gave Kate an idea.

"Did Professor LeGrande say anything about how he beat the machine?"

"Not that I recall."

"I have an idea, and I was hoping he might have said something that would suggest if I'm on the right track," Kate said. "I can count, and we're almost out of keys."

"Hang on then," Julian said. "I was asleep in my chair when Francois beat the machine, and he woke me with the news. He did say something, but I can't recall. Give me a minute."

"I know what it was," Keisha said. "I had no idea what he was talking about, but the word stuck in my mind. Like something you might say to a beautiful woman or a brilliant sunrise."

"What did he say?" Julian asked.

"Dazzling," Keisha replied. "He said dazzling."

"Does that mean anything to you?" Julian asked.

"We're about to find out."

Kate drew White and prepared to start the clock and make her opening move. *Enough with conventional play,* she thought. *You've seen it all and studied it all, and none of it makes you even break a sweat. Well, chew on this one.*

Kate launched the game with a King's Pawn Opening, considered comical among serious players, and she waited.

"Have you lost your mind?" Julian asked.

"Wait for it," she said.

"For what? Is it going to laugh?" he asked, and waited. "Why hasn't it moved?"

And when it moved, Kate noted her plan's first success.

"That was double its average response time," Kate said, and she pressed her advantage.

The more disorienting Kate's moves, the longer the machine struggled to deduce the strategy and unmask the trap. The machine had no concept of a psych out. It didn't realize it was already in the trap. In any other style of play, or against an opponent with a brain, this might not have worked, but in Blitz Chess the clock tips the scale. She didn't need to beat the AI, she only needed to run out the clock.

"Got you!" Kate shouted. "You, my digital friend, have just been dazzled."

"Is that a thing?" Julian asked.

"It is now."

"My turn," he said and took control of the console. "This might be a good time for you to get something to eat, maybe take a nap."

"Don't worry about me," Kate said. "I opened the door, but you've got to bring the heat. Wake up those zombies of yours and turn them loose. I'll pray we have time to find Jake's files. You know now that there's more at stake than a few memories."

My job now, she thought. *Is to make sure no one gets in here until we're done and gone.*

Chapter 82

NOMAD'S FORTRESS, MANHATTAN, NY

KATE LEFT JULIAN TO work, and found Keisha in the kitchen, sipping from an Army logo coffee mug.

"Can I get you some?" she asked. "Or something else?"

"No. Thanks," Kate said. "Former Army?"

"Yep. Nurse. Joined for the adventure, stayed for the free mug."

"Where did you serve?"

"Balad Air Base."

"Fallujah?"

"So you know it?"

"I know the stories, and my husband lived it."

"I'm sorry about your husband," Keisha said.

Kate could see that Keisha was struggling to find the words, so she changed the subject. "Jake was there. Fallujah I mean," Kate said. "For all I know, you were on the team that stitched him up."

"Might have been. The choppers were dropping wounded day and night. We didn't have an empty operating room for eight days straight."

"How did you manage that?"

"You don't think about it, you just do it. You worked twenty-four, slept four, if you could. And we never knew what day of the week it was," she said. "Most of us had never seen combat injuries. Missing limbs. Shredded bodies. Hundreds of patients."

"I'm so sorry. I didn't mean to pry."

"No, I'm sorry," Keisha said, and she wiped away tears. "You didn't need to hear all that."

Kate wrapped her arms around Keisha and gave her a hug.

"Sometimes we just need to say it," Kate said. "A friend told me that tears cleanse the soul."

"Thank you. I'm guessing you didn't come in to hear me ramble. What do you need?"

"Now that Julian's doing his thing. Time for me to do mine."

"What's that?"

"Keep him alive," Kate said. "We can't move, and we can't hide, so…"

"We defend."

"Yep. I need you to show me every way in and out of this place. The crash barriers at the roll-up door are a good start. Can we lock them in place?"

"Yes. We'll take your Jeep, and I'll show you how."

The two women left the kitchen and walked past Julian's workspace.

"Where are you two going?" he asked.

"Time to lock this place down," Kate said.

"Oh. Good idea."

The two women walked down the ramp, and Kate said, "Turning a parking garage into a home and office is definitely…"

"Weird."

"I was going to go with unique," Kate said. "But weird works."

"It takes some getting used to, but after a while you see the beauty of it," Keisha said.

They passed Julian's van and stopped in front of the jeep.

"I need to grab a few things before we start," Kate said, and Keisha followed around to the back.

Kate popped open the rear. Jake clipped their tactical vests to the interior roll bar. She grabbed hers and slipped it on.

"Is that body armor?"

"Yes. It's 3A, small arms."

"Can I have the other one?" Keisha asked.

"Sure, but it's my husband's, so it may be pretty big."

"You're sweet, honey. But in case you haven't noticed, I'm a big girl."

They both laughed. Kate offered to help slip it on and lock it down, but Keisha didn't need it.

"What's that?" Keisha asked, pointing at the black cabinet that spanned the width of the jeep.

"You'll see," and Kate punched in the combination, turned the handle and rolled out the truck vault's main drawer.

"Holy Mother of God. Those weapons might fly in Texas or somewhere like that, but don't get caught with this rolling armory in New York City. They'll lock you up and throw away the key."

"Let's not get caught," Kate said, and she wrapped a battle belt around her waist and clipped the cobra buckle. The belt had a G-Code Glock 19 holster and leg strap. She secured the strap around her leg and pulled a G19 from the vault's foam cutout. With a quick press check to confirm the weapon's condition, she pressed the handgun into the holster with a satisfying click.

Every inch of Kate's belt served a purpose. She had spare pistol and rifle magazine pouches, an IFAK trauma medical kit, magazine dump pouch, knife, and flashlight. A few minutes later, every slot was full, and she set about configuring the vest. More ammo, a pair of smoke grenades, and a fixed-blade knife rounded out the setup.

"Last but not least," Kate said, and rolled out the lower level drawer. Four AR pistols lay side by side in the foam tray. Kate grabbed the first one, locked the bolt back, and slipped the sling over her shoulder.

"Is that a silencer?"

"Technically, it's a suppressor, but that's the idea. Of course, it's nothing like the movies. These short-barreled rifles are so loud that this is more about protecting your hearing than pretending the shots can't be heard."

Kate shoved a thumb into the top of a rifle mag, tested the spring depth, and loaded the rifle.

"See anything you'd like?" Kate asked.

"I'll take one of those," Keisha said, pointing at Kate's rifle.

"Good choice. Know how to shoot?"

"Like my life depends on it."

Kate selected another AR pistol, checked the brightness on the red dot, and got the sling adjusted for Keisha. With a couple of spare mags loaded into Keisha's tac vest, she was ready to go.

"Alright, Jake never handed anyone a weapon, including me, without asking them to quote the safe-handling bible, so let's hear it."

"OK. Let's see," Keisha said. "Assume every gun is loaded."

"Correct."

"Keep the muzzle pointed in a safe direction."

"Two for two."

"Finger stays off the trigger."

"Until you're on target, and the Red Dot is sitting on something you intend to destroy," Kate said. "And the last one?"

"Know your target."

"And what's beyond," Kate added. "We've got cement all around, so we don't need to worry about penetration and neighbors, but the goal is to keep all fire as far away from Julian and his systems. Are we good?"

"Good."

"One last thing. We don't separate. I move, you move."

"Copy that."

Kate clipped a radio to her tac vest and pressed an earpiece into her left ear.

"I'll get Julian set up on comms, and then we'll have a look around."

Julian turned when Kate called out, and his eyes widened. "Jeez. I hope you don't need all that."

"You and me both," Kate said. "But I've seen how Moore's men operate, and we both know what Zhukov can do. So, how's it going?"

"Smooth so far, but it's a bit like walking through a minefield. One wrong step —"

"Game over," Kate said. "So, slow and steady wins the race. We're headed downstairs, but your radio is on VOX. I can hear everything you're saying, so shout my name if you need something, or find something."

Kate hoped Jake's files were somewhere inside Moore's mountain of data, and there would be time to find them. *Would the files contain answers or just raise more questions,* she wondered. *Jake's team played a role in Global Economic Council's regional meeting. Did someone on the US delegation have concerns about the GEC's agenda? Could Moore be angling for a seat within the fabled Coalition? Could he have orchestrated the attack? What would he have to gain?* Kate's brain was spinning with conjecture and speculation. *That's pointless,* she reminded herself. *Stay in the moment.*

She walked back to the Jeep, and the two women climbed in. They wound their way down to the entrance ramp, and Keisha helped Kate lock the ram barriers into place.

"Nobody's coming through that door," Kate said, and standing at the entrance to Nomad's lair, she couldn't help but marvel at the simplicity and brilliance of the concept.

This is Julian's reinforced concrete fortress of solitude, she thought. *And all under the watchful eye of his security cameras and motion senors.* The building's isolation was a gift. From the outside, it blended seamlessly with its surroundings, a chameleon in the urban jungle, virtually invisible to prying eyes. And tucked away from the bustling world, the garage offered solitude and silence—a veil of obscurity. Few stumbled upon it by chance, and none entered without invitation.

"What's next?" Kate asked.

"The elevator," Keisha said. "Oh, and the ground floor stairwell doors."

CHAPTER 83

MOORE TOWER, MANHATTAN, NY

DREW CHECKED AND DOUBLE-CHECKED the results. He had to be certain before he called Moore.

"You better come down," Drew said. "I found him, and you were right. He's been right under our nose this entire time."

"I'm on my way."

Moore's private elevator opened, and he stepped into the control room.

"Alright. Let's see it."

Drew put the location up on the monitor.

"You're sure?" Moore asked.

"Positive. Every packet I've traced across dozens of proxy servers originates and terminates at the same building."

"That brilliant, ruthless bastard," Moore said. "He played us. Offered up the Frenchman like a pawn, and I fell for it."

Moore texted the address to his team leader and added that he'd be coming.

"Get me the bag," Moore yelled, and he ripped the Frenchman's NanoVault out of Drew's examination vice. With the device in his hand, he asked again, "Where's the damn bag?"

"Here," Drew said and handed him the courier's Faraday bag.

Moore dropped the NanoVault inside and sealed it.

"I wasn't finished with that," Drew complained. "There might have been something I could discover."

"Or it's a Trojan Horse," Moore said. "Think about it. Nothing gets in here, but we can't wait to get our hands on this, and it lands right in the middle of our operation. I can't believe I fell for it."

"You think Nomad sacrificed LeGrande to break in here?"

"He might have thought we'd just steal it, and leave the old man alone," Moore said. "He tried to save him, but he was wasting his breath. Whatever the Frenchman's role, I couldn't risk the exposure. And I might have given Nomad exactly what he wanted."

"We're secure," Drew said. "If you're right about Nomad, whatever he hoped would happen didn't work, and now it can't."

"Let's hope you're right about that," Moore said, and checked his phone. "The team's almost ready," he said and headed for the elevator. As the doors closed, he added, "The hunt for Nomad, ends today."

Chapter 84

MONDAY, APRIL 20
9:23 AM EDT

NOMAD'S FORTRESS, MANHATTAN, NY

Julian was still hard at work when Kate and Keisha returned from surveying the building's security.

"How does it look?" he asked.

"Not bad," Kate replied. "This is quite the fortress. I just want to a do a sweep of this level, and the living space above. Then I'll head for the roof."

"Do you need Keisha?"

"No, she can stay, but stay together. If something happens, I need to know you're both in one place."

Kate walked up the vehicle ramp toward the top level, and the minute she was out of sight, Julian turned to face Keisha.

"You need to see this," he said, and brought up a video feed of Moore Tower's underground parking.

"They're prepping for an assault," he said.

"I count ten."

"At least," Julian agreed. "And look at these guys. I think Moore's private security is all former special forces operators."

"We need to tell her."

"No. We can't," he said. "She'll want to fight, and she'll die trying. I can't have that on my conscience, not after everything I've done. Francois should be enjoying his retirement. Kate's friend Pete, the security guard, would be home with his wife. Kate shouldn't be here, and she wouldn't be if it wasn't for me."

"I still think it should be her choice," Keisha said. "But I'll help. What do you need?"

"Both of you need to be in the safe room before they get here."

"You've seen her," Keisha said. "Equipped and ready to repel anyone that even tries to get in here. She'll never go voluntarily."

"Agreed. Do you have anything that might knock her out for a while? Chloroform? Or something she could drink?"

"That's movie nonsense, and besides, we don't have the time. Moore Tower is twenty minutes away, and they'll be leaving soon," Keisha said. "No, the only thing we have that would work is a Propofol IV, but she's not exactly gonna sit still while I find a vein."

"Then we need to prey on her moral code."

"How the hell do we do that?"

"You'll see," Julian said. "First, you need to move the Jeep. Take it up to my level."

"What if she sees me?"

"She's on the roof right now, so be quick. I'm the one they want, so they won't stay long, and when they're gone, give her this note. But I need your word. You won't give this to her until it's over."

"What is it?"

"An explanation and apology. Now, promise me."

"Fine. I promise."

Keisha slipped the note into her tactical vest, and they watched three of Moore's blacked-out SUVs start rolling.

"They're on their way," Julian said. "Open the safe room."

Keisha stood in front of two huge, floor to ceiling steel storage racks filled with scrap computer parts, cables and monitors. She twisted an ancient hard drive, and a magnetic lock released the two racks. Now they slid easily apart, revealing the safe room's vault door. Keisha punched in the code and pushed in the door.

"Go lay in the far right corner of the room," he said. "I want to be sure she can see you from the door. When you're ready, I'll call her down."

"What about the door?"

"I've got that, now go."

Julian watched the monitors, and as soon as he saw Kate descending the roof top stairs, he yelled into the radio,

"Kate! Come quick. Keisha's fallen. Please, hurry."

Kate came running. "Where is she?" Kate asked.

"Over there."

Kate saw Keisha laying on the floor and rushed in.

"What happened?" she asked and knelt alongside. She checked for a pulse.

"Her pulse is strong, fast and —," Kate began. "What are you doing? Julian!"

"I'm sorry, Kate," Julian said through the last gap in the vault door. "It has to be this way."

With another key press on his chair's command console, the steel cabinets slid back together and the magnetic lock engaged.

Chapter 85

NOMAD'S FORTRESS, MANHATTAN, NY

KATE POUNDED ON THE safe room door.

"Julian Pryce, you open this damn door right this minute or so help me God, when I get out of here you won't know what hit you."

"He can't hear you," Keisha said. "It's completely sound proof. You could shoot in here, and there's no way to know this room even exists."

"Are you OK?" Kate asked.

"I'm fine."

"So it was a trap?"

"Yes. I wanted you to know. I thought the choice should be yours."

"Know what?"

"Moore's team is on the way," Keisha said. "Julian showed me the video feed from Moore's garage. At least a dozen men loaded into three vehicles. I saw them Kate — they're equipped like you."

"And now they'll enter unopposed," Kate said. "He's giving up."

"It's not that," Keisha said. "He couldn't bear the thought of you getting hurt, or killed, trying to protect him, and he has a point. Death is hovering over his work. Francois, your friend Pete, and now you, all because of him."

"Yes, people have died. Good people. But Julian didn't kill them. Moore did," Kate said. "How many will die if he's not stopped? Now, help me get out of here."

Keisha punched in the code. Nothing happened. She tried again. Same result.

This can not be happening, Kate thought. *Not again. No explosives this time. I guess that's something.*

"I don't understand," she said. "If he changed the code, how do we get out?"

"We're not supposed to get out," Kate said. "Not until it's over. He probably set the door on a time lock. It's the right code, but the wrong time."

"How do we know when it's the right time?"

"We just keep trying," Kate said, and she studied the room. A row of monitors was mounted on the sidewall. *Security monitors,* Kate wondered. *Makes sense. He'd want to watch what was happening outside the room.* She pressed the power buttons. One by one, the monitors filled with security camera feeds from around the building. They could see Julian sitting at his workstation, and hear him issuing commands.

"That doesn't look like a man waiting for an assault team," Kate said. "Do you recognize what he's watching?"

"Those are Moore's vehicles, but I don't recognize the building," Keisha said. "Wherever they just stopped. It's not here."

"Julian lied to you," Kate said. "For some reason, he wanted us out of the way."

"But those are Moore's men, and look —," Keisha said. "Devin Moore is with them. Where are they?"

"Exactly. Where did Julian send them?"

CHAPTER 86

NOMAD'S FORTRESS, MANHATTAN, NY

JULIAN WATCHED THE SUV's arrive and fan out around the rear of the Overwatch Nexus building. The vehicle doors flew open, and the operators split into three teams, each headed for a different entrance. Alexei's Samoan bodyguard picked the wrong moment for a smoke break and caught a round in the head before he could reach for his weapon.

The building's warehouse access had three entry points. Stairs at each corner connected to emergency exit doors. In the center was the loading ramp, a warehouse roll-up door, and an adjoining side door. The breachers assessed the entry options. All three locations had hardened steel security doors, with deadbolt locks, and ram-resistant steel plating. They deployed charges and moved back up the stairs or away from the loading bay door to await a synchronized entry.

Julian spotted Devin Moore standing near one of the vehicles, surrounded by bodyguards. Moore remained a safe distance from the operation, but close enough to watch his men taking position. Their target, Alexei Sumarov. The former KGB, Russian hacker-for-hire, and owner of the popular twenty-four-seven Overwatch on-line gaming center.

I knew he would come, Julian thought. *The prospect of capturing the mysterious Nomad was just too tempting. And Keisha was right. I wanted to destroy Alexei for his part in Francois's murder, but this is better. It was only a matter of time before Moore traced my location, my real location, and now his men are my arms and legs. They will do what I could only dream.*

The team leader's hand signal set the stage. Everyone was in position, and safe behind cover, when the doors blew. The teams rushed in and deployed throughout the building to locate the man they believed to be on site, Alexei Sumarov, AKA Nomad.

At the sound of the explosives, Alexei grabbed a handgun from under his desk and jumped to his feet.

Moore's men were closing in on Alexei's position, and when they were about to reach him, Julian pressed PLAY on the recording he had queued. *This is for Francois.* Julian said, and the sound of gunfire erupted from Alexei's computers and basement speakers.

Alexei froze in the confusion of the gun battle happening all around him. He dropped his gun, but it was too late. Bullets ripped through Alexei's chest, puffs of wool flew from his sweater, and bursts of red sprang from his chest and back. He was on his knees when the final round passed through his right eye, shattering his glasses and blowing out the back of his skull.

Julian killed the soundtrack. The teams closed ranks around Alexei's body and searched for other combatants. There were none, and that led to whispered confusion among the men.

Moore entered the building and approached Alexei's bloody, crumpled body.

"I wanted him alive," Moore said. "At least for a little while."

"I'm sorry, sir, but our rules of engagement were fire if fired upon."

"Was anyone hit?"

"No, sir."

"Did anyone see him fire?" Moore asked the group. No one spoke up.

The team leader retrieved Alexei's gun. It was cold. A quick press check confirmed a round in the chamber. He released the magazine and checked the capacity.

"He didn't shoot."

Moore began slowly clapping and looked around for a security camera. When he found one, he turned to face it.

"Nicely played," Moore said. "Honestly, you surprise me, and that's difficult to do. I never imagined you capable of orchestrating such an elaborate execution. I guess I should be relieved the execution wasn't mine."

"He deserved to die," Julian said over the speaker system.

"Ah, there you are. Nice to hear your voice again," Moore said. "You know, in all fairness to the late Alexei Sumarov, he didn't know the Frenchman would be killed. He just gave me a name and a location, a purely financial transaction. Considering that you and Alexei are in the same business, have you ever wondered how many of your transactions had, shall we say, unintended consequences? I suspect not. Easier to assume you're above all that. Well, not anymore."

"Are you done?"

"Not yet," Moore said. "Is the girl with you?"

"No, I haven't seen her since she left Richmond Pinnacle," Julian lied. "When she didn't make contact, I figured your men caught up with her."

"Perhaps they did," Moore said. "I'll know soon, and that just leaves you. I know you're here. In New York, so it won't be long now."

"I agree," Julian said. "And I'm tired of running, hiding."

"Forgive me if I don't believe you. My gut tells me that's a ploy, a setup for another surprise."

"You're right about the surprise. Have a seat at Alexei's workstation. There's something you need to see."

Moore pulled up a seat at Alexei's desk and waited. A moment later the monitor displayed the live feed of Julian Pryce.

"Hello, Devin."

"Pryce?" Moore said. "It can't be."

"It's been years," Julian said. "I wondered if you'd recognize me."

"How could I forget the annoying little shadow that followed me everywhere? But I don't understand. We all went to your funeral."

"Sorry I missed it."

"He lied to me," Moore said. "My father said it was handled, and when I heard you were dead, I was actually proud of the man for the first time in my life."

"Your father was a great man," Julian said. "Truly brilliant, and kind and generous."

"And weak," Moore said. "But get to the point. What do you want?"

"I want in," Julian said. "Whatever it is you're building. Whatever the endgame. None of it would have been possible without me."

"Are you insane?" Moore asked. "When I find you, and I will, the only thing coming your way is a bullet in the brain, and since Julian Pryce is already dead, no one is going to care."

"Ah, you don't know," Julian said. "It wasn't you."

"What are you talking about?"

"The NanoVault's hidden core, the way it communicates and propagates, that's my worm code," Julian said. "I'm sure you've been scrambling to figure out how I breached your system. Well, the code has a backdoor."

"That's impossible," Moore said. "Drew wrote —"

Moore froze mid-sentence, and Julian watched him wrestle with the concept and consider the facts.

"Drew said the MIT Mystery Hunt hack was his. He showed me the code," Moore said. "It was stunning. I'd never seen anything like it, and the minute Drew graduated, I hired him."

Moore snapped back into the moment, and back to the ruthless businessman his father feared he would become.

"What do you want?" Moore asked. Ownership? Recognition?"

"Look at me," Julian said. "I'm a prisoner in this body, this chair, and the clock is ticking on the time I have left."

"You're dying?"

"Could be months, maybe a year, two at most," Julian said. "And you can ensure that whatever time I have left is spent in luxury and comfort.

"And what's in it for me?"

"I can fix the code," Julian said. "When I close the door, the NanoVault will be invincible."

"Why should I trust you?"

"You don't have a choice," Julian said. "If something happens to me, the code to the NanoVault's core goes public. No one will use them or buy them. Your venture will collapse. I imagine a swat team of Federal Agents will sweep in and cart off everything that's not nailed down. And your high-priced attorneys will vanish when the well runs dry."

"How do I know you won't do that, anyway?"

"Because, like your father, I am a man of my word. I don't care what you do with the criminal organizations, corrupt politicians and judges, they deserve what they get," Julian said. "But millions of ordinary people have no role in your grand power grab. They're innocent, and I won't hurt them unless you give me no other choice. You have my word."

"Where are you?"

"Do we have a deal?"

"Yes," Moore agreed. "Now where are you?"

"The address is on the screen. It's an old parking garage. You'll find the main entry door open, and you can drive right on in. You'll find me on the fourth floor."

"Oh, I won't be coming. I'm not taking a chance that this is an elaborate trap."

"Fair enough, but as you can see, I require some assistance to travel," Julian said. "Your men will find I have a van, and the keys are in it."

CHAPTER 87

NOMAD'S FORTRESS, MANHATTAN, NY

THROUGH THE SAFE ROOM's building monitors, Kate heard everything Julian said. She leaned against the wall and sank to the floor. Keisha cried.

"I don't understand," Keisha said. "I trusted him."

"We both did."

"I thought he wanted to stop Moore. Was that a lie?"

"I honestly don't know. I like to think I've got good instincts, but if it was all a lie, he sure fooled me."

"But why join forces with Moore? Why help him succeed?"

Those are two different questions, Kate thought. *Joining doesn't mean helping, but if that's true, he's in serious trouble.*

"Is Julian dying?" Kate asked.

"Not on my watch."

"Another lie," Kate said. "Did he say anything to you when he set up this little ambush?"

"No," she said. "I thought he was genuinely concerned for your safety, and mine. He wanted us both in here. I guess he just needed us out of the way"

"Both things could be true," Kate said. "He could want to keep us safe, and he needed us out of the way. If he's doing what I think he's doing, I would have stopped him. Where's my Jeep?"

"He asked me to take it up to the fifth floor."

"Of course, he wouldn't be able to explain it. He told Moore he hadn't seen me."

"Maybe he thought Moore would stop looking for you."

"True, but I think he wanted Moore to believe I was off the board. Permanently."

"What do you mean?"

"Julian's moving the pieces around. We can't see it, not yet, but he wanted us in here for a reason. He knew we'd see and hear everything and that didn't matter."

"You've got an idea."

"Just a hunch," Kate said. "I've played Julian many times. He's fond of misdirection, and he's good at it. He gets you thinking one thing, while he does another."

"The note!" Keisha said. "I was so upset, I nearly forgot. He made me promise not to give this to you until they left." She handed Kate the note. "I think under the circumstances, this is one promise I can break with a clean conscience."

Kate read the note and began pacing the room.

"Well, what is it? What did he say?"

"I was right," Kate said. "Julian's gambling with his life, and we need to find a way out of here."

CHAPTER 88

MONDAY, APRIL 20
10:27 AM EDT

NOMAD'S FORTRESS, MANHATTAN, NY

JULIAN WATCHED THE THREE SUVs approach. The lead vehicle broke off, and set up a rearguard position, angling the vehicle to engage anyone that might try to enter the building. The other two raced up the ramp, using speed as a shield. Their wheels screeched as they took each corner, and the engines roared as they sped up up the ramp from level to level.

When they hit level four, the trailing vehicle set another rearguard position, leaving one to park and block the van. The drivers remained with each vehicle, but four men spread out, rifles hot and low ready. The men scanned over the tips of their barrels and climbed the ramp toward Julian's workstation.

Julian was facing the men, and did his best to ensure his hands were visible. He didn't want a repeat of Alexei's gun battle.

"Hello, Gentleman," Julian said. "You made good time."

The team leader stayed with Julian, while the others spread out to search the rest of the floor and signal the all clear.

The team leader pressed the mic button on his radio and listened via the earpiece in his left ear. Julian was able to follow one side of the conversation.

"We have him."

"No Sir. He's alone."

The team regrouped around Julian, "Load him up, but the chair stays here."

"But I need the chair," Julian pleaded. "It's an extension of my body and I'm nearly helpless without it."

Back on the radio, he went. "Sir. He claims he needs the chair."

"Understood. Yes, sir."

"The chair stays. Look around for an old wheelchair. The boss says there's likely to be a transport chair around somewhere."

While the others searched for a chair, the team leader grabbed one of the operators.

"You're staying here," he said. "No one gets near this system until the geeks arrive to examine it. If anyone does return to the building, detain if you can, kill if you must, but nobody touches this system."

"Yes, Sir."

"Where's that chair?"

"Found it."

"Good. Now, pick him up, and strap him in. We're leaving."

CHAPTER 89

MONDAY, APRIL 20
10:45 AM EDT

NOMAD'S FORTRESS, MANHATTAN, NY

KATE CRUSHED JULIAN'S NOTE and tossed it on the floor. Keisha scooped it up.

"We need to find a way out of here," Kate said and started pulling everything away from the walls.

"What are you looking for?"

"An exit hatch," Kate said. "A safe room's not a vault, so they often design them with an emergency exit, but it won't be obvious."

While Kate dragged heavy cabinets full of freeze-dried food, water and medical supplies, Keisha read Julian's note.

"I don't understand any of this," Keisha said. "Root access. Proximity trigger. What does this all mean?"

"Julian lied to me," she said. "It was never possible to bring down Moore's system remotely. He didn't have root access."

"Try again, only this time pretend I'm not like you."

"It means there was no way he could launch Omega. And it means he could never find Jake's files."

"So, he really is helping Moore?"

"No, it's worse."

"Jesus, what would be worse?"

"The damn fool's playing a Knight Fork," Kate said. "Here, give me a hand with this one."

The two women tried to move a steel cabinet that wouldn't budge, and after multiple strenuous attempts, they rested.

"What's a knife-fork?"

"It's Knight Fork, think Knight of the Round Table. It's a powerful chess tactic. You sacrifice the Knight hoping to trap the King or at least make him vulnerable."

"So, Julian calling Moore was a trap?"

"When Julian revealed his identity, he counted on Moore not being able to resist his offer. He was right about that, but he didn't count on Moore's paranoia."

"So, what's this bit about a proximity trigger?"

"That's the problem, and it's why we need to get out of here. Now," Kate said. "The time clock on that door won't release for another three hours. Julian will be dead by then, and it will all have been for nothing."

A cabinet that their combined strength couldn't move had Kate wondering why. She searched for something small, metallic, and found a paper clip. She lay down next to the base of the cabinet and released the clip. When it stuck to the base, she had her answer.

"This is it. There's an electromagnetic lock holding the cabinet in place."

"Oh, like the entry cabinets that hide the safe room door."

"How do those open?"

"The shelves are full of old clutter and junk, and there's an old hard drive. When I turn it, the cabinets separate and I can slide the cabinets out of the way."

"OK. Let's find the switch in here," Kate said. "Start turning, and pulling. Anything and everything. Something in here is the key to getting out."

Kate watched the paper clip fall. The magnet was off.

"That's it. You found it," she said, and pulled the cabinet away from the wall.

A two-foot square door was cut into the side of the room, with electromagnetic bars mounted above and below the exit. *That's over two thousand pounds of holding force,* Kate thought. *No wonder it wouldn't budge.*

Kate put a finger on her lips to signal they needed to be quiet. *Can't count on the room's sound proofing once I crack this door.* Kate twisted the lever handle and pulled the door into the room. With the flashlight from her tac vest, she looked inside and whispered to Keisha, "It looks like this runs about twenty feet north, and then turns east. Any idea where this might come out?"

"Maybe the kitchen? There's a return air vent near the floor. That could be it, and that might be a problem."

"Why?"

"There's a large recycle bin in front of it. It will be full of glass and aluminum cans."

"Keisha, imagine I'm in the tunnel, and staring at the back of the bin. Which way can I slide it and not hit something?"

"Right," Keisha said. "Definitely right."

Kate set her rifle off to the side, took off the tactical vest, and removed her gun belt. She grabbed two Glock mags, stuffed one in her left front pocket, and another in the left rear. Kate tucked the front of her shirt in behind her appendix holster and tested her gun's fit. With a master grip on the pistol, she gave a slight tug, just enough to break the gun free of the kydex, and then she pressed it back in with a click.

"What are you doing?"

"I can't risk anything that could make noise and reveal my presence," Kate said. "I need to move fast and count on surprise."

"But he's wearing body armor, and now you aren't."

"Yep. But there's only the one guard, and he thinks he's alone," Kate said. "I should have surprise on my side. If all goes well, you'll hear me shout down the tunnel and then it's your turn."

"Through there?"

"It's bigger than it looks."

"And so am I," Keisha said.

"It's your choice, but crawling out beats staying in here, and I may need your help."

"But couldn't I just give you the door code and have you open it from the outside?"

"Outside, inside, it's all the same to the time lock," Kate said. "For the next three hours, there's no way to open this door."

Keisha got down on her knees and peered into the darkness. "I don't know about this."

"You can do it," Kate said. "But if you don't hear from me, close the hatch and lock it. No one can get in from that side, and you could stay in here for a year. No matter what you see or hear, do not come out if you see Moore's people return. They won't hesitate to kill you."

Kate slipped into the tunnel and started crawling in the dark. When she made the turn, she could see light ahead. Another twenty feet and she was at the grate. Keisha was right. This is the kitchen. The lights are on. Kate listened. *Sounds empty,* she thought. *Good boy. You stay right where you are.*

The challenge now was removing the grate quietly, and it just got harder. *The damn thing's hinged. That probably seemed like a good idea, but I can't push it open without hitting the can.* With Plan A out the window, Kate didn't have a choice. *I need to push the can into the room, and hope he doesn't come in. I hope this thing slides. If it tips over, I won't be alone for long.*

She took a minute to war-game the worst-case scenario. *If I have to burst into the room, is there any cover? Maybe the side of the refrigerator. The table and chairs are worthless. OK, not pretty. Let's hope it doesn't come to that.*

Kate was relieved when the recycle bin moved, but then it stopped. *It's stuck on something. The grout lines in the kitchen tile.* She pressed harder, and then more. It broke free, but the recycle contents rattled, and she froze. She was ready to push in and lunge out, but no one came. The bin slid far enough to let her crawl out, and she moved it out of Keisha's way.

Glock in hand, Kate approached the open kitchen door, but stood well back of the opening, gun up, and in tight. She could see the edge of Julian's workstation, and leaned right to take in more of the room. When that view was clear she stepped right, exposing more of the room while keep her body obscured behind the kitchen wall.

The guard was right where she expected, his back to her, so he could watch the monitors. Believing the interior was secure, he took advantage of the security cameras to track the exterior.

Heel toe, Kate thought, and she moved one step at a time to close the gap between them. *Watch the monitor. Can't let him see my reflection. Twenty yards, fifteen, ten. At this distance, I can shoot one-hole groups. Kate placed the red dot on the back of his neck, in the gap between his plate carrier and his helmet.*

"Move and you're dead," she said, and she watched him flinch. She took up the slack on the trigger. "Don't even think about it."

When Kate saw him accept the situation, she moved on to the next order. "Put your hands on your head and interlock your fingers."

He did as he was told. "Now turn around. Slowly." He turned and Kate's aim pivoted from the back of his neck to the front, then up to his face. She wanted him to see her finger on the trigger, and the gun pointed at his head. Everything from her stance to her grip was part of the message.

"I've killed three men in the last forty-eight hours," Kate said. "If you don't want to be number four, you'll do exactly what I say."

"With your left hand, release the sling and let the rifle fall."

The rifle hit the deck.

"Now, kick it away"

The rifle slid across the cement floor.

"Left hand, thumb and index finger only. Pull the Beretta from the holster and let it fall."

Her eyes followed the left hand, down from his head, across his chest, over to the grip of the Beretta. He turned his shoulders, just a few inches, to aid in reaching around to grip the weapon. Kate didn't see the right hand move until he turned back toward her and his gun was clearing the holster.

Kate's shot hit the bridge of his nose. The fluted NovX poly/copper bullet shattered bone pushed into the center of his brain. The Beretta crashed to the floor, and a moment later, so did he. *You stupid bastard,* she thought. *Why the hell did you do that?*

CHAPTER 90

MONDAY, APRIL 20
11:00 AM EDT

NOMAD'S FORTRESS, MANHATTAN, NY

The drive from the garage-fortress to Moore Tower gave Julian time to think. *Without my chair, this isn't going to be easy,* he thought. *Now, I need hands-on access.* Given the physical limits, that would be a challenge, but he had an idea.

The van pulled into the Tower's underground parking and stopped in front of Moore's express elevator. Julian's transport wheelchair was handed off to a member of the building security detail. He conducted a thorough electronic and weapons scan, and bagged Julian's smart watch and phone, before stepping into the elevator.

Julian and his escort ascended to the seventieth floor and exited past another member of the security team, who nodded and, using his wrist mic, radioed their arrival.

The pair waited outside Moore's office doors for a few minutes and when the automated doors opened, a smiling Devin Moore stepped out.

"Welcome to Moore Technologies," Devin said, and passed through the gigantic doors.

"Are we good?" Moore asked Julian's escort.

"Yes, Sir. The only electronics were his phone and watch, and both are in the bag."

"Then I'll take it from here," Moore said, and he took the handles of Julian's wheelchair, and pushed him through his office entry.

"Was the body search really necessary?" Julian asked.

"Yes, my apologies, but you've proved to be so resourceful that I couldn't take the chance."

"That's an impressive entrance," Julian said, and they rolled through Moore's massive office doors. "And, wow, what a spectacular view."

"You should see the view from the penthouse. I have the top two floors, and that affords a remarkable three-hundred-sixty degree view of my city."

"*Your* city?" Julian asked. "That's a bit of a stretch. Don't you think?"

"Yes, that's true," Moore replied. "But it turns out that with your help, the citizens of this fine city have practically been handing it to me. But come, I know you're eager to see it for yourself, and I can't wait to show it to you."

Moore reached under his desk and toggled the office controls. First the main entry doors closed, and Julian heard the locking bolts engage. Then the library walls parted. Flickering light and music drifted into the office.

"I feel privileged to be entering your inner sanctum. I imagine this is an honor very few enjoy."

"Very few, but it's not every day you entertain someone who has risen from the dead."

They approached Moore's chessboard and the unfinished game.

"May I?" Julian asked, and Moore drove him in for a closer look at the board. "Let me guess. You're playing white."

"I am."

"Checkmate in five moves."

"Funny you should say that," Moore said. "Another visitor suggested I would lose."

"Oh, I'm sorry. That's what I meant."

"I beg to differ, but with LeGrande dead, we'll never know."

Julian felt his face flush at the thought of Francois's murder, and Moore's heartless disregard for the man's life. *If I had the strength,* Julian thought. *I would kill Moore where he stands and be done with it. But while this system lives, someone would just take his place.*

"It is breathtaking," Julian said, and Moore rolled him into the center of the control room. The two men melded with the living art of light and color swirling around them. "Extraordinary. And the detail."

Julian found it hard to focus on any one monitor. It was sensory overload, at a scale his brain couldn't fathom. The data collection rate was beyond all expectation, a technical achievement he could scarcely imagine. And the fact remained, it was his brilliance, his code, that made all of this possible. He was at once astounded and horrified.

"Remarkable, isn't it?" Moore asked. "And to think I owe it all to the annoying little boy I pushed off the balcony. What irony."

Julian was speechless. With his skull fractured and his memory fragmented, he didn't know what happened. The accident, which is what everyone called it and what the papers wrote, was a blur to him. He ignored the sounds and images that plagued his nightmares, and eventually they disappeared along with the life that would never be.

"You...you pushed me?" Julian stammered.

"Oh, I see. You don't recall," Moore said. "Sorry, spoiler alert," he said and laughed. "When you were in the coma, I worried you might wake up and spill the beans. I confess I even thought about how to make sure that never happened, but then you died, and problem solved."

At that moment, Julian realized Moore's father wasn't just protecting MIT or the fraternity, or even his son as the fraternity president. The deal Julian's parents made was to keep Devin out of jail and clear the way for the rise of the future entrepreneur, humanitarian and philanthropist, Devin Moore. Julian thought he might vomit, but swallowed the bile rising in his throat.

Moore turned the wheelchair away from the door, so Julian couldn't see who entered the room, but he heard the footsteps.

"Drew, I have a little surprise for you," Moore said. "There's someone I want you to meet. Andrew Freeman, let me introduce you to the infamous Nomad."

Moore spun the wheelchair around and Drew's eyes darted back and forth between Julian and Moore.

"Julian?" Drew asked.

"Surprise!" Moore announced. "Yes, our long, lost, MIT brother is back from the dead. And, a funny thing happened while Nomad and I were catching up. He seemed to think I'd stolen his code."

"Let me explain —" Drew began.

"That won't be necessary," Moore said. "Frankly, I'm relieved to solve one of life's great mysteries. I never could reconcile how you produced something so remarkable, when everything else you've ever done has been so, well, pedestrian. And, now, I know."

"Julian, I'm sorry," Drew muttered. "I never thought. Didn't know. Would never —"

"Drew, relax," Moore said. "Your job's safe, if that's what has you so flustered. You've been with me for years, and loyal to a fault. Julian is going to show us the backdoor you never knew existed, and when that's patched, our worries are over."

Moore turned his attention back to Julian, and asked, "Shall we begin?"

"Just one more thing," Julian began. "As much as I would like to take your word, I'm going to need something in writing, something binding."

"Given our history," Moore said. "I certainly understand. But we are a bit pressed for time. Let me draft up something while you two begin work. Will Andrew's signature, as a witness, be sufficiently binding?"

"Yes, that's fine."

"Excellent. Let me just make sure I capture the spirit and intent of our agreement. You agree to show Andrew where the remote access code is located, assist in the removal of said code, ensure the ongoing integrity and viability of the remaining code. And you agree to provide instruction and maintenance, if needed, for the remainder of your life?"

"Agreed," Julian said. "And in exchange, you will provide a luxury, ADA compliant, apartment here in the tower. A minimum three-bedroom, with a gourmet kitchen, fully furnished, and a skyline view — I've been trapped in a cave long enough. Oh, and since I'm on the payroll, a monthly retainer, for myself, and my live-in nurse."

"A retainer?" Moore asked. "What did you have in mind?"

"You know the rule: whoever says money first loses," Julian said. "But given the success of the NanoVault, and the prospect of losing it all, I'd say you can afford to be generous."

"Fine," Moore said. "Give me a few minutes to draft up an agreement, and I'll make sure that you and whomever you designate for nursing care are generously compensated. In the meantime, you and Drew can get started. Given that Julian Pryce is dead, what name do I use?"

"Your father arranged for a new legal identity," Julian said. "My name is Julian Fischer."

"Geez, as in Bobby?" Moore asked. "That sounds like my father. So, how long is this going to take?"

"If I had my chair, this would be easier, and faster, but an hour, give or take, depending on how Drew configured his development environment."

"Alright. Drew, give Julian whatever help he requires. I would imagine you'll be his keyboard-monkey as he guides you through the code, but the development system only," Moore said, and wagged a finger. "Can't have Nomad here tweaking production code. You understand, right Julian?"

"Of course."

"Very good, then I'll leave you boys to it. Chop. Chop," Moore said. "I'm close if you need me, and remember the eye in the sky. We'll be watching."

CHAPTER 91

NOMAD'S FORTRESS, MANHATTAN, NY

KATE DRAGGED THE GUARD's body away from Julian's workstation and searched him. She held on to his phone, wallet, and the access card she found hanging around his neck. Kate retrieved a black plastic garbage bag from the Kitchen and draped it over his head. *No reason for Keisha to see that,* she thought. *The trail of blood smeared across the floor is bad enough.* As Kate looked at the bloody mess, she was thankful the 9mm round stayed in the man's skull. *The good news is that it's only blood, no brains.*

She turned to face Julian's security cameras. "Keisha," she said. "It's clear. You can come out now. I'll meet you in the kitchen."

When Keisha reached the end of the escape tunnel, Kate helped her crawl out and stand. They headed back out to Julian's workstation, and Keisha's eyes were fixed on the guard's body.

"I wish there was another way," Kate said. "But we're Julian's last chance."

"I know. I watched," Keisha said. "You gave him a choice. He chose poorly."

Kate scoured Julian's chair and nothing jumped out at her. She and Keisha tipped the weighty chair on its side and continued the hunt.

"What are you looking for? Maybe I can help?"

"I honestly don't know," Kate said. "Julian's note said the chair has the proximity trigger. This was a critical part of his plan. He turned his chair into a kind of Trojan Horse, assuming Moore would let him stroll right in with it. We see how that worked out. The chair's here, and he's trapped."

"But what does it do?"

"Same core principle as the NanoVaults. It will connect to whatever electronics it can find," Kate said. "But what it needs, the piece Julian was missing, is a computer that has enough security clearance to launch Omega."

"So Julian finished it?" Keisha asked. "Omega's ready to go?"

"Well, the note said, 'Release the Kraken' — but I'm sure that's what it meant. He's such a nerd."

"OK, whatever it looks like, there's no way it's underneath," Keisha said. "Bring the chair back upright and take a seat. You need to imagine Julian's limited mobility. Where could he physically hide something?"

Kate sat in Julian's chair. She'd seen him type, but it was difficult, so he relied heavily on voice commands. She closed her eyes and pictured Julian working. His elbows remained anchored to the chair's armrests, forearms and wrists did most of the work. She opened her eyes and examined the padded arms.

"The structure's solid. I don't see where he could attach or hide anything."

"What about the joystick?" Keisha asked. "It's fairly small, and shaped like a small box."

"Let's have a look. Do you have a phillips screwdriver?"

"Like the one laying on his desk?" Keisha asked, and they both laughed.

"That's encouraging."

Kate removed the joystick cover and reached inside. "Bingo!"

She held a miniature Bluetooth tracker in the tips of her fingers. "Julian, my friend, you are a brilliant little devil. Foolish to go it alone, but undeniably brilliant."

"What is that?"

"It's a tracker. The kind of thing you'd put in your purse or your luggage. With these, you can monitor your stuff, and if you leave it somewhere or it's stolen, you can track its location."

"That's cool, but I don't see how that helps?"

"Normally, it wouldn't, but with Julian, all bets are off," Kate said. "Lord knows how Julian modified this one, but one thing is certain. Julian believed he could bring Moore down, and all he had to do was get this in close."

"So now all you need to do is wander into Moore Tower and ask real nice if you can visit their super-secret data center."

"I didn't plan on asking," Kate said, and hid the tracker in her boot sock. "I've got the dead guy's access card, so that's a start."

Glass shattered. Keisha screamed, and Kate yelled. "Cover your ears!"

Kate grabbed Keisha and took her to the ground. The combination of flash-bang and smoke grenades had both women disoriented and choking. Kate regretted not retrieving her tactical gear from the safe room, or grabbing more from the Jeep. That was a mistake. Armed only with her handgun, fighting wasn't an option, so she stayed face down, placed her hands on the back of her head and told Keisha to do the same.

"No sudden movement," Kate said. "Don't give them a reason to shoot."

Kate heard boots smacking the floor. *At least four men, she thought.* And that voice, the man shouting bursts of tactical commands, his accent unmistakable. *Russian. Zhukov.*

"Look for weapons," Zhukov said. "She will be armed."

Kate kept her hands interlocked behind her head, while someone patted down her arms, back, waist, and legs. From her right ankle, they removed her trauma medical kit, and from the left, a boot knife. She did what they asked and rolled on to her back. The pat down continued, underarms, breasts, and waist. They pulled the Glock, and the Benchmade pocketknife. *Good,* she thought. *They missed my bra knife, and the tracker.*

"Bring them here," Zhukov said, pointing to the chairs at Julian's workstation.

"Sit down," he said. "Please."

Did Mikhail Zhukov, the Butcher of Beslan, just say please, Kate thought. *What's going on?*

Zhukov looked at Keisha. He appeared confused, but finally spoke.

"Are you Nomad?"

"I'm Nomad," Kate said, before Keisha could speak. "I'm the one you want."

"If only that were true," Zhukov said. "But I know that you are not."

"He's gone," Kate said. "Whatever you were planning, it's over. Nomad may already be dead."

"Then there is no harm in telling me where he is."

"Moore Tower," Kate said. "If he's still breathing, he's with Devin Moore."

"You are certain of this?"

"I'm as certain as that man is dead," Kate said. "Moore's men collected Nomad about thirty minutes ago. They left this one behind to ensure no one tampered with Nomad's equipment."

Zhukov walked over to the body and lifted the plastic bag.

"Did you kill him?"

"No," she said. "He accidentally shot himself in the face."

Zhukov walked down the parking garage ramp, made a call, and waited.

"What do you think he's waiting for?" Keisha asked, straining to keep her voice down.

"Best guess, his employer," Kate said. "Zhukov is a mercenary. Somebody else is pulling this puppet's strings."

The SUV that drove up the third floor ramp and turned toward Zhukov had diplomatic plates. *She's riding a little low,* Kate thought. *Must be armored.*

The vehicle stopped, and Zhukov opened the passenger door. Kate couldn't see the face of the man that stepped out. *He's tall,* she thought. *Maybe six feet, with a full head of wavy gray hair. Finely tailored suit. Looks trim, fit, for his age.* But it was the greeting that shocked Kate. *He hugged and kissed Zhukov like a brother. Who is this guy?*

The two men walked up the ramp and directly to Kate.

"Ms. Preacher," the distinguished gentleman began. "I am—"

"Vitali Moshenski," Kate said. "Ukrainian Oligarch, and Attaché to the Ukrainian Embassy, not to mention suspected war criminal and crime boss. I've seen your file. It's not pretty."

"Yes, of course," Moshenski said. "Given your prior career, I'm sure you've read a good many things about me. Some of which are undoubtedly true, but that is a conversation for another day."

"Why are you here? And why send your attack dog?"

"Yes. Yes. I will answer all of your questions," Moshenski said. "But please let me take a moment to express my deepest sorrow on the death of your husband. He was a remarkable man, and a hero beyond my ability to express."

"Don't pretend you know anything about my husband."

"It's true. I know very little about the man, but I owe him a debt I can never repay."

"You can start by letting us go."

"And I will," Moshenski said. "You have my word that we will do our utmost to ensure no harm comes to you or your friend."

"But what?" Kate asked. "I'm sensing there's more."

"As you've already seen, there are forces at work that are determined to stop us, stop you. In fact, I understand you have already killed three men—"

Zhukov interrupted and whispered in Moshenski's ear.

"I stand corrected. You've killed four men, so clearly you know what is at stake."

"How does *he* know about the other three?" Kate asked.

"Mikhail has been tracking Nomad, trying to make contact, and when your paths crossed, he tracked you as well."

"That's not an answer," she said, and looked at Zhukov. "How did you find this place?"

"I was at your cabin," Zhukov said. "And we placed a GPS tracker on your vehicle. The one that is here, now."

"You were there? You saw?"

"Yes. Everything," Zhukov said. "My sniper witnessed you kill Moore's man, and he dispatched the second."

"You saw the fight with the bounty hunter?"

"Yes, and the entire area has been sanitized."

"Wait a minute," Kate said. "You removed the bodies? All of them?"

"The bodies. The vehicle. Everything," he said. "But not to worry. I heard what you promised. His body will be found."

"Kate, what's he talking about?" Keisha asked.

"It's a long story," Kate said. "But I suspect you knew I had a little trouble getting here, given my bruises and swelling."

"What's important at the moment is that we are here, and we're not your enemy," Moshenski said. "Like you and Nomad, we only hope to stop Moore from going any further and destroy what he has collected."

"That doesn't add up," Kate said. "Wall Street had you pegged as the White Knight who bankrolled the Moore's venture when he was facing ruin. Now, you expect me to believe you want to stop him?"

"Yes, I backed Moore. It began as a legitimate tool for secrecy and an opportunity to conduct business without the meddling of greedy corporations and corrupt governments. That was a promising and lucrative investment," Moshenski said. "But it has become emblematic of both the corruption and greed I hoped to fight, and it will soon be more powerful than anyone could imagine."

"On that, we agree," Kate said. "I've seen what Moore can do with power he has already amassed, and that makes me wonder what he has on you?"

"A man in my position has many secrets," Moshenski admitted. "Some I would kill to protect, others I would take to my grave, but that is not what motivates my pursuit. Do you know of the Coalition?"

"I've heard the term," Kate said. "And I understand the concept. A group of male lions banding together and hunting together. At the Agency, there were rumors of a group of powerful men manipulating currencies, politicians, and countries, but it was never anything more than conspiracy theories."

"Yes, the easiest way to hide the truth is to wrap it in hyperbole and call it fiction or delusion," Moshenski said. "But in this case, the Boogeyman is real. The Coalition is a secretive group buried deep within the Global Economic

Counsel. And Moore hopes to join them. His path to a seat at the table is granting exclusive access to the data he's collected, and the burgeoning AI that will support the Coalition's quest to shape humanity's trajectory. I lived this nightmare under Russian rule and lost all that was dear to me. I have no desire to see others repeat the mistakes of the past and enslave future generations."

"That's why you wanted Nomad," Kate said. "You discovered he had a way to get inside Moore's network."

"It is. Despite Moore's attempts to hide the facts, when I learned of the system breach, I could smell the fear, and realized the opportunity. But it seems we're too late. If he is with Moore, Nomad has either succumbed to Moore's influence or he's dead."

"While I pray my friend is still alive, there's still a chance to stop Moore."

"How?" Zhukov asked.

"Nomad planted code deep inside Moore's system," Kate said. "It can destroy everything he's collected."

"And what of the NanoVaults? Will they remain a threat?" Moshenski asked.

"That's the beauty of Nomad's plan. The same mechanism that Moore used to collect all the data will reset all the devices," Kate said. "Nomad understood that millions of people rely on them, and he didn't want their lives destroyed."

"If he had this capability, why has he not used it?" Zhukov asked.

"That's the catch. He couldn't do it remotely. He needed to get close, so he convinced Moore he was tired of running, and hiding, and willing to show him how to eliminate the vulnerability."

"What would prompt Moore to agree? What sort of leverage could he possibly have?" Moshenski asked.

"Nomad is Julian Pryce, is he not?" Zhukov asked.

"You knew?" Kate asked.

"I suspected," Zhukov said. "Nomad would not be my first encounter with a dead man."

"Julian's code powers the NanoVaults," Kate said. "That's how he breached Moore's system, and that was Julian's leverage. He threatened to release the code to the public. If he did, the entire company would collapse."

"I don't understand why Julian didn't just do that," Keisha said. "Bring the bastard down."

"It would be the end of Moore, but not the data," Kate said. "Who knows what our government would do with it, and what they would do with the technology they gained dismantling Moore's data center?"

"How do we stop him?" Moshenski asked.

"With this," Kate said, and she pulled the tracker from her boot sock. "I need to get this inside Moore's data center, and ideally within about ten feet of a console with admin level access."

"You can't get in," Moshenski said. "But Zhukov can."

"No offense, but we've only got one shot, and we can't take the risk."

"I don't understand. What risk?"

"Zhukov, let me ask you," Kate said. "You've been inside, right?"

"Twice."

"Does he let you bring in any electronics? Watch? Cell phone? Anything?"

"No. They bag everything before heading up in the elevator."

"That's what I thought," Kate said. "When Moore wouldn't let Julian bring his chair, I suspected there was more to it. No one gets close with anything that could harm his baby."

"Then what's the answer?" Keisha asked.

"I had no clue until these guys showed up," Kate said, and turned to Zhukov and Moshenski. "Look, I can't believe I'm going to say this, especially to *him*, but if we work together, we can get this inside and end this."

"Whatever you need," Moshenski said.

"Alright. Here's the plan."

CHAPTER 92

NOMAD'S FORTRESS, MANHATTAN, NY

KATE WALKED EVERYONE THROUGH the plan, handed out the assignments, and retrieved her equipment. The Glock went back in the holster, and the knife back in the boot sheath. *If I'm going to sell this,* she thought. *I need to look the part. Everything was back where it was.*

"First, we set the stage," Kate said. "The camera will be here, and I want Moore to see that his man is dead. Zhukov, prop the body up against the wall here, and remove the plastic. Moore needs to look into the face of death and believe I'm a serious threat."

"What can I do?" Keisha asked.

"I think it's best you stay clear. If you're standing over there, you'll be out of the shot," Kate said.

"Mr. Moshenski, you should go. It's best you're nowhere near when we start."

"Very good," Moshenski said. "I have some arrangements of my own to make. Mikhail, Katherine, good luck and Godspeed to you both."

Kate watched Zhukov escort Moshenski back to his car. They hugged, and Moshenski left. *Moshenski's much more than Zhukov's boss,* Kate thought. She couldn't imagine what brought the Ukrainian and the Russian together, but the bond was unmistakable.

When Zhukov returned, Kate drew her Glock. She released the magazine and cleared the chamber.

"Here," she said, handing everything to Zhukov. "You start on this, while I'll get back into Moore's system."

Kate pulled one of the spare NanoVaults from Julian's stash. *Only three left,* Kate thought. *Julian said we had plenty. Another lie.* But this one made her smile. *He didn't want me to panic. That's sweet.*

Armed with insight gleaned from her last battle with Moore's AI, Kate was confident she could make quick work of the game. She drew black, but even with the AI's first move advantage, it had not adapted to Kate's nonsensical and disruptive play. She didn't need to win. She just only needed to run out the speed-chess clock, and three minutes later, she was in.

Now, let's see what we can use to get Devin's attention. It didn't take Kate long to discover the peripheral devices connected to Moore's network. Between the video distribution system that controlled every monitor in the room, the sound system's overhead speakers, and Moore's eye in the sky security camera, Kate had everything she needed. *This is perfect.*

"Alright. I'm ready," Kate said. "Places everyone."

Kate piped the microphone from Julian's workstation into Moore's sound system and fed her web cam into the video distribution. The control center's panoramic ceiling camera gave her a bird's-eye view of the entire room. Andrew Freeman was sitting next to Julian. *I didn't realize Andrew was on Moore's team, but that explains it,* she thought. *Now, I know how Moore got Julian's code.* Moore was nowhere in sight, but she expected he would show up the minute she took over the security camera and started broadcasting.

"Show time."

All the monitors in the control room's massive half-circle wall filled with Kate's face, and her voice echoed throughout.

"Julian Pryce, what the hell do you think you're doing?"

"Kate!" Andrew shouted. "You're alive."

"Yep, still breathing," she said. "No, thanks to you and your boss. Now, where is he?"

"Hello, Kate," Moore said. "I would say it's nice to see you again, but it's not. I see one dead behind you, and the men I sent to your cabin?"

"They've retired."

"It appears Julian showed you how to exploit the vulnerability," Moore said, and placed his hands on Julian's shoulders. "He claimed he hadn't seen you since Richmond Pinnacle."

"He told you the truth," Kate said. "When I arrived, Julian was gone, and your man's Moore Technologies badge told me exactly where to find him."

"So what happens now?"

"Simple," Kate said. "The world needs to know what you've been doing. When I hit enter, Julian's code goes public. He didn't have the courage to do it, but I do, and I wanted you to watch your world crumble."

Kate's hand hovered over the keyboard, and the second she moved, Moore shouted, "Wait!"

"Why should I?" Kate asked.

"Because if you press that button, Julian dies."

"He's already dead, and he knows it," Kate said. "Why else would he be there? Today, tomorrow, next month, it doesn't matter. Just look at him. Anyone can see he's living on borrowed time, and I'll bet he sold you his services for a chance to live in luxury and die in peace. Am I right?"

"And here, I thought saving your life in Richmond would count for something," Moore said. "But I do have something else that might interest you."

"I seriously doubt that."

"We'll see," Moore said, and Kate watched Moore sit down at one of the control room's consoles. "I have your husband's files. Some of them are really quite touching. I dare say he really loved you. That makes him unusual in my book. And with a little detective work, his files might reveal what he was working on, and who killed him.”

Kate hesitated, and without realizing it, pulled her hand away from the keyboard.

“That's better,” Moore said.

The flash-bang explosion filled the room with a blinding flash of light and an ear-splitting roar, and Kate cut the feed to Moore's control room. She probed and pulled the ear protection she had stuffed deep in her ears, but her eardrums still throbbed in protest of the sound that reverberated. Smoke billowed from the grenade's canister, and between the light and the smoke, she struggled to clear her vision.

“Are you OK?” Keisha asked.

“Yes. I think we sold it,” Kate replied. “Let's give Moore a couple of minutes to digest and consider what he just saw.”

Keisha gave Kate a cold rag for her eyes, and it helped her focus enough to check her watch. “That should do it,” Kate said. “I imagine Moore's sweating bullets by now. Zhukov, your turn.”

Zhukov called Moore, and the moment Moore answered the phone, he said, “I have her.”

“Brilliant timing,” Moore said. “I don't know how you managed it, but I was starting to panic that the FBI, or even one of Nomad's clients, had breached his location.”

“Your man is dead.”

“I know,” Moore said. “Bring her straight up and make sure no-one goes anywhere near the computers. Understood?”

“I will post one of my men,” Zhukov said. “If there is anyone else in the building, my man will not be killed so easily as yours.”

The call ended, and Kate prepared for the second phase of the plan. “Keisha, are you OK?”

“My ears are ringing a bit,” she said. “But I kept them covered, and my eyes closed this time.”

Keisha walked over to Kate and gave her a hug. "I sure hope you know what you're doing. We've only just met, but Julian was right about you, and he's lucky to have you as a friend. Please, bring him home."

"I'll do my best."

"I know you will," Keisha said, and turned away to fight back tears. "Kate? Have you seen this?" she asked and pointed at one of Julian's monitors. "It says it's done."

Kate had completely forgotten about the audio broadcast Julian had captured from Jake's device. The decryption algorithm finished, and between being locked in the safe room, and exploding grenades she never noticed. She searched for a headset and plugged it in. *Whatever this is,* Kate thought. *No-one else needs to hear it.*

She pressed play, but it was barely audible, as if whatever it captured was a whisper. Kate cranked the volume and played it again.

Kate's relentless. She will...

Kate played the recording again and again. *That's definitely Jake,* she thought. *No question about that. Who is he talking to? What does he mean by relentless, and what will I do?* The timestamp on the file answered one question, but raised even more. *This was the last thing Jake said to Marcus.*

"We should leave," Zhukov said.

"There's something I need to do," Kate said. "Whatever happens next, there's something I need to know before we go." She pulled one of the burner phones from the messenger bag.

Marcus answered on the first ring, "Preacher?"

"Yes, and before you ask, I'm fine. Where are you?"

"The cabin. When I didn't hear from you, I gambled you might be here," Marcus said. "From the wine and popcorn, I can see you *were* here. Tell me where you are, and I'll put together a team."

"No need to drag you into this."

"You're not dragging me. I'm offering to help," Marcus said. "Did you figure out what was going on?"

"Still working on it."

"Do you still have whatever those guys were looking for?"

"No. It's gone."

"That's too bad."

"Why do you say that?"

"I thought it might give you some leverage or something. Not important."

"Look, I'm going to stay dark a while longer, but you'll hear from me about Jake's arrangements."

"Of course, thanks," Marcus said.

"Marcus, before I go," she said. "I need to ask, and I'm sorry if this is hard, but I need to know. Did Jake say anything? You know at the end?"

"Oh, Preacher. I'm sorry. I should have said something long before now," Marcus said. "Jake said that thing. You know. The thing you guys say all the time."

"Always?"

"Yeah, that's it," Marcus said. "I know he said 'Kate' and pretty sure he said 'Always' — I'm sorry I can't give you something more. It was hard to hear over the chaos, and he was struggling to speak."

"Thanks Marcus, that means more than you can know."

"I'm glad," Marcus said. "Stay safe, Preacher."

"That's the plan," she said, and hung up.

"Are you ready?" Zhukov asked.

"Almost. I just need five more minutes," Kate said. "This can't wait."

Kate's ace up her sleeve was the sleeper code she planted on Deputy Director Boucher's laptop. She didn't know if she would need access, but she knew he would have access to the cafe's street cam video, and by now, possibly more. Her command-and-control code was sending periodic pings to show it was active and waiting. Kate woke up the malware and mirrored Boucher's screen to her monitor.

Good, Kate thought. *It's locked. He's away.* The key-logger in the malware captured Boucher's credentials, and within seconds she was logged on and checking his activity. *Here they are.* Kate found the street camera video and copied it to a private cloud address. She spotted some files and notes that might help her investigation, but, for now, those would have to wait.

She disconnected from Boucher's laptop and drafted a quick email to Martin Hayes, a former colleague at Langley. Kate passed along the audio file Julian decrypted and the address to the Paris video she'd stolen. Martin was the Agency's leading audio analyst and speech-reader. She had rebuffed his advances when she was single, but prayed she could count on him for a favor. If anyone could isolate the words on the recording, or read Jake's lips from the video, it was Martin.

"Now we can go," Kate said.

Zhukov cuffed Kate's hands, and they walked down the garage ramp to his vehicle. *All part of the show,* Kate thought. *Cuffing her hands in front made them easier to pick. Zhukov would know that, but Moore wouldn't.*

Chapter 93

MONDAY, APRIL 20
12:00 NOON EDT

MOORE TOWER, MANHATTAN, NY

DEVIN MOORE MONITORED THE security feeds in anticipation of Zhukov's arrival and his prize. He grinned when he saw their vehicle pull into the garage. *This worked out better than I could have imagined,* he thought. *Imagine the odds.* The thought made him uneasy. There was something. He couldn't put his finger on it, but he couldn't let it go.

Moore watched Zhukov and Kate enter the elevator, accompanied by one of his men. They stepped off at the office entrance and Zhukov filled a Faraday bag with their electronics. The elevator guard headed back down, while the office guard began searching Kate.

"Hey, watch the hands buddy," Kate protested.

"She is clean," Zhukov insisted, but he knew the protocols. "Use the wand."

The guard ran the metal detector over every inch of Kate's body, and nothing registered beyond the buttons on her pants.

"Follow me," the guard said, and he escorted them both to Moore's massive office entrance.

"Geez, what is this King Tut's tomb?"

Moore was about to open the doors, but he hesitated. *Was this too easy,* he wondered. *The timing too perfect?*

He pulled up the security recording of Kate's video feed and watched it again. *I could have missed something,* he thought. *My focus was on the incursion and the risk of releasing the code.*

Until the moment of the explosion, there was nothing unusual, just the banter between the two of them, then the sparks that obscured the picture, and it was gone. He backed it up and stepped frame by frame from the moment Kate appeared to hesitate. *I thought I had her. But Zhukov's arrival made the point moot. Wait. What's that? A reflection on the monitor.*

Moore captured the screen and enlarged and enhanced the image. *It's a black woman. Her eyes shut tight. Hands covering her ears. The assault was staged.*

He launched from his chair and paced the room. *Zhukov betrayed me. He's working with Kate. Moshenski will regret sending his dog to do his dirty work. If only they'd stayed at the cafe two minutes longer, they'd already be out of my hair.*

Moore considered his options and realized that seeing his opponent's trap had advantages and presented a unique opportunity for closure on his terms.

Chapter 94

MONDAY, APRIL 20
12:10 PM EDT

MOORE TOWER, MANHATTAN, NY

KATE WATCHED AND WAITED. Minutes passed, and she grew concerned. When the giant doors parted, she took a deep breath. *Here we go,* she thought. *This is it.*

Devin passed through the gigantic doors, and with open arms and a broad smile, he greeted Kate as he would a celebrity guest.

"Welcome to Moore Technologies."

As he always did, Moore asked the security guard standing next to Zhukov if the electronics had been secured. "Are we good?"

"Yes, Sir. Everything's in the bag."

"Let's be sure," Moore said. "Run another scan."

Kate raised her arms, and the guard scanned her from head to toe, and front to back. "She's clean."

"And him," Moore said, and the guard hesitated to approach Zhukov. "It's alright. Mikhail understands the protocol, and you don't mind, do you?"

"No," Zhukov said, and extended his arms. The scan registered Zhukov's firearms, but no electronics.

"You, stay right here," Moore said, directing the guard to remain just outside the office.

Moore led the way into the control room, and Kate saw Julian working alongside Andrew, and when they stopped to watch, Moore snapped at them.

"Don't stop," He insisted. "This doesn't concern you."

"I have to admit, Kate," Moore said. "I'm relieved to see you in handcuffs."

"Do I scare you?" she asked.

"Yes, a little. It appears you killed a few of my men."

"She did not use her bare hands," Zhukov said. "She shot them. With this."

Zhukov pulled Kate's gun from his waistband and handed it to Moore.

Moore did a press check and confirmed Kate's gun had a round in the chamber. *Didn't see that coming,* Kate thought.

"Don't look so surprised," Moore said, and he popped out Kate's magazine, took a quick look, and then shoved it back into the gun.

"I'm no stranger to firearms, courtesy of my father's legal career," Moore said. "He prosecuted some nasty characters in his time, and insisted that if we had firearms in the house, we should know how to use them."

"Smart man."

"Brilliant, yes. Smart? Maybe not," Moore said. "Julian and I have agreed to disagree on my father's virtues. But one thing I learned from my father was to trust my instincts. To understand that the brain captures so much more than it can process, and intuition is often little more than the subconscious processing minute details which surface as flashes of insight."

Moore pointed Kate's gun at Zhukov.

"For example, the off-Broadway theater production you staged was very convincing," Moore said. "For a moment, I thought Mikhail had actually saved the day. Drop your weapons," Moore commanded Zhukov. "All of them. And trust me, I will pull the trigger with a smile on my face, so I wouldn't test my resolve."

"Vitali will be furious when he learns of this," Zhukov protested.

"Your boss doesn't scare me. Not anymore. I know what Vitali's been hiding," Moore said. "Now, nice and slow. One by one. Drop everything, and kick them away."

Zhukov's CZ-75 pistol hit the deck, and he swept it away. He reached behind his back, and Moore brought the pistol up as a warning. Zhukov reached back slowly and dropped a large fixed blade knife at his feet.

The blade caught Moore's eye, and Kate's too.

"That's a beautiful piece," Moore said. "Damascus steel is mesmerizing. Persian?"

"Syrian," Kate said, and turned to Zhukov. "Where did you get that?"

"You already know the answer."

"But how?"

"When you were kidnapped by the Al-Shammar, you were just CIA," Zhukov said. "And an opportunity to find out what you knew about our operation, and learn how you found me. But when I realized who you were, I warned Suliaman not to harm you. He was told to guard you with his life."

"You sent the photo," Kate said. "You're the reason the team found me, but not before that sadist did this."

Kate pulled down the top of her blouse, snapped off a button, and revealed a small portion of the scar tissue that covered her chest and breasts.

"I never thought I could feel such pain and fury, not again," Zhukov said. "But when I saw what he did, I cut out his heart and shoved it down his throat."

"Shut up!" Moore shouted. "I don't know what any of that is about, and I don't give a damn. But I'm glad you're familiar with the concept of retribution. It's my turn."

Moore pointed Kate's gun at Zhukov, but he didn't care.

"Nothing to say?" Moore asked.

"What did you expect?" Zhukov asked. "That I would beg for my life. Do you imagine you are the first to point a gun at my head?"

"Where are you going?" Moore demanded, but Zhukov kept moving. "Stop!"

Zhukov turned back to face Moore and smiled. "Come," Zhukov said. "If I'm going to die. Do it here. Right in the center of your glorious new world."

The center console. Kate realized. *Moore's AI workstation. It must have full access. Zhukov's drawing Moore closer.* With Drew and Julian mesmerized by the scene, no one noticed Kate's hands. She fished a tiny, black, plastic handcuff key from a coin pocket and unlocked the right cuff. She was careful to preserve the illusion that it was still secure, but loose enough to slide out.

Moore obliged Zhukov's taunt and followed him into the center of the room. Still wary of someone with the Russian's skill, he didn't dare approach too close. But when Zhukov retreated, Moore stepped forward, unaware he was a puppet on Zhukov's string.

"Perhaps you *are* afraid of death," Moore said. "Time to join your wife and daughter."

With the Glock's red dot squarely in the center of Zhukov's face, Moore pressed the trigger. Kate saw Zhukov's head move slightly, just before the shot's sound wave rang in her ears. The bullet struck just above Zhukov's left eye. His head jerked left, and his shoulders followed. Blood and bone sprayed across the AI's console. Zhukov's feet gave way, and he tumbled like a massive timber. His limbs stiff and body rigid, his face and head slapped the floor with a sickening thud.

"Let's be sure, shall we?" Moore said and approached Zhukov's body. Now, standing within inches of the AI console, Moore was exactly where Zhukov wanted. *He sacrificed himself,* Kate realized. *That's not the act of a mercenary.* Blood seeped from Mikhail's wound and pooled around his misshapen face. There was no reason to shoot again, except for the blood lust Moore had ignited. He pointed the gun at Zhukov's head, but the room went black. The lights and monitors. All Dark. All except one.

"What's happening?" Moore screamed.

"I have no idea," Drew replied. "I'm locked out."

The one remaining monitor displayed the worldwide map and the count of connected NanoVaults. Like the infection rates of a global pandemic, a wave of red flowed out from Manhattan, consuming everything in its path. Within seconds, the continental United States changed from green to red, and then black.

Julian's Omega wave traveled like a tsunami ripping apart Moore's world. Every device it touched disconnected from Moore's network, and could never broadcast again. The number of connected devices was falling so fast the count was a blur, and the number of digits dropped like a launch countdown, eight-figures, seven-figures, six-figures, and down.

Moore waved the gun at Julian. "You did this. Make it stop."

"I can't," Julian said. "Drew's right, the console's frozen."

"If I'm going down, you first," Moore said, and he raised the gun.

"Wait!" Kate yelled. "I can stop it," she lied.

"Get down here."

Kate raised her handcuffed hands, pressed together just below her face, and lowered her eyes like a woman praying.

"Yeah," Moore said. "You better pray this works, or you're both dead."

Moore pressed the gun into the side of Kate's head and used it to shove Kate toward the AI console. She was the perfect picture of a terrified woman. Hands in prayer, tears streaming, body trembling, slow, small steps. *Wait for it,* she thought. The barrel of the gun smacked the side of Kate's head again. *Now!* Her right hand slipped out of the cuff, and panic raced across Moore's face.

Kate's left arm shot straight up, swept the gun away from her head, and trapped his arm. Moore fired and tried to step back, but his arm was locked to Kate's left side. She launched a right hand spear strike at Moore's chest. With open palm, thumb spread wide, her hand grazed his collarbone on the way to her target. The adrenaline backed strike carried every ounce of muscle Kate could summon and slid into Moore's throat.

She felt his trachea crush and compress against the vertebra in his neck. The gun crashed and skidded across the floor. She released his arm and pushed him back. Both of Moore's hands raced to his throat. He coughed and choked, and fell to his knees. Eyes bulging, pleading, he looked up at Kate. Unable to speak, or draw a breath, he moaned and wheezed, wasting what little air remained in his lungs.

Drew scrambled for Kate's gun. Julian tried to grab Drew's belt and toppled out of the wheelchair.

"Kate!" Julian screamed, but Drew had the gun up and pulled the trigger. Click. He tried again. Still nothing.

"Didn't think you had it in you, Andrew," Kate said, and swung her foot up into his groin, and followed with an elbow to the back of neck. Drew went down. Out cold. And Kate picked up the gun.

It worked, she thought, and released the magazine. Visible now, wedged deep in the magazine, was Julian's proximity trigger. When Moore checked the gun, as Kate feared he might, all he could see was the round in the chamber and the one at the top of the magazine. Moore didn't have the tactical experience to know the magazine was light, too light to be full.

Bringing the gun into the room was easy enough. How they would get it near an admin station was the part of the plan that Kate couldn't answer, but Zhukov did. He taunted Moore into carrying the means of his destruction to the very place it could do the most damage. She pocketed the magazine and holstered the empty gun. *An extra mag would have been smart.*

Kate was snapped back into the moment when Moore's head hit the floor. The gurgling death rattle of Moore fighting for breath sent chills through her body. Kate picked up Zhukov's knife, then started searching Drew's desk.

"What are you looking for?" Julian asked and dragged himself along on the floor.

"A tube," she said. "Anything I can use as a tube?"

Kate found a pen and knelt next to Moore. The cyanosis had begun. Moore's face was turning blue. Starved of oxygen, he panicked, and struggled. *He'll be unconscious soon,* Kate thought. *And dead within minutes if I don't help.*

She took the pen apart. *This should work. It's not ideal, but some air beats no air until he can get to the hospital.*

Kate ripped open Moore's shirt to fully expose his neck. A gold plated NanoVault dangled on a chain and slid to one side. Moore's hand wrapped around the device and he thrust it at Kate. *Is this a bribe,* she wondered. *After everything he's done, he still thinks he can buy what he wants?*

She hesitated, and Moore panicked. He ripped the NanoVault from his neck and shoved it into Kate's hands. With his right hand, he flashed three fingers, then one, then four, and kept repeating that sequence.

"Pi?" Kate asked, and Moore nodded.

With Zhukov's knife hovering over Moore's throat. Kate pictured the procedure, the training. The Cric technique was the field trauma, emergency, version of the tracheotomy. She needed to open his airway, and insert the tube. She'd never done it, and there were risks, but certain death was the alternative. Kate probed Moore's thyroid and prepared to make the midline incision. Moore's eyes fluttered and closed. *He's unconscious*, she thought. *It won't be long now.*

Kate squeezed her eyes shut, imagined her next move, and her heart raced. She was drowning in images of death. Francois swaying at the end of a rope. Pete lying in a pool of blood. Senator Cahill on the floor of his suite, the girl, bound and gagged. The bounty hunter at Ruby's Corner. Rojas and the men Moore sent to Jake's cabin. *All of this blood is on Moore's hands. And how many others,* she wondered. Images of Jake were there, too. Racing to stop the Paris attack. Sacrificing himself to save others. *Evil exists,* he would say. *And my job is to protect the innocent.*

She looked at Julian, willing his body to move, and pictured Keisha waiting to hear if Julian was alive. *They'd both be dead if Moore had his way. If I hadn't been there,* she thought. *Jake was right. Some people are born to do our unpleasant jobs for us. I'm one of them.*

Kate stood up, stepped back, and looked down at the man dying on the floor. *You're in God's hands now,* she thought. *I'm not that kind of preacher.*

"Kate!" Julian yelled.

The security guard burst into the room. He charged the woman standing over his boss with a knife and slammed her into the wall. The knife flew out of her hand and clattered on the floor. Dizzy and wobbling, Kate tried a groin strike, but he caught her leg, and threw her back against the wall. Her head shattered a monitor, and glass dug into her scalp.

Kate was on her knees when his left arm wrapped around her throat. She knew the escape. *Turn your shoulders away from his elbow. Get inside. Find a target.* But on her knees, she had no leverage.

Her right hand dug inside her blouse. She wrapped two fingers around the T-handle hilt of the ceramic blade. In one continuous move, she drew the blade, shoved it deep into the underbelly of his forearm, and yanked from his elbow to his wrist. The knife split muscle and severed tendons, veins, and nerves. A tortured scream pierced the air and blood flowed down Kate's shirt.

Kate was free, and turned to thrust the blade into his neck, but he pivoted, and she missed. She readied another strike, but he drew his weapon and raised the gun. Again, Kate charged and trapped the arm. With an elbow strike to the side of his head, she twisted and stripped the gun free. It discharged, and a round struck the floor. But now gun in hand, Kate turned and fired point blank into his chest. He grabbed at Kate's shirt, sunk to his knees, and fell over.

The elevator's arrival ding sent Kate leaping for cover. She didn't know how many of Moore's men would step out, but she knew the odds weren't good. *This isn't going to be pretty,* she thought, and waited for the assault.

She saw Julian crawl in beneath the AI console, struggling with little more than forearms and wrists, to pull himself into the chair. "Julian!" Kate shouted. "Get down!"

But Julian ignored her and kept fighting to get into the chair. *Whatever he's doing, he must think it's worth dying for,* Kate thought. *We may both be going out in body bags.*

"Don't shoot!" Moshenski shouted, and Kate recognized the voice and the accent.

"All clear," Kate said, and stood. Gun at the low ready, just the same.

Two of Moshenski's men raced into the room, and Moshenski stepped over the bodies they left in the elevator. One man knelt alongside Zhukov.

"There's a pulse," he said. "Faint and thready. He's fading fast."

"Quickly then," Moshenski said. "Get him into the elevator. Medical transport is waiting in the garage. Now, go."

Moshenski surveyed the scene, and the blood on Kate's shirt. "Are you injured?"

"No," she said, and glanced at the security guard. "Not my blood."

"And Moore?"

"He's gone," Kate replied.

"Did you shoot him?"

"Crushed trachea."

"Ah, that's useful," Moshenski said. "We can work with that."

"What does that mean?"

"It's just that holes are harder to explain," Moshenski said. "It's much easier to construct a narrative around a broken neck or, in this case, a throat injury."

Kate realized that Moshenski was already managing the scene and the story. The others could simply disappear, but Devin Moore was a prominent international figure. His death needed to be scripted.

Moshenski kicked Andrew's foot. "And this one?"

"Unconscious," Kate said. "I'm lucky my gun only had two rounds."

Moshenski noticed the blood dripping down the back of Kate's head and neck.

"You are injured."

"It's not bad," Kate said and reached up. "Ow. That hurts."

"We'll have the medical staff look, to be sure."

Moshenski picked up Zhukov's knife and studied it for a moment.

"Here," he said. "Mikhail would want you to have this."

"I don't think so."

"I know what this knife means to him, and you," Moshenski said. "Taking it can't change what happened to you, or lift the burden Zhukov carries, but take it. At least, for now."

"Zhukov said when he realized who I was, Suliaman was warned."

"That's true."

"But I don't understand. They had my CIA file. I saw it at the compound," Kate said. "Suliaman knew exactly who I was. That's why I was grabbed, so what did Zhukov mean?"

"You ask questions I cannot answer."

"Can't or won't?"

"Both can be true," Moshenski said. "Let us pray my friend survives. Zhukov is the only one who can help you understand."

"And if he dies?"

"Some things one takes to the grave. This may be one," Moshenski said. "Now, we should go."

"I better leave this here," Kate said, and set the security guard's gun near the body. "I assume your people are going to sanitize everything?"

"We were never here."

Moshenski's men dragged a pair of bodies out of the elevator and helped Julian into the wheelchair.

"I'll take him," Kate said, and she backed the chair into the elevator. "What was so damn important you wouldn't take cover?"

"This," Julian said, and he handed her Moore's gold-plated NanoVault. "It was just laying on the floor, and it was exactly what I needed."

"For what?"

"For Jake's files," he said. "Now, I can't promise it's all there, or that everything's intact, but it's everything Moore collected."

Kate knelt alongside Julian's chair, tears streaming down her cheeks.

"You don't know what this means to me," Kate said. She wrapped her arms around him and smothered him in kisses. "I don't know what to say."

"Say you forgive me."

CHAPTER 95

MANHATTAN INTERNATIONAL TRAUMA CENTER (MITC), NY

MOORE'S PRIVATE ELEVATOR OPENED, and Kate guided Julian into the parking garage. Moshenski's men had overwhelmed Moore's private army and corralled them in a corner of the garage.

"I assume those are your men?" Kate asked.

"Yes," Moshenski replied. "You may recall I had my own arrangements to make. Getting into Moore's world was your task. Getting you all out was mine."

They loaded Kate and Julian into an ambulance.

"I will meet you at the hospital," Moshenski said.

"Wait," Kate said. "How do I... What should I..."

"Not to worry" Moshenski said. "I arranged everything. There will be no questions, no police. But it would be wise to bag the weapons."

Moshenski handed Kate the electronics bag that held her watch and phone. She added Zhukov's knife and her gun and magazine.

"Where are we going?" Kate asked.

"Manhattan International Trauma Center," Moshenski said. "One of the perks of being a billionaire benefactor is the ability to count on the hospital's quality and rely on their discretion."

They took Kate and Julian to the emergency entrance of a private wing, where a pair of medical teams were waiting to escort them to the examination rooms. *Moshenski was right,* Kate thought. *No questions, explanations, or signatures.*

Julian was fine, but his medical team insisted on a thorough examination. Kate's team cleaned her scalp, removed the shards of glass. And confirmed stitches weren't required. A butterfly bandage took care of the cut above her eye, but when she looked in the mirror, Kate realized how bad her neck looked. *Guess I'll be wearing a scarf to the funeral,* Kate thought. *Can't have people thinking I tried to hang myself.*

Moshenski knocked and Kate invited him in.

"Are you alright?" he asked.

"It's nothing. I'll be fine," Kate said. "Any news on Zhukov?"

"Mikhail's in surgery, so it's too soon to say, but he's alive and that's a miracle," Moshenski said. "It's been my experience that he's a hard man to kill."

"I have to admit, I'm surprised," Kate said. "A head shot from that range is a devastating injury."

"Mikhail's head is harder than most," he said, and laughed. "And there's a plate in his skull. A remnant of another time, a different life."

"I know who he is, who he was," Kate said. "The Butcher of Beslan is not something you forget."

"Of course. I understand," Moshenski said. "How old were you when you lost your Mother and brother? Six or seven?"

"I was seven," Kate said. "And you seem to know more about my past than I expected."

Kate noted that Moshenski ignored her observation.

"Ah, seven. Just a child," Moshenski said. "And you blame Zhukov for their deaths?"

"I was too young to understand what happened or why," Kate said. "All I knew is that I walked to school with my mother, and my little brother, and three days later I was an orphan. They say I was one of the lucky ones, but it didn't feel that way."

"You have no recollection of Mikhail before the Beslan School attack?"

"No, why would I?"

"Just curious," he said. "I know your father was also in the military. I thought perhaps you might have crossed paths before he was killed."

"I see you've done your homework on me," Kate said. "Now, tell me why."

"I thought about this on the way to the hospital. As I prayed for my friend, I felt there were some things about Mikhail you should know. If you will indulge me for a few minutes, I will start where we met."

"This is important," she said. "Please, go on."

"Very well. I met Mikhail in Lefortovo Prison, Moscow. As my power and wealth grew, Putin considered me a threat. Prison is where you are taught to remember your place. I was still there when Chechen rebels seized your school. With over three hundred dead, half of them children, Russia needed a scapegoat."

"The Butcher of Beslan."

"Yes, that name was born while Mikhail was in the hospital. An explosion tore away part of his skull, and he was in a coma. He was the perfect—what you Americans call, the patsy. They claimed Mikhail charged into the school, without regard for the lives at risk or the consequences. And so the former war hero became the butcher, and since he wasn't expected to live, no one would object. But he survived."

"They tried and convicted him."

"Yes, and his conviction was a forgone conclusion, as are most in Russia, but the man who arrived at Lefortovo was a mere shell of the warrior he once was. I used what little influence I had inside to nurse him back to health, and when he was well, he repaid my kindness with his strength and loyalty."

"What does that mean?"

"Russian prisons aren't country clubs, and when I needed protection, he was there."

"None of this explains why you both seem to know so much about me."

"We became friends. No, brothers. And I learned that Mikhail, too, suffered a great loss at Beslan. Few knew, or seemed to care, that his wife and daughter also perished that day, or so he believed."

"You don't think I'm —"

"No. We know that you are not," Moshenski said. "But your journey from a Russian orphanage to adoption in the US was one of the many trails we followed until we were certain. Eventually, we confirmed that Zhukov's wife and daughter are buried together in a mass grave with many others at the Beslan memorial. And when I could finally purchase my release, I bargained for Mikhail's as well."

"So that's what Zhukov meant. In Syria," Kate said. "He discovered I was a Beslan survivor. That's why he warned Suliaman."

"That much is true."

"What else is there?"

"That is not for me to say," Moshenski said. "I may have said too much already. If he wants you to know more, he will have to tell you himself."

"But what if he doesn't make it?"

"Then he will take the rest to his grave."

"The rest? How much more is there?"

"Say a prayer Mikhail lives, and you can ask him yourself," Moshenski said. "Now, if you will excuse me. I will check on your friend."

More questions than answers, Kate thought. *Deflection. Misdirection. Half-Truths. And outright lies. I might as well still be working at the CIA. Martin!* Kate had compartmentalized, and focused entirely on saving Julian and stopping Moore. But she wasn't done.

Martin was the Agency's top audio analysis expert, and Kate needed a favor. She and Martin hadn't been colleagues for years, and weren't exactly on speaking terms when she left, but she still hoped he would help.

Kate reached for her messenger bag. *That's heavy,* she thought, and glanced inside. *Right. The electronics bag, and the weapons.* She pulled out the burner phone and called Martin's cell phone. She hoped he would answer even though the number might come through as potential spam. Kate was relieved when he answered.

"Martin Hayes," he said.

"Hi Martin. It's Kate," she said. "Thanks for answering."

"I didn't recognize the number," Martin said. "But I figured you'd be using a burner."

"Yes, and before we go on, I want to apologize—"

"Kate, what's past is past," he said. "And I just want to say how sorry I was to hear about Jake. I know you two were very happy. He was a remarkable man."

"Thanks, Martin. I really appreciate that," she said. "I hated to ask for help, and I wouldn't have asked if it wasn't important, maybe even a matter of life and death."

"I understand," he said. "I've been studying the street cam video you sent, and I know better than to ask how you got it, but it helped me try to piece together what Jake said. I overlaid the audio file you sent with enhanced images of Jake's lips during those final moments."

"Were you able to work your lip-reading magic?" Kate asked. "Do you know what he said?"

"You know how this goes," he said. "I can't be sure. Not one-hundred percent."

"Martin, I can hear it in your voice," Kate said. "It's OK. Whatever it is. I can handle it, but I need to know."

"Well, like I said, the process isn't perfect," he said. "But I believe Jake said *Kate's relentless. She will kill you.*"

Kate took a minute to absorb that message, and the context. The only other person there, the one that had just fought to save Jake's life, was Marcus. *Why would he say that to Marcus? What does it mean?* She considered the possibility it was a twisted joke, something passing between warrior-brothers, but she recalled

Jake's face on the video, the look in his eyes. *He wasn't joking. That wasn't pain. It was anger.*

"Kate?" Martin asked. "Are you still there?"

"Yes. Sorry," she said. "And the other audio clip I sent? Were you able to get a voice print match?"

"I did, and you were right," he said. "The voice on the *Mission First* clip is Marcus Jones."

"Thanks, Martin," Kate said. "You're a good friend. And let's just keep this between us."

"Of course, Kate," he said. "Please, let me know if there's anything I can do."

"Thanks."

***

MOSHENSKI RETURNED, GUIDING JULIAN.

"They have discharged him," Moshenski said. "I have a car coming around to take you both back to Julian's loft."

"Can't wait to tell Keisha we live in a loft," Julian said. "That sounds so much better than parking garage."

"You're in good spirits," Kate said.

"We've earned it. The Quantum NanoVaults now function properly. The mountain of accumulated data is gone, and we're still breathing."

Moshenski handed Kate an envelope, and she pulled out a diplomatic license plate.

"What's this?"

"Can't risk having you stopped on the way out of New York," Moshenski laughed. "Mail it back to the consulate when you get home."

"That's thoughtful. Thank you," Kate said, and she took Moshenski's arm. "Julian, if you'll excuse us for a minute. I need to have a word with Mr. Moshenski."

"Please, call me Vitali. After all of this, you're practically family."

"I'm glad you think so, because I need a favor," Kate said. "I can't go home right now, and I need a place, away from everyone, and especially the press."

"Friends can be comforting at times like these," Vitali said. "Are you certain you want to be alone?"

"Yes."

"Very well. I have an estate in Upstate New York. Between the gated entrance and nestled among towering trees, you'll find complete seclusion and privacy. I will let them know you're coming and arrange transportation. To be safe, your vehicle should stay here, and we'll secure it in the embassy garage."

"It's staffed?"

"Yes, it's a large estate, but aside from providing whatever meals you require, they will make themselves as scarce as you desire."

"Here," Kate said, and handed Vitali back the license plate envelope. "Best you hang on to this for now, and your people will find the keys tucked above the driver's visor."

Kate returned to Julian and gave him a hug.

"This is where we part company, for now," she said, and pulled Moore's golden NanoVault from her pocket. "And thanks for this. I don't know what's on it, but at least now there's a chance I can find out what Jake wanted me to know."

"I don't understand," Julian said. "I thought you'd be coming back with us. Your Jeep's there."

"No, I need a little time," Kate said. "I bury Jake in a few days, and in the meantime, there are still some things I need to sort out. And it wouldn't kill you to tell Keisha you're grateful for everything she does for you. She was ready to fight. I don't think you know how lucky you are to have her in your corner."

"Keisha!" Julian said. "Oh, my God. She doesn't know."

"Are you kidding me?" Kate asked. "You haven't called her? Boy, you are in BIG trouble. Well, good luck with that."

Kate kissed Julian's cheek and watched as a medical tech pushed him down the hallway toward the exit and his mobility van.

She turned back to Vitali. "I'm ready when you are."

Chapter 96

ARLINGTON NATIONAL CEMETERY, VA

Kate sat alone in the limousine that crawled down Memorial Avenue. Just ahead, the funeral coach carried the remains of Senior Chief Jake Church. The motorcade behind her stretched for half a mile. The cars that followed brought the men and women of Jake's executive protection team, the closest thing he had to family. Behind them were the SEALs from nearby Virginia Beach, some with their spouses.

The rest of the invited guests knew Jake or Kate personally or professionally and asked to attend to pay their respects and to offer Kate their support. While Jake's actions drew worldwide attention, Kate insisted his burial was a private matter. She denied all Congressional office requests and asked the media to stay away.

The funeral coach stopped alongside the horse-drawn caisson, and Kate's Town Car stopped well behind to give the men and the horses ample room. Kate stepped out of the limo and walked up to the caisson. She knew all six men in Navy dress whites. Three of the SEALs were still active duty, but fast approaching their twenty. Forest, Deon, and Mike wrapped up their twenty and found a home with Trident Executive Protection. All were among Jake's personal last wishes and dropped everything to attend.

Jake's honor guard marched up to the funeral coach and stood ready to receive Jake's casket. Each took a hand in guiding the casket out of the coach and marched at Jake's side during the transfer. All uniformed military saluted and held their salute until Jake's flag-draped coffin reached the caisson.

The guard flanked the caisson, three on each side, and escorted Jake to the burial site. Kate walked a few steps behind and remained alone. This was a journey she didn't want to share. One last stroll with her husband before his journey's end.

Nearly one hundred walked silently behind Kate. Horse hoofs marked the cadence as they walked, and muffled tears echoed in the background.

All saluted again when Jake's pallbearers lifted the coffin and began the march to his gravesite. When the coffin rested on the pedestal, the transfer team grabbed edges of the flag and snapped it aloft. The flag stretched tight in the hands of his brothers, like a shield, floating above Jake's polished wooden coffin.

Jake's last commanding officer, Commander Lewis and Chaplain Miller, saluted, and then the Chaplain turned to address the gathering.

"Ladies and gentleman, I am Chaplain William Miller, and it is our honor to be present with you as we lay to rest your beloved, and our comrade-in-arms, Senior Chief Jake Church."

"For over one hundred and fifty years, Arlington National Cemetery has honored our fallen warriors and patriots as their final resting place. These sacred grounds are a memorial, a lasting tribute to the men and the women who faithfully served this nation.

"As you look out across these fields, and upon the rows of headstones, know that there are over four hundred thousand such Americans buried here.

"Every headstone is a brick in the foundation of freedom upon which we stand today. Let these stones be a stark reminder of the cost of freedom, and I encourage you also to remember this.

"You cannot purchase a place at Arlington National Cemetery. It must be earned.

"Those of us who knew the Senior Chief know he earned his place in this sacred ground with remarkable distinction in the service of this nation. Recipient of the Silver Star, and two Purple Hearts, none would question his heroism or commitment to his country and his brothers.

"And today the entire world knows his name, and can bear witness to his unwavering determination and character. It is our privilege to include Jake among the graves of our honored fallen.

"For his honorable service to the United States Navy, for our comrade-in-arms Senior Chief Jake Church, our nation bestows military honors. In life, he honored this flag, and now this flag will honor him.

"Ladies and gentleman, if you'll please stand for the military honors. The firing party is located just slightly off to the left, but we invite you to gaze upon your beloved as we honor his service and sacrifice."

Commander Lewis's booming voice rang out. "Present arms."

The row of seven sailors moved with machine-like precision. All in uniform saluted the casket, Kate placed her hand over heart, and three volleys of fire rang out.

The bugler stood alone among gleaming white headstones. He pressed the bugle to his lips, and the haunting melody of Taps filled the air, echoing off the trees and headstones. The mourners bowed their heads, some closed their eyes, most fought back tears.

The bugle's lilting tones played through the sorrow and pain of the moment. When the last note faded away, the mourners slowly opened their eyes, wiping tears from their faces. The silence that followed was heavy with emotion, and it seemed as if no one wanted to break the stillness of the moment.

Commander Lewis called out, "Order arms." And the firing party marched away.

Chaplain Miller asked everyone to sit. The Navy band played *America the Beautiful,* while Jake's honor guard folded the flag. The honor guard smoothed every edge, tucked corners and presented the flag to Commander Lewis.

Commander Lewis took a knee in front of Kate, one hand below the flag, one above.

"Ma'am, on behalf of the President of the United States, the United States Navy and a grateful nation," he said. "Please accept this flag as a symbol of our appreciation for your loved one's honorable and faithful service."

He stood, stepped back, and raised his right hand in a long, graceful salute.

A member of the Army's Old Guard approached Kate with the Arlington Lady on his arm. She wore a long black skirt and a tailored black blazer.

"Mrs. Preacher," she said. "I'm Margaret Packwood. Please accept my condolences and this card from the Chief of Staff and his wife, as well as one from the Arlington Ladies."

"Thank you," Kate said, and she slipped both cards into Jake's flag.

"I am honored to be here with you today," Margaret said. "Your husband's service, and his selfless sacrifice, that others might live, is a reminder that there are some among us who answer the call. They do not hesitate, and never waiver, no matter the cost. God bless you, and may your husband rest in peace."

Margaret took the arm of her escort and returned to the side.

Chaplain Miller approached and offered his condolences, and then the honor guard formed up and marched away.

The cemetery representative announced that the service was over, and that the family may approach. The gathering of SEALs, Jake's brothers-in-arms, formed a line. One by one, they set their tridents on Jake's coffin, and with a fist, pounded the trident into the wood. The men Kate knew stopped to take her hand or kiss her check.

Kate tried to thank them for coming, but she struggled to speak.

Some women placed roses on the casket, and Kate's boss, Leslie Dodd, came and sat alongside her. Neither could speak at first. Leslie wrapped her arms around Kate, both hugged and cried.

Kate wiped away the tears and broke the silence.

"I won't be coming back to work," she said. "I can't."

"I know," Leslie said. "When you left for Paris, I suspected you might not return. When Pete was killed, I was certain. You were there, weren't you? In the office?"

"Yes, I was. The men that killed Pete were looking for me," Kate said. "And Pete's wife? How is she doing?"

"Grieving, of course," Leslie said. "But she's surrounded by family. Did you know they have nine kids?"

"And something like a half-dozen grand kids," Kate added.

"There is someone here that I would like you to meet."

"Oh, Leslie, I don't know if I can."

"She just wants a moment. It would mean the world to her, and I think you too."

Leslie waved over a young woman and her son. Kate recognized them from photos in her case file.

"Katherine Preacher, let me introduce you to the family you saved through sheer audacity and perseverance," Leslie said. "This is Maya and Caleb Washington."

Kate stood and faced the beautiful young woman and her handsome little boy. The last thing Kate did before leaving for Paris was ensure that Maya was cleared of the embezzlement charges and reunited with her son.

Maya hugged Kate, and whispered in her ear, "I know words mean so little right now, but if you ever just want to talk to someone, call me anytime, day or night."

Kate knew Maya had lost her husband in Iraq shortly after Caleb was born, and he never got to hold his son.

"Thank you," Kate said. "Does it get any easier?"

"Easier? No, not really, but different. I think about my husband every day, but I see him in our son, and in the miracles that come our way. I like to think he sent you. An answer to a prayer."

Kate choked up at the notion she was the answer to someone's prayer, and turned her attention to Maya's son.

"Caleb, what have you got there?"

Caleb held up the Rubik's cube for Kate to see.

"He doesn't say much, not yet," Maya said. "But with the settlement, and Leslie's advocacy, he's starting school next week. I know in my heart it will help."

"May I see that?" Kate asked, and Caleb handed Kate the cube. She examined it for a moment, then holding opposite corners, she spun the cube like a top. The pattern of colors streamed past. *He wasn't trying to solve the puzzle,* Kate realized. *That was probably too easy. He created a work of art, with a distinctive repeating pattern of diagonal colors.*

"It's beautiful," Kate said. "Do you know how many moves it would take to solve the puzzle?"

Caleb nodded. Kate leaned down and tilted her head. "You can tell me. It will be our secret," and she tapped her ear, suggesting he whisper. To his mom's surprise, Caleb whispered in Kate's ear.

Kate stood and smiled. "He's going to be just fine," Kate said. "Reminds me of a boy I knew once. A fine man now, with a good heart and a brilliant mind. And we're all a little safer today because of him."

Caleb smiled and gave Kate a hug. When Kate turned back around, there was an older gentleman standing nearby in a Marine Corps uniform. In his dark blue coat and red trim, matching trousers, and crisp white shirt, Kate didn't recognize the homeless man she passed every day on the way to work.

Gunnery Sergeant Tyrone Walker took Kate's hand, and with a tear in his eye, he tried to speak.

Kate threw her arms around him, "It's OK, Gunny. You don't have to say a word. It means the world to me you're here. And look at you. You're going to have to beat the girls off with a stick."

"I'm so sorry, Kate," he said. "Jake was one of the finest men I have ever known, and when I saw what he did, I thought about all the times we talked and laughed. And how you two tried to help me, and I pushed you away. I said to myself, you coward. Don't you dare throw this life away."

Kate saw Amy, the barista she saw most mornings, and called her over.

"Amy, it's OK," Kate said. "Please, join us."

"I didn't want to intrude," Amy said.

Kate gave her a hug and asked, "Did you have something to do with this?"

"No, this is all Gunny, but I was happy to bring him here today."

"It's OK," Tyrone said. "You can tell her. We're family."

"I brought Gunny a little something to eat, and he was crying. He had Jake's business card in his hand and asked if I would call the number on the back, the number for the veteran assistance program."

"They took me right in," Gunny said. "I know I've got a long way to go, but it's a start."

"It's a beautiful sight," Kate said. "Jake would be proud."

The procession of SEALs was just wrapping up, and the three remaining were Forest, Deon and Mike. They pounded their tridents into Jake's coffin and took a knee in front of Kate's chair. Forest took Kate's hand.

"We don't know what happened over the last week," Forest said. "But Marcus not making Jake's funeral doesn't add up. Are you going to tell us what's going on?"

"I will," Kate said. "Just not right now. Marcus will be coming soon, but I need to speak with him alone."

"Just remember," Mike added. "Whatever you're planning, and whatever comes next, if you need us, we'll be there."

"I know," she said. "But right now, I need you three to step into Jake's shoes. Forest, you're the new team lead. Deon, Mike, you two need to back him up. The three of you are the heart and soul of Trident Security. You are gifted leaders with instincts and skills Jake trusted with his life."

"I don't get it," Deon said. "We all thought Marcus would step up."

"Marcus is leaving."

"What the hell?" Mike said. "With Jake gone, how could he do that to us?"

"It's complicated, but it's for the best," Kate said. "Jake built this team around trust and competency, and we have clients that are depending on us."

"Us?" Forest asked. "Are you stepping in?"

"Yes," Kate said. "It's something Jake wanted, and I think it's time. I have a few things that need my attention, and I don't know how long they will take, but I know that Trident Executive Protection is in capable hands."

"Would you like us to stay?" Forest asked.

"No, you should go. Join your brothers, have a few drinks, tell some lies," Kate said. "I'm going to sit awhile and visit with Jake."

A lone member of the Old Guard remained at a respectful distance. He stood watch over the gravesite, hands at his side, eyes fixed forward. He would remain present until all were gone, and it was time for the caretakers to lower the casket and close the grave.

Kate approached the casket, Jake's flag under her left arm, her right hand resting on the coffin. She swept her fingers across the rows of tridents and fought back the tears. *So many brothers,* she thought. *Loved and respected by all.*

"I hope you know how angry I am," she said, as if Jake was standing there, watching, listening. "I didn't think we had secrets. Not like that, anyway. You nearly got me killed. Seriously? Claymores?"

"I can hear you now... But you didn't die," she said. "That's not funny."

"When I catch my breath, I'm going to spend a few weeks in that vault of yours and wrap my head around everything you were doing. But I can't go back to the cabin right now, not yet."

"And your NanoVault. It's a miracle that I have your files, or at least some of them. There must be thousands of pages of documents, receipts, video and God knows what else. My mind has been spinning for days. How long have you been collecting this data? Keeping it secret? And why is it that every time I think I have an answer, I find more questions?"

"But one thing recent events have shown me is that you were right. I have been hiding. Thank you for letting me find my own way back, and teaching and training me along the way. You call *me* the Shaman, but I think you always knew this day would come. Not the when or the how of it, but the inevitability of lightning striking."

"You need to know. I'm sorry. I was hurt, angry. But I see it now. You kept your promise. You said you would always be there, and you were."

"Not the way I hoped. I can't hold you, kiss you. But I saw you. Standing there, and heard you guiding me. Maybe it wasn't real, but I like to think it was. I hope it was. Like right now. Standing by my side. The gentle breeze that grazes my cheek is your hand. I will remember, and know that you will *always* love me."

"In Paris, I said that I didn't know how to live without you, and I never will. I choose to live with you. You will always be in my heart, and I know that when I need you most, you will be there. In my darkest moments, you will be my light. When I can't take another step, you will show me the way. And in the end, when the angels ask me what I loved most, I will tell them every moment with you."

Chapter 97

ARLINGTON NATIONAL CEMETERY, VA

KATE KISSED THE TOP of Jake's coffin and turned away. She nodded to the cemetery staff waiting nearby, and when she reached the street, they lowered Jake's coffin. The Old Guard PFC that stood watch over Jake saluted and when the coffin rested, he lowered his hand and left.

The street, once filled with cars, was now almost empty. Kate's driver stood dutifully by the Town Car's passenger door. She raised a hand to signal she would stay a while longer. There were two other cars, a blacked-out SUV and a limousine. Standing alongside the limo was Margot Ryder, Deputy Director CIA National Clandestine Service.

"Thank you for coming," Kate said.

"It surprised me to get an invitation, and thought it best to keep my distance," Margot said. "But I'm grateful for the chance to say goodbye to one of the most remarkable men I have ever known. He and I did not always agree, but I never questioned his motives or judgment. In my business, that was extraordinary."

"Are you OK?" Margot asked, pointing at the bruises Kate's scarf and makeup couldn't hide from trained eyes.

Kate touched her neck. "Yes, a bit sore, but nothing serious."

"I wanted to thank you for arranging Jake's return," Kate said. "Things were going south with the DGSI's Deputy Director. I'm sure Boucher meant well, but it was looking like it could take days, even weeks. I had no idea when or how I could bring Jake home, and then everything changed."

"How did you know it was me?"

"It was a short list of candidates with the clout and the reach to pull that off," Kate said. "Do I have you to thank for Arlington finding space so quickly?"

"For that you can thank the President."

"He's a busy man," Kate said. "I'm guessing you whispered in his ear."

"Close. His chief of staff is former CIA, so I made a suggestion," Margot said. "You know how DC works. It's all relationships."

"And whispers and lies," Kate said. "Did you bring it?"

"I did," Margot said. "But I have to admit I'm torn."

"I still have clearance."

"It's not that."

"Then what?"

"You put Syria behind you years ago," Margot said. "Why open old wounds?"

"They're already open," Kate said. "Now I need closure. I haven't played chess since Syria, but I had no choice recently, and there was a fleeting image from my captivity. Something I can't quite recall."

"And you think photos of being beaten and tortured will help?"

"I know how it sounds," Kate said, "But I realized something this week."

"What's that?"

"I'm stronger now than I have ever been."

Margot reached inside her limo and pulled out a classified document folder.

"It's all here," Margot said, and handed it to Kate. "I hope you know what you're doing, but I know you well enough to know I couldn't talk you out of it."

"Thank you," Kate said. "Seeing Zhukov again, hearing his voice, and learning a bit more about his unwritten story shed some light on what happened."

"Alright, let's hear it."

"Zhukov killed Suliaman," Kate said. "Brutally, I might add."

"I've seen the photos from the scene," Margot said.

"Zhukov had Suliaman's knife," Kate said. "I have it now."

"That's information you do not want to share," Margot said. "Assad took in Nizar, Suliaman's son, and he exceeds his father's savagery. There's nothing he wouldn't do to reclaim the instrument of torture his family wielded for generations."

"Thanks for the warning," Kate said. "I also discovered Zhukov sent the photo with my GPS location."

"Zhukov? Why would he reveal where you were being held?"

"If he lives," Kate said. "I'll ask him."

"I'm glad you're not set on killing him on sight."

"You're not surprised," Kate realized. "And you already know Zhukov might die."

"I'm the Deputy Director of the CIA," Margot said. "Of course, I know. Zhukov may have some diplomatic privileges, but when he travels, I'm informed. And don't worry about Moore Tower. The accidental death cover story will hold. We'll see to that. The press loves nothing more than to watch the mighty fall prey to their foibles, but we both know Devin Moore didn't die in the throes of an auto-erotic asphyxiation episode."

Kate hugged Margot and noted the surprise on her face.

"This doesn't make us even," Kate said. "Not even close."

"I know," Margot said. "But if you wanted to come back, I could make that happen. Your linguistic skills alone would be invaluable, but in concert with your other unique talents, you would be a tremendous asset to the Agency and the country. Don't answer me now. Just promise me you'll think about it."

"I already have," Kate said.

"And?"

"Maybe someday. But right now where I need to go, and what I need to do, it's best there's no link to the Agency. In fact, it would help if you looked the other way."

"I can work with 'maybe someday', and while I can't guarantee we'll stay clear of whatever you have planned, I will try."

"I can work with 'try'," Kate said, and they hugged again.

Margot stood at the door to the limo and nodded at the SUV parked down the road.

"Should I be concerned about those two?"

"No, they're with me," Kate said. "I have a little unfinished business and they're on loan from a new friend."

Margot raised an eyebrow, and slid into the limo, but before she closed the door, she looked back up at Kate.

"Stay safe."

"I'll try."

Chapter 98

ARLINGTON NATIONAL CEMETERY, VA

Margot's limo pulled away, and Kate walked over to her Town Car. Her driver held the door, and Kate placed the classified folder inside, then set Jake's flag on top.

"Please, drive around for a while," Kate said. "I have your number, so I'll text when I'm ready to be picked up. It shouldn't be long, but this isn't a good place to wait."

When her driver left, Kate pulled a cell phone from her clutch.

"Send him in," Kate texted, and she waited by the edge of the road.

A few minutes later, a motorcycle rocketed up the road and stopped directly in front of her.

"Preacher," Marcus said. "I am so sorry. I don't know what happened. The MPs ran my ID, and the next thing I know, I'm stuck in some holding room. I begged and pleaded, and pounded on the door, but they wouldn't budge."

Marcus removed his helmet and over-suit, revealing his Army Service Uniform's dark blue coat, matching trousers, and black bow tie on a dress white shirt. When he had pulled himself together, he stepped up to give Kate a hug, but she held up a hand.

"You're pissed," Marcus said. "And I get it, but I swear I was here on time. It wasn't my fault."

"I asked them to hold you at the gate."

"I don't understand. Why the hell would you do that?" Marcus asked. "You kept me from my best friend's funeral. How could you? How dare you?"

"Does this sound familiar?" Kate asked. She pressed play, and an audio enhanced version of Jake's last words echoed from her phone.

Kate's relentless. She will kill you.

"Where did you get that?"

"It doesn't matter. What matters is that you lied to me."

"Is that what this is all about?" Marcus asked. "I lied. I'm not proud of it, but I wanted Jake's last words to be something loving, memorable, not him giving me a bad time."

"What are you saying? That this is some kind of inside joke?"

"Hold on. You thought Jake was serious?" Marcus asked. "Whoa! Preacher, you've got this all wrong."

"Then explain it to me."

"We're brothers, teammates," Marcus said. "I was supposed to have his back, you know that, and so did Jake. He was telling me you're going to kill me. Not because he believed you would, but because I should have been there. I could have made a difference. If it wasn't for me, he wouldn't have even been there. If it wasn't for me, this would have been something we saw on the news."

"It surprised you when Boucher showed me all the equipment Jake had with him."

"Of course." Marcus said. "Whatever work he was doing, it wasn't for the company, so I couldn't imagine why he needed it. You think this has something to do with me?"

"Giving me back Jake's phone was a mistake."

"I knew you would want it. What's wrong with that?"

"Turns out the phone Jake cloned was a burner, and the last text message sent was a single word."

"And you think it was mine?"

"I know it was yours."

"This is insane. I know you're grieving. Maybe this is shock or something, so I'll cut you some slack, but I will not stand here while you accuse me of... what? Being complicit in my best friend's death."

Marcus took one step toward his bike, and the tire exploded.

"What the hell?" Marcus yelled. "You've got a sniper on me?"

"Snipers. Plural," Kate said. "Aren't you even curious about the word Jake captured, or do you already know?"

"Enlighten me."

"Albatross."

"That's it? That's your proof?" Marcus asked. "What the hell does that even mean?"

"You know what it means, and you sent it the moment you left Jake at the table," Kate said. "I've seen the video. You turned, texted and tossed the phone."

Marcus flinched at the whizzing sound of another sniper round, and they heard the sharp crack of the high-velocity bullet striking the other tire.

"What do you want from me?"

"The truth."

"I can't tell you the truth," Marcus said. "My life isn't the only one at stake."

"Good Lord," Kate said. "You're on BountyHunter."

"What do you know about it?"

"More than I'd like."

"Then you know they were hunting for you."

"They tried."

"When I saw your bounty, I asked to join the hunt," Marcus said. "I wanted to monitor their progress, and then I saw they headed for the cabin. I went to help, but by the time I got there, you were gone."

"Is that why you were curious if I still had the NanoVault they were after?"

"Yeah, I thought maybe that might give us some leverage."

"Or maybe a big payday?"

"You obviously have a very low opinion of me, and I understand, but I swear my only interest in your bounty was to help. I owed it to Jake to try."

"Who's your collateral?"

"I can't tell you that," Marcus said. "It's not safe."

"Well, you can talk to me, or you can talk to them," Kate said. She nodded at the two large Ukrainians standing by the SUV and waved them over.

Kate continued, "I don't know what role you played in Jake's death. Maybe none. I'd like to believe that. I'd like to think you sent the Albatross mission abort code genuinely hoping they would stop. If they had, you might have saved Jake, and so many more. But they came anyway, and for what? Money? Position? Politics? Did you trade innocent lives, Jake's life, for yours, or your collateral?"

"Preacher, you wouldn't understand," Marcus said. "But wherever you think those goons are taking me, I'll never get there. You won't get answers. They'll just dump my body in the woods and be done with it."

"I think you're wrong about that. At least, I hope you're wrong, but I'm willing to take that chance," Kate said. "Because with you or without you, I will get answers. I already know you killed Francois LeGrande. Just a harmless old man. You slipped a rope around his neck and kicked out the chair. Why? Because that was the mission. And Marcus Jones is always *Mission First,* and you, AKA Ronin, had a reputation to protect."

The two Ukrainians cuffed Marcus's hands behind his back and led him toward their car.

"Preacher," Marcus begged. "Don't go down this path. You don't know who you're dealing with, and there's no way you can stop them. Not alone. Let me help."

"Like you helped Jake?"

"I didn't know what Jake was doing. I swear," Marcus said. "If I'd known, I would have warned him, tried to stop him. Like I am right now, with you. These people have connections everywhere. If they think you're a threat, they won't hesitate to put another bounty on your head, and there's always someone, somewhere, waiting to take the contract."

"I believe you," Kate said. "I don't know who's pulling the strings, not yet. But they don't know what's coming, and Jake was right. I am relentless."

Epilogue

ARLINGTON NATIONAL CEMETERY, VA

KATE WATCHED MARCUS DISAPPEAR into the back of the SUV, and she walked toward the one remaining vehicle. *I need Moshenski,* she thought. *But he can't know everything. Not yet. Jake said not to trust anyone, and Moshenski's connection to the GEC puts him at the top of the list.*

Moshenski's palatial home in upstate New York helped Kate rest and focus, and escape media attention. The estate was also an opportunity to dig through everything on Moore's NanoVault. Julian's miracle retrieved Jake's files before all of Moore's data was wiped from the planet. As expected, some of the files were corrupt, but the vast majority were intact. That fact confirmed they were transmitted the night before Jake was shot.

Kate approached Jake's files like she was back in the CIA and handed a treasure trove of intelligence data. The sheer volume was overwhelming, but a picture was beginning to form. *"See what everyone else is missing,"* Kate thought. *"Solve the puzzle. And take them down."* Those were Jake's instructions.

It was too soon to draw conclusions, and the picture was far from complete, but her original suspicions were confirmed. The files were peppered with references to the Global Economic Council and the Coalition, and the investigation took a surprising turn with the help of Moore's personal files. Using his NanoVault was opportune, and it was also a gift. His files confirmed the Coalition was real. Its members remained a mystery, and their motives unclear, but Moore was on the fast track to joining.

Kate reached the limo, and the driver opened the passenger door. She slid in next to Moshenski and shook his hand.

"Mr. Moshenski, thank you for your help today."

"Please, call me Vitali."

"Vitali, I'm not hopeful that your men will learn much from Marcus."

"Give them some time," he said. "They can be very persuasive."

"I'm sure they're very capable, but Marcus is a highly trained operator," Kate said. "But, we have to try. If Marcus was in any way involved in the planning and execution of the Paris attack, or knows anyone connected to the attack, I need to know."

"Everyone breaks, eventually," Vitali said. "You and I know this better than most."

The memory of her own capture and torture reminded her of the man the CIA hunted, the man she located. But without Zhukov's sacrifice, the mission to take down Moore and destroy his intelligence network would have failed. It was difficult for Kate to imagine the man she tracked to a Syrian chemical weapons cache was the same man who just helped her survive, both then and now.

"Any news on Zhukov?"

"Mikhail remains in a coma, but he's stable enough to travel," Vitali said, and he checked the time.

"He should be in the air soon."

"Where are you taking him?"

"Paris. I need to return, and want to keep him close, and I will leave at the conclusion of our meeting."

"When we met, you said that you owed Jake a debt you could never repay. What did you mean by that?"

"That day in Paris," Vitali said. "He saved my grandson."

"Was he the young man —"

"That your fatally wounded husband fought to save? Yes, that is my grandson. And Stephan owes your husband his life."

"I understand his fiancée was among the victims."

"Yes, and he's heartbroken. Those two had such a bright future," Vitali said. "We were celebrating their engagement just moments before the attack."

"You were there? At the cafe?"

"I was, but Mikhail insisted we leave. I don't know why, but it wasn't the first time his instincts have saved my life."

"Do you believe you were the target?"

"Yes, I fear so," Vitali said. "Several men pursued us down the alley, and Mikhail lost two of his men in the fight."

"Does the DGSI know you were there?"

"We haven't spoken, but they will have all the street camera video, and would have collected the bodies from the alley," Vitali said. "Zhukov's men, professionally dressed and licensed, would be easily identified, and the others readily linked to the attack."

Of course, Kate thought. *There are thousands of cameras in Paris. One may have caught Jake's sniper approaching the building when they set the overwatch. Boucher will have access to the video, but he wouldn't know where to look or why.*

Kate had connected to Boucher's laptop once already and the video she borrowed helped her solve the mystery of what Jake said. Now she wondered if it might help her find who pulled the trigger, and lead her to who orchestrated the attack. *The only person who walked away that day was the sniper. I need to find him or her.*

"I want you to hire me," Kate blurted out with more intensity than she had intended.

"Are you in need of employment?" Vitali asked, and Kate could hear the surprise. "If you require financial assistance, I would be happy —"

"That's kind of you to offer, but it's not the money," she said. "In fact, I've recently come in to a rather significant sum."

"Of course," Vitali said. "Moore's Bitcoins. You have them?"

"Yes," Kate acknowledged. "I'm returning to Paris, and they may help fund my search for answers. And the sooner I go, the greater the odds there are breadcrumbs I can still follow and information I can acquire for the right price."

"And you believe that working for me would be of some use?"

"I do," Kate said. "If I was in your employ, and investigating the attempt on your life, I would have access and leverage that I wouldn't have on my own. Something tells me, as your representative, I could pry open a few locked doors."

"Very well," Vitali said. "But I have one condition."

"What's that?"

"When you discover who is behind the attack, you bring the proof to me personally. No one else must know, and absolutely no police. Do we have an agreement?"

"Yes, we do," Kate said, and she shook Vitali's hand. "I need a day or two before I can leave, and I'll need a quiet place to stay in Paris. The Crillon might attract unwanted attention."

"Yes, of course. Let me think," Vitali said. "Ah, yes. The Hôtel de Pourtalès would be perfect. It is a small luxury hotel, known for its discretion, and frequented by high-profile celebrities escaping the paparazzi. My team will arrange for a private flat with an open-ended reservation."

"Thank you again. For everything," Kate said and shook his hand again. "I'll see you in Paris."

My Shameless Request for Your Review!

As an independent author, my success or failure is in your hands. Indie authors don't have the distribution reach of traditional publishers. You won't spot a copy of my book at the airport or the grocery store. But your review can reach dozens, hundreds, even thousands of readers looking for a good book and a new author to follow.

I hope you enjoyed *Relentless*. And if you did, please let others know — feel free to include the *Good, the Bad, and the Ugly* (for you Clint Eastwood fans) — just no spoilers please!

My sincere thanks!

Michael Maloof

 Review Here!

Dedication

JAKE CHURCH ISN'T THE only one who believes in love at first sight. I still remember the first time I saw Michelle. I knew. She was the one.

Our first date was on New Year's Eve, and seventeen days later, I asked her to marry me. Remarkably, she accepted my awkward proposal and blessed my life ever since.

I dedicate this book, with all my love, to my lovely bride. Like so many things in our lives, this book is a dream made real. We learned, long ago, there's nothing we can't do together, and this book is more proof.

Michelle, you are my best friend and my biggest fan. You knew I could do it, and with a gentle guiding hand, you would say, *Michael, go write.*

You are my muse, my sanctuary, my heart and soul.

I will *always* love you.

Your Grateful and Adoring Husband,

MICHAEL MALOOF, A SEASONED entrepreneur with a knack for turning ideas into multi-million-dollar acquisitions, marks a thrilling new chapter in a dynamic career with his debut novel, *Relentless*.

Born with an insatiable curiosity and a genetic case of wanderlust, Michael's foray into the world of thriller writing brings his rich tapestry of personal experiences to the page in a heart-pounding, globe-trotting adventure.

His wanderlust has taken him to over forty countries across six continents, each trip adding another chapter to his already rich life story. Michael's adventures read like a thriller novel in themselves: from dredging for gold in Honduras and hunting Mayan artifacts in Guatemala to acquiring uncut diamonds in Liberia and dodging an elephant charge in Kenya.

Michael's most treasured experiences include remarkable opportunities to train with the likes of Navy SEALs, Marine Raiders, Army Rangers, Green Berets, and Flight Medics. In these men, Michael found a deep well of inspiration and respect that informs his writing, bringing authenticity to his action scenes and characterization.

Now, with the release of his debut novel, this serial entrepreneur, international adventurer, and self-confessed Starbucks Frappuccino addict is poised to transport readers into a world filled with high-stakes intrigue and relentless action. Michael Maloof is not just writing thrillers; he's lived them.

Visit him at MichaelMaloof.com
Follow along on Facebook, X and Instagram
@MichaelGoWrite

Acknowledgments: Freedom Isn't Free

FIRST, I MUST EXPRESS my sincere gratitude to the Special Forces Operators and Army Flight Paramedic, whose invaluable input and insights were instrumental in the development of this book. Your unwavering dedication to our nation and your teams defines genuine heroism. Your exceptional skills, depth of knowledge, wit and humor, have not only inspired me but have enriched the content of this book. It's an honor to call you friends. I am profoundly grateful for the time you generously shared, and your help turning my dream into a reality.

I must also recognize the contribution of two remarkable men, my father and father-in-law, who were both my life's foundation and inspiration. My wife and I are proud children of *The Greatest Generation*. Michelle's father piloted B17s. At the ripe old age of twenty-four, he completed 26 missions over Germany. On one mission, he returned to base with unexploded ordinance lodged under his seat. Another flight nearly ended in disaster when an aircraft in the formation damaged his aircraft's tail. Given the opportunity to turn back, he and the crew agreed to press on and complete their mission.

My father, a Pearl Harbor survivor, was helping the chaplain prepare for Sunday morning services when the attack began. His bunkmate didn't survive the fire that ensued when a bomb struck the USS Tennessee and punched through the deck's surface plating. As the war in the Pacific expanded, my father took on the harrowing task of radioman and observer on a catapult team. Aboard an OS2U seaplane, he rocketed off the side of the battleship. He'd scout for hours at a time, land in the open ocean, and a crane would latch on to pull the aircraft back on board. He claimed he did it for the hazard pay, which he sent home to his wife, but it was essential duty, and I know he did it for the safety of the ship and crew.

Both men embodied the spirit of God and country, and they instilled in us the American ethos that's born from sacrifice, honor and responsibility. We learned early in life the value of hard, honest, work, and that "Freedom isn't Free." We understood what it meant to embrace the spirit of "All Gave Some, and Some Gave All" and to be grateful for life's blessings and opportunities.

And these pages would not contain the level of detail, heart, and warrior spirit I tried to capture without the contributions and support of two extraordinary military and veteran support organizations. It is with a spirit of responsibility and gratitude that we are proud to be affiliated with two outstanding military and veteran support organizations:

Troops Direct supports active-duty military by fielding requests for mission-essential, often lifesaving, equipment, that deployed forces require and can't acquire. Through Troops Direct founder, Aaron Negherbon, over the past few years I've met and trained with members of the US Special Forces. While the training was exhilarating, exhausting, and humbling, meeting these men, hearing their stories, and now calling them friends was life changing.

Unbroken Spirit founders, Colonel Peter Champagne and Major Marlene Champagne, both with distinguished military service records themselves, founded a community-based charity. Focused exclusively on veterans and led by veterans who have overcome adversity in their lives, they offer a life-affirming program toward long-term wellness and growth. Supporting their mission, meeting the veterans they've helped, hearing these veteran's stories, and drawing these men and women into our home and lives, gave us a renewed appreciation of honor, service, and sacrifice.

I am forever grateful and thankful to the men and women of our armed services who have touched my life and for those unseen, unknown heroes who touch all our lives.

 Troops Direct:
https://troopsdirect.org/

 Unbroken Spirit: https://unbrokenspirit.org/

Cover Design by Patrick Kang

Revised Edition December 2023

Library of Congress Control Number: 2023920949

ISBN 979-8-9893659-0-6 (eBook)
ISBN 979-8-9893659-1-3 (Paperback)
ISBN 979-8-9893659-2-0 (Hardcover)

Golden Oak Writer's Guild, LLC

Printed in Great Britain
by Amazon

52332504R00261